THE JENNY WILLSON MYSTERIES

IN RHINO WE TRUST

A Jenny Willson Mystery

DAVE BUTLER

DUNDURN
TORONTO

Publisher: Scott Fraser | Editor: Allison Hirst
Cover image: istock.com/rusm | Cover designer: Laura Boyle
Printer: Webcom, a division of Marquis Book Printing Inc.

Library and Archives Canada Cataloguing in Publication

Title: In rhino we trust / Dave Butler
Names: Butler, Dave, 1958- author.
Series: Butler, Dave, 1958- Jenny Willson mystery.
Description: Series statement: A Jenny Willson mystery
Identifiers: Canadiana (print) 20190051701 | Canadiana (ebook) 2019005171X | ISBN 9781459740877 (softcover) | ISBN 9781459740884 (PDF) | ISBN 9781459740891 (EPUB)
Classification: LCC PS8603.U838 I52 2019 | DDC C813/.6—dc23

1 2 3 4 5   23 22 21 20 19

We acknowledge the support of the Canada Council for the Arts and the Ontario Arts Council for our publishing program. We also acknowledge the financial support of the Government of Ontario, through the Ontario Book Publishing Tax Credit and Ontario Creates, and the Government of Canada.

VISIT US AT

 dundurn.com | @dundurnpress | dundurnpress | dundurnpress

Dundurn
3 Church Street, Suite 500
Toronto, Ontario, Canada
M5E 1M2

To the many men and women who are committed to ensuring that black and white rhinos, elephants, lions, and other iconic wildlife species survive and thrive, for many generations, in the wild landscapes of Namibia.

CHAPTER 1

MAY 24

Sam Mogotsi climbed to the top of a ridge, slowly, quietly. The dry, crystalline soil crunched beneath his boots. It was midday and the sun was high and hot, sucking the moisture from his skin. Since leaving his remote house at dawn, he had been driving and walking for more than five hours and was keen to be home by the time his two boys returned from school. After checking the ground for snakes and scorpions, he lowered himself and sat in the limited shade of a large boulder, his back against the rust-coloured sandstone. He could feel its warmth against the shirt of his uniform, its tan fabric dark with sweat.

Mogotsi began to search the opposite hillside with a slow pan of his 10x50 binoculars. He knew they were close. As he did each day, he'd been following their tracks since he'd spotted them on the road. They were old friends. If he was patient, he would eventually spot them.

Seeing nothing through the high-powered optics, Mogotsi dropped them to his chest and let his experienced eyes scan the slopes unaided, watching for the hint of movement that would reveal his targets against the rugged browns and greys. The rainy season had ended a month earlier, and already, most of the trees and shrubs on the far hillside — the acacias, mopanes, and shepherd trees — were showing signs of drought, their leaves drooping or edged with brown. Surprisingly, a few were still vibrant green. He used these as landmarks while his eyes moved in a practised pattern. He slid his *Save the Rhino Trust* hat from his head, its dark-green brim ringed with salty white. A slight breeze blew from the north, carrying with it the smell of heat, of parched grasses, of the baking rock at his back, of something vaguely organic.

His eyes continued the sweep.

After a few moments of silent observation, Mogotsi finally saw motion. He again raised the binoculars and watched as the creatures cautiously emerged from behind a grove of mopane trees. It was a pair of black rhinos, a cow and a calf. The pointed lip and lack of hump on the cow confirmed the species. They were moving from right to left, the calf behind and partly obscured by the mother's larger body. He saw the notch in the cow's left ear and knew it was Linda. The calf was Buhle, or "Beautiful." Mogotsi had been given the honour of naming her because he was the first to see her after she was born.

Linda was leading Buhle away from the shade of the trees, though they'd normally be napping at this time. Mogotsi knew Linda's eyesight was not keen enough to see him at this distance, so he wondered if she'd heard his footsteps as he came up the ridge, or if she'd caught his scent on a slight shift in the wind. Or had she detected the scent of something more dangerous?

Mogotsi smiled. Seeing wild rhinos always gave him pleasure, even though he saw them almost daily. Ten years ago, that pleasure had come from the thought of a quick payday. Then, he had carried a .303 rifle in his hand and a large axe in his backpack. Like today, he'd slowly stalked the animals, staying downwind. His goal would have been to get close enough to the cow so that he could shoot her and, as quickly as possible, hack the two horns from her skull, the larger one in the front, the much smaller one behind. On the two-hour drive to meet his buyer in the town of Kamanjab, he would not have given any thought to the fate of the orphaned calf.

But Mogotsi's days as a poacher were over. As a full-time rhino ranger hired by the local ≠Khoadi-// Hôas Conservancy, he was a valued member of the team and could now comfortably support his family with a regular salary. Having grown up with a father and a grandfather who had both hunted illegally and sold horn and ivory to shadowy buyers, or used illicit bushmeat to barter with hungry neighbours, it had taken Mogotsi two years to shift his thinking. But he now understood the saying "A dead rhino will feed a family for a week; a live rhino will feed a family for a lifetime." He knew it, his family knew it, and so, too, did his community. His wife and sons no longer had to endure boom-and-bust cycles, with money for food or clothing there one day and gone the next. His family and friends respected him, and he was free of worry over going to jail or paying hefty fines. Life was better now.

In his notebook, Mogotsi recorded the rhino pair's condition and direction of travel, using a handheld GPS unit to determine their exact location. Even though he knew the animals by name, he sketched in the length of their horns, the size and shape of their ears, and descriptions of their tails. Most importantly, he noted his distance from them and their reaction to him at that distance. He knew that this data would be used to fine-tune the guidelines they followed when they brought out guests from the local eco-lodge to watch these and other rhinos.

Mogotsi rose, pulled his cap down low, and moved out of the shade. He began to walk parallel to the path of the animals, stepping carefully around rocks the size of soccer and cricket balls, moving downhill along the spine of the ridge he had climbed earlier. He looked toward where he expected the rhinos to be heading: a water hole in a low draw, visible in the distance as a copse of green trees. There, he saw a herd of elephant cows and calves, the adults feeding on acacia leaves above their heads, the youngsters cavorting in and out of a tiny pool of water.

Picking his way carefully along the rocky ridge while keeping his eyes on the rhinos and on the ground at his feet for any sign — tracks or scat — that other animals were around, Mogotsi almost missed it — something lay in an opening to his left. When he saw it, he knew that things had changed, suddenly and dramatically. After two days of searching as he'd shadowed the rhinos, it was the very thing he had hoped not to find.

Mogotsi froze, Linda and Buhle forgotten for the moment. Myriad tracks — he recognized those of black-backed jackals, spotted hyenas, and vultures — led to the gruesome pile. Though the bones were mostly picked clean of flesh, he knew they hadn't been there long; he saw traces of blood and sinew in their crevices. Where sharp molars and incisors had cracked open the bones, the marrow was still red. The action of the scavengers had most likely erased any evidence of the cause of death.

The only portion of the skeleton that still resembled its original structure was a length of spine, and only because the lobes, tongues, and planes of the vertebrae fit together like pieces of a jigsaw puzzle. The circular pelvis sat next to it, as if resting, waiting for its owner to return. Turning in a slow circle, Mogotsi saw the rest of the bones scattered over a vast area. The skull there on the slope just above him, laying on its right side, empty sockets staring, the lower jaw missing, as was most of the left side of the skull. A lone femur lay a few feet away.

Mogotsi stood quietly, shocked by the ghastly sight, frightened of the implications it would have for the safari lodge and the lucrative wildlife-viewing program that brought new visitors to the conservancy each week. He had to report his find; if he didn't, someone else would eventually. But most of all, he wondered about the effect this discovery would have upon him and his family.

Deep in the Klip River Valley, the sun was dropping steadily toward the horizon, and Mogotsi scanned the scrub brush around him. Was he in danger of becoming the next meal for the area's predators and scavengers, which had tasted human flesh, perhaps for the first time?

Slowly, Mogotsi fished the portable radio out of his pocket and raised it to his lips. "Klip River Lodge," he said in a near whisper, "this is Sam. I have found what we have been looking for. I need you to send the police." He was purposefully obtuse in case any lodge guests were listening.

The voice of the dispatcher crackled in his ear. "What did you find, Sam?"

"I think … I think it's Chioto."

"Where are you?"

Mogotsi gave the dispatcher the local name for the area — DuRaan East — and his coordinates from the GPS, just in case.

A response came five minutes later. "Sam, the police are on their way. I also reached the manager on the phone. He is in Windhoek but will come back right away. He wants you to stay there until the police arrive."

"I will," said Mogotsi, again turning slowly to look around.

The radio crackled again, but this time came the voice of his partner for the day, a man who was watching a second pair of rhinos about a kilometre away: "I copy that, Sam. I will come to where you are."

Mogotsi hesitatingly took a step toward the skull, respectfully. Knowing he shouldn't, but unable to help himself, he gingerly picked it up, turned it to face him, and stared into the empty sockets. "I am so sorry this happened to you, my friend." A clump of soil fell from the right side of the skull, revealing a hole the diameter of his thumb, opposite to where a chunck of the skull was missing.

For Mogotsi, there was no doubt that this was all that remained of Chioto Shipanga, a fellow ranger who'd been missing for two days, the subject of an intensive search by friends, family, and colleagues. Mogotsi thought about his sister, Martha, and the devastation that his brother-in-law's death would cause, not only for her, but for their whole family.

CHAPTER 2

MAY 24

The late afternoon traffic on Windhoek's Independence Avenue was heavy, with cars and trucks and motorbikes jostling for position at the end of the workday. Horns beeped impatiently. Engines roared and paused. Music blared from open windows. It could have been a typical rush hour in any city on earth.

Danny Trang sat alone at a café on the corner of Independence and Fidel Castro Street, the pedestrian traffic on the sidewalk just inches from his right elbow. He'd finished his first full day of work in Namibia's capital city, a sprawling metropolis of more than three hundred thousand people. He felt like crap and was frustrated that his internal clock had been painfully slow to shift to his new time zone. He'd endured a nine-hour flight from Calgary, Alberta, to London, England, an eleven-hour flight from Heathrow airport to Johannesburg, and then a two-hour flight from there to Windhoek, but he was a seasoned traveller and had expected to hit the ground running, as he always did. It was a badge of honour for him. In his career as an adventure travel photojournalist, he'd learned all the tricks of the trade: changing his schedule before he left to match the time zone of his destination, using noise-cancelling headphones and compression socks on the plane, and going to bed when appropriate to the local time when he arrived. But despite having done all that, he still felt like a first-timer. The previous afternoon, in his first meeting — an interview with a source for his story — he'd yawned so many times that his jaw ached and he felt as though he'd gone eight rounds with a dentist.

When he left his hotel that morning, he was almost hit by a truck as he crossed the street; he hadn't yet remembered that vehicles drove on the left side of the road here. He'd have to constantly remind himself to look right instead of left when crossing the street.

He'd spent the day dragging his ass around to craft centres, the Parliament Gardens, the Independence Memorial Museum, the Supreme Court building, and the dramatic Christuskirche, the red-towered Lutheran church built in the early 1900s that dominated the downtown skyline.

Once he'd finished for the day, still feeling foggy and jelly-legged, he'd walked two blocks from his hotel to the coffee shop, intending to top up his caffeine level while getting a better feel for the rhythm of the city buzzing around him. It wasn't a quiet or particularly relaxing spot, but it offered him a good vantage point to watch the world go by.

Trang studied the plastic menu. He'd heard that Windhoek Lager was good, but knew he'd fall asleep if he had one at this time of the afternoon. Perhaps later, before bed. Instead, it was time for a big mug of strong, black tea with lots of sugar. *Not* that caffeine-free rooibos tea he'd heard so much about.

Trang twisted in his seat, trying to catch the eye of one of the roving servers. For the third time since he'd arrived, one of them glanced at him and his waving arm but quickly looked away.

Five minutes later, he tried again, this time waving with both arms. After the same surreptitious snub from the same server, Trang ignored his Canadian tendency to polite nonconfrontation, stood, and walked directly toward her. If he was rebuffed again, he would keep walking. "I'd like to order a big pot of black tea," he said quietly, almost apologetically. "I'm sitting at that table over there." He pointed. "And have been for at least ten minutes. But then, I think you already knew that."

"Oh yes, sir, sorry, sir," said the server, dropping her eyes to the floor. "I thought someone else had taken your order."

Trang returned to his seat, wondering when the drink would arrive, whether the water would be hot, what organic material might be in the tea bag. He gazed across the street at the shady retreat that was the city's Zoo Park, at the pairs of elderly men sitting on benches and the women and groups of children who were scattered around on blankets, claiming space among the trees where they were protected from the afternoon sun.

Trang had wandered into the park earlier that day on his way back to the hotel, pondering the elephant column, a bas-relief of an elephant hunt topped with a sculpted elephant skull. It was a reminder of why he was here. Pausing at the nearby German war memorial, he'd reflected on Namibia's history of more than one hundred years of foreign occupation, thirty years by Germany, then seventy-five under the rule of South Africa. Its independence had only recently been granted in 1990; the country had come a long way in a very short period.

With a bang, a china plate holding a pot of water, a tea bag, a large mug, and a spoon landed on the table. Trang had been jostled by locals on the sidewalk yesterday and again that morning, he'd been ignored by servers, and now one of them had served him as if he had somehow disrupted her entire day. He couldn't help but wonder if his arrival had somehow pissed off all the people of Windhoek. Even the taxi driver he'd hailed at the airport and the hotel clerk at check-in had been abrupt at best. As a journalist on assignment, he'd visited more than seventy-five countries and had never felt like he wasn't welcome. What was going on? His experience thus far didn't match the stories he'd heard about Namibia's hospitality, about the smiling, helpful residents who lived there. He'd have to ask someone about this — that is, if he could find anyone who would actually talk to him about it.

As he sipped his tea, Trang stared down the tree-lined street. Hints of German colonial architecture abounded. Windhoek resembled a capital city in northern Europe more than it did other African cities, with their frenetic pace and constant noise. Despite the clamour of the main street traffic, the city was refined, understated, and evoked a pleasant combination of history and anticipation of the future. At 1,700 metres above sea level — six hundred metres higher than his home in Kimberley, B.C. — and bordered by hills to the east and west, it was also much cooler than he had expected. But that would no doubt change the next day when he headed north to lower elevations.

Trang opened his book to review the notes he'd made in his meeting yesterday with the executive director of Namibia's community conservancy association, a key player in the country's approach to adventure travel. Unlike the servers and taxi drivers and the hotel clerk, the executive director had been not only friendly, but also very responsive to his many questions. She'd talked about how the conservancy model, which created self-governing local groups with responsibility for wildlife management, had opened the door for joint venture eco-lodges. Some of those lodges had built global reputations for the quality of their experiences and for their commitment to wildlife conservation. Her passion and pride had shone through, and Trang had left the meeting excited about visiting some of the lodges during his four-month stay.

"Here," the director had told him, "in a country that is less than thirty years old, we've successfully tried a new model." With eighty-two conservancies covering about 20 percent of the country, forty-two joint venture lodges, and the populations of iconic animals like elephants and rhinos generally doing well, she was convinced that this new model was working. And she'd been clear in stating that the conservancies weren't areas locked up to humans, sealed against any use. They were working landscapes with ecotourism and grazing and even, in some places, hunting. Trang loved finding juicy hooks for his travel stories — this was clearly a treasure trove. And the potential comparisons to British Columbia, where the provincial and federal governments were still debating who had jurisdiction over wildlife, might add significant contrast. Over the next few weeks, as he wrote his article for *Outside* magazine and maybe other outlets, he would peel back the layers of the story, looking for details on how the lodges worked, who invested in them, and what they meant for animals like the rhinoceros and the elephant. With luck and hard work, this trip might provide him with enough ideas and background for multiple pieces.

As he reached for his mug, something banged forcefully into his right elbow. His hand knocked over the mug, spilling tea across his notebook. "Hey!" he said to the large man passing by on the sidewalk. "Please be careful."

The man turned and snarled, "Go back to where you came from. And leave our daughters alone." He glared at Trang, his fists clenched as if he were considering something more than angry words.

Trang, surprised and frightened by the venom in the man's voice and eyes and by his veiled threat of violence, replied before his brain re-engaged, before his Canadian tendencies had him apologizing. "You want me to go back to Canada?"

"No!" the man yelled. "Go back to China. Leave our daughters alone. And stop poaching our rhinos."

DAVE BUTLER

As the man walked away and the other faces in the café turned back to what they'd been doing before the outburst, Trang blotted the sodden notebook pages with a stack of napkins. It wasn't the first time he'd been mistaken for Chinese, and it wouldn't be the last. It happened even in Canada, in cities large and small, but mostly in rural areas where white faces were the norm. The product of a Vietnamese mother and a Caucasian father, Trang believed — mostly because an ex-girlfriend had told him so — that he had the finest characteristics of both backgrounds: jet-black hair, tawny skin, and deep-blue eyes. But some people assumed a face like his could only have come from China, Japan, Vietnam, or some other Asian country. To them, even though he'd been born and raised in Vancouver, he was still different, foreign.

The local man's anger was a shock, mostly because it seemed so misplaced, but Trang was not surprised to learn that people here — at least this man — didn't like the Chinese. China's growing influence over global economies and politics was an issue in almost every country he'd visited over the last five years. However, he'd never felt such overt and dramatic anti-Chinese sentiment. It was normally subtle, not spoken out loud, expressed by looks rather than words. But here he felt it was just below the surface.

The man had been angry enough to take it out on a stranger sitting in a café, enjoying the afternoon sunshine. *Stay away from our daughters* — what had he meant by that? And then there was his comment about poaching. The official Trang had met with yesterday had suggested that the conservancies, the joint venture lodges, and the fact that communities were recognizing the value of wildlife for ecotourism had all contributed to a reduction in poaching. Was there something going on that he hadn't picked up on in his pre-trip research? Maybe he'd have to dig deeper.

Rather than wait for more tea, Trang stood, gathered his notebook and cellphone, and slid them into his camera bag. He handed the server twenty Namibian dollars as he left, the amount — roughly equivalent to a Canadian toonie — indicating his displeasure with the service. He then headed north along Independence Avenue. He needed a long walk to shake off the jet lag and the disturbing feeling that he wasn't welcome in this country.

CHAPTER 3

MAY 24-25

After clearing passport control at Windhoek's Hosea Kutako International Airport, Jenny Willson and her friend and colleague Tracy Brown muscled their way past a crowd of tourists, grabbed their bulging duffles from the luggage carousel, bypassed the broken X-ray machine, and walked through the sliding doors into the arrivals area.

Willson paused. Her only travel experience outside Canada or the northern U.S. was an ill-advised university spring break trip to Cancun that she remembered little about. As a result, she was amazed by the sea of faces in front of her, some white, but mostly black. They stared at her, shouted at her, waved signs with offers of taxis and shuttles. Willson prided herself on her self-confidence, but she found this first African scene overwhelming and slightly unsettling.

"Welcome to Namibia," said Brown, grinning widely as she grabbed her friend's elbow and urged her forward through the crowd. "We're looking for the shuttle to the Avani Windhoek Hotel downtown. There should be a sign here somewhere."

"It's like we're in a different country," said Willson wryly, following Brown through the throng of people toward a smiling man holding a sign for their hotel. Brown turned and grinned at her but didn't respond.

They waited outside for the hotel shuttle. The air was warm and heavy, the sky big and blue with no clouds in sight. Willson thought of her grandmother, who had visited Namibia nearly thirty years ago, when it had been called South West Africa and was still under the governance of South Africa. She remembered the post-cards her grandmother had sent, with images of people and wildlife so strange and different from what Willson saw every day in Canada, that as a young child, she had been captivated. What must it have been like back then for a young woman to step off a ship into this strange country so different from home? She felt an unexpected connection to her grandmother, who had died of cancer five years ago, when her sixty-seven years of hard drinking and hard living had finally caught up with her.

Willson was tired, sweaty, and jet-lagged after the twenty-one hours of travel from Calgary to Windhoek via Frankfurt. The shuttle ride into the city passed in a blur. At one point, she thought she saw a troop of baboons observing them from the top of a bluff. But being in a state of exhaustion, she wasn't sure.

As soon as they arrived at their accommodations, Willson automatically thought she should send her mother an email to confirm her safe arrival. Then melancholy hit her, a wave of sadness and loneliness. Her mother was not there to receive any emails. She had committed suicide just two weeks ago. Her mother's despondency and subsequent decision to take her own life had been the gut-wrenching, heartbreaking outcome of Willson's last case. Now she was alone in the world, without parents or siblings, without a place to call home, and with a grim feeling that she wasn't worthy of love. Only her deep shock acted as a barrier, kept her from being completely overwhelmed by grief.

It wasn't until she and Brown were sitting at Joe's Beer House later that evening, large glasses of cold Windhoek Lager in hand, that she finally began to relax. Apparently sensing her mood, Brown raised her glass. "Here's to your mom, here's to us, and here's to our Namibian adventure!"

"To Mum ... and to us," said Willson with a small smile at Brown. "I still can't believe she's gone. Being so far away makes it even harder to grasp the fact that she's not back in Golden, working in the library and waiting for a message from me."

"You know I'm here for you, Jenny. Let me know what I can do."

Willson opened the large menu. "Right now, you can help me choose an entree. I'm hungry enough to eat a zebra."

"You can't get a whole zebra, Jen," said Brown, pointing at the last item under *Mains*, "but you can chow down on a damn big zebra loin steak."

"Oh, man, I was just kidding. Can you really order zebra here? They eat it?"

"Yup. And apparently any of the members of the antelope family, as well: oryx, kudu, springbok. Or you could try crocodile? I read they're all raised on game farms or are harvested legally from private game reserves, and it's all popular meat for the *braai* — that's 'barbecue' in Afrikaans."

Coming from Canada, Willson had no aversion to eating game meat, if it was hunted legally. "So instead of shrimp on the barbie, it's zebra on the *braai*?"

They ordered their entrees and another round of beers. The lager was cold, crisp, and pale, perfect for quenching throats parched by the dry air circulating in the plane cabins during their long flights.

Willson scanned the large room. Brown had told her that the restaurant was famous in Windhoek for its food and quirky atmosphere. Along the front of the bar, toilets stood in as seats. Empty Jägermeister bottles lined the wall to their left. Two entwined kudu skulls hung behind the bar, their horns wrapped together in a fatal spiral. The floors were rough wood, the surfaces uneven and pockmarked.

Willson turned her attention back to Brown. "So, now that we're here, what happens next? I'm itching to get started."

"Believe it or not, we're leaving on safari tomorrow for seven days. The folks at Wild Dog Safaris will pick us up tomorrow morning at eight. I think we go to their compound on the edge of town for a briefing and to meet the others on the tour. From there, we all head north together for a seven-day camping trip."

"That's news to me," said Willson, confused. "I thought we were going to meet the people we'll be working with."

"Oh, yeah, I got a text just after we arrived. You were in the washroom. Plans have changed … in a good way. Anita Ghebo — that's our contact in the Ministry of Environment and Tourism — says they're busy this week with unanticipated meetings, so they're sending us north to get an initial look at the areas we'll be working in. But she'll meet us for breakfast tomorrow before we leave."

"Have you been to the places we're going?"

"Nope," said Brown, sipping her beer and leaning back in her chair as the server slid a steaming ceramic plate of oryx lasagna in front of her. "When I was here three years ago, we were in the south, near Fish River Canyon. What we see over the next seven days will be as new to me as it is to you."

"And after the tour?" In her fog of grief, Willson hadn't asked many questions about their itinerary.

"As far as I know, we'll be heading up to the new law enforcement training centre in a place called …" She checked her phone. "Waterberg Plateau Park. We'll see how things are running there and begin teaching after that. I expect we'll be at the centre for a month or so before heading out in the field."

"Sounds good. And I think I'm going to like this, too," Willson said, digging in to her sizzling zebra steak with a sharp knife.

The Wild Dog tour group left Windhoek early the next morning in a fourteen-passenger Toyota Dyna truck, a lumbering beast with high windows and a pop-up roof for wildlife viewing. It wasn't luxurious by any means, but it was perfect for carrying everything they needed for their northern tour — food, tents, bedding, a stove, and all their luggage.

As they travelled north, Willson marvelled at the unfamiliar landscape: wide open spaces, red soils and rocks as far as she could see, and few trees, but hundreds of termite mounds. The peaks of the Erongo Mountains poked out of the distant western horizon in two pronounced bumps.

During the drive, they passed troops of baboons who sat and watched as the truck passed, and a pair of ostriches running along parallel to the highway. There were also several lone impala and a few sightings of springbok — their size and colour were reminiscent of the antelope in southern Alberta.

For a midmorning break, they pulled in at the woodcarving market in the city of Okahandja. Willson and Brown wandered down the two rows of small tarp-covered shops tended by polite but persistent vendors. "Hello, ma'am. Come and see my shop, please, ma'am." They bought nothing, knowing they would be back at some point.

For lunch, the group stopped under the wide branches of a lone acacia tree by the highway north of Otjiwarongo. They assembled their own sandwiches and sat down to eat them in canvas camp chairs in the shade as traffic hissed by on the asphalt road.

Still suffering from jet lag, Willson fell asleep in the middle of the afternoon, her face plastered against the back window of the truck. She awoke with a start to discover they'd reached the Von Lindequist Gate at the eastern entrance to Etosha National Park. Her right cheek was red and sweaty, her brown hair was matted against the side of her face, and her neck was sore. When she turned to look at Brown, her partner burst into laughter. "Nice look you're rockin' there, Jenny."

"I stink," said Willson, sniffing her armpit. "I need a shower."

They arrived at Namutoni Camp in Etosha National Park near dusk. After checking in at Namutoni's main registration centre, the group watched the sun go down from the tower of the old German fort, originally built in 1896. Willson and Brown walked to the campsite, detouring to check out the covered viewing area at Namutoni's water hole. Sitting quietly, while dark bats and large moths flitted in and out of the spotlights, Willson whispered to Brown, "I can't believe I'm really here."

After dinner, the campfire lit the faces of the Wild Dog guests in dancing pulses of orange and white. As the dry mopane wood crackled and popped inside the metal firepit, sparks floated up, creating red streaks in the black sky. Seated on a camp chair, Willson — freshly fed and showered — looked over the top of a mug of Amarula liqueur at her fellow travellers circled around the fire.

Tracy sat to her left, talking with Kathy and James, a forty-something British couple who were missionaries. They'd brought their three children to Windhoek from a village in Dorset a year earlier, but this was their first visit to the northern regions of the country. To Willson's right were Werner and Angelika, an older German couple who spoke little English. They were apparently on their fourth visit to the country and had with them a pile of Nikon photography gear that rivalled the stock of most small-town camera stores. Beside them sat Danny Trang, the seventh guest, a quiet man in his late thirties with Asian features. He'd introduced himself that morning as a photojournalist from British Columbia, but since then had spoken little, spending much of his day shooting images and scrawling in his notebook. Willson assumed that he was either very shy or very private. Recently, while working on an investigation back in Canada, Willson had had a painful experience with an American journalist — he had betrayed her, both personally *and* professionally — so she thought it wise to stay as far away from this journalist as possible. She'd been burned more than once and had no interest in being burned again.

With her belly full and a soothing drink in hand, she tilted her head back to look at the stellar display above them. It was a very different sky than she was used to in the Rockies. Here they sat at almost 19 degrees of latitude below the equator. She quickly found the Andromeda constellation, which at home was visible only in autumn. There on the horizon was Orion; in the mountains at home, that appeared only in winter. And replacing the familiar North Star, she saw the Southern Cross for the first time in her life. Her time on the web while sitting in the Frankfurt airport had paid off.

"Could I have everyone's attention, please?"

Willson lowered her head to look at the speaker, illuminated by the glow of the flames.

"My name is Ian Kamanya, and I am from the Herrero tribe. My home is near here, on the north side of the park. Welcome to Namibia and to Etosha National Park."

Kamanya was a tall man with ebony skin. His head was shaved close, and his brilliant smile revealed a single gold canine tooth.

"Before joining Wild Dog as a guide," he continued, "I worked for the Ministry of Environment and Tourism in wildlife management. I was chosen for this tour because of my knowledge of the area's geography and wildlife. Please ask me any questions, any time."

He stood on the far side of the crackling fire from his seven guests. "I know that was a long and hot first day, but it was necessary to get us up here. Now that we're in the north, we can take things slower." He smiled again. "As you know, we're now on the eastern edge of Etosha National Park. It is one of the largest national parks in Namibia, and one of the largest in all of Africa. It's been a park since 1907, and depending on what local language you speak, its name means either 'great white place,' 'place of mirages,' 'lake of a mother's tears,' or 'the place where no plants grow.' Tomorrow, when we see the expansive salt pan that dominates the park, you'll understand. You can decide which name fits best."

As the wind shifted, he moved around the fire, closer to Willson and Brown. "We'll have an early start tomorrow because we're going to drive some of the park roads in search of animals and birds. Breakfast will be at six, so I encourage you to get up earlier to pack your tents and sleeping bags and have your luggage ready to load in the truck."

Over the next two hours, Kamanya and his assistant wandered off to bed, as did the other five guests. Headlamps flashed in the dark, silhouettes danced in canvas tents, voices whispered. Finally, the campsite was quiet, and Willson and Brown remained alone by the dying fire. They sipped their drinks in silence.

Off to their left came a series of moans, a long sequence of deep roars, then grunts. Willson turned to Brown. "What the hell is that? Is someone having more fun than we are?"

"Lions," Brown said. "They've started their night hunt."

Then came a series of whoops, yowls, and grunty laughs.

"And that?" whispered Willson.

"Hyenas," said Brown. "They're either hunting on their own, or they're following the lions."

Willson's eyes were wide. "They're outside the fence, right?"

"They are. Their calls do carry, but I think they're close to the fence. Exciting, huh?"

Willson shivered. "Can you imagine being an ungulate out there in the dark, hearing that?"

"That's fear at its most primal. And they deal with it every day of their lives. Some unlucky kudu, hartebeest, or zebra will be chosen tonight. Lions are the top predator here, and they're very efficient. They take only what they need to survive."

"Unlike humans," Willson said, staring into the darkness. "Which is why we're here."

CHAPTER 4

MAY 25

Leaning against the dusty side of the police truck, Sam Mogotsi stared into the back at the black vinyl bag containing what he now knew were the remains of Chioto Shipanga. After his initial radio call, it had taken four hours for members of the Namibian Police's Crime Investigation Directorate, their Regional Protected Resources Unit, and the National Forensic Science Institute to arrive at the scene, which was located in a remote area of the Klip River Valley. When an officer with an ancient metal detector uncovered a ring from the dirt near the scattered bones of one hand, Mogotsi immediately recognized it as a unique piece of jewellery that had belonged to Chioto. A few moments later, under a shoulder blade, they found a single misshapen bullet, expanded at one end like a mushroom.

Then the entire entourage had returned to the Klip River Lodge. Now the men and the emergency vehicles were congregated in a remote corner of the maintenance yard, so as not to upset the guests or set local tongues wagging unnecessarily. The setting sun lit the canyon to the west so that it looked like the valley was on fire.

A burly police inspector by the name of Nashili, with greying temples and three gold suns shining from his dark shoulder epaulets, shifted in front of Mogotsi. "Tell me again how you found the body," he said, his pen poised over his notebook.

"Like I told you, I found it on my regular patrol today. I was following two rhinos when I saw the bones. At first, I thought they were from an animal. Then I saw the skull. It was upside down, the upper jaw facing up. The lower jaw bone was not there."

"And you touched it before telling the lodge what you had found?"

"I knew I shouldn't, but I did. I wanted to know for sure if it was human."

"Did you touch anything else?"

"No. As soon as I saw that the skull was human, I put it down exactly as I found it."

"Did you see the hole?"

"Not right away. But when I turned the skull over, a piece of dirt came out of the hole. It was obvious what had happened."

Nashili stared hard at Mogotsi. "Do you *know* what happened?"

"I'm not a trained policeman. But I used to be a ... a hunter. I'm guessing Chioto — if it is Chioto — was shot."

"You may be right," said the officer. "But let's change course. When we found that ring today, you immediately said you knew who it belonged to."

"I did. We've been looking for Chioto for two days, ever since he didn't report in from a patrol. He and I have been ... *were* friends for a long time. Since our school days. I remember that ring. It came from his grandfather. He always wore it."

"You knew him well, then?"

"I did. He is also my brother-in-law. He married my younger sister, Martha."

Nashili again stared at Mogotsi. "How well did you two get along?"

Mogotsi froze, realizing for the first time that the police might consider him more than just the man who had found the body. He could be a suspect. "Good. Very good! He's like a brother to me. Both Natasha — my wife — and Martha will tell you that."

"We will certainly talk to them. When did you last see Shipanga?"

Mogotsi looked toward the canyon as the sun dipped below the horizon. He felt a sudden chill despite the lingering heat. "The day before he went missing. We were at their house for dinner that night. He and I talked about plans for the following day, and where he might find rhinos in the middle part of the valley."

"And where were you the day he went missing? Why weren't you with him?"

"I was in a different part of the valley."

"Did you see him that day?"

"No, but I heard him on the radio. Neither of us had

partners, but we wanted to cover as much ground as we could, so we went separately."

"What about yesterday? Where were you?"

"It was my day off. I had to drive Natasha to Outjo because she had an appointment with the doctor. She's pregnant."

"Were you there all day?"

"Most of it. The appointment was at ten in the morning, so we left home around eight o'clock. We had lunch after the appointment, picked up a few things at the store, then drove back. I think we were home by four."

"Did you know Shipanga was missing when you went to Outjo with your wife?"

"I knew he hadn't reported in, but sometimes he stayed out overnight. We all do, now and then, if we want to follow some tracks, or get an early start the next day."

"Did you see anyone out there the day before yesterday, the day Chioto went missing?"

Another change of direction.

"No," said Mogotsi, shaking his head. "We always look for signs of other humans while we're out there: tire tracks, footprints. We listen for vehicles, people talking, low-flying aircraft, gunfire. I didn't see or hear anything."

"Speaking of guns, do you own any guns, Sam?"

Mogotsi paused. The inspector was making him uneasy with his constantly shifting questions. "I … I own a .303 rifle. That's all."

"Where is it?"

"At my home, between here and Kamanjab. It's locked in a shed outside."

"Do you mind if one of my officers goes to your house to get it?"

"It hasn't been fired in a few years." He put his hand in his pocket and pulled out a ring of keys. "Here is the key to the shed. Why are you interested in my rifle?"

Inspector Nashili took the key and passed it to a sergeant standing next to him. "We don't yet know the calibre of the weapon used in this offence," he said. "By verifying that it was not your rifle that shot the bullet, we can cross you — or your rifle, at least — off our list." He paused, looking down at Mogotsi's feet. "Have you been wearing those boots all day today?"

"Yes," Mogotsi said, "I wear them every day to work."

"We must take them as evidence, to compare to any tracks we found near the body." He motioned to the same sergeant.

Mogotsi's discomfort was growing. "Uh, okay. I have some old shoes in my truck."

The inspector tucked his notebook into a breast pocket. "I think those are all the questions I have for now, Sam. We may want to talk to you again, so stick around. If this does turn out to be your brother-in-law, then please accept my condolences. We will do our very best to find out who killed him."

In a daze after the day's unexpected events, Mogotsi gave the sergeant his boots, replacing them with a pair of worn leather shoes, and stumbled over to the staff car park. He leaned against a post and stared at the dark sky to the west. He thought about Chioto, about loss, and about the wave of trouble his brother-in-law's death was going to unleash … had already unleashed. For the lodge, the conservancy, their family, and perhaps most of all, for him. Twenty minutes later, he walked through the main lodge entrance and entered an unmarked side door to the small staff lounge. He needed a beer, so he helped himself to one from the bar fridge, then wrote his name on a list so the cost would be deducted from his salary. He didn't normally do this, because Natasha liked his paycheques to be the full amount. However, this was a day unlike any other.

With the lodge guests out on the patio enjoying their "sundowners" (gin and tonics traditionally enjoyed at sundown), the serving staff focused on keeping the guests happy, and the kitchen staff preparing dinner, Mogotsi had the lounge to himself. He sat by himself in a corner. He had to figure out how he was going to tell Martha and Natasha about Chioto's death ... unless, maybe, the police visited them before he got home. If they hadn't, maybe he could persuade his wife to give Martha the bad news. The wailing and crying would be unbearable.

The door to the lounge blew open with a crash. "There you are, Sam," said Hans deVilliers in his heavy Afrikaans accent. Tall with a massive brown beard, deVilliers was the manager of Klip River Lodge. "I've been looking everywhere for you."

"I was talking to the police. They just finished with me, and I needed a beer. It's been a very long day."

"I came from Windhoek as soon as I got the call."

Mogotsi finished his beer in two long gulps. Still trying to collect his thoughts and control his emotions, he stood and walked across the room to put the empty bottle in a recycling bin.

"What the hell happened?"

Mogotsi relayed the day's events for his boss, including his interview with the police inspector.

"Are you sure it's Chioto?"

"Yes, fairly sure. We found his pinky ring near the body. I would know that ring anywhere. And no one has seen him for two days."

"Do they know yet how he died?"

Mogotsi took a moment to answer. The inspector had warned him about sharing the details of what he'd seen. But in his shock, he felt that he couldn't help himself. "It ... it looks like he was murdered, sir, shot from the right side. I saw a bullet hole in the skull, and a large exit hole on the other side. The police took his remains with them. I guess they'll know more after the experts look at them."

"Do you think he was shot where you found him?"

"I do not know. The animals had discovered the body long before I got there, so all that was left were scattered bones. We found a bullet near the body, but that doesn't mean he was shot there. It could have happened anywhere."

"Who do they think did it?"

"They do not know. But I think I'm on their suspect list because I found the body."

"What?" asked deVilliers. "They can't be serious. You and Chioto were friends for ages. And he married your sister!" The manager stared at his ranger for a moment. "You didn't have anything to do with it, did you?"

"Of course not," Mogotsi said, a tear sliding down his dusty cheek. "He's like a brother to me."

"Chioto was one of my best rangers, like you. And he was a good man," deVilliers said. "Why would someone kill him?" His face suddenly darkened. "*Diep in die kak.*"

Mogotsi understood enough Afrikaans to know that his boss thought they were in deep shit.

The manager paused his pacing, apparently noticing the tear on Mogotsi's cheek. "I'm sorry, Sam, I should have asked how you're doing. Finding a body is one thing, but if it was Chioto … I can't imagine how you feel right now."

Mogotsi stared vacantly at a small window. His heart raced and his vision blurred. His grief and guilt and sense of loss over Chioto's death were palpable, impacting his entire body. "I don't know how I feel. This is a real shock. My family will be devastated."

DeVilliers ran his fingers through his thinning grey hair, which was a dramatic counterpoint to his massive beard. When Mogotsi had first met deVilliers, he couldn't help but think that the man's head was upside down on his neck, with the hair on the bottom instead of at the top.

"This is bad on so many levels," deVilliers said. "I'll have to deal with the police. The bloody media will come calling, which could devastate our reputation and our bookings. And I'll have to report to the conservancy's management committee. All seventeen of those people will want to know how this happened and what I'm going to do about it." He moved across the room to grab Mogotsi's hand. "Again, I am sorry. None of that is your concern. We will make it right for your family, Sam. For Martha and her daughter. You have my word."

Mogotsi knew that his boss meant it; he would do all he could to help the family through this tragedy. But there was only so much he could do.

CHAPTER 5

MAY 27

After a quick breakfast and a well-practised breakdown of the tents in the pre-dawn darkness, the Wild Dog Safaris group left Hoada campsite, one of the most dramatic places Danny Trang had ever camped. Now they were heading west toward the Atlantic Ocean and Skeleton Coast National Park.

The early morning air was surprisingly cool as the tour van finally crossed the 1,645-metre summit of Grootberg Pass. For the last hour, the pass had been an obvious notch ahead of them in the rugged pre-dawn sky. Even now, the sun had yet to rise over the Grootberg Plateau to their left. The gritty taste of dust filled the air.

Danny Trang sat across the narrow aisle from Jenny Willson, his fellow Canadian, on a bench seat near the rear of the truck. Wrapped in a red-and-white scarf he'd picked up on a trip to Jordan, he huddled with his hands deep in the pockets of his light jacket. Across the aisle, Willson was doing the same. Next to her, Tracy Brown slumped against the window, asleep.

After two days driving in and around Etosha National Park, filling his memory cards with thousands of images of the landscape and its wildlife — lions, rhinos, elephants, giraffes, birds, reptiles, spiders, and scorpions — Trang was a believer. Like the marketing people had promised, Namibia was the least densely populated country in Africa, a mosaic of dramatic landscapes, from grasslands to woodlands to pure deserts. And the wildlife was more diverse and plentiful than he had imagined. The ecotourism potential here was incredible, and he was excited to share the story with readers back in North America.

Trang saw Willson shift in her seat. "What do you think, Danny?" she asked in a muffled voice just loud enough to be heard above the roar of the truck, but not loud enough to wake their fellow travellers. "Is Namibia what you thought it would be?"

Trang turned to look at her. Between her hat and scarf, only her eyes were visible. "I'm struggling to process it all; it's so much more than I expected." His gaze shifted forward again and he kept his voice low. "So far I've just been taking notes and shooting all the images I can, but at some point, I'm going to need some quiet time to figure out what it all means, and figure out how I'll weave everything I've seen, heard, smelled, tasted, and touched into stories. I've been to a lot of places around the world, but this country overwhelms me … on many levels."

"What strikes you the most?"

Trang paused. It was a tough question. "It would have to be the conservancies and the eco-lodges we've seen so far. It makes me think about the challenges we face back home and how we've dealt with them. Other than maybe grizzly bear viewing on the B.C. coast, I think we're still in a resource extraction mindset in the West. Tourism is seen as an afterthought, and often, a threat to wildlife. Which is hypocritical when hunting, logging, oil and gas, and mining are such big deals in B.C." Trang felt Willson watching him.

"Do you really think it's different here?" she asked. "They face many of the same pressures."

"Maybe," he said. "Maybe not. They seem to have developed a bold model for a country that's still in its relative infancy. From what I've seen so far and from what people have told me, it's not perfect. But it sure turns democracy and wildlife conservation on its head. And like I said, tourism seems to be at the centre, rather than on the outside looking in. I'm looking forward to being here long enough to dig deep into how things are really working. But I'm rambling. What do you think?"

"I haven't been here long enough to agree or disagree. But I do recognize that we're only scratching the surface on this trip. There is so much more to learn. Like you said, it'll take time to connect all the dots. How long are you here?"

"Four months, give or take, depending on what assignments I can dig up along the way. *Outside* magazine is covering my airfare, but I'm a freelancer, so I always keep in touch with a number of magazine and newspaper editors while I travel. The fact that I'm already here in the country makes it less of a risk for other editors to agree to one of my pitches."

"What'll you do after this safari?"

Trang smiled. "I'm excited. I have a camping truck rented for the rest of my time here. I got a heck of a deal for a long-term rental. It has a pop-up tent on the top, accessible by a ladder, and everything I need inside the canopy, — sleeping bag, cooking gear, stove, lanterns, you name it. All I'll need to buy is food and water now and then. I can basically go wherever I want and be self-sufficient."

"That sounds great." Willson sat up to catch the first rays of the sun as they snuck in through the window. "That black rhino we saw yesterday was so cool, wasn't it? It was my first rhino."

"I saw a rhino in a national park in India a few years ago, but it wasn't the same as that big bull coming out of the bush so close to the van. I got some great images when he was moving toward us."

"I think we pissed him off. I'd love to see your pictures." Willson grabbed the top of the seat in front of her to pull herself into an upright position. "I guess this tour is a prime example of what you were saying about wildlife viewing. Everyone was trying to get pictures of that rhino when it appeared, and at the same time, no one said a word. It was as if something magical was happening. No wonder people pay good money for this experience."

Trang turned back to Willson again. "Did you notice, when the rhino appeared, that our guide gave me a really aggressive look and said the animal was on the move, so it wouldn't be in the same place a day or a week from now?"

"I did notice. I figured he just hates journalists."

He could hear from her voice that Willson was joking, but he couldn't tell if she was on the same page as him. "He was clearly sending me a message," Trang said. "I've asked him questions about rhinos a few times on the trip, but he always changes the subject, like he's trying to keep it all secret from me."

"He must assume that you're Chinese ... and therefore a poacher?"

"I think you're right. Ever since I arrived in Namibia, people have been less than friendly to me. It took me twice as long to get through airport security as anyone else. The officer must have asked me ten times what I was doing here. I had to show him copies of my articles and assignment emails from editors to prove I was a journalist, and he went through my phone like all the mysteries of the universe were in there. I've been jostled on the street, ignored by taxi drivers and waiters. I even had a guy in Windhoek yell at me to go back to China. Maybe I need a shirt that says, 'I am not Chinese,'" he joked.

"Could it be that people just don't like your personality?"

Trang shook his head but chuckled. Willson was clearly trying to lighten his mood. "Seriously, though, it's going to make my job tough if people won't be open with me. I knew this might be an issue, but I'm surprised at how overt it is."

"Have you told anyone that you're Vietnamese-Canadian, not Chinese?"

"I told the customs guy, but it didn't seem to make any difference to him."

"You're going to have to really charm people into talking to you," Willson said.

Trang felt the truck slow down and saw a petrol station through the front window. "This must be Palmwag." He could see the wires and poles of the veterinary fence at the north edge of the tiny town, a demarcation line they'd already crossed three times in their trip. Ten feet high, it prevented cattle and meat and dairy products from being transported south, to stop the spread of disease. "On the map, it looks like about another two hours to the coast from here."

"Jesus. My butt will definitely not thank me tomorrow," Willson quipped as she shifted to a more comfortable position on the slippery seat.

The interior of the country had been dramatic, yet still, Trang was unprepared for the famed Skeleton Coast. It was like the surface of Mars, except with oxygen. There was plenty of ocean and rock and sand, and little of anything else.

They stopped for a lunch, then continued to Cape Cross, where they all got out of the truck to see the enormous colony of Cape fur seals that could be observed from the wooden boardwalks and viewing platforms. The beach was covered with tens of thousands of the blubbery, barking, fighting, stinking animals. Just as many swam and dove in the waves offshore.

With the wind blowing off the ocean and fog swirling around them, Trang, Willson, Brown, and the others listened intently as Ian Kamanya described the seal's life cycle. The massive bulls spent most of their time offshore, he told them, while the pregnant cows came ashore to give birth in early December. Two of every three pups died from trampling, drowning, or predation by the hyenas, jackals, and desert-dwelling lions that hunted the edges of the colony at night.

Trang quickly realized that the smell emanating from the colony came as much from dead animals as from live ones. The carcass of a massive bull lay bloated and rotting under the walkway; Trang almost lost his lunch when he understood what he was seeing and smelling.

"Ian," Brown asked the guide, "why does Namibia still cull almost ninety thousand of these seals every year, despite all the international pressure to stop the hunt?"

Kamanya grimaced. "This comes up nearly every time we come here. Personally, I'm opposed to the cull, just so you know." He lifted his right hand in the air, palm upward. "On the pro-cull side, we have fishermen who see the seals threatening their livelihoods. We have local businessmen who create jobs and make lots of money from the oil derived from the seal blubber — they call it 'Namibian Sunshine.' It's allegedly high in omega-3 fatty acids and more easily absorbed by humans than fish oils are. We have international buyers who pay good money for the furs, too, which are made into coats, mostly by one Turkish fashion tycoon who sells them to Russian and Chinese buyers. And even the bull penises are sold for use in traditional Chinese medicines."

He looked at Trang every time he referenced China.

This was starting to piss Trang off. "Ian," he said, "for the record, I'm Canadian, and my mother is originally from Vietnam. I have no connection to China whatsoever."

"China, Vietnam, there's no difference as far as we're concerned," said Kamanya. "People from those countries come to Namibia pretending they're tourists, then take as much as they can from us, legally or otherwise, with no care about the mess they leave behind."

Willson turned and stared at the guide, her eyebrows raised. But then, as if a switch had been flipped and Trang had not spoken up at all, Kamanya raised his left hand and continued his lecture.

"On the other side of the argument, we have biologists and conservationists who say the cull is not sustainable and that the seals don't measurably impact the commercial fishery. And, as Tracy pointed out, more than thirty-five countries around the world have banned the import of products of commercial seal hunts. That includes the United States." He turned to Willson. "It does not include Canada, which still has its own seal harvest."

"The difference, Ian," said Trang, trying to reinforce the fact that he was a Canuck, "is that in Canada, the hunt is largely carried out by Indigenous Peoples — the Inuit — who have a legal right under treaty to follow their traditions. Regardless, many in the country aren't one hundred percent comfortable with it, either." He changed course a little. "But considering how successful the other wildlife programs are, rather than kill the seals, couldn't Namibia develop seal tourism? Seal viewing, like we're doing now, or swimming with the seals. That would create jobs and bring foreign money into the economy."

"We could," said Kamanya, "but until some nations stop demanding fur coats, bull penises, and Namibian Sunshine — or, for that matter, rhino horns and elephant ivory — it's going to be difficult to make that transition." With that, Kamanya turned toward the van. "Time to head to Swakopmund, folks!"

As Kamanya lead the group away, Trang and Willson lingered on the edge of the viewing platform. The seals had vanished behind a dense bank of fog, but he could still hear and smell them. He glanced at Willson and could see that she might just be starting to comprehend how complex Namibia was. There were many layers to its conservation story — some conflicting, but all complicated. It was a story begging to be told by a certain curious photojournalist. As if following choreography, they both shrugged, turned, and walked over to join the group picking their way back to the vehicle.

CHAPTER 6

JUNE 1

Willson and Brown sat on hard wooden chairs at the back of the warm lecture hall — the solar-powered air conditioner on the roof was trying but failing to cool the room. The class was sparse; sixteen experienced Namibian rangers, wardens, and police officers sat at a scattering of small desks, their backs to Willson and Brown. Some wore uniforms of green and khaki, others dark-blue police uniforms, and still others were in civilian clothing. Willson noted that of the sixteen students, four were women.

At the front of the room, Anita Ghebo, the senior official from the Ministry of Environment and Tourism, launched into her introduction. "Welcome to the Waterberg Wildlife and Law Enforcement Training Centre," she said. Ghebo was a small woman with smiling eyes and curly black hair pulled into a large bun at the back of her head. "All of you should know that this past summer, the Namibian government amended the Nature Conservation Ordinance to show its commitment to ending the practice of poaching. Now, there are large penalties for illegally hunting elephants and rhinos. Convictions can result in fines of up to twenty-five million Namibian dollars, twenty-five years in prison, or both."

Willson leaned toward Brown. "They *are* serious," she whispered.

Brown kept her voice low. "Talk is cheap. We'll see if they truly are serious. I've seen this kind of thing come and go in the U.S. I believe actions, not words."

"The opening of this training centre is part of that commitment," Ghebo continued. "You are the first class in the advanced wildlife law enforcement program. You'll be here for a month of classes and exercises, covering everything from patrols and navigation to crime scene handling, investigation tactics, and intelligence gathering, as well as wildlife law and court procedures. If you pass the course, we'll expect you to be leaders in your own regions of the country, to participate in increased joint-agency patrols on the ground and in the air, and to work with your colleagues to *thoroughly* investigate wildlife crimes." Her emphasis on the word *thoroughly* was not lost on the two North Americans.

Ghebo pointed at Willson and Brown, and the entire class turned toward them. "I want to offer a special welcome and thanks to two of our visiting instructors. They are here as the result of an appeal for assistance from my minister directly to the secretary-general of Interpol, who was here last year on a familiarization trip. Jenny Willson is a national park warden and law enforcement specialist from Banff National Park in Canada."

Willson stood and waved to the students.

"She recently cracked an international poaching case that involved animals being illegally shot in Canadian national parks and trophies being taken from there into the United States. This is Jenny's first time in Namibia, so please make her welcome."

Ghebo turned toward Brown. "Jenny's partner in that investigation was Tracy Brown. Tracy is from the U.S. Fish and Wildlife Service. She was here a few years ago when her agency was running Operation Crash, a massive, successful crackdown on the smuggling of elephant ivory into her country." Brown, too, stood and waved. "Jenny and Tracy will be with us here at Waterberg all month, teaching parts of the course. Then, they'll spend up to six months in the field working with those of you from Etosha National Park and the Kunene region."

Willson knew that Brown shared her discomfort at being introduced as an expert. They'd certainly come to help, to do their part to save rhinos and elephants. But they both fully appreciated that much of Africa's history involved strangers — so-called experts, in some cases — coming in from other countries to "help." The entire continent had been negatively impacted by centuries of colonization, from the Romans and Egyptians in the north, to the Arabs in the north and east, to Belgium, Britain, France, Germany, Italy, Portugal, and Spain in the south. That was not a club Willson wanted to be associated with.

"You are the sharp edge of a new spear," Ghebo said to the students as they turned back to face her, "a spear built to curb unprecedented levels of poaching in Namibia." She pointed at each of the students one by one. "We need every one of you to take this very seriously. Poaching threatens our safety and security, our economy, and the growing number of communities that depend on wildlife for their livelihood." She paused, letting the significance of her words sink in.

"During the course of my own studies, I have heard instructors and schoolteachers use the same metaphor … that being taught different lessons is like receiving many stones to place in your bag. That your bag will get fuller and fuller as the years go by. Perhaps some of you have heard this metaphor also. Some instructors would suggest that you should keep only the stones given by African teachers and discard those from white teachers. But that would be a very big mistake. If you want to succeed in this fight against poaching, you will keep every stone in your bag, because at some point, you will need each and every one." Ghebo paused again. "Now I'll turn you over to your first instructor. He will lead you through the details of our new wildlife laws. Thank you, and good luck."

Ghebo walked to the back of the classroom and motioned for Willson and Brown to join her outside.

The three women stood in the shade of the building. It was still early morning, but Willson could feel the air heating up already, like an oven rising to its baking temperature.

"I received some bad news late last night," said Ghebo, wringing her hands, "which makes your presence here that much more important."

"What happened?" asked Willson.

"We found a rhino carcass in the ≠Khoadi-//Hôas Conservancy, southwest of where you were in Etosha. It was killed about a week ago."

"I remember seeing the sign for the conservancy on our way from the Hoada campsite through Grootberg Pass," said Willson. She thought back to the night they'd spent at the Hoada Camp, one of the most dramatic and intriguing places she had ever stayed in. The facilities, including a small swimming pool, braai area, toilets, and showers, were tucked amongst massive granite boulders in the middle of the desert. The braai heated water for the showers, a simple yet brilliant innovation. That night, too, she'd stayed up late beneath the array of stars, this time talking with Danny Trang as the low fire reflected against the giant boulders and shadows danced on the rock faces. Afterward, she'd realized with surprise that she'd spent two full hours talking to someone she'd initially vowed to stay away from.

From her constant probing, not unlike interrogating a suspect, Willson learned more of Trang's story. He seemed the type who was shy in a group, but less so one-on-one. His mother, along with her widowed mother, had immigrated to Canada from Saigon after it fell to the North Vietnamese in 1976, and his parents had met while studying medicine at the University of B.C. Both were doctors now. Trang — who was four years older than Willson — had earned a diploma in journalism from the B.C. Institute of Technology and now worked full-time as a photojournalist, writing stories and taking pictures for travel and adventure magazines around the globe. He mentioned that he lived in Kimberley, which was not far from where her recent Canadian poaching case had occured. "You've got to be joking me!" she'd blurted, bringing a smile to his face. His teeth had glinted in the firelight.

"So, of all the places you could live," she had asked, "why'd you choose there? With your job, I guess you could live anywhere."

"Well, I stopped in there because a buddy of mine was an instructor at the ski resort," he'd said. "He did odd jobs in town for the other seven months of the year — bartending, construction, some rafting guiding — all so he could ski in the winter. I love the mountains but can't stand the towns like Whistler and Banff — they're so crowded and everything's ridiculously overpriced. Kimberley struck me as the perfect mountain town. Lots of things to do, great restaurants, fun atmosphere, friendly people, and the real estate's affordable. I bought myself a small house on the edge of town, and I love it."

Willson's thoughts returned to Ghebo, who was looking at her quizzically.

"The carcass was a cow rhino, and a calf was nearby," Ghebo said. "Someone killed the mother and took her horns. Unfortunately, we think the calf died of thirst or malnutrition. It probably lasted only a day or two near its mother's body. Because none of our rangers heard shots, and based on the amount of blood around her, my collleagues think the perpetrators shot the cow with a tranquilizer and hacked off her horns while she was still alive. It's unclear whether she was shot afterward or died of blood loss. They haven't got the necropsy results yet so these are educated guesses."

Willson's heart raced with anger. "That's horrendous. I'd like to catch them and —" She stopped short of saying what she'd like to do to the poachers. She had resolved to be politer, more culturally correct during her secondment to Namibia, at least for the first few weeks. But she thought back to the illegal trophy hunter she'd successfully chased back home. "It makes me so angry."

"I agree," said Ghebo. "It's all about the money. We estimate the value of rhino horn on the international black market to be as high as sixty-five thousand dollars U.S. per kilo. Some say it's as valuable as cocaine or heroin. More valuable than gold. Even the poacher can get as much as twenty-five hundred dollars U.S. from a middleman for one horn. In cash. That's one-fifth of the average salary in Namibia. For someone who doesn't have a regular income or who makes much less than the average, that is a windfall."

"Do the authorities have any idea who did it?"

"From what I hear, no. They followed the spoor for many kilometres but then lost it at ..." Ghebo stopped when she saw Willson's confused look.

"Spoor?"

"Sorry, Jenny. A spoor is any sign of an animal that we can follow in the wild, including tracks, scents, scat, even broken foliage. I think it originates from Afrikaans."

"Thanks. I'm sure I'll have other questions along the way."

Ghebo nodded. "But the worst part of it is that one of the rhino rangers was also found dead nearby. He had been shot. We don't know yet if the two are connected, but for now we must assume they are. The poachers may have killed him to get to the rhino cow."

"Geez, this is intensifying. Do many rangers get killed here?"

"Thankfully, no," Ghebo said. "Not like in central and east Africa, where poachers and mercenary armies murder dozens every year while they try to protect elephants and rhinos. In Namibia, even one such murder is too many."

"Anita," said Brown, "could this new violence be a result of your increased commitment to catching these guys? Now there are larger fines and longer jail sentences, there's more at stake for them."

Ghebo looked at Brown in surprise, as though she hadn't previously made the link between increased risk and increased reward. "I suppose it's possible. But along with increased penalties, we have also increased the reward for reporting such incidents to sixty thousand dollars Namibian. We're hoping that might encourage locals to come forward if they know something has happened, or even if they suspect something *might* happen."

"You've got no choice but to be aggressive," said Willson, aware that her voice was a bit louder than usual. "It's not like you can back off and let the bastards have free reign to kill as they wish. You'd have no wildlife left. Go after those cowards. Go after them hard." Those poachers she had helped to catch back home had been driven by greed to cross legal, moral, and ethical lines — just like the ones here. And whenever people crossed those lines in the context of wildlife, Willson saw red, no matter what country she was in. She began to pace, doing her best to stay in the shade. They were talking instead of doing, and that drove her crazy. But she knew she must first fully understand the background of the case to have any chance of succeeding.

"You're right," Ghebo said, her thin eyebrows raised at Willson's bluntness. "But that's not all we're doing. There are three key approaches here. The first is law enforcement and strengthening our criminal justice system. That's where you two come in. We must get solid, thoroughly investigated cases to court, and we must get convictions, and then sentences, using the new maximum penalties."

"Will that be a problem?" asked Brown.

"Yes," Ghebo said. "Suspected poachers are often released on bail but fail to return to court. Cases are tossed out because of poor evidence. Convicted poachers are given minimal fines or jail time. Even then, I think we've achieved only two or three convictions. So, the laws may be tougher, but we've got to enforce them better and implement them in a much tougher way."

"What are the other two things?" Willson asked. She swiped at a bead of sweat beside her eye.

"We're continuing to work with NGOs from around the world to better support our community conservancies, because we believe that the communities will look after their animals if they see and experience lasting value in wildlife tourism. The rangers in those conservancies and the joint venture eco-lodges they work from are prime examples. You'll get a better sense of how that works when you get out in the field. And finally, we're working with CITES — the Convention on International

Trade in Endangered Species — and the UN and others on programs to persuade the people in countries like Laos, Vietnam, and China that rhino horn has little to no proven medicinal value — because it doesn't — and that there are much more effective remedies for what they claim it can treat."

"You've mostly been talking about rhinos," said Brown. "What about elephants? That's where I'm hoping to have the greatest impact while I'm here. I've loved them ever since I was a kid."

"Killing elephants for their ivory is not as much of a problem here as it is in countries like South Africa, Chad, South Sudan, or Tanzania. I don't know why. Maybe we're just lucky, or maybe it's tougher to move elephant ivory out of the country. We've lost a few from the Caprivi area, near our border with Angola and Zambia. We haven't talked about lions yet, either. They're being poached across Africa for their bones, which are also used in traditional Chinese medicines. But our major problem here, at least for now, is loss of rhinos."

"Is it still true in countries like China and Vietnam, men use powdered rhino horn because they think it's an aphrodisiac, or a cure for erectile dysfunction?" Brown asked, curving her index finger downward to make her point.

Ghebo shook her head. "No, actually, that's not true. That myth has been around a while. Ground rhino horn is still used in traditional medicines for its alleged cooling properties; it's prescribed for things like fever and inflammation. There was a rumour circulating in Vietnam a few years ago that a high-ranking official had been cured of his cancer after taking rhino horn. It's been debunked, but the story persists. In fact, we've been told that unscrupulous types — some of them doctors — creep through the halls of Vietnamese hospitals offering to sell rhino horn to people who have just been diagnosed with cancer."

"But it's just keratin," said Willson, "the same stuff as our fingernails and hair!"

Ghebo nodded. "Yes. But that doesn't stop desperate sick people from trying anything they think might cure them, including drinking illegal powdered rhino horn. Apparently, horn is increasing in value so much that I hear officials in China and Vietnam and some other countries are hoarding it as an investment ... so they can cash it in later."

"In the West, people keep gold in safety deposit boxes and bank vaults," said Brown. "Here, it's on the heads of endangered animals, waiting to be stolen."

"A fair comparison, and a sad one," said Ghebo.

Willson thought again about Danny Trang and the overt racism he'd experienced since arriving in Namibia. In light of the links to illegal trade in China and Vietnam, everything made sense. She recalled Ian Kamanya's comment about Asian people coming to the country pretending to be tourists, when in fact they had other agendas.

She stared out at the acacia savannah that surrounded them. In the sparse trees, the buzz of thousands of cicadas was like an orchestra of tiny, tinny electric engines. Willson was coming to associate the sound with the heat, which was unlike any she'd experienced before.

"Wow," she said. "We've got our work cut out for us."

Brown and Ghebo both nodded.

Willson pulled her boonie hat from her head and wiped her brow with her sleeve. She felt sweat running down between her breasts and in places that had never sweated before. Ignoring her discomfort, she turned and grinned. "But you know what my colleagues in Canada say? 'Where there's a Willson, there's a way.'"

Ghebo offered a hopeful smile. "I hope they're right, Jenny."

CHAPTER 7

JUNE 2

Because Sam Mogotsi wasn't a member of the Himba tribe, he would simply be an observer at Chioto Shipanga's funeral. But he had to attend. After a few wrong turns due to the loose directions given by his sister, Martha, just before her abrupt departure from her home a day ago, he and his wife finally found the location outside the small village of Omarumba.

Driving slowly on a rough track through the scrub bush, they heard chants and whistles and knew they were close. A group of men appeared as if from nowhere, chanting, waving long sticks, stomping their feet. One man led the group, using his stick like a drum major would use his baton. He kept the others walking forward slowly, in a straight line, one small step after another. Mogotsi and his wife, Natasha, followed slowly in the truck. He could not understand the men's language, but knew their singing was a traditional display of strength and a show of respect for the deceased. All at once, the chanting stopped, and the men disappeared into the bush.

Mogotsi saw a group of women sitting in the shade of a tree, so he parked under another tree close by. As he and his wife walked toward the women, he saw Martha, the grieving widow, in their midst. The Himba women surrounding her were all dressed in traditional fashion, wearing skirts made of leather or colourful blankets, bare-breasted, their skin coated with red ochre. Their hair was caked in mud and fell down their backs in tufted braids. Small horn-shaped headpieces made of animal skins sat on their heads. Many of them cradled babies. His little sister was wearing her best dress. Her husband's Himba family had accepted her as one of theirs when she'd spent three months there after the birth of their daughter. The women circled around Martha were supportive, protecting, sympathetic. Martha's daughter was not present; she had been left with Martha and Sam's mother, along with Sam's two boys. At four years old, she was too young to understand that she'd lost her father before she'd had a chance to really know him.

The women sat quietly, some fanning themselves. Mogotsi noticed the jewellery and other adornments they wore on their ankles, wrists, and necks: beads, metal, and leather. He assumed they were family and friends of his deceased brother-in-law. In all the years he and Chioto had been friends, he'd only been to Omarumba once, and that was for Chioto and Martha's traditional wedding seven years ago. He wondered why they had chosen this spot as Chioto's final resting place. To his mind, it was no different from dozens of other spots they had passed on the way in from the paved road. However, it clearly held a significance that he did not comprehend.

While Natasha sat down with the women, Mogotsi stood to one side, shaded from the sun by his wide-brimmed hat. He was not part of the women's group and not part of the Himba men's procession, either; he was an outsider, yet bound to them all by friendship and family marriage. He thought about Chioto — his brother-in-law, friend, and colleague — and all their times together in school, in ranger training, in the conservancy. They'd walked many miles together tracking rhinos, shared many stories and dreams for the future, guided many groups of picture-taking visitors, and, when it was just the two of them, watched in awe as rhinos and elephants and other wildlife grazed steps away from them. Chioto had been the one who persuaded him to shift from poaching rhinos to saving them. That was a decision that had changed Mogotsi's life. Now, working for the rhinos had cost Chioto his life. In his honour, Mogotsi vowed he would never go back to that old way of making a living.

The men's chanting resumed without warning, interrupting Mogotsi's thoughts. Three groups of men came into the clearing from different directions, and as they did, the women stood as one and began to wail and moan. Mogotsi had grown up in this area, not far from Kamanjab, but this was his first time at a Himba funeral. It was as if an unspoken message had passed quietly through the crowd, a message he was incapable of perceiving. The sounds made by the men and women seemed part sorrow, part celebration. Some of the women smiled, others shed copious tears.

From behind him, Mogotsi heard approaching vehicles. In a cloud of dust, a line of cars and trucks came down the same road he had travelled with his wife, then slowed to a stop. Men pulled an ornate coffin from the bed of the second truck. With little ceremony besides a short prayer, they lowered the casket into a deep hole in the red soil that had been hidden behind the women. At the head of the hole stood a grey granite headstone. Chioto's full name was carved in the stone, along with the names of Martha and their daughter and the dates of his birth and death. Across the top was the dramatic silhouette of a rhino, its dominant horn long and pointed. Mogotsi remembered the poached cow rhino they'd found, and near her, the young calf that had died a horrible and lonely death. That had been the day after he'd found his friend's body. He knew that Chioto's dedication to these animals and to his job had been the cause of his death.

The hole was filled and a large square stone placed on top of the grave. Mogotsi watched his friend's family pound a stick adorned with cow horns into the soil beside it. This signified Chioto's wealth during his lifetime; the number of cattle he had owned meant more for his status in his community than any other possessions had.

Mogotsi was surprised at how quickly the funeral ended after that last act of respect. The Himba women wandered off into the bush in small groups, on trails used by generations of their ancestors, while the men drove away in an army of dilapidated vehicles. He stood with Natasha and Martha by Chioto's fresh grave for one last goodbye. His sister remained overwhelmed with grief. With her head on his shoulder and tears pouring down her face, she shuddered and sobbed. They stood like that for many moments, Natasha supporting Martha on her other side. When Martha was ready, the three of them, too, drove away. In the truck, Martha twisted in her seat beside him and stared at her husband's final resting place through the back window until they could no longer see it.

The next day, men of the village slaughtered Brahman cattle, and three days of ritual feasting began in honour of Chioto Shipanga.

Mogotsi sat on the ground with Natasha and Martha in a circle of Himba men and women on the outskirts of Omarumba. Smoke from cooking fires swirled around them, and the smell of roasting beef caused their stomachs to gurgle with hunger. Small dusty children wandered from adult to adult, clearly enjoying the gathering but not comprehending the reason for it. Farther away from the circle, Mogotsi saw the scattered mud huts built by Shipanga's family. Beyond the huts, walls made from the stems of mopane and ironwood encircled the entire area. He wondered which hut had been Chioto's birthplace and, for a moment, imagined him as one of the contented children wandering the yard,

playing with dogs and other children, loved and supported by the entire village.

With that image in mind, Mogotsi turned to his
sister. "Do you think anyone here knows who killed
Chioto?" He had tried to keep his tone of voice as soft
as possible, but he felt her stiffen beside him. It was as
if she had been anticipating and dreading the question,
yet was still unprepared for it.

"Yes," said Martha after a time, her eyes cast downward. "But if they do, they will not speak of it."

"Why not?"

Martha's eyes came back up to meet his. He saw sadness, but also a hint of fear. "Because," she said, "because
they are afraid."

"Afraid of what?"

"Not of what … of *who*."

"Okay then, who are they afraid of?"

Martha shifted closer and glanced around to ensure
no one was eavesdropping. "The men are powerful," she
said in a whisper. "People here believe that speaking of
these men, or of what they do, will bring harm upon
them and their families. So, they remain silent."

"But someone here might know who did this? Who
killed Chioto and slaughtered the rhino mother and
took her horns?" He scanned the men and women all
around them.

"I think they do, but I've heard no names."

There had been a time when Mogotsi had killed
animals illegally and sold their parts. But the amount
of money exchanged between buyers and sellers was
small back then, as was the risk of being caught and

convicted. The people who looked after the animals weren't killed for doing their jobs then. Now the money had changed everything. He knew that better than anyone.

"When you say talking about these men brings harm, what do you mean?" he asked.

"I'm not fluent in OtjiHimba, but I hear the old women speaking of some men who have visited a local witch doctor to get strong *muti*, or magic, to protect them and their business. People hear this and they believe it, whether it is true or not. You see these men in Opuwo and Sesfontein and even in Kamanjab. We know who they are. While most people are poor, barely making a living, these men build new houses, buy more cattle, drive fancy cars."

"And what's their business?" asked Mogotsi, though he already knew.

"They're the middlemen," said Martha. "People say they're the ones who pay others to kill the rhinos — and elephants, when they can — and then they sell the horns and ivory to others for big money."

"Do these men hurt people if they talk?"

"It is assumed by all that if anyone does speak of them, they will meet the same fate as Chioto … or be stricken with a strange fatal illness. Fear of the muti guarantees silence."

"But the police are investigating Chioto's death. Won't they know about these men and question people about it?"

Martha smiled, but it was a sad smile, full of resignation. "They will. But people are scared, so the police won't find anyone willing to speak. That's *if* the police officers haven't been paid to look the other way."

"So," Mogotsi said, "these men in the shadows won't be caught or charged. Despite what the big men in Windhoek say, justice is a rare thing here. Big money and big muti together are very powerful."

Mogotsi leaned back, staring up at the cloudless sky. High above, he saw a lappet-faced vulture riding a thermal, the white stripes on its thighs and under its wings clearly visible. The scavenger was awaiting its next victim.

When he'd found his friend's remains, Mogotsi, in the midst of his own guilt and sorrow, had given no immediate thought to what came next other than knowing his life had irreversibly changed. He'd immediately reported his discovery, and the police investigation had begun surprisingly quickly. As soon as he'd given them the key to his shed, the inspector and another officer had gone to his house to seize his old .303 rifle. They had frightened Natasha and forced their way into the house. At the end of their search, they'd told her that they had not found the rifle. Now, a week later, he'd heard nothing more from the inspector.

Mogotsi turned to look at his sister. She was suddenly a widow with a four-year-old daughter. The lodge manager, deVilliers, had promised to make things right for her, but still, the main wage earner of her family was gone. From now on, her life would be very different. Mogotsi and Natasha would have to take more responsibility for Martha and their niece. The girl would grow up with as many opportunities to succeed as he could give her. And she'd learn about her father, come to understand what a great man he was. How committed he was to doing the right thing.

Mogotsi shifted his gaze from one person to the next, searching for that one surreptitious look, that one glance that said, *I know who did this*. He saw nothing.

CHAPTER 8

JULY 3

Jenny Willson watched the final team of four students burst through the door of the Waterberg classroom. Carrying plastic bags, notebooks, and cellphones, they were dusty and appeared exhausted and nervous. Their excited chatter filled the room like a cloud of sound. The other teams, one of which consisted of the class's four women, had arrived earlier. With just a few minutes to spare, the groups huddled in each of the room's four corners, quietly going over their final presentations. They stole quick glances at Willson, Brown, Anita Ghebo, and the three guests — two women and one man — sitting in chairs along the far wall. It was the end of the month-long advanced investigation course, and this was the final day of the last field exercise before their graduation ceremony. They were all clearly feeling the pressure to perform.

Willson grinned at Brown, who was on the far side of the classroom, peering over the shoulders of one of the all-male teams. They had pushed the students hard over the last four weeks. With only a short window of time, the training had to be intense and focused. And with so much at stake, not least of which was the survival of rhinos and elephants in Namibia, it was never going to be easy. Ghebo had asked Willson and Brown to impart the greatest possible amount of knowledge and experience to students who would soon be out in the real world, facing complex situations and making life-or-death decisions.

One of the most important things they had impressed upon the students was Locard's Exchange Principle, developed by famed French criminalist Dr. Edmond Locard. In class, they had reminded the students of the principle repeatedly: "Any time two things — be they people or objects — come in contact with each other, something is given, and something is taken." This final exercise they'd drafted on the plane ride over. During their month at Waterberg, as they'd learned more about the situation in Namibia and listened to other instructors, they'd tweaked and changed the exercise to make it more challenging and relevant.

The set-up for the exercise had kept them busy for the better part of two days. They'd had to find four fresh animal carcasses in appropriate condition, then place them in different convincing field scenarios. They had brought in other Namibian officers recommended by Ghebo to convincingly play the parts of witnesses and potential suspects.

Willson looked at her watch. She clapped her hands to get the attention of the noisy room. "Group One, you're up first." She paused for effect. "And Groups Two, Three, and Four, I want you to leave the classroom now and go back to the dorms. We'll call you, one team at a time, when we're ready for you. I'm sure that after each team is finished, they will say nothing to help the remaining teams ..." Willson grinned. "But I'm *not* certain whether teams that are finished will say things to distract, confuse, or undermine the others' approach. You're all trained investigators, so you have the skills necessary to pick out the truth from the lies and be confident in what you're doing. The team that does the best job today will receive a special prize at the ceremony tomorrow."

The noise level in the room exploded as twelve of the sixteen students gathered their materials and equipment and piled through the door, many turning their heads for one last look, as if hoping for a hint of what was to come, before Willson closed the door behind them. They would all be wondering about the identity of guests, too. She hadn't introduced them, and the guests themselves had purposely refused to give their names to the two sharp female students who tried to engage them in conversation in an overt attempt to figure out who they were. Unbeknownst to the students, they'd received extra marks from Willson for their initiative.

"Group One, I'd like you to meet today's special guests," said Willson, turning to face the seated visitors. "We're excited and pleased that they've agreed to participate in this final exercise. On the right is Supreme

Court Judge Yvonne Chomba. Judge Chomba will be hearing the case you present today; this will be her court-room. Next to Judge Chomba is Fred Mokgoro, a highly regarded prosecutor from Windhoek. And beside Mr. Mokgoro is Dinnah Usiku, a successful defence lawyer from Keetmanshoop. Mr. Mokgoro and Ms. Usiku will question you today on the evidence that you bring before this court. I have given them a detailed briefing on the scenario you investigated in the field. You'll start by pre-senting your case to them. Anita will act as court reporter of sorts, taking notes on what she sees and hears today. Judge Chomba will make a ruling on your case, and she will also decide on today's winning group." Willson paused, relishing the looks of concern on the students' faces. "And no, her decision cannot be appealed." The stu-dents laughed nervously, and Willson turned to Brown.

"We're going to give you ten minutes," Brown said, "to make final decisions about how you will state your cases, in what order, and who will present which piece. Good luck."

While the students huddled in a corner in a frenzy of final preparation, arms waving and opinions flying, Willson and Brown quickly rearranged the furniture to make the space into a mock courtroom. Judge Chomba presided at the front, clearly amused by the wooden chair and tiny desk she sat behind, so different from the high bench in the Namibian Supreme Court.

The four scenarios that Willson and Brown had set up were similar, but each had a unique variation at the scene that added to the challenge. In some cases, it was physical evidence that was confusing or misleading, while in others, it was phony witnesses who took great pleasure in misleading them with statements didn't match the physical evidence.

"Your Honour," began the leader of Group One, "we received a radio call from our dispatch at eight forty a.m. on July 2, 2017, asking us to respond to a suspected poaching. The call came from a local resident who refused to leave his name, and the dispatcher was unable to get a return phone number for the complainant. We arrived at the site, located twenty-two kilometres northeast of this location, as shown on the map, at nine twenty a.m., to discover the carcass of an oryx … *Oryx gazella* … also known as a gemsbok."

In a step-by-step manner, the prosecutor, Fred Mokgoro, pushed each witness for details. He allowed them to continue if they presented their evidence logically and concisely, but if they were awkward or imprecise, he would jump in with pointed, yet open-ended questions that gave them no hint about what they were missing. Mokgoro would never be this vague in a real case but was doing so for educational purposes. "When you and your team were on the way to the scene, what did you talk about? What were your first steps when you arrived? How did you prevent contamination of the scene? How did you know that this was an oryx? Please show the court the photographs you took at the scene. How did you determine the cause of death?"

Meanwhile, Judge Chomba and the defence lawyer, Dinnah Usiku, interrupted and fired questions meant to throw the witnesses off their game, to dig deeper into the facts, or to tease apart fact from supposition. They did the job so well that some of the students, even some of those with experience in the field, withered under the pressure. Their discomfort was obvious in their sweating brows, wandering gazes — as if searching for divine intervention — and mumbling, incoherent answers. Chomba and Usiku's questions sometimes demanded yes-or-no answers, which frustrated the less experienced students, forcing them to reconsider how they presented what they knew. Willson enjoyed this; she could see the light of understanding switching on in their faces as they realized what a real courtroom would be like and how difficult it was to face a lawyer whose sole purpose was to trip them up, make them look unprepared and unprofessional or, even worse, unreliable as a witness. Watching Usiku's aggressive and unrelenting interrogation style, Willson could see that she was undoubtedly a force in the courtroom, her fierce reputation well-deserved.

In the end, all four groups did well, making Willson and Brown proud. But each made a mistake or two that might have resulted in their cases being dismissed. For one group, that mistake was breaking the chain of custody of key evidence taken from the scene, so that they could no longer guarantee that it had stayed free of contamination. For another, it was failing to find a bullet at the scene that would have helped convict the man who owned the gun. If they had used a metal detector, they likely would have found it. The third group made the mistake of using a paper towel to blot blood samples, rendering them unusable for DNA analysis. And the fourth failed to properly match tool marks on an oryx skull to the teeth of a saw found at the house of the main suspect.

Willson was pleased to see, though, that it was the all-female group who, through solid preparation and a calm, thorough approach, best handled Usiku's aggressive cross-examination. That got her thinking ...

After each group had completed their courtroom presentation, Willson, Brown, Chomba, Mokgoro, and Usiku took turns providing feedback, with Willson always concluding. Ghebo stayed in the background, letting her experts take the lead. At the end of the day, they brought all four groups back to the courtroom for a summary session, sharing with them the good and the bad as a final opportunity to learn. Then the students were released for the day. Willson knew they'd be racing to change clothes or drop off their exhibits and notebooks in the dorms before heading into Otjiwarongo, a town of 28,000 people an hour to the west, to unwind and celebrate.

Willson and Brown thanked their colleagues, who were clearly exhausted from an intense day, but had seemed to enjoy themselves. Brown suggested they follow the students' lead and head into town for some much-needed food and drink.

"I'll buy dinner," Judge Chomba agreed, "because I had so much fun. It took me back to law school, our mock trials."

"Everyone will fit in our truck," said Willson. "Let's go!"

The Windhoek Lager flowed freely at the Crocodile Ranch Restaurant three blocks off the main street of Otjiwarongo. The students were at an establishment with cheaper food and beer, so the instructor group was free to relax and exchange thoughts about the day's exercise.

Afterward, as they sipped small glasses of Amarula, Willson raised the idea that had been percolating in her brain over the last month. "What would you think about putting those four women together as a unit? You saw how well the team did in the exercise …"

"Yes," said Judge Chomba, "they were clearly the best team and will win the prize in tomorrow's ceremony. Dinnah, you threw everything you had at them, and they were professional and thorough, and they stayed calm."

"Well," Willson said, "what if they worked together on a permanent team, an all-women anti-poaching unit? They could be sent to areas of the country where the risk of rhino poaching is greatest and be given extra resources."

Judge Chomba chimed in first. "I think it's an intriguing idea, Jenny. However, I'm not sure the country is ready for such a move quite yet."

"Why not?" asked Willson. She saw herself working with the talented team as they moved about the country, acting as an adviser of sorts. And she couldn't help thinking of the rhino cow and calf and the ranger who had been murdered near the Klip River Lodge a month earlier. She was here to make a difference, with action, so spending the month inside a classroom had just about killed her. In the last two weeks, another rhino had been found killed. For Willson, it was three animals too many. It was time to get out there and do something, instead of just talking about it. But she knew that Chomba originally came from a Herrero community in the north, and her knowledge and opinions were priceless.

"It's a cultural thing," said Chomba. "Village leaders, most of whom are male, would be threatened by a team of strong and confident women. Even more so if they showed up with guns and power of arrest."

"Keeping people off balance is what I do. I've had good success with it."

"But the people you most need to be honest with you might end up less willing to co-operate. It could back-fire. And you'd end up with less information, not more. With so much at stake, you can't afford to erect barriers before you even start."

"So, should I forget about the idea?"

"No," said Usiku, "I don't think it's off the table. But you might want to take it a step at a time. For example, if you or Tracy were to join the team, while also adding at least one male police officer, you'd have the respect of many community leaders. You're here to help, and they will appreciate that, but only if you are not the one in charge. And if you add a male officer who is local, someone they trust, you'll have a much better chance at positive and productive interactions."

"I agree," said Mokgoro. "The same thing applies in our courts. Most of our magistrates and judges and many of our lawyers are white or male or both, although that's changing fast." Willson saw Judge Chomba nodding. "But if you start the way Dinnah suggests, it would give the women a chance to prove themselves. Once that happens, I can see all-woman teams eventually being successful."

Willson thought about her own experiences in her last few major cases back home. Canada and Namibia were a world apart, but some things weren't that different. Throughout her career, Willson had had to climb or circumvent barriers set up just for her, intentionally or not, by a male-dominated system.

"But will a male officer get the credit for successes? Will prejudice lead people to assume we caught the bad guys because of him, or even because of me? How will we ensure the women get the recognition they deserve?"

"This is a concern," said Judge Chomba, nodding, "but if we pick the right officer, a man who's comfortable being supportive rather than dominant, and if you ensure that your team stays at the front of the investigation and any media coverage, I think this has a chance of working the way you want it to."

Willson knew the judge was right. "All I really want is to work with those women to kick some rhino poacher ass, but it makes sense to do it in a way that'll succeed on all fronts." She turned to Anita Ghebo. "What do you think, Anita? How do we make it happen?"

"I like it. The deputy minister has given me latitude to develop new approaches, so I'm sure I can persuade her to agree to this ... if the women officers are willing, that is."

"I'm sure they will be," Willson said, now full of excitement. "They know what they can achieve together. It'll take some courage on their part, but from what I saw of them this month, they're up to it."

The excitement didn't last long, unfortunately. "We might have a bigger problem," Mokgoro said.

"What's that?"

"Most of the courts are presided over by male magistrates hired by the Ministry of Justice. In my mind, this is a big piece of what's going wrong. I've been in front of many of them, and it's really frustrating. They set ridiculously small bail amounts, so these poachers disappear, or, soon after, get arrested for doing the same thing again. Even when they are convicted, the penalties are no deterrent at all. We've got the harsher laws now, sure, but I'm not convinced that the magistrates have received the message. One of my clerks did some analyses on cases over the last ten years, and the preliminary results are shocking."

"In what way?" asked Willson.

Mokgoro shook his head. "As a group, magistrates clearly don't see poaching as a serious problem. For some reason, they're not willing to use the full force of the law." He turned his head to look at Judge Chomba. "But I'm more worried that in key areas of the country, some of the magistrates may have been compromised ..."

"You mean bought off?" Willson asked.

"Bought off, coerced, blackmailed ... or they may be willing members of the groups moving horns out of the country. That's the only thing that could explain some of what I've seen. There's a hell of a lot of money involved. And with money comes the potential for corruption."

"That's awful."

The judge frowned, her eyebrows dipping to match the downward curve of her mouth. "Unfortunately, there's truth to what Fred says. It's an issue we're actively addressing because it has made our entire system look weak, not only to our citizens, but also to the rest of the world. With the recent changes to the laws, the Ministry is rolling out a series of training programs to magistrates across the country. That's a good start. Beyond that, we're aware of the problem in specific areas. All I can say is that we are ... aggressively looking into it. I'd sure like to see your research, Fred."

Willson scratched her head. "If there's corruption or resistance in the justice system, doesn't that make our training program less likely to succeed?"

"No," said Judge Chomba, "I don't agree. This is a multi-pronged approach. What you're doing with these students is a critical piece in our plan to deal with the problem. Through training these students, we can move toward flawless investigations, indisputable evidence, and getting perpetrators into custody so that the magistrates have no choice but to convict and punish them to the full extent of our law. Dinnah, do you agree?"

"I do," said the defence lawyer. "It's my job to give my clients a strong defence. But as a Namibian, I'm disgusted by the idea of our animals being slaughtered so their horns or tusks can be sold to losers in other countries. That's why I agreed to be part of this program at Waterberg."

Judge Chomba smiled and turned back to Willson. "If anything, what you are doing here, Jenny, Tracy, and Anita, and what you'll be doing out into the field, is more important than it's ever been."

Willson felt buoyed by the judge's words of encouragement. She looked at Brown. "What about you, Tracy? Are you in?"

Brown dropped her eyes. Willson immediately sensed that something was wrong. Her friend's face didn't show the enthusiasm she'd expected, but instead, an apologetic sheepishness. "What is it?" asked Willson.

"I'm sorry we haven't talked about this yet, Jenny. I spoke with one of the other instructors, Jimmy Maharero. He's from the Caprivi Strip area. Bwabwata National Park. In the northeast." Brown's short, clipped sentences showed her discomfort. "It's that narrow strip of the country between Angola and Zambia and Botswana. They're trying to stop the loss of elephants there and block the movement of illegal ivory to South Africa, and then to buyers around the world. I know how passionate you are about putting an end to rhino poaching, Jenny. I feel the same way about elephants. Well … Jimmy asked if I'd like to spend time up there to help them."

The air in Willson's lungs left her in a rush. The entire restaurant disappeared — the sounds and smells, their companions, the other diners. For an instant, it was just her and Brown sitting across from each other as if in a narrow tunnel. "And what did you say?"

Brown took a moment to respond. "I told him I wanted to go … but that I had to talk to you first."

"For how long?"

"Probably a few months. I'll need at least that long to understand what's going on."

The two of them had been through a lot together, and they'd come to Namibia with an idealistic if somewhat naive plan to always work together. Panic rose in Willson at the idea of being left alone. She pushed her chair back with her hands firmly on the table. "We've only been here a month and we're already splitting up? I thought we came here to work together."

"I know," said Brown. "I'm sorry, Jenny. But I thought —"

"It's fine, Tracy. Do what you have to do." Willson rose from her seat. She struggled to keep her voice level, to keep her anger in check. This wasn't the time or place. "We should head back to Waterberg now, if anyone needs a ride."

The return trip to the law enforcement centre was quiet, uncomfortably so. In the darkness, the truck's headlights providing a single cone of illumination on the road ahead, Willson dodged small groups of baboons and solitary warthogs that appeared and disappeared out of the shrubs on each side. For now, the need to concentrate on the road was her excuse to be silent and focused, alone with her thoughts.

In the darkened cab, her cheeks burned over her outburst in the restaurant. Where had this intense emotion come from, why had she jumped on her friend so quickly and so harshly? She was just starting to realize how extremely vulnerable she'd been feeling over the last few months, more vulnerable than she'd been in the last twenty years, ever since her father died in a railway accident. That journalist whom she'd trusted, more than she should have, had betrayed her. She'd been shot in the arm. And her mother had taken her own life just six weeks ago. The thought of making this trip with Brown had been the only thing sustaining her, and now Brown was leaving. The fear of being abandoned by significant people in her life was clearly an emotion Willson had buried up to this point. But now it was exposed, laid bare for all to see and for her to experience like a knife in her guts. The pain of loss and loneliness was suddenly excruciating. As a person who liked to be in control of everything around her, she despised every second of this vulnerability.

No one in the vehicle spoke during the long drive, as if they understood that something deep, yet undefined had shifted within the Canadian officer. But only Tracy Brown had any idea as to what Willson was dealing with inside.

CHAPTER 9

JULY 5

The early morning air was cool as Sam Mogotsi stood on the north side of C40, the main gravel road from Palmwag to Kamanjab, then on to Outjo. The sun had yet to rise, so the semi-desert scrubland around him remained in shadow. In the pale light of near-dawn, the scattered plants on these stony plains harboured all manner of movement as creatures large and small migrated to the places where they would spend the day, protected from the hot sun.

After another sleepless night, Mogotsi had eaten a quick breakfast, then walked the kilometre from his house to the main road, leaving his pregnant wife and two boys asleep in the darkness. His sister and his niece were also there; they'd moved in after the funeral, making the small house feel even smaller. Now that there was another baby on the way, the available space would continue to shrink.

Far to the west, Mogotsi could see a dust trail coming toward him on the road, a single vehicle travelling at a rapid speed. Checking his watch, he assumed it was his ride. He absentmindedly kicked a golf-ball-sized stone around as he waited, letting his tired thoughts wander. Small puffs of dust rose with each kick, then settled on his new boots. The lodge had bought him a new pair since the police still had his old ones. He knew that the chances of seeing them again were slim. Once the police realized the boots were of no help to their investigation, they would likely be thrown in the trash or given to someone who needed them more than he did.

Mogotsi's thoughts shifted back to his sleeping family. He desperately wanted to be sleeping a restful sleep, too, but until things sorted themselves out, that was unlikely. His mind was too busy. As soon as he woke up, no matter what time of night or morning it was, his brain would take over, and he couldn't control where it went, or how quickly. Sleep was a rare commodity now and would be for a while yet.

Mogotsi kicked the stone harder this time. He wondered how long Martha would stay with them, how much time would pass before she was ready to move out on her own. But he would never ask her that question directly. Instead, he would continue to be patient and supportive, waiting until she decided for herself. Natasha felt the same. It was the least they could do.

But in the privacy of their double bed, with their whispering faces nearly touching so as not to wake their younger son where he slept on the floor by their feet, Natasha had shared her growing fear that she might lose him the same way they'd lost Chioto. The danger of the job was a topic that had remained unspoken about in the ten years since he'd changed careers. Ironically, he was probably more at risk now than he'd been when he'd been poaching animals. But Natasha could no longer keep her rising dread to herself, not after Chioto's violent death. For the past month, she'd been pushing him, pleading with him to get out of the rhino business, to do something less risky. They both knew, however, that there were few other jobs available to him that would pay a regular salary and give him so much satisfaction.

As if it would somehow protect her from becoming a single mother herself, Natasha had tearfully confirmed her willingness to support his sister through her time of mourning. No matter how long it took. They both knew that she might be with them for many years. Despite pressure from Chioto's mother and extended family, Martha had refused to move to the Himba village near Omarumba. And there was little prospect for work for a single mother with a preschool-age child. Mogotsi was now supporting them all. He truly hoped to stay alive long enough to see all the children grow up to have families of their own.

A flash of headlights and the roar of the approaching Land Rover shook Mogotsi from his thoughts. The driver geared down aggressively before reaching him, slowing down and saving him from being enveloped in a dusty cloud. He reached for the door handle and made out the gold background and black lettering of the Save the Rhino Trust Namibia logo on the side, nearly invisible due to the brown film covering the vehicle from one end to the other. Unconsciously, he wiped the logo clean with his palm.

"Good morning, Sam," said the driver. "Sorry I'm late."

Mogotsi got in and reached across the cab to shake her hand. Carolina Musso, a red-haired woman in her early forties, was one of the field directors for the organization known locally as SRT, Namibia's largest and most successful non-governmental organization solely dedicated to protecting its rhinos. Mogotsi had met Musso, a conservation biologist by training, eight years ago when she'd first arrived, having been seconded there by the Minnesota Zoo. He'd immediately liked her. She was passionate about rhinos, but more importantly, she understood the need to work with local communities. The fact that her zoo's non-profit fundraising foundation paid for much of his training and his equipment and part of his salary didn't hurt, either.

"This should be interesting today," said Musso, her eyes intermittently scanning the land to her right for signs of rhinos and other wildlife.

Mogotsi was confused and didn't mind showing it. "Would you please explain to me why we are going to Kamanjab? All Mr. deVilliers said was that he wanted me to attend a meeting about rhinos and poaching. I am not sure why he wanted *me*. I am not good in meetings and I do not like speaking in groups. I prefer to be in the bush taking care of my rhinos."

Musso flashed a brilliant smile. "You and me both, Sam. I know you're very modest, but you're one of our top rhino rangers now. Your perspective is extremely valuable. We're going to talk to the new anti-poaching squad that the Ministry of Environment and Tourism has sent to our area. They're going to be based in Kamanjab for a while, maybe the next few months. They want to meet us and listen to our ideas and concerns."

"How is this any different than what the government has tried before?"

"There are a couple of differences. This squad is mostly women, which is interesting to me. It includes a female park warden from Canada who I really want to meet, and the police, the Namibian Defence Force, and the Ministry of Environment and Tourism are also involved. They've been given extra resources: vehicles, weapons, access to camels and donkeys and dogs for patrols, like we already use. I'm guessing they'll have a few other tricks up their sleeve, as well."

"Hmm," said Mogotsi. "Sounds like they might be serious this time." He thought about Chioto. Would he still be alive if the government had acted sooner? Were they serious enough to prevent any other rangers from being murdered?

Musso stole a quick glance at him. "Seems like they are. We may not lose many rhinos here, but even two or three is too many." She turned her gaze back to the road. "How is your family doing, Sam?"

"Martha is still in shock over Chioto's death. We all are. She's keeping her daughter happy and occupied, but wondering what the rest of her life will be like without him. And with all five of us living in the same house, it's tough on everyone. But we're making it work."

"Maybe we could find some things for Martha to do at SRT once your niece starts school."

"That would be much appreciated, Carolina … by all of us."

The sun cracked the horizon ahead of them. Light shone down the gravel road like a beacon. Musso pulled down the visor to shield her eyes and slid her sunglasses down from the top of her head.

"Have you spoken to the police lately?" asked Musso. "Do they have any leads?"

"I haven't spoken with them in a week or so, but I'm not in the clear yet …"

"What do you mean?" Musso's head snapped left to look at him. "You're not a suspect, surely? I don't believe it."

"I don't know. They wanted to seize my rifle so they could eliminate me — or at least eliminate *it* as the murder weapon. They think the same type of rifle was used to shoot the cow rhino. But when they went to my house to get it the day we found Chioto, it wasn't there."

"Your rifle wasn't there? Where was it?"

"I do not know. I remember seeing it a few days or a week earlier in the locked shed where I normally keep it. I gave them the key so they could go get it. They coerced my wife into letting them search our house, too. She was scared because she was alone. The next day, they said they couldn't find it anywhere on my property."

"Did they say anything about the shed — was it locked when they arrived?"

"They said that there was no lock on the door, and no rifle inside."

"Where do you think it is, Sam?"

"I have no idea. Either someone stole it from the shed … or the police *did* find it and something else is going on."

"What do you mean?"

"I know the rifle was in the shed, Carolina. I saw it there, and I was the only one with a key. If someone took it to kill Chioto, then I'm in big trouble. If the police found it but are telling me they did not, then I don't know what to think."

"Who is it you're dealing with in the police?"

"Inspector Nashili and his sergeant — I think his name is Kugara."

"Oh," Musso said, turning away for a moment. "They can't really think for a moment that you'd kill your own brother-in-law, who was your friend for years …"

"But I am worried. Nashili keeps showing up when I least expect him, always asking more questions about the gun and what I was doing the day Chioto went missing. I do not know what he is thinking. I keep wondering if he is going to appear one day and arrest me. If they find my gun and if it was the murder weapon, then I could go to jail for a very long time."

"Why would anyone set you up like that?"

"I have been thinking about that. I keep wondering if this is about something from my past. You know I used to live on a different side of the law … but I left that life behind ten years ago. At least, I thought I did."

"Is there anything I can do to help?"

"I don't think so but thank you for asking. I just have to wait and see where this goes."

Mogotsi knew that his deep concern over the situation was showing, so he was glad when Musso changed the subject.

"Tell me what's happening in the Klip River Valley these days," she asked. "What have you seen on your patrols?"

"It is not the same without Chioto there. I'm devastated that the cow and calf are gone, too. I really miss them. There is a big hole in that valley without them. But we still have three pairs of cows and calves in there, including Linda and Buhle, and at least three bulls. We watch them every day, but I never take it for granted. And when I am with the guests from the lodge, I realize how special it is to see them. They cannot get enough of watching the rhinos, particularly if we see a calf with its mother."

"That's one of the reasons we do what we do," said Musso. "And what about the other animals?"

"Still lots of Hartmann's mountain zebras, oryx, giraffes, and the elephants seem to be doing well. Lots of babies this year. Springbok and klipspringers are everywhere."

"Excellent. That bit of rain we had worked wonders. Other than rhinos, the oryx are still my favourite. I love how they prance when they run, like Lipizzaner stallions. Except they're wild … and no high-priced trainer has been anywhere near them."

Mogotsi smiled for the first time that morning. "Me, I like the meerkats. There's a colony not far from our house. I love how they work together, how they take turns watching for danger. I've sat out there quietly and had one of the males climb up and stand on top of my head, so he could see farther."

"That kind of co-operation is a lesson we could all learn, isn't it," said Musso, returning his smile.

They were finally at the edge of the town of Kamanjab, and the sun was now fully above the horizon. Musso turned right off C40 into the new police station that had been commissioned the summer before. The police officers based here covered a large area of the Kunene region, so the complex included new offices, male and female barracks, and fuel tanks for their vehicles. To Mogotsi, it felt like entering the lion's den. The inspector who kept interviewing him had his office here. Mogotsi had no desire to spend any time inside the new block of holding cells.

Musso parked her dusty vehicle between two white crew cab trucks and grabbed her nylon briefcase from behind her seat. Before opening the door, she shifted to look at Mogotsi. "Ready, Sam?"

He reluctantly reached for the door handle, his mouth a thin line. "As ready as I'll ever be. But don't expect me to say much."

CHAPTER 10

JULY 5

During her career in government, Jenny Willson had, unfortunately, had plenty of experience with meetings. They were usually incredibly dull and unproductive, and she was always the first to leave as soon as they were adjourned. Like a convict released from prison, she'd pop out the front door of the building, pulling freedom and fresh air deep into her lungs. But she was optimistic that her first meeting at the new Kamanjab police station would be an exception.

Willson and her new unit met the Kunene region's key players in a small boardroom. Seated and standing around the room, shoulder to shoulder in the tight space, were local police officers, prosecutors, staff from the Ministry of Environment and Tourism, experts from Save the Rhino Trust and two other NGOs, and a scattering of local eco-lodge managers. Willson noted that at least a third of the people in the room were women. At one point, she thought of Tracy Brown, who was now 750 kilometres away to the northeast. Her bitter anger over Brown's surprise decision had softened to a dull ache of disappointment.

Willson was introduced to the locals as an adviser to the new anti-poaching unit that would be stationed in the area for an indeterminate time. She'd driven over from Waterberg the day before with the four women who'd won the prize for best investigative team at the graduation ceremony. Veronica Muafangejo was an inspector with the Namibian Police. She was tall with dark, piercing eyes and a no-bullshit approach — she would lead the team. Two ranks below her at warrant officer was Monica Hauwanga. The two police officers were a study in extremes; while Hauwanga was stocky, muscular, and reserved, Muafangejo was tall, graceful, and enthusiastic. Army captain Gaby Bohitile, born in Sesfontein about two hours to the northwest of Kamanjab, was the team's representative from the Namibian Defence Force. She was fit, disciplined, and knew weapons as well as anyone in the room. She also had experience on a shadowy military squad dealing with domestic terrorism. The fourth woman was Behati ("call me Betty") Tjikuzu, an anti-poaching specialist from the Ministry of Environment and Tourism who clearly struggled with the shackles of bureaucracy.

They'd decided that wearing uniforms might be intimidating or simply too obvious for the work they would be doing, so the team were dressed in drab clothing, combinations of greens and tans and light blues. In the language of Willson's field back in Canada, it was more plainclothes work than undercover. In addition, before arriving, Willson, Bohitile, and Tjikuzu had been given Namibian police badges granting them all the powers of regular police officers.

Based on Judge Chomba's recommendation to have at least one male officer on the team, Inspector Muafangejo had persuaded Windhoek police sergeant Benjamin Mushimba to join the unit. Mushimba was a wiry officer with twenty-two years' experience. More importantly, though, he was a K-9 handler. He had arrived separately this morning with his partner, Neus, a three-year-old Belgian shepherd who'd been trained in South Africa to sniff out horn, ivory, weapons, and ammunition. Willson had laughed upon learning that the dog's name meant "nose" in Afrikaans. Mushimba had left him in the truck with the air conditioning running, a much better place for him than a crowded boardroom filled with strangers.

With Mushimba in place, Willson knew that the team of five specialists (six, including Neus) was a diverse and formidable unit. She thought of herself as the Canadian-style icing on that cake, adding value wherever she could. She assumed that, once the meeting today was done, word of the team's arrival in the area would spread quickly, as would rumours about why they were there. She wondered if that alone might act as a deterrent to some would-be poachers.

Once the introductions were complete and Inspector Muafangejo had offered the attendees a superficial summary of why they were in the area, the meeting slid into a pattern that Willson knew well. First, there was push-back. The local police inspector, a burly man named Nashili, suggested that the new unit was wasting time and resources coming to Kamanjab because he and his officers had everything under control.

Willson watched Muafangejo's response with interest. It was polite but pointed. "With all due respect, Inspector Nashili," she said with a polite smile, "if everything was, as you suggest, under control in this area, we would be assigned to a different part of Namibia. The fact that we are here today, and for some time to come, is an indication that few people — perhaps only you — believe that things are under control."

Willson dropped her head and covered her mouth to hide a smile. This was going to be an intriguing few months, and she had no doubt this wouldn't be the only time there'd be friction between these two senior officers. She'd liked Muafangejo when they'd first met at Waterberg, and she liked her even more now. They were like sisters from different mothers.

While Muafangejo spoke, Willson surreptitiously studied the dynamics in the room — the subtle body language, the furtive glances, the smiles and frowns — that provided more clues about the environment the unit would be working in than words ever could. She wondered if this group of people had ever worked together or if they tended to work in isolation. Did some in the room know more about rhino poaching — such as who was involved — than others did? Were some in the room involved in it themselves? There were many layers to this situation, lots of history and culture, and different agendas, both overt and hidden. It was confusing and exciting, and Willson knew she had much to learn. As an outsider, it was going to be that much more of a challenge to understand the nuances of this complex situation.

She snuck glances at the trio of rhino rangers from three of the local community conservancies. They were dressed in simple khaki uniforms, said little, and looked utterly out of place. According to what she'd heard from Anita Ghebo and others, they were likely some of the most knowledgeable in the room. But their body language indicated they wished they were somewhere else, anywhere other than this crowded meeting room. That was something she had in common with them.

The meeting shifted then, with a few speakers completely dominating the conversation while the rest remained silent. In the background, Nashili scowled in what had to be part humiliation, part anger. His second-in-command, Sergeant Kugara, took up most of the remaining oxygen, demanding to know exactly what the unit planned, how they would operate, and whom they would chase.

"The way we operate will remain confidential for reasons that should be obvious to everyone in this room," said Muafangejo. "We can't take the chance that information about our activities might be shared with the targets of our investigations. You will be advised on a need-to-know basis."

"I hope you don't think you will be operating out of this complex," said the sergeant. "We don't have space for you, and we can't be distracted from the important police business we do here."

Inspector Muafangejo smiled again. "Don't worry. We have rented a building in town for our base. We have our own communications network and our own computer systems. We'll operate on our own tactical radio channels, but we can contact you if we need to. When we make arrests — and we *will* make arrests — our suspects will be transported to magistrate courts in other cities so we don't burden the court here. We certainly don't want to get in your way."

Willson watched the local inspector's eyebrows rise with obvious surprise at the news that Muafangejo's unit would be completely autonomous. She wondered what he was thinking. Would he welcome the new unit now or ever? Did he think they posed a threat to him? No doubt he was upset about losing control. People were unpredictable when they lost control. He would be one to watch.

In contrast, when the SRT's Carolina Musso took her turn to speak, Willson was intrigued by the woman's obvious passion for and commitment to protecting rhinos inside and outside conservancies.

"I completely agree with enforcement," said Musso to Muafangejo, "and we'll do everything we can to support what you're doing. On behalf of the SRT, we heartily welcome your team's presence here. A strong commitment to law enforcement is overdue."

Willson didn't miss her quick glance at the local inspector. She was sending him a message. Did they have some history?

Musso continued. "But I want to remind everyone here that arresting someone after they've killed and mutilated a rhino is too late. The damage is already done.

Our biggest success in protecting rhinos in this area is in continuing to show our communities how valuable they are alive. We want them to care about these animals. We're making good progress, and we won't let a few bad actors distract us from that." The smiles and nods of those around the table showed Willson that Musso was well respected and that many here agreed with her sentiments. That was something they could work with. Anita Ghebo had told her about the conservancies and SRT's work, but it was clearly a subject she needed to better understand.

Willson's experience told her that some of the most productive conversations were yet to come, after the official meeting had adjourned. In rural parts of Canada, these were often called "bumper meetings" or "tailgaters": people would stand around in the parking lot afterward, usually with one foot up on the bumper of a truck, and say what they had wanted to say, what they should have said in the meeting, but hadn't, for whatever reason. It drove her crazy — when people were reticent to speak up, it made meetings even more useless. Why the hell did they show up if they weren't going to contribute?

Today was no exception. In the dusty lot outside the police station, Willson stood with Sam Mogotsi, the rhino ranger from the ≠Khoadi-//Hôas Conservancy. She'd shaken his hand before the meeting started, but this was her first chance to talk with him. They leaned against one of the anti-poaching unit's new white trucks. A warm breeze blew through, doing nothing to cool them down in the heat of the afternoon.

"Thanks for coming today, Sam," said Willson. "I hope you found it useful."

Mogotsi shrugged. "My boss told me to be here. I don't like meetings."

"You and me both. How long have you been a ranger?"

"I have been working for the SRT for ten years, mostly in and around the Klip River Lodge area."

"What did you do before that?"

"I was a hunter, putting meat on the table for my family. Some people called me a poacher."

"And why did you become a rhino ranger?" Willson watched him pull and push the toe of his brown boot through the dusty dirt.

"At first, it was about money. But also, instead of doing something my family, friends, and community were ashamed of, I wanted to find a job that made them proud. The conservancy asked me to work for them because I know the land and the wildlife. They pay me a regular salary, and they give me a uniform, equipment, and lots of training. It was hard to turn down. They made it easy for me to say yes."

"And now? How do you feel about it now?" She had caught some glances exchanged by Mogotsi and the local inspector. They clearly weren't friends.

"I'm proud of what I'm doing. I'm using my bush skills to do something good."

"As I learn about the program, I am more and more impressed with what you and your colleagues do out there every day."

Mogotsi smiled at the recognition. "Because our communities are managing wildlife through our conservancy status," he said proudly, "and because the animals bring in so many tourist dollars, it's good for everyone. I'm proud to be a part of it."

Willson paused to kick some dirt herself. "Are there any people in your community who don't feel the same way?"

Mogotsi paused, then looked up at her. "There are. Some people don't like it because it affects their grazing. They cannot move their cows and goats wherever they want to because the conservancy managers have divided the area into zones. Some zones don't allow grazing."

"Are there people who don't like the conservancies for … other reasons?"

"Yes. Some people still think the animals' only value is in their horns and tusks."

"Do you know who those people are?"

Before Mogotsi could answer, Willson heard her name being called. Inspector Muafangejo was standing in the door of the station with her cellphone pressed to her ear. "Time to go, Jenny," she yelled. "I'll brief you on the way."

Willson raised her hand in acknowledgement, then turned back to Mogotsi and reached out to shake his hand again. "I hope we can talk more later, Sam. You're based out of the Klip River Lodge, right?"

The ranger nodded. Willson noticed his eyes narrow and follow Inspector Nashili as he came out of the building, climbed into his patrol car, and drove away.

"I'd like to go out in the field with you one day, talk with you about what you do, learn from you. I'll come out to the lodge one day if that's okay with you."

Mogotsi nodded again.

Willson picked up her pack and jogged over to join Muafangejo. "What's up, Veronica?" she asked.

"We got our first tip. An anonymous caller said there is a rhino horn hidden in the bush north of the Galton Gate, west of the C35 road."

"That's on the western edge of Etosha National Park, isn't it?"

"Yes. We're all going there now. Why don't you ride with Ben and Neus?" She gestured toward Mushimba, who stood beside his truck, waving. "He has the details."

Willson sprinted over to Mushimba's dusty truck, slid into the passenger seat, and twisted around to look behind her. Neus was in a large cage in the back, his eyes bright and excited. His hide was a mottled mix of blacks and chocolate browns.

"I saw you talking to Sam Mogotsi," said Mushimba as he steered the truck out of the parking lot and onto C35, heading north.

"Only for a few moments. I asked him if he knew of any locals who might be involved in the rhino trade. But Veronica called me over before he could answer. Do you know him?"

"I do. Did he mention his brother-in-law?"

"No, why?"

"Chioto Shipanga, the rhino ranger who was killed a month ago, was married to Sam's sister. I wouldn't be surprised if Sam knew who did it, or at least suspected someone. There's no doubt in anyone's mind Shipanga's murder is linked to the deaths of two rhinos in the same area. They called me and Neus up from Windhoek to do a wider search after they found the body. While we were looking, we found the dead cow rhino and the young calf nearby. It was very sad." He glanced at Willson before shifting his gaze back to the road. "You should know that Inspector Nashili, that arrogant man you met in today's meeting, seems to think that Sam was somehow involved in both the murder and the poaching. I don't believe it myself, but now you know, for what it's worth."

"Ah, that explains it. I saw Nashili staring at him in the meeting. Sam was clearly intimidated. And then later, Sam was watching the inspector like a hawk when he came out of the building. I wondered what was going on." Willson stared out the window. "This is a complicated place."

"Welcome to the Kunene," said Mushimba, "where things are rarely as they seem."

CHAPTER 11

JULY 5

It was 2:00 p.m. and the sun had begun its slide from its noon zenith toward the horizon. The anti-poaching unit's three unmarked vehicles stopped in a line on the side of the C35 road, about a kilometre from the reported location of the cached rhino horn. To the east was Etosha National Park, while to the west lay a wild scrub area of the Kunene that was used for wildlife and cattle grazing. The rocky, rolling land seemed to go on forever.

Inspector Muafangejo gathered the group on the shady side of the trucks. Without uniforms or logos on their vehicles, passing motorists might take the assembled officers for a group of safari clients stopping for a break. And that was just the way they wanted it.

"This is our first real work together as a team," the inspector said. "We need to think this through carefully, take it slow, like Jenny and Tracy taught us." She folded her arms across her chest and smiled at Willson. "I'm sure that Neus and Ben could lead us to the cache. We could simply find and seize the horn. But if we all go in there, we're going to leave a messy network of tracks. The perpetrators will know we've been there, and that will be the end of that. They will not return."

Muafangejo scanned the group. "Thoughts?"

Gaby Bohitile was the first to speak. "Have there been any reports of poached rhinos in the last few days? That might tell us whether the alleged horn in this cache is fresh or has been hidden for a while."

"I checked the reports and call logs this morning," Muafangejo said. "There was nothing. So, the horn could be old, or from the Klip River kill, or from a fresh kill we don't know about yet. I've heard that this is an increasingly common way for poachers to deal with horns and ivory. It's like Mother Nature's safety deposit box. They make a deposit, then come back later to make a withdrawal once they find a buyer, or when the price goes up, or if they need cash."

"Did the caller who reported the horn give any information about the people involved?" asked Willson.

Warrant Officer Hauwanga had listened to the anonymous call, which came in to the police station moments after the meeting adjourned. The entire team knew the timing of the call was no coincidence. Someone knew that the unit was in town. Perhaps it was someone who had attended the meeting. "They didn't give a name," Hauwanga said. "They just said that a local farmer was involved. And that we'd see vehicle tracks leading near to where the horn is."

"I'm guessing that doesn't narrow things down much," asked Willson.

"Only to a few hundred suspects," Hauwanga said.

"Was the caller a man or a woman?"

"The caller sounded male, but I think they were trying to disguise their voice. It was muffled. But even if we did know who it was, word travels fast around here. If we do any digging into the locals or start watching them, the guilty party will go underground fast. Unless they think for some reason that they won't be caught."

Neus whined and strained at his leash as if he wanted to speak.

"We can't let the horn sit out there too long, or they'll retrieve it," Mushimba said, calming the dog with a back scratch. "Then we'll have nothing. If Neus and I go in there alone, we could at least see where the cache is, confirm that it is a horn, take pictures, look for evidence."

Betty Tjikuzu spoke next. "What if we send in the drone? It'll give us almost the same information as if Ben and Neus went in." She smiled at Mushimba. "No disrespect, Ben … or Neus." She gave the dog a pat on the head. "But it would leave no tracks. Once we know what we're dealing with, we'll have more options."

"Do we have enough information to send the drone to the right place?" asked Mushimba. He was obviously eager to get out with Neus to show what they could do.

"We do," said Hauwanga. "We can fly the drone up the highway from here until we cross the vehicle tracks the caller mentioned. With the sun getting lower, it will be easier to see them now than at midday. We'll follow them 'til they stop, then do a grid search from there, following any human tracks that lead from the vehicle."

After more discussion, the group finally came to a consensus: they'd go with the drone.

Tjikuzu unpacked the drone, set it up, and sent it on its way. The unit members huddled around a laptop on the tailgate of one of the trucks to watch the live video from the drone as it flew to the north.

Willson had no experience with drones; she was intrigued by the technology, by the possibilities it presented. Previously, she'd thought of drones as kid's toys to be crash-landed into a pile of broken pieces in the driveway on Christmas morning. Now, her mind raced with ideas of how they could be used in national parks in Canada: surveying wildlife; inspecting and monitoring waterways, wetlands, and lakes; tracking fuel or chemical spills; inventorying forests and trails; viewing avalanche paths and debris piles; monitoring for illegal human activities …

She snapped back to the present and watched the path of the drone as it flew up the highway. A small panel on the laptop screen showed the drone's position relative to its launch point, along with its elevation, speed, and direction of travel.

"There," said Bohitile, pointing at the screen. She had regularly used drones in her army career. The drone was 1.1 kilometres north of their position. "There are two sets of vehicle tracks leaving C35 there." She tapped Tjikuzu on the shoulder. "Get in closer." She studied the screen as the drone hovered less than a metre above the ground. "No. Not two. It looks like the same vehicle.

One set of tracks going in, and one coming out. See the tread patterns? But we won't know for sure until we see the other end. It could also be two vehicles with very similar tires. In that case, they could still be in there ... or they may have left the area by a different route."

The drone hovered at the edge of the secondary highway. Tjikuzu ensured that the video was recording on the laptop's hard drive, then, with a subtle shift of the joystick attached to the computer, steered the aircraft to the west, slowly following the vehicle tracks across the parched landscape. The tracks swerved around small trees and larger bushes and the occasional termite mound. The drone did the same, zigging and zagging.

Five minutes later, the vehicle tracks ended at the edge of a dry creek bed. Tjikuzu slowed the drone. She swivelled the camera slightly to reveal footprints: a single person had stepped out of the driver's side, walked to the back of the parked truck, then headed west. The returning set of footprints came directly back to the driver's side. No visit to the back of the truck, so theoretically the person had taken something from the truck but brought nothing back. They could also see the tire prints where the driver had backed up, executed a three-point turn, and left the area using the same route. They now had their answer. It had been a single vehicle, likely with a single driver. That meant there was less reason to worry that the drone would be spotted right now.

Tjikuzu had the drone circle the area at a higher elevation to ensure they hadn't missed anything, then dropped it down and followed the outgoing footprints toward the west into a low, rocky area where water had apparently once flowed. In many places, the incoming footprints were covered by the outgoing footprints, which again confirmed the team's assessment that one person had gone in and come out the same way.

Willson continued to monitor distance on the technical panel on the laptop's screen. The footprints looked large, like a man's. But with nothing to compare them to and no way to accurately measure them, that was only a guess. Just over two kilometres from the truck, the tracks ended at a single dense shrub, one of the largest in the area. In this kind of terrain, a large bush like this was a landmark.

Tjikuzu circled the drone low to the ground. The footprints covered each other repeatedly as though the person had been dancing. But on the west side of the bush, it was obvious to all what had happened. The soil at the base of the bush had been disturbed, likely dug up and then carefully replaced. The surface was loose and higher than the surrounding ground.

Veronica Muafangejo was the first to speak. "Damn. It looks like something is buried there. Our guy must've had a shovel with him. I guess our anonymous caller knew what he was talking about. He wasn't joking when he said it was hidden. I'd sure like to know who called this in, and why ... and how he knew where it was."

"Agreed," said Monica Hauwanga. "If our suspect was retrieving a horn to take with them, then why would they replace the soil back into the hole?" She stepped back from the group and looked westward. "Something is buried there, and we need to know what it is."

Willson watched Muafangejo. Her face told the story. The team leader was clearly struggling with what to do next. On the one hand, she wanted the team to continue making decisions as a group. But on the other, she knew what needed to be done. Willson could see that the inspector was trying to figure out how to lead the team to the idea without their knowing it.

"If it is a rhino horn or horns buried there," said Muafangejo, "I don't think we can leave it. We can't risk losing it, because there's a good chance it's evidence of a crime. Agreed?"

"What about covert surveillance?" asked Bohitile. "I'm guessing they'll come back at night, rather than in broad daylight. We could hide an infrared camera close by that only captures an image if there's movement. We'll get some great wildlife shots … but we might also catch the bad guy in the act. Those batteries last for months."

"I've got one here, ready to go," said Hauwanga.

"But that means checking it regularly," Mushimba said, "which means leaving footprints, which would be noticed … and we can't guarantee we'd get a good picture of our perp."

"Even if we did get a clear image," added Hauwanga, "we still might not know who it is if they're not from around here. And we'd still lose the evidence …"

"In my mind," said Muafangejo, "there's only one option. We've got to go in and get whatever is buried there. We'll try to do so as carefully as possible. We will also leave a hidden infrared camera and fly the drone over the site every few days to see if there are any new tracks, or if the spot has been disturbed again.

If we see any signs, we go in on foot and get the camera, see what we've got. Assuming it is rhino horn, like our caller said it was, someone's going to be very angry when they realize it's gone. We might get a picture of that person, and we'll have the horn. And maybe our caller will phone again to give us more info. If our suspect is angry enough about the empty cache, we might just hear about it ..."

All the team members nodded in unison.

The inspector gave her orders. "Ben and Gaby, I want you to go to the site from here. Take a circuitous route so that it's not clear from your tracks that you headed directly to the cache. Leave Neus with us. Our perp would recognize his dog tracks and find them highly unusual. When you get to the site, dig up whatever is buried and — if it's at all relevant — bring it out with you. Take lots of pictures of the site and whatever you find in the hole. Hide the infrared camera nearby as best you can. Once you're done, head north, again taking a circuitous route, and when you're about two kilometres north of the site, start heading back toward C35. We'll pick you up close to the main road." She turned to Willson. "Jenny, do you want to go with them?"

"I thought you'd never ask."

Hauwanga, who had clearly taken a liking to Mushimba's K-9 partner, jumped in quickly. "I'll take your truck, Ben. Neus and I will keep each other company until we pick you up."

Willson pulled her pack from Mushimba's truck. He tossed her a water bottle and she dropped it into the pack. Her two colleagues entered the coordinates of the site into their handheld GPS units, then the three of them headed across the road and into the scrub bush, Willson carrying a shovel over her shoulder. They could hear Neus barking behind them; he was clearly unhappy to be left behind.

As they began their trek around the low shrubs and sparse trees, all of them strange and new to Willson, her mind churned with an idea. What if they somehow could mark whatever was in the hole with a GPS or RFID chip and let it be recovered? She'd used one in a previous investigation to track a stolen polar bear skin to its eventual buyer. Once the suspect, whoever it was, came to claim the horn, perhaps the team could follow their route? She needed to talk more with Betty Tjikuzu. The young woman understood technology and electronic gizmos much better than Willson did. As much as Willson was confident in her own experience, she was starting to comprehend just how much more she had to learn. And these amazing team members would be her teachers as much as she had been theirs.

A loud screech and sudden movement shocked Willson from her thoughts. She whipped her head around, shifting her hand automatically to the pistol on her belt. A large warthog, its tail high, crashed around a bush and feinted toward her. She jumped back, knowing that the animal's sharp tusks could easily slash open her leg. Instead, it darted between her and Bohitile, who was a good ten metres ahead of her. Behind it, four small piglets raced to catch up to their mother. In an instant, they disappeared into the brush to Willson's right. She stood still for a moment, letting her heart rate slow, wondering what would have happened if she'd been faced with something bigger and more dangerous.

When they finally reached the cache, Willson dug down about twenty centimetres to uncover what was buried there: a single rhino horn. They left an infra-red game camera nearby, disguised in a pile of rock and brush, its lens pointed at the target location. After replacing what they'd taken with some short, stout tree branches, they filled the hole back in. It put Willson in mind of pack rats back home, which always left something behind if they took something — sort of a different take on Locard's Exchange Principle. *Something given, something taken.*

They pondered for a moment how long it would be before someone returned to discover what they'd done, then Willson, Mushimba, and Bohitile headed back toward the highway, trying to make their path appear aimless. The rhino horn was heavy in Willson's pack.

CHAPTER 12

JULY 5

After a quick goodbye and thank you, Sam Mogotsi closed the door of Carolina Musso's truck. He stood on the rocky shoulder as she accelerated, heading up to Grootberg Pass. As the vehicle moved away, the truck's red tail lights dimmed and winked out in a cloud of dust, though the sound of the engine lingered for much longer.

Mogotsi was alone under the vast star-filled sky, a bowl of black interspersed with millions of points of light. People from the city might be frightened by the immensity and uncertainty of this darkness, by the thought of unknown predators lurking in it. But for Mogotsi, it brought comfort. This was his home, and whether it be day or night, he knew its sights and sounds and smells intimately. They were chapters of a story he'd heard since he was a young boy, learning some from his father, some from his grandfather, but reading most of it through his own experience.

A light breeze blew from his right, bringing with it the single scream of a black-backed jackal. Even though it was likely kilometres away, he could sense the animal's hunger and knew the hunt was on.

Hands in his pockets, he thought about the meeting in Kamanjab. From all that he'd heard, it seemed to be good news that this new unit was in the area, with that inquisitive Canadian woman advising them. He remembered her question, the one he hadn't answered: *Do you know who those people are?*

Maybe Jenny Willson and the new unit would do what the police inspector had so far failed to do. Maybe they would identify the man who'd killed the cow rhino and caused the death of her calf.

He remembered Inspector Nashili's glowering stare across the table after he'd been embarrassed by the woman inspector. Sam had returned the stare, not blinking, not turning away, not willing to give the inspector any sense that he might be afraid or worried. It was not merely that the man did not like Mogotsi; he clearly believed Mogotsi was the murderer. And now, with this new team on his turf, Nashili must have something to prove. That made him more dangerous. The fact that Mogotsi had not yet been arrested gave him no relief. He wondered, as he did many times a day, what had happened to the missing rifle. Had someone stolen it, or had the police found it? If they had found it, why had they told him otherwise? And if they had it in their possession, had they successfully matched it to the bullet found at the scene?

Mogotsi clutched the bag of leftovers he'd brought for his family from the post-meeting meal to which Musso had treated him. He crossed the C40 and walked up the side road to his house. Noticing the dark blotches of a snake against the lighter gravel, he paused to let it cross the road in front of him. For a second, he wondered if it was a poisonous adder, but then he saw that it was a common egg-eater. The ridged scales on its flanks hissed as it traversed the road surface. With sinuous waves, the reptile moved from Mogotsi's left to his right, intent on reaching something important on the other side of the road.

When Mogotsi reached the edge of his property, he saw with alarm that his house was dark. His wife, his sister, and the children should all be at home, doing schoolwork and preparing meals and clothing for the next day. He sprinted to the front door. It was then he saw that one of the windows facing the road was broken.

"Natasha?" he called out. "Martha? Are you here?"

He slowly turned the handle and pushed the front door open. The interior of the house was dark.

"Is anyone here? Natasha? Martha?"

He heard a small whimper, a sound that was immediately muffled. It was the sound of a frightened child.

"It's Papa," Mogotsi said. "I'm here now and you are safe. Is anyone here?"

He reached into his pocket for a box of matches and lit one. The scraping of match against striker was loud against the silence of the house. The flare of light reflected in the eyes of his family — his wife, his sister, and the three small children — where they were huddled on the floor in the corner of the small living room, clutching each other. It was a sight he would never forget.

He quickly moved toward them. "Natasha! Martha! Are you all right? What happened?"

His wife stood, her tear-streaked cheeks shining in the light of the dying match. "Thank god you are home."

Mogotsi clutched his wife to his chest. "Martha," he said to his sister over his wife's shoulder, "can you please get a light on?" His two boys raced over and clutched his legs. Both were trembling.

"It is better we stay in the dark," said Martha, "in case they come back."

"In case who comes back?"

"The men in the car."

"What men?"

"A car came an hour ago. Some men got out and shouted. We shut off the lanterns as fast as we could. Then they threw a rock through the window."

Mogotsi looked at the broken glass on the floor and saw a rock the size of a cricket ball on the floor near their threadbare couch, where his two boys normally sat after dinner to do their schoolwork. Fear and anger boiled up in him. "What were they shouting?" he asked.

Natasha looked up at him. "They yelled for you to mind your own business. One spoke English, another OtjiHimba." She sobbed and then gathered herself again. "They said that if you do not back off, the same thing will happen to us that happened to Chioto."

"Back off from what? Did they say?"

"No. One yelled that you would know why they came."

"How many were there?"

"I do not know," said Natasha. "We were too scared to look, and we did not want them to know who was here. Maybe three or four." She looked up at her husband. "Why did they come, Sam? What do they want?"

Mogotsi clutched his wife tighter. "I am so sorry this happened, Natasha. I don't know who these men are, or why they came."

"The last thing they said was that they would know if you told the police. And then they laughed."

Mogotsi thought back to the meeting, to Nashili's angry looks, to his own hard stare, as if he'd dared the man to do something, to act against him. And then he'd had a discussion in the parking lot with Jenny Willson, out in the open where anyone could see them, without knowing what he was telling her. Had that simple act, that quick conversation with the Canadian officer — which *she* had initiated, not him — suddenly raised the threat against him and his family so dramatically? If tonight's violence had indeed been caused by that moment, then he had to figure out what it was they didn't want him to talk about. And what role, if any, Nashili played in it.

He realized that he was in the middle of something big now, something he did not completely understand. It was confusing, yet he knew that it was all tied together. Whoever was involved did not want him talking to the police. The trouble was, he didn't know what they were afraid he'd say.

"We should get the kids to bed," he said. "Things will seem less scary for them in the morning."

And maybe for us, too, he thought.

CHAPTER 13

JULY 6

Jenny Willson took a sip from her mug of instant coffee and grimaced. Even though she'd been drinking this coffee-that-wasn't-coffee-at-all for over a month, it still tasted like lighter fluid mixed with motor oil to her. And that was on a good day. She had experimented with rooibos tea, which everyone in Namibia seemed to like, but had desperately missed the caffeine buzz.

She was at the apartment she shared with Veronica Muafangejo. It was an apartment only in the loosest sense of the word: basic furniture, running water (most of the time), bare walls and floors with peeling yellow paint, and just enough pots and pans and other housewares with which to prepare basic meals. Not that either of them was a gourmet chef. The windows, covered with threadbare curtains, looked out onto the dusty street. This was one of the three places the team was renting in

Kamanjab. In style and decor, it matched the new office they'd set up in an old warehouse two blocks away: spartan, but functional.

Willson flipped open her laptop and checked her inbox. There was no Wi-Fi in the apartment, so she'd downloaded her emails at work the night before. Along with a message from someone in Parks Canada's HR Department, which she ignored, she had emails from Tracy Brown (the first since they'd parted company at Waterberg) and from Sue Browning, her closest friend back in B.C. Willson loved what she was doing here in Africa, but at the same time, she envied Browning, who was spending another summer in the Rockies — hiking, climbing, mountain biking. But the envy lasted only a moment, and Willson smiled when she thought of how far she was, literally and figuratively, from the tourist hordes that descended on towns like Banff and Jasper like ravens on roadkill.

"You can wait, Tracy," she said, as she clicked on Browning's message first. She hated to admit it, but she was still pissed off with her American colleague, though her feelings were softening by the day.

The message from Sue had been sent the previous day:

> Jenny,
>
> I hope you're well. How's everything wherever you are in Namibia? Hooked up with any muscular African dudes yet? I've been busy with guiding the last few weeks, but I've finally found some time to write.

Summer here in the Rockies has already been hot as hell (but I bet not as hot as where you are ... why did you go there again?) and everyone is freaked out about the wildfires. I keep wondering when the government's going to kick us out of the bush, not only from Crown land, but also from national and provincial parks. The forests are tinder dry, and even though my guests all want to be up high, we still have to get there through the lower elevations ... unless they want to pay for a heli. Fat chance. I'm hoping I can keep working until the end of September.

Two things: first, you'll be happy to hear that I bundled up four bags of Kick Ass coffee for you. I'll mail them to the new address you gave me in Kamanjab. Are you going through Kick Ass withdrawal yet? If so, glad I'm not there to see it. I bet it's not pretty. You owe me big time. As you often do.

The other thing is that I ran into Brad Jenkins yesterday. Does the mention of his name get your heart pounding and your juices flowing? I hope so. 😊 You'll be happy to hear that he asked about you. He also asked me to pass on that, if you're ready to leave the warden service, there might be a conservation officer job opening up in the East Kootenay, if you're interested. Apparently some guy is retiring. If you don't already have his email, it's brad.jenkins@gov.bc.ca. I'm sure he'd love to hear from you, but don't scare him off with too many kissy faces. Okay?

Stay safe. Let me know how you're doing.

Sue

Willson laughed as she reread the message. Browning was as funny and irreverent as ever, and she missed her. They'd talked about her coming over to visit, but that likely wouldn't happen until the fall, after her summer guiding was done and before she started work in December as a heli-ski guide.

Kick Ass coffee — Willson missed that as much as she missed the mountains. But how long would it take for a package of coffee to get to her from Canada? How many security checkpoints and sniffer dogs would it have to pass? Sighing, Willson realized she might be back in Canada before the package reached this remote part of Namibia. If it made it here at all.

And a job as a CO in the East Kootenay area of B.C.? Now that was intriguing. She'd left Canada under a small dark cloud, with her Parks Canada bosses telling her she'd have to toe the line when she came back or find other work, so the idea of moving to a different enforcement agency was appealing. She'd be able to continue doing what she loved, but start with a clean slate. A change might do everyone good — her most of all. The job was in the mountains, which was a key criterion for her. And it was close to Sue Browning, to her old crush Brad Jenkins, and even to Danny Trang. *Why did Trang suddenly come to mind?* She resolved to send Brad Jenkins a message after work, without any kissy faces. But not Trang. Not yet.

Before she had a chance to open Brown's message, Veronica came in. "I'm heading to the office. I'd like to fill everyone in on what you and Gaby and Ben dug up yesterday. You coming?"

"Sure."

The rest of the unit had already arrived by the time Willson and Muafangejo walked through the office door. Neus came over to greet them, his tail wagging vigorously. Ben Mushimba and Neus had chosen to bunk in a back corner of the warehouse building, not only because the team was one apartment short, but also to ensure that the office, their communications equipment and computers, and their files were safe from prying eyes. The room was as bare as their apartment: paint peeling from the walls, a concrete floor scuffed by the previous industrial tenant, barred windows facing a dusty back alley.

Absently scratching Neus behind the ears while she walked, Willson headed immediately to the main work table in the centre of the room. Laid out there were the results of their search from the day before.

Willson used two gloved hands to pick up the massive rhino horn from the table. It was about ninety centimetres long from base to tip, dark, and still covered in dirt. The tip was shiny and slightly worn. The base, marked by the sharp knife or axe that had been used to forcibly remove it from the animal, still showed a stain of blood. She turned it from side to side, closely studying the cracks and fissures in the surface. These horns were referred to as "African gold," were valued around the world as raw material for carving and, as Anita Ghebo had told her, for bogus medicinal purposes. She felt the rough texture of the horn and thought about the life its owner had lived. Through the latex gloves, her fingertips traced cracks that ran down the length. It was like studying the trunk of one of her favourite coniferous trees in the Rockies, or the textured, curling horn of the bighorn sheep that had been at the centre of her poaching investigation back home; the marks and lines told a unique story of age and violence and weather.

Willson placed the large horn back on the table, then stood back to consider it. The tool marks on the base of the horn meant only that it had been forcibly removed from the skull. They weren't proof that the animal had been murdered to get it. However, the fact that the horn had been buried in a remote place, awaiting a clandestine retrieval, was proof that someone knew they were breaking the law.

Muafangejo spoke as Willson respectfully ran her fingers down the horn again. "What do you think, team?" she asked. "Is this fresh?"

"I think it's quite fresh," said Mushimba. "The fact that I can see blood stains in the keratin means it wasn't off the animal very long, and not in the ground long, either." Neus sat beside him, staring at the table, his tail thumping. Mushimba told them the dog was looking for a reward for "finding" the horn on the table that morning. They all laughed.

"I tend to agree," said Monica Hauwanga. "We might have a fresh kill site out there somewhere. And given the size of this horn, it must have been a very large and/or very old animal."

"Makes sense," said Willson, nodding. "But this is big country to be wandering around, looking for a kill site. From what I've seen and what little I know of the number and diversity of predators and scavengers you have around here, carcasses can literally turn into piles of bones in days, if not hours. To minimize wasted time, we need a network of informants who will tell us when they find something."

"I wonder how long it'll be before someone discovers their treasure is missing," Muafangejo said. "We've got a horn here weighing almost five kilograms. To a local guy, the one who sells it to the first buyer, it would be worth as much as three, even four thousand U.S. dollars. But the final street value of this baby could be as high as a quarter of a million."

"Someone is going to be extremely pissed off," Willson said, smiling at the thought. "And I wonder when we'll hear about it through the local grapevine … or whatever you call the rumour mill around here." Willson ran her fingers down the horn once again, her touch light. "What about DNA analysis?"

"Already crossed my mind," said Muafangejo. "Ben, I want you and Neus to go to Windhoek today. Leave as soon as you can and take the horn with you. We need to get it to the University of Pretoria's rhino database specialist. There's a police courier going from Windhoek to South Africa tonight with other samples. Dr. Harper can run the DNA and tell us if the horn is from here in the Kunene, and if it matches any local samples they have on file. That will confirm if this is a local problem or the horn is simply in transit from another region, or even another country. But as soon as he's taken the necessary sample, I want the horn back."

"Sounds good, boss," said Mushimba. "We'll leave right away. It'll give me a chance to see my kids for a few hours."

Muafangejo ran her fingers through her hair. "When I heard that the local police 'lost' the DNA samples they took from the Klip River rhino, I was angry, but not at all surprised. Those would have helped us determine if this horn here came from that case."

"Having met Nashili, I don't believe we'll get any help from him or his officers," Gaby Bohitile said as she watched Mushimba cover the horn in bubble wrap and place it back in the labelled evidence bag. "They're either incredibly incompetent, or they're involved. But considering all the people in the room yesterday, and all the people in this area who now know that we're here and why, I'm sure we'll hear something — sooner than later. Maybe we get the word out to remind locals about the new sixty-thousand-dollar reward. That's got to be an incentive to loosen some tongues."

"If it is locals doing the killing — though we don't know yet that's what it is —" said Willson, "they must be willing to risk arrest because they have a buyer. Or, maybe there's some other reason they're not worried about getting caught. Veronica, are you thinking about going after the sellers here, or the buyers?"

"Both," said Muafangejo, scanning her colleagues' faces for agreement. "We need to go after both simultaneously. We're here to shut down poaching in this area, to put the bad guys away. I intend to do that." She pointed to the bag on the table. "I'm predicting that by quietly seizing this horn, we've just inserted a healthy dose of uncertainty into the market around here. We don't know who they are yet, and it's only our first step, but there are buyers and sellers out there somewhere who are going to be wondering what's going on very soon. So, we've got to beat the bushes and get the word out about that reward. Around here, that's a big chunk of money."

CHAPTER 14

JULY 7

The Klip River Lodge sat high above the river valley for which it was named. When Jenny Willson first strode out onto the large front deck, her breath caught at the splendour of the view. She sensed Betty Tjikuzu silent behind her, letting her absorb the scene. Willson had visited many backcountry lodges in the Rockies, all of which sat amongst dramatic peaks and vistas, but this was very different.

Below the wooden deck, a small infinity pool was perched at the edge of the Klip River canyon, the blue of the water a dramatic counterpoint to the browns of the rocky canyon beyond. Empty deck chairs faced west, waiting for guests to sit and savour the view. Like the Grand Canyon, though not as wide or deep, the Klip River canyon was an imposing gash in the earth created over thousands of years by the erosive power of water and wind. On both sides, the Grootberg Plateau created a distinct line between the earth and the early morning sky. From there, the steep sides of the canyon were broken by three distinct bands of rock. In that way, they were reminiscent of the shape of the peaks in the Rockies.

A large eagle soared in the thermals that rose along the cliffs, a black silhouette against the lightening sky. In the distance, a scattered carpet of vegetation, mostly low shrubs, some in leaf and some bare, covered the walls and floor of the canyon. Along the river at the bottom of the canyon, larger trees created a dark ribbon that followed the course of the water. The air was cool, and the sun had yet to crack the eastern horizon.

Willson held her cup of real coffee with both hands, allowing the aromatic steam to rise and fill her nostrils. Freshly brewed, the coffee was dark and rich. With each luxurious sip, she felt life seeping back into her tired body and mind.

The plateau was lit by the pre-dawn light, but the canyon still lay largely in shadow. To her left, small cabins built of reddish stone with thatched roofs clung to the hillside. Lights shone through the small windows.

Tjikuzu came up and stood beside her. Wordlessly, they watched as the rising sun grew brighter, revealing more and more of the harsh landscape around them.

At last, Willson broke the silence. "This is amazing," she said.

"It certainly is."

"Are those guest cabins over there?" Willson asked, pointing.

Tjikuzu nodded. "Fourteen of them. They're powered by solar, and each has a shower, toilet, and washbasin, along with a comfortable bed. And, of course, this amazing view."

"And the business is owned and operated by the conservancy?"

"It's a joint venture between the conservancy and outside private investors. The investors put up the money and the conservancy gets a share of the profits, guaranteed employment, and a say in the management. Almost everyone working here — about forty-five people — comes from the local area. A management company operates it; they bring in a few specialized people and do all the training. This lodge, along with the Hoada campsite we passed on the way here, provides consistent, well-paying jobs that weren't here before. It's made a huge difference to the community. And, as you can see, it's an amazing experience that tourists are willing to pay good money for."

"What does it cost to stay here?" asked Willson.

"If you're a single, I think it's about twenty-three hundred Namibian dollars. That's for one night, including dinner and breakfast. Any activity you want to do while you're here, like rhino or elephant tracking, sundowners, or a massage, is extra."

Willson smiled, her eyes returning to the view. "That's not bad for all of this. Not bad at all …" Spending a night here would cost just over two hundred Canadian dollars.

"And part of that money goes into the lodge's education fund," said Tjikuzu, "which ensures that disadvantaged children from the area can go to primary or secondary school. Guests can also donate money to it when they pay their bills."

The more she heard about it, the more Willson liked the model. And she couldn't help but wonder if it had any relevance to parts of western Canada that were struggling to find a sustainable alternative to an economy that had relied for decades on the boom-and-bust cycles of resource extraction. "I've heard so much about how this model links tourism and conservation, how locals see the value of protecting animals, rather than killing them. Even though there's still some poaching, it's got to be making a difference."

"It truly is," Tjikuzu said. "The proof is in the numbers. But that's not the whole story. At a lodge like this, for every predator sighting by a guest — that includes lions, cheetahs, wildcats, and spotted hyenas — the lodge puts twenty-five dollars in their Predator Fund. The money is used not only to collar animals, so managers can warn farmers when the animals are close to their livestock, but also to compensate farmers if one of their cows or goats is taken by a cat."

"Brilliant," said Willson. "A practical approach that goes beyond just the wildlife viewing."

The women turned at the sound of a door opening, releasing the hum of guests enjoying their breakfast in the lodge's dining room. Sam Mogotsi, dressed in his ranger uniform, closed the door behind him. The silence returned. "Good morning, Jenny. Good morning, Betty."

Willson reached to shake his hand. "Great to see you again, Sam. I've been looking forward to spending the day with you."

"My pleasure. I have three other guests coming with us today. We're ready to go when you are."

"I'm ready," said Willson. "Are you sure you don't want to come, Betty?"

Tjikuzu shook her head. "No, thanks. I'll stick with our plan. I'm going to chat informally with all the staff today to see if anyone knows anything about the poached rhinos. I've been here many times, and they all know me, so I'm hoping one of them might trust me enough to share something."

As they walked to the waiting truck, Willson asked Sam what the strange-looking trees on the edge of the cliff were. "I've seen quiver trees, and I know that's not what those are." She pointed to a stocky tree to their right, its trunk thick and squat, smooth and light-coloured, the bark slightly peeling like a stunted version of the arbutus trees she'd often noticed in Vancouver while she was at university. At the top of each branch was a whorl of bright green leaves and flower buds. If someone had shown her a picture of it, she would have assumed the tree was from somewhere in Africa. It just had that look.

"That is what we call the cobas, or butter, tree. It grows in hot, arid, rocky places and is a protected species. It stores huge amounts of moisture in its trunk, and that light, smooth bark reflects the heat and protects the water from evaporating. This is one of the few places I've seen them."

"It looks more like cartoon broccoli head than a real tree."

"I have heard that before from other guests," said Mogotsi, laughing, "although I have never seen a broccoli, so I cannot disagree with you."

Fifteen minutes later, after the truck had bounced down the steep, rocky road from the lodge to C40, spooking a lone klipspringer, they headed east. When they turned onto a secondary road, Mogotsi pointed out his house to Willson and beeped his horn. Two women and a small child waved from a small garden plot in the dusty yard.

Willson watched Mogotsi out of the corner of her eye. He turned to look back a few times after they'd passed, and she was sure he was watching his house in his side mirror until they finally turned a corner.

"It must be tough leaving them in the morning. This is remote out here. And you start very early and get home late, don't you?" She saw his eyes move to the rear-view mirror.

"Yes," he said, "although I do get to drive by here twice nearly every day."

"Do you worry about them?"

He glanced at her, and she thought she sensed fear in his eyes.

"More so lately," he said. "After my brother-in-law was killed and we lost the two rhinos from the area we're going to today, someone threatened my family. It happened the day of the meeting in Kamanjab, after I met you and we talked in the parking lot."

"What do you mean, 'threatened'?"

"When I got home that night, my family was sitting in the dark, frightened, because some men had come and thrown a rock through our front window. Before the men left, they yelled that I should mind my own business."

"I'm so sorry to hear that. I hope no one was hurt."

"Not physically. But my wife, my sister, and our three children were very scared. They still don't like me to be away from home when it's dark."

"Did you report it to the police?"

"That's not really an option for me now," said Mogotsi. To avoid sharing too much with the three guests sitting on elevated seats behind them, he kept his voice low as he explained how he'd been questioned about his brother-in-law's murder by the police inspector. "And my rifle is still missing."

"Wow, Sam, this sounds serious. Do you know who those people are or why they want to keep you quiet?"

Mogotsi did not answer. Instead, he slowed the truck, then turned onto a very rough road strewn with rocks. "Okay," he said to Willson and the other guests, "we're now entering the main Klip River Valley. This is a very rough road, so you're going to bounce around a bit. If anyone feels carsick, please yell out, and we'll stop and take a break. I'll go slowly, not only to give you a smoother ride, but also so we don't make too much noise. It should take us about thirty minutes or so. We're very lucky that trackers from Save the Rhino Trust are in the valley today, so we're going to meet up with them. It will be a good chance for you to see them at work and ask them questions. Until we find them, keep your eyes peeled for animals. Please talk very quietly and hold on to your packs and cameras so they don't bang around or fall off the seat. This is a very special place, and I'm pleased to share it with you."

The sun was now up, and the first hint of the day's pending heat began to enter the open cab of the truck. Within the first kilometre, Willson realized that Mogotsi had not overstated the quality of the road. She bounced around on the seat, left, right, up and down, twice almost banging her head on the roof despite gripping the grab bar tightly.

Not long after, Mogotsi stopped the truck and hopped out. He came around to Willson's side of the vehicle and motioned for her to join him. He pointed at a track on the ground. Squatting, Willson saw that the track was about 250 millimetres in length and showed three distinct toe marks coming from a larger mass, like a misshapen three-leaf clover. Where it wasn't bare rock, the ground here was not quite soil, not quite sand, but it showed the print as clearly as if it had been purposely left there for them to find.

"Rhino?" she asked.

"Yes, a big bull. This is a print from his rear left foot. See the lines in the sand made by the bottom of the main pad? I can identify those like a fingerprint — this is probably the one we call Michael. He's very large and has lived in this area for a few decades. He's likely the father of many of the younger animals in the valley. I see him, or his tracks, every few days."

"Where was he was going?" Willson lifted her head to look around. She saw the three guests in the truck listening and looking in the same direction.

"He was travelling east, probably a few hours ago." He held his hand across the track, with his fingers pointing to their right. "He was likely moving from a water hole, where he spent the night, to a shady place for the day."

It was another twenty-five minutes before they rounded a corner to find a white truck with the distinct SRT logo on its side parked in an open area, in terrain that reminded Willson of Joshua Tree National Park in California. Granite boulders the size of steel shipping containers were stacked in naturally occurring piles, and trees clutched at their bases as if seeking shelter or companionship. Three men, all dressed in the same uniform of light-tan shirts and dark-green pants, sat on the tailgate of the truck. Mogotsi parked the lodge truck next to it, then helped the guests out of their seats. Willson introduced herself to the men, then listened as they gave the group a safety briefing. They'd be walking for about twenty minutes. If they found a rhino, they would not approach closer than a hundred metres, and they would stay for only ten to fifteen minutes so as not to disturb it. They explained what might happen if the rhino approached them, either curiously or aggressively, and how everyone should react if that happened. The talk was illuminating and impressive in its attention to detail. Above all else, its focus was on protecting the animal.

Led by one of the trackers, the group began walking single file, following a rough track that meandered through spiny shrubs and leafless trees. The tracker pointed out the soccer-ball-sized dung from a herd of elephants that he said had passed through the day before. The track from one of the elephants was more than twice the size of the rhino's, and didn't show the toes. Along the way, they also saw dung from zebras and giraffes.

Willson hung back with Mogotsi, marvelling at the landscape, which was so different from the Rockies. Baseball-sized rocks, always threatening to trip her up, were strewn across the reddish soil in every direction.

"Sam," she said, "I asked you on the day of the meeting if you knew who might have killed your brother-in-law and who took the rhino's horns. You didn't give me an answer, but I'd really like to hear what you have to say.

I know your family is at risk, but they won't be freed of that risk unless we catch these guys."

"I know. I have my suspicions, but I don't know for sure who it was."

"Could you put me in touch with people who *do* know?"

"Martha, my sister, thinks there are women in Chioto's village who may know who is responsible."

"Would Martha talk to me? Would she take me there to meet with them?"

"I could ask her, but if she's seen with you, that might put us at even greater risk. She is very angry and grief-stricken about losing her husband, though, so she might be willing."

As the group reached the top of a low ridge, the lead tracker raised his hand as a sign to stop, then pointed across a small gully. "There," he said, his voice low.

At first, Willson couldn't see anything. But as she focused her eyes on a single point, allowing them to pick out movement against the background of greys and browns, she at last saw the large bull rhino travelling slowly across the steep hillside. Willson had been in Namibia for nearly two months, but this was her first live sighting of a big bull. Her heart quickened, and goosebumps rose on her arms. She raised her binoculars. Looking like a prehistoric tank, the large male was surprisingly nimble on the challenging terrain. His ears were forward, and small clouds of dust swirled around his feet with each deliberate step. Capable enough on this hillside, Willson knew that on flat ground, the bull could outrun the fastest human. But it was the largest of its two horns that gave Willson the greatest thrill. Holding and touching the seized horn at the office had made her appreciate just how large and heavy it was, and she saw how integral the horn was to this incredible animal's identity. On this bull, it was a massive display of power, a dangerous weapon, dark and sharp and wielded with amazing dexterity. And yet, it was also the greatest threat to the rhino's survival.

Willson lowered her binoculars, then turned to Mogotsi. He was making notes in his rhino ID book. She looked over his shoulder as he described the sex, the age class by the size of its horns, and the body condition. On the forms, he sketched in the notches he could see in the ear facing them, which gave him the animal's number and confirmed that it was the bull named Michael. Finally, he checked their location on his GPS, noted it on the form, then calculated their distance from the animal with his electronic rangefinder: three hundred metres. Well beyond the hundred-metre minimum separation distance that researchers thought was the distance beyond which rhinos could not see movement.

Mogotsi completed the sighting record and returned the notebook to his pocket.

"This is what it's all about, Sam," Willson whispered. "This is why I'm here. Will you talk to Martha?"

Mogotsi nodded once and raised his binoculars.

CHAPTER 15

JULY 9

Danny Trang laid his paddle on top of the kayak. Saltwater dripped from the blades. He slid his camera out of the waterproof bag between his legs and scanned the waterfowl around him. There were hundreds of lesser and greater flamingos in the shallow waters. The whites, pinks, and reds of their feathers, beaks, and stilt-like legs, along with their goose-like honking, all combined to create a cacophony of colour and sound. Between them, ducks and geese, herons and egrets searched for food and space. On the shore of Pelican Point, he saw more shorebirds bobbing, feeding, and darting in the intertidal zone. Hundreds of avocets, oystercatchers, and plovers picked their way along the flats exposed by the low tide. His shutter clicked rapidly, the long lens's autofocus moving constantly as it tried frantically to pick out individual birds. The potential images were overwhelming in their quality and quantity.

At one point, Trang realized that this was one of those times when it was best to put down the camera and relish being where he was, to live in the moment. He leaned back and closed his eyes. The salty air was sharp in his nostrils, the late afternoon sun warm on his face. A slight breeze came in off the Atlantic Ocean, smelling of enormous distances, of power of inhuman proportions.

Trang felt the kayak tremble slightly, so he sat upright and opened his eyes.

"Amazing place, isn't it?" The kayak guide had quietly manoeuvred his own boat beside Trang's. They were a tour group of eight people; the other six were three couples, each in a tandem kayak. The guide, who was about Trang's age, had introduced himself as Jason when they'd paddled away from Pelican Point four hours earlier.

"Walvis Bay is a major stopping point for hundreds of bird species moving north and south," Jason explained, "and each year, it becomes more popular with birders. You can see why. In my opinion, there's no better way to experience it than from a boat."

Trang smiled. "And the smaller the better, right?"

"Absolutely."

"How did you come to be a kayak guide, Jason?"

"I grew up in Swakopmund and always spent time at the beach. My father comes from the San Bushmen, so he wasn't comfortable in the water. But my mother is white, and she was a competitive swimmer. Mum was always taking us to the ocean. I came to love it and realized I could make a living doing exactly this. I took some guide training courses, apprenticed under other guides, and now I run my own business here in Walvis."

When Trang had first arrived on the coast more than a month earlier, like most newcomers, he had pronounced Walvis, the name of the bay and the adjacent town, the way it was spelled. But after only a few hours, he'd realized that locals pronounced it *Valfish*, like Jason had just done.

"You and I are both mixed race," said Trang. "My mother is Vietnamese, and my father is white."

"It must have been difficult to grow up being part Vietnamese." The guide's brow furrowed beneath his wraparound sunglasses.

"Not particularly. I mean, sometimes it was confusing to grow up mixed race, straddling two different cultures, not fully fitting into either one. I don't have to tell you. But in Canada, people of Asian heritage are somewhat common, so I wasn't that different from many of my friends in Vancouver."

"I see. That's good — around here, honestly, locals aren't too fond of Asian guys."

"So it's not just my personality?" Trang said dryly.

"What do you mean?"

"Just a joke. Yeah, I've noticed."

"There's a lot of prejudice here against the Chinese, and of course many are unable to tell the difference between Chinese, Vietnamese, or other Asians."

"It shouldn't matter what ethnicity I am — I'm a proud Canadian. That's where I'm from."

"It shouldn't matter, but unfortunately, Asian men, no matter where they come from, are disliked."

"Well, I'll get over it," said Trang. "Can I buy you a beer after our tour is over, Jason? I'd like to talk to you more about your business."

"Sounds good." Jason looked at his watch. "I better get the group back to shore before this wind picks up any more." He began paddling toward the rest of the group. "It'll take me some time to stow the boats and hang the lifejackets and spray skirts. Why don't we meet at six at Anchors Bar on the jetty? You said you're buying, and I'm *very* thirsty!" With a big smile and a trio of seemingly effortless paddle strokes, he left Trang to catch up.

The warm evening breeze rustled palm fronds on the edge of the roof over Trang's table for two on the patio. His notebook was open on the table, his pencil abandoned in the crease. After ordering a beer from the waiter, he'd made notes about the day's kayak trip. It was important to capture the sights and sounds and smells before they were lost in the coming days. This was something he tried to do every evening when he was travelling. It was those little details — the place names, the quality of the light, the way the air smelled and tasted, the travel times and distances from one place to another — that made his articles come alive. And it helped him to accurately label the thousands of images he'd upload to his computer when he got home. Despite his best intentions, however, tonight he was distracted by the sight of the Atlantic in front of him and the seals and pelicans in the water that lapped the shore below. Instead of writing, he sipped his beer and simply watched and listened. The sky was massive, and the ocean stretched out until it disappeared beyond the curvature of the Earth.

Jason arrived at the table in a flurry of movement, a beer already in his hand.

"This is my favourite spot to come after a day of paddling," he said, settling into a high seat across from Trang. "If you're hungry, you have to try the deep-fried calamari. People say it's the best on the coast, and I think they're right."

The two men clinked glasses. "Thanks for a great day out there, Jason," Trang said. "I've been in the drier interior of the country for the last few weeks. It's like a different world here. And it's unlike Swakopmund. More down-to-earth, more real."

"You're right. Walvis Bay has always been a port city focused on fishing. Now, it's starting to become more of a tourist destination, mostly because of the birds. More restaurants like this and more traveller-friendly hotels are showing up. But most importantly, it sits at one end of the TransNamib railway, which is a major entry point for goods to all parts of the country. And because we have no pipelines in Namibia, it's where all our fuel comes in. It all goes on the railway from here. So, the economy here is diversifying, which is good."

"I had no idea of Walvis Bay's importance to the country," said Trang, jotting a couple of quick notes on the open page of his book.

"Not many visitors do, especially if they spend their time on safari up north, or visiting the dunes at Sossusvlei or Fish River Canyon to the south.

And if they do come to the coast, it's most likely to Swakopmund. They may not even know Walvis Bay is here. Some locals are fine with that, because they've experienced cruise ships visiting the port. Having hundreds or even thousands of tourists spewing into the community for a few hours can't help but dampen some residents' impression of tourism. There are a few of us trying to change that, to show them what high-value, low-volume adventure tourism looks like."

Trang raised his glass. "Music to my ears, Jason. That's why I do what I do."

Later on, after they'd eaten plates of beer-battered calamari, hake, and oysters, washed down with a few more beers, after they'd spoken at length about adventure tourism and Jason's guiding business, Trang asked the question that had been eating at him since that afternoon. Despite the loud laughter and conversation around them, he kept his voice low. "I now know some of the reasons why people in Namibia don't like Asian men. But can you give me *your* take on it?"

The young guide did a double shoulder check, then shifted his chair in closer.

"I don't normally like to talk about this. I'm in tourism, so I prefer to … I *need* to focus on the positive. But because you asked, and because you've clearly experienced discrimination, I will share what I believe. It's a complex subject, with many layers."

Trang closed his notebook so the guide would feel more free to speak.

"From a big-picture perspective, there is a significant amount of new Chinese investment coming in to

Namibia. Companies are investing in highways and buildings and mines. From what I hear, those investments always come with big strings attached, and it's the Chinese government that pulls the strings. They demand to bring in their own workers, and they don't like to follow our labour laws or human rights laws. A Chinese company was recently involved in a multi-million-dollar corruption case. So, people like me get nervous when we hear about their growing influence."

"I get that," said Trang. "I did a lot of research before I came over here, and that kept coming up. It seems to be an issue across sub-Saharan Africa."

"But it goes much deeper than that. At the next level, individual Chinese people have also started showing up with money to start businesses. They work hard and are often successful. But some of my friends who have worked for them say they pay low salaries, make employees work long hours, and don't pay overtime. These Chinese businessmen have a reputation for being dishonest and trying to defraud the government of tax money."

"That's starting to sound like racism, isn't it?"

Jason nodded. "But relationships are important here, and it's a feeling that's becoming more prevalent, rightly or wrongly. And now there are stories about an increasing number of abandoned part-Chinese babies in Windhoek. Girls get pregnant, have no support from the fathers, and they know their families won't accept a 'China baby,' so they give them up. You can understand why opinions are shifting. It's affecting families and communities."

"Well, that certainly explains some of my experiences."

"Without knowing anything different, people probably assume that all Chinese people are of the same unscrupulous type. It also explains why Chinese businesses are often raided by government authorities looking for criminal activity, why Asians at the airport are often given the third degree by customs officers, and why Chinese applicants are having a much harder time getting work permits and visas."

"This is definitely not a side of Namibia that people hear about."

Jason waved at their waiter to bring two more beers to their table. "I'm glad. But it *is* our reality. And I haven't even spoken about poaching yet."

Trang immediately remembered his fireside conversations with Jenny Willson, the Canadian park warden. He'd exchanged emails with her a couple of times over the last few weeks, but she didn't seem like the email pen pal sort. Her responses were always abrupt, just a few sentences with little detail about what she was doing. During the safari, he'd been intrigued by her, as much by her bold confidence as her natural beauty, but it seemed that she didn't feel the same about him. "Right, poaching."

The beers arrived then, so Jason waited until the waiter had moved on again before continuing. "We lose some animals each year to poaching — rhinos, elephants, other large species. It's not much compared to other African countries. But when it happens, and when the cases are made public, it seems that many of them have some connection to Asian buyers — mostly from China, but also Vietnam and Laos and even North Korea. It's a big issue even here in Walvis Bay."

"Why here?"

"Because I've heard rumours that some of the illegal products — ivory, horn, skins — are coming through here, being put on foreign ships in this port."

"But why Walvis Bay?"

"Because of the link between the interior and the ocean."

"You mean the railway?"

"Yes. Contraband taken from around Etosha and the northern areas of the country is allegedly hidden in shipments of copper ore and other minerals, brought down here by rail, then shipped overseas."

"Where did you hear this?"

"A buddy of mine who works on the docks. He told me he sometimes sees guys hanging around, waiting for trains. He never sees them take anything with them when they leave, so he figures they're just there to confirm the arrival of their special cargo and its safe transfer onto the ship."

"Why haven't the police noticed? Has your friend told them?"

Jason flashed a wry smile. "My friend is smart enough to know that if this is happening, someone in the police force must be involved. He wants to keep his job and stay healthy, so he hasn't reported it."

Trang turned to look out at the ocean, his hand lingering on his empty beer glass. A flock of gulls worried at something at the tide line below the patio, squawking and swirling and battling in the darkness. If he were an investigative journalist, this would be a trail he'd follow without hesitation. But he knew he should leave it to someone with more authority and expertise than he had, someone willing to investigate in the shadows. Someone like Jenny Willson. She'd impressed him with her dogged determination and her desire to see justice done. And she was cute, too. If he shared this information with her, maybe she'd answer his next email with more enthusiasm. Maybe it would be an excuse to see her again. But if she wasn't interested, then what? This was a fascinating story that needed to be told.

CHAPTER 16

JULY 10

Abruptly, Sam Mogotsi awoke from a deep sleep. For a few seconds, he was dazed, on the edge of consciousness. Was it a dream, or had he heard banging? He felt Natasha stir beside him. Startled and confused, he rolled over and began to rise from the bed. He looked at his watch: 4:30 a.m. The banging came again. It was real, and it was coming from their front door. Then a deep voice shouted, "Police! Open the door!"

Mogotsi's heart raced. Having the police show up — if it *was* the police — at the front door in the middle of the night couldn't be a good thing. Mogotsi knew they weren't here to deliver bad news such as an accident involving a loved one — they were all safe in the house with him. Likely, they were here for him. In developing nations such as this, that probably meant something sinister.

He padded down the short hallway, then paused at the closed door.

The same deep voice: "It's Sergeant Kugara from the Namibian Police. Open the door. We're looking for Samuel Mogotsi."

Mogotsi paused, his hand on the doorknob. They knew he was here, so there was no use pretending otherwise. He turned the knob slowly, opened the door just as slowly, and immediately raised his arm to his face when three flashlights shone directly into his eyes. Three shadowy forms held the flashlights. He could see no faces. For an instant, he wondered if the three men were really police officers. A quick glance to his right, to their vehicles with flashing multicoloured lights that illuminated his yard, confirmed their identity.

"I'm Sam. What do you want?"

The officer standing closest to him lowered his light and spoke first. It was Kugara. "We're here to arrest you for the murder of Chioto Shipanga. Come with us."

"What?" said Mogotsi, incredulous. "I didn't kill Chioto! I was the one who found his body and reported it. You were there that day. He was my friend. My brother-in-law!"

"You'll have a chance to tell your story to a magistrate," Kugara said. "Turn around. Arms behind your back."

Mogotsi stood still for a moment in shock. He slowly turned his back to the three men at the door and saw Natasha standing barefoot in the hallway. Her eyes were wide with fear, her hair sleep-mussed, and she was wrapping a light cotton sheath around her nightclothes, the bump of her pregnancy now clearly showing. "Sam? What's happening? Why are they doing this?"

Mogotsi felt the handcuffs tighten around his wrists, then a hand grabbed his right arm above the elbow and began to pull him toward the door. "I don't know, Natasha. I don't know."

"They're arresting you for Chioto's murder?"

"I'm going to need a lawyer, Natasha. Please phone one for me in the morning."

"Who … who do I phone?"

"I don't know. Martha was talking to one about Chioto's affairs after his death. Start there?"

Natasha wrapped her arms tight around her chest, one hand resting on her swollen stomach, as if protecting the unborn baby from what was happening to its father. In the quiet of their bed, they'd talked about the risks of his job, but being arrested for the murder of a family member was not something they'd discussed. Mogotsi had wondered whether this day might come ever since the rifle had gone missing. But he hadn't shared his speculation with Martha or Natasha. It would have caused too much of a worry. That was a moot point now.

"Where are you taking him?" Natasha asked the sergeant.

"To our cells in town, in Kamanjab, at least until he sees the magistrate."

"Will that be tomorrow?"

"I can't say," the sergeant said. "It will happen when it happens."

The hand gripping Mogotsi's arm was now pulling him more insistently. He felt another begin tugging on the handcuffs.

"Can I at least put some shoes on?" Mogotsi asked.

"You don't need shoes where you're going," said a voice behind him. "We'd just take them from you anyway, when we book you in the cell."

As he was led through the door backward, Mogotsi kept his eyes locked on his wife's, trying to comfort her, hoping to leave her with the impression that she should stay calm, that it would all work out. But the truth was that he and his family were now deep into a dangerous situation where anything could happen, and he had little to no control over the outcome.

As he stumbled across the rocky yard in his bare feet, his world crumbling around him, he recalled his last conversation with Jenny Willson. He'd connected her with his sister as agreed, and Martha had then set up a meeting between Willson and a pair of elders in the Himba village where Chioto had grown up. Through their conversations, he felt that they'd built up a level of mutual trust and that she was an honest professional looking for the truth. He'd done the Canadian officer a favour — now, maybe, she would do one for him in return. He didn't know how exactly, but anything would help.

"Natasha!" Mogotsi yelled as the officers pushed him into the back of their vehicle. "Call Jenny Willson. Martha knows how to reach her. Tell her what's happened and ask for her help."

With his hands cuffed behind his back and pressed against the seat, Sam Mogotsi's shoulders ached by the time the officers pulled him from the police car at the Kamanjab police station. The cuffs were removed, and after a quick pat-down, he was hustled into a cell. He'd never been arrested before, but he expected there would be paperwork or his fingerprints and picture would be taken — something official. Instead, they simply shoved him into a cold concrete cell without a word. The six-by-eight-foot space smelled of urine and strong chemicals. After the steel door banged shut behind him, Mogotsi sat down on the hard bed, his back to the wall, and wrapped his arms around his legs, as much for comfort as for warmth.

During the ride to the station, Mogotsi had repeatedly asked Sergeant Kugara why he was being arrested. Finally, either tired of the question or taking pleasure in Mogotsi's predicament, Kugara had said, "The inspector will talk to you in the morning. You'll be properly processed then. But I can tell you that we have your rifle. And it matches the bullet that killed Chioto … and the rhino."

"You found the rifle? Where was it?"

"That's a question for the inspector when you see him. And you better hope that the fingerprints on the rifle don't match yours. That, combined with your bootprints by the body, would make this an open-and-shut case."

Mogotsi thought it obvious that his prints would be on the rifle, given that it was his. But wisely, he chose to say nothing.

Now, listening to the hacking coughs of the man in the cell next to him, Mogotsi closed his eyes and breathed deeply, trying to calm his mind. But he could not stop the swirling jumble of random thoughts and questions that leapt around wildly in his head. In that first interview by the inspector after the body was found, he'd immediately given the police the key to his shed, hoping his co-operative attitude would reinforce his claims of innocence. But in hindsight, he'd made a mistake. It was like he'd signed his own arrest warrant with that one action.

In the cool of the cell, Mogotsi began to shiver. He wrapped a threadbare wool blanket — the only item he'd been given — around his shoulders and tried to concentrate. Suddenly, the reality of his predicament hit him hard, and he lowered his head and began to sob. Based on his previous experiences, he had no confidence in lawyers or the justice system; the chances of his going to jail for a long time were very high.

Three months ago, Mogotsi's life had been as good as he ever could have hoped. He had a wonderful family. A great job with a good income. Respect from the community. A house on a small piece of property he could call his own. Now, all that was at risk.

Late the next morning, Inspector Nashili entered the holding cell wearing a smug smile. He leaned against the wall, crossed his arms, and stared at Mogotsi silently. The smile was frozen, as if it were painted on a mannequin. The cell next door was quiet. The man who'd been there earlier was either asleep or had been taken away.

"You're in serious trouble, Sam," said Nashili. "You told me you had nothing to do with your brother-in-law's death, or with the poaching in Klip River. But all the evidence we have collected so far suggests otherwise."

"I don't care what you say. I did not kill Chioto … and I did not kill the rhino."

"The courts will decide that, Sam ... and we have a very compelling story to tell them. All the evidence points to you, so I can't imagine they'd do anything but convict you. I'm guessing it will be a quick trial. That will put your family in a very difficult situation. They won't see you for many, many years. You should think about that."

At the mention of his family, Mogotsi had the sudden urge to jump across the small space and grab the inspector by the throat. But that would only make his situation go from bad to worse. Instead, he clasped his hands tightly and remained quiet.

Nashili shoved his hands into his pockets and raised one leg, resting his foot against the concrete wall. In his casual stance, Mogotsi read the man's confidence and arrogance.

"My officers tell me you instructed your wife to ask Jenny Willson for help," the inspector said. "Why do you think she can help you?"

"Because," said Mogotsi, glaring, "she wants to uncover the truth about what's going on. Not everyone seems to share that interest."

Nashili laughed once, crossed the cell, and stepped outside, calmly closing the steel door behind him. "You need to understand something, Sam," he said, peering back through the bars. "You're in my world now. And in my world, *I* decide what is the truth."

CHAPTER 17

JULY 11

Jenny Willson burst through the door of the Kamanjab apartment, dropping her clothes piece by piece as she headed for the shower. She knew that the probability of feeling hot water was slim, but even if it was only tepid, she wanted to beat her roommate in getting water and soap onto her skin, which would feel good after a dusty day in the field. By the time she reached the bathroom, the trail of clothing behind her made it look like something much more interesting was going on.

In the cramped fibreglass stall, as the water ran down her body, she worked the sweat and dust out of her wind-tangled hair. After their day in the Himba village, she realized how privileged she was to have access to plumbing, refrigeration, and restaurant meals. While the apartment she shared with Veronica Muafangejo was basic compared to most North American homes, it was a far cry from village life.

Early that morning, she and Muafangejo had driven Martha Shipanga to the village near Omarumba, passing stick-carrying men herding goats along the road and family groups walking in what seemed to be the middle of nowhere. Like most of this part of Namibia the country was open, with sparse vegetation, some of which was leafless, and some still green. They stopped the vehicle outside the village, which was more of a transitory compound than anything permanent. It was bounded by a fence constructed of large pieces of ironwood stuck in the ground and wrapped with barbed wire.

They entered the compound on foot and were immediately overwhelmed by a group of smiling, curious, and dusty children. Circled around them was a group of fifteen huts, some built of sticks and some of mud, all with roofs made of thatched grass. A separate fenced animal corral stood to one side, its gate facing what they were told was the sacred fire.

It was Willson's first time in a Himba village; she followed a young woman of about eighteen years on a short tour. Speaking passable English, the woman explained how far they walked to get water, how they kept themselves clean and fed, and the importance of goats and cows in their culture. Inside one of the huts, which was surprisingly cool, she asked if Willson was married, and when she said no, the woman talked at length about a young man from a nearby village whom she had her eye on and wanted to have babies with. *Young love*, thought Willson, *is the same everywhere.*

Like the Himba women she'd seen in Kamanjab, Willson's tour guide was barefoot, her ankles enclosed in beaded bracelets. She wore a red fabric skirt tied with leather belts and went bare-breasted. Her skin was coated in a red mud that protected against both the sun and insects. Her neck was covered by many layers of woven necklaces. But it was her hair that most fascinated Willson; it was tied in many tight braids, each coated with thick red clay. The ends were left untied, creating an effect like black pompoms dangling at the tips. And on the top of her head, a hide headpiece sat upright like a pair of cattle horns. The girl's brother accompanied them on the tour. A young boy, his skin was also reddish, but his black hair was tied in two tight braids that fell forward in front of each eye.

After the tour was complete, Willson thanked the young woman, then she, Veronica Muafangejo, and Martha Shipanga sat in a circle with two women elders who were clearly respected by all. The children ran by, chasing a rolling bicycle tire that one young boy kept moving with a stick. At the request of the older woman, the one with a lazy, cloudy eye, they had chosen a spot to talk that was distant from the rest of the villagers. Willson understood that she and Muafangejo were permitted to be there only because the recent death of Chioto, a son from this village, was a grave matter; because they had been brought by Chioto's widow, Martha; and presumably because they were women.

Willson was keen to get to the meat of the subject — who might be involved in the murder and the poaching — but was (uncharacteristically for her) patient, allowing time for the women to trust her, to be open and relaxed with her. They spoke about their daily lives, building a level of comfort. The Himba women's English was weak, so Martha took the lead, switching between English and OtjiHimba as needed.

Around midmorning, they heard an approaching vehicle. Martha explained that it was a group from the conservancy's main eco-lodge. They paused their conversation to watch. The group of seven tourists entered the compound, led by a lodge guide, and were immediately met by the same rambunctious youngsters and the same young woman. This time, though, when the group entered a hut with the young woman, other women from the village and from villages to the north and south appeared like ghosts, each carrying bulging fabric bags. They formed a large circle in the middle of the compound, sat down, and on pieces of fabric, laid out selections of wood carvings, beaded necklaces and bracelets, and decorated gourds. Willson smiled. The tour of the hut was not only educational, it also gave the women time to set up their impromptu market. When the visitors came out of the hut's low door, it was clear they were expected to bargain with the women for their local crafts.

Once the visitors drove off in the lodge van, the saleswomen drifted away, and Willson and the other four resumed their conversation.

"Can you please tell them that we are very sorry about Chioto's death?" Willson asked Martha. "We offer our sincere condolences to his family and to the whole village. Neither of us had a chance to meet him, but we understand that he was brave and strong and well respected ... and a good husband to you, Martha." She waited while Martha translated and saw the elders nod their heads. One put her hand on Martha's arm as if to comfort her.

Upon seeing that simple act of tenderness, Willson felt a sob bubbling in her throat. She'd suddenly thought of her mother, her own loss, of the things they did together after her father's death: hiking, reading, sharing meals, taking short trips in the car. Her loneliness came to the surface in a single moaning sob, more like a cough than a cry. Tears poured from her eyes and dripped onto her lap. She lowered her head and let them come. The elder sitting next to her laid her hand on Willson's arm — Willson sensed that the elder knew the tears were not for Chioto, but someone else — and waited until they stopped flowing.

When she'd regained control, Willson turned to the woman, looked into her eyes, and said the only Himba word she could remember. "*Okuhepa*. Thank you."

Willson wiped her eyes on her shirt sleeve, then turned and again addressed Martha. "I'm sorry about that. Please also tell them that we are not investigating Chioto's murder — the police are doing that. They have not included us in their investigation, so we don't know what progress they have made. But we believe that Chioto's murder is somehow connected to the poaching of the rhino in the Klip River ... and perhaps, to other poaching that's happening in this area." She purposely used the dead man's name as much as she could to honour him, to show her respect for him, and show her understanding of the depth of loss created by his passing. As she spoke, she noticed that the women were watching her intensely. Perhaps they knew more English than they were letting on.

"We wonder if you know anything about the people involved in that."

While Martha translated, Willson watched the two women as intently as they had watched her. This time, there was some emotional discussion between the widow and the two women that was clearly more than an explanation of Willson's question. She wished she could speak the language herself.

Martha turned to Willson and Muafangejo. "They do not know who killed Chioto," she said, "although they wish they did, so that they could tell us." Martha's cheeks were wet with tears. "They want to see his death avenged. They want justice. But concerning the poaching, they say they know of men coming in to Kamanjab, Sesfontein, and Outjo who are willing to buy horn or ivory at very good prices."

"Do they know who these men are?" asked Muafangejo.

"Not their names, but they've been seen on the streets of those towns."

"How do they know they're buying these illegal products?" Willson asked.

"They have approached them and their husbands outside stores and at the market in Kamanjab, asking if they have horn or ivory to sell. Other members of the village and of nearby villages have been approached in the same way in Sesfontein and Outjo."

"Do they know if Chioto ever met these men?" Muafangejo asked.

Martha asked the question, and both women shook their heads.

"What else can they tell us about these men?"

Martha again turned back to the two elders. The exchange between them was even longer this time.

"They think they're from Helao Nafidi," she said, "the main border crossing into Angola in the north."

Willson had heard of Helao Nafidi, Namibia's busiest border port to Angola, and she knew of its importance as an economic centre for goods moving north and south. It was not surprising that the men they were looking for were from there. "How many of them are there?" she asked.

"There are always three. Two of them are Ovambo men, native to that area."

"And the other?"

"The other man is Chinese. They think he is the boss because the other two men always defer to him."

"Chinese?" Willson turned to Muafangejo. "Does that make any sense to you, Veronica?"

"It does," she said. "The EU helped to set up Helao Nafidi as an export processing zone, which encourages investment, particularly in manufacturing. New plants seem to pop up each year. I was up there two years ago to raid a warehouse, searching for elephant ivory. Since 2005 or so, Chinese businesspeople have settled in the area and bought up large chunks of land. Some say it's because they're involved with corrupt local officials. But certainly, the new zone designation has made a difference. These new investors have become a powerful economic force in that area, taking advantage of its growing commerce. It doesn't surprise me that one of them might be involved in this."

Willson recalled the conversation she'd had in Waterberg with Anita Ghebo and Tracy Brown. They had talked about the involvement of Chinese, Vietnamese, and Laotians in the illegal horn trade and the demand for rhino horn in traditional Chinese medicines. For the first time, she felt they had a link to something tangible. They were no longer dealing with shadowy unknowns, conceptual bad guys. Now, they had three specific men to identify, pursue, and, ideally, convict.

"Please ask them to describe the men," Willson said with a hopeful smile.

This time, the younger of the two women spoke directly to Willson. She did understand English. "Ovambo men are very big." She held her hands out in front of her to show that their stomachs were large. She then pointed to her front teeth. "One has gold smile. Chinese man is small." She shifted her dark, heavily veined hands so they were outstretched, palms facing downward, one above the other, to indicate someone very short. "Chinese man always smoking. Always. Drive a big black truck."

"You don't know their names?"

The woman shook her head.

"Do they come every month? Every week?"

"I do not know," the woman said with a shrug. "I only see them when I in town."

Without prompting, the older woman began speaking to Martha in her native language. Willson saw Martha's eyebrows rise in surprise. As the woman spoke, she was animated, full of emotion — her hands waved in the air, her fingers fluttering.

"She says she knows of a local man who shot two rhinos in the Uukwaluudhi conservancy north of here," Martha said. "Three days ago. He buried the horns not far from here and is waiting until the three men come again so he can sell the horns."

This was unexpected news, to say the least. "Does she know where he buried the horns?"

Martha smiled. "She tells me that her family is hungry. If we make sure they have a good meal, she will take us to where the horns are buried. She heard that you will give her money if she tells. I think she means the reward."

"Ah," Willson said. "Please thank her and tell her that if we find and convict the man, I will request that she get a reward."

The trip to the village had been surprisingly productive, more so than she could have hoped. However, she was shocked at the way a single act of kindness had triggered her emotional outburst. In that moment, she had found herself wondering if anyone would ever care for her.

Shivering, Willson turned the creaky faucet off and stepped out of the shower, wrapping herself in a thin towel. Without bothering to get dressed, she padded out into the apartment, leaving a trail of wet footprints behind her.

Muafangejo was hunched over a laptop at the dining table.

"You might have to wait a while for the water to heat up again, Veronica. Sorry about that. I was deep in thought about today."

"That's okay, Jenny. After the Himba women showed us the burial site today, I had Betty and Gaby race up there and put up a surveillance camera. They buried it in a pile of brush near the big termite mound we saw. I've got the site plugged into Google Earth here. I wonder if it's the same guy who buried the horn west of the park. He hasn't come back for that one yet, as far as we know. Betty has been running the drone by there every other day, and Ben and Neus have also been in to look. There are no new tracks."

Willson nodded. "Whoever this guy is — if it *is* the same guy — he's building quite a stockpile."

"Agreed. What we don't know is if there's any link to Chioto's shooting." Muafangejo pulled back from the computer and ran her hands up and down her dusty pants. "This guy seems to be comfortable taking a rhino or two, burying the horns, then selling them to a buyer when the time and money are right. Unless Chioto stumbled onto what he was doing, it seems a big jump from that to murder."

Willson clutched her towel. "What makes me most nervous is having to wait for this guy to return for the horns ... or for the buyers to come get them. It would take only a minute or two for someone to dig each site up and then disappear. If we happened to miss it, we'd have to start again."

"What are you thinking?"

"Two things," said Willson. "The first is that I'd love to find a way to get a transmitter into the two new horns so we can trace their movements once they leave the ground."

"Betty does have transmitters. They came in yesterday with that package of coffee you received from back home. I'd love a cup of that, by the way."

"Great idea. I'll get some started." Willson moved into the kitchen and put the water on to boil.

Muafangejo spoke from the other room. "Yeah, the transmitters are each the size of an AA battery. We'll have to drill holes into the horns, place the transmitters in, close them up so no one can tell they've been tampered with, and rebury them. Then we can follow them with a receiver like we use for collared wildlife. Or we may even be able to track them on our cellphones."

"You guys are well ahead of me, then. That's excellent. We need to get those into the horns tomorrow. We can't wait any longer." Willson banged around the kitchen, pulling a French press and mugs from a cupboard.

"Agreed. And the second thing?" asked Muafangejo.

"I was reading my university alumni magazine online last night, and there's a guy in the biomedical engineering school who's developed a way to create artificial bones with a 3-D printer. I guess they're starting to do it with other body parts, like ears. What if they could print rhino horns and insert a tracking device in them?"

"Have you been drinking, Jenny?"

"No, I'm totally serious. Think about it: it would allow us to track each horn along its illicit path, from the first to the final buyer. And think about how it could disrupt the supply chain, creating confusion amongst buyers about whether or not they were buying the real thing."

"Even if that is possible — and it sounds like science fiction to me — we'd need a way to get the fake horns to the buyers. And we don't even know who they are yet."

"One step at a time," said Willson. "It seems like such an obvious step if we can figure it out."

"Can you contact this guy to see if it's even possible to build an artificial horn?" asked Muafangejo. She seemed to be reconsidering the feasibility of the idea. "I suppose it is only keratin, after all. I'm no scientist, and I can't even figure out how to change the ink in my printer at home ... but it makes some sense. It might take a few years' supply of fingernail and toenail cuttings, but why not?"

"I'll send him an email tonight."

Later that evening, after dinner with Veronica at the Oppi-Koppi Rest Camp, Willson sat down with a glass of whiskey and her laptop full of downloaded emails. First, she crafted a message to the UBC professor, asking whether it was possible to build artificial rhino horns on his 3-D bioprinter and whether he'd be willing to give it a try. Would he respond, or think she was a crackpot? Or someone trying to make a quick buck selling fake rhino horn to unsuspecting buyers?

Her oldest unread email was from Tracy Brown, the second one she'd received since they'd parted. It was just another *Hi, all is good, wish you were here* message. She pounded out a similarly neutral response, then hit send. Her disappointment over Brown's departure was diminishing, but she wasn't yet ready to write anything more.

The second message was much more interesting. It was from Brad Jenkins, the B.C. conservation officer, confirming that there *would* be a position open in their Cranbrook office at about the time her Namibian secondment was done. She reread twice the sentence where he urged her to apply for it and hinted that he'd put in a good word for her if she did. She'd been thinking about this opportunity ever since that first message from Sue Browning. At first, she'd wanted to jump on it. The mental scars from her experience in Yoho Park hadn't yet healed. But then, her thoughts bouncing around, she'd reminded herself that Parks Canada had always been her dream job. Now, with even more weeks' reflection under her belt, she was back where she'd started, thinking it was time for a change. During her stint in Namibia so far, she'd come to appreciate that her drive and her set of professional skills were valuable in many different settings. And why not use those back in the mountains of B.C. — but without the Parks Canada bureaucracy looming over her shoulder? She didn't kid herself that working for a different government would make a huge difference. But it *would* be a new start. She emptied her glass and banged it down on the table, the decision made: she would throw her name into the hat.

Of the three new personal messages in her inbox, the email from Danny Trang was the most intriguing.

Hi Jenny,

I hope you're having success up north. I discovered something here in Walvis Bay that you might find interesting. And before you write me off because of your last experience with a journalist (yes, I was listening on that early morning drive!), I assure you that I have no interest in pursuing this story. I'm an adventure travel writer/photographer, not

Sebastian Junger. I'll leave the cloak-and-dagger investigative stuff to you.

Starting in two weeks, I'll be at Klip River Lodge for a week, doing a story on community conservancies for *Outside* magazine. If you'd like to meet, I can tell you more about what I've dug up. I'd love to catch up and see how you're doing.

Danny

Willson crossed the room and poured herself another whiskey, taller than the first. Glass in hand, she stared out the window at two children riding a bike down the street toward town. In a single day, she'd discovered new information from the Himba women about rhino poachers and horn buyers here in the northwest, and then, moments after she'd decided to apply to become a B.C. conservation officer, she'd reconnected with someone who lived right where that job was located — someone who apparently wanted to see her and might have some valuable information. Was it a coincidence, or was it a sign? She shook her head. As nice as Danny Trang seemed, he was still a journalist, and in her mind, that meant he shouldn't be trusted.

On first sip, her second whiskey was better than the first, seasoned with the intoxicating taste of progress. But at the back of her tongue was a subtle aftertaste of uncertainty.

CHAPTER 18

JULY 12

Sam Mogotsi jerked awake from a fitful, sweat-soaked sleep. For a moment, he couldn't remember where he was. But the bare cinder-block walls were a stark, immediate reminder. The sunlight slanting through the high, barred window of his cell was his only clue that another day had arrived.

Three distinct sets of footsteps echoed down the long hallway. He sat up. He was the only prisoner here, so he assumed he was about to get another visit from the inspector. He waited as the steps came closer.

Since Mogotsi's early morning arrest three days earlier, Nashili had tried without success to persuade Mogotsi to confess to Chioto's murder. The inspector normally came alone and tried threats, lies, promises of leniency. Occasionally, he brought one or two junior colleagues with him, presumably to create extra tension and make Mogotsi wonder if and when things would get physical. Perhaps this would be the time.

With this ever-present threat of violence, Mogotsi had begun to question just what they had on him, if anything. Despite the inspector's arrogant swagger and the lack of visits from a lawyer, Mogotsi suspected that if the evidence really were strong, he would've appeared before a magistrate already. But that had yet to happen, even after two full days behind bars.

When he saw Jenny Willson's face, Mogotsi stood up and smiled, his cramped back and leg muscles complaining. Hers was the first friendly face he'd seen since the steel door had first swung shut two days ago. Behind Willson was Veronica Muafangejo, the female police inspector who'd stood up to his nemesis during that meeting he'd attended with Carolina Musso. Kugara, the sergeant who'd arrested him, stood next to her.

"Hi, Sam," said Willson. "Sorry it took me a while to get here. I was out in the field for the last two days. Are they treating you okay?"

"Thank you for coming to see me, Jenny, Inspector. I was wondering whether you'd received the message from my wife." He glanced sideways at the sergeant. "I'd really like to get out of here. They've been very … *persistent* in trying to get me to confess to something I did not do."

"They haven't hurt you, have they?" asked Muafangejo.

Mogotsi again looked at Kugara, knowing that everything said in the cell would be reported back to Nashili. Saying the wrong thing could impact his future comfort and safety if his time here lasted any longer. His gaze popped back to Muafangejo. "They have not," he said. "But I'd feel better if I were home with my family. I'm hoping the lodge will keep paying me until I get out of here, so my wife can keep food on the table. Even so, it won't last forever. And they surely won't support her if I'm convicted. I need to get this sorted out."

"Well, you'll be pleased to hear that we're taking you home," said Muafangejo. "At Jenny's urging, I reviewed your file … such as it is." It was the inspector's turn to look at Kugara, clearly sending a message to her counterpart through him. The sergeant suddenly took an interest in the shine of his shoes.

"After seeing how little they have in the way of hard evidence," Muafangejo continued, "I spoke to the local magistrate on your behalf. She agreed to release you on the condition that you'll come to court … *if* your case ever goes to trial."

Mogotsi nodded his head vigorously, looking from Muafangejo to Willson and back again. "I will, I will."

"We'll make sure of that," said Inspector Muafangejo. She turned to the sergeant and pointed to the locked cell door, saying nothing, her meaning clear.

Kugara clumsily tried to stall. "My superior officer will not be happy with this or with me," he said, fumbling in his pocket for keys. "It is his case, and this is his prisoner. He is in Windhoek today, but he would want to be consulted."

"Mr. Mogotsi is no longer a prisoner, Sergeant. You've seen the magistrate's order, and it does not allow your boss any discretion in the matter. We are taking this man with us. Open the cell and stand aside."

Once Kugara unlocked and opened the door, Mogotsi left the cell as quickly as possible. In the hallway, he gave Muafangejo a vigorous handshake, and then Willson. He felt her strong grip, and she placed her other hand on his shoulder. Tears of relief came to his eyes.

"Sergeant," said Muafangejo, "where are Mr. Mogotsi's shoes?"

"He … he wasn't wearing any when he was arrested."

"You brought him here without his shoes?"

"Yes, sir … ma'am. Our orders were to bring him in as we found him."

Mogotsi watched the sergeant shrink under the inspector's glare.

"I have half a mind to demand that you take off your own boots, Sergeant. Get this man some shoes immediately."

While Kugara reluctantly walked away from them, down the hallway, Mogotsi turned to Willson. "Jenny, I —"

"Don't say anything, Sam," said Willson quietly, her eyes serious. "Let's just get you out of here."

A short time later, the three stood in the gravel parking lot outside the police station, Mogotsi wearing a pair of battered flip-flops that were a couple of sizes too big for him.

They got into the truck, Mogotsi sliding in behind Muafangejo, who was driving. "Thank you both for getting me out. I owe you. My family owes you."

"We need to find out everything you know," said Willson. "And we couldn't do that while you were in there."

"I told you everything I knew when we talked in Klip River," Mogotsi said.

Willson twisted around to look at him. "I don't think you did, Sam," she said. "We've seen the evidence, and while I don't think it's enough to convict you of anything, there has to be more to this than you're telling us. Or perhaps more than you're aware of."

Mogotsi slumped in the seat, his head back. His relief at being released from jail was replaced by dark foreboding, as though the worst was yet to come. And on top of that, he was exhausted; jail was not the place for deep sleep. "I'd really like to go home to my wife and family."

"We'll take you home soon," said Willson, "but first, we're going to our office, so we can go through every detail of your story. We need to know every question the police asked you before your arrest and while they were holding you."

"Why don't you believe me?"

"It's not so much that we don't believe you, Sam. We've just got to figure out what's going on here. Chioto's murder and your arrest are somehow linked to the rhino poaching. I don't know how yet, but I will find the connection. Whether you like it or not, you're at the centre of something big. Now you're one of the keys to figuring out what it is."

Mogotsi shook his head in resignation. He was losing perspective on what to say or not say. As they reached the paved road at the edge of Kamanjab, he saw the Sentra grocery store and gas station. "Could we possibly stop at the store?" he asked, his hand on his stomach. "I haven't eaten anything since yesterday."

Muafangejo parked outside the store, and Mogotsi and Willson climbed out of the truck. As they started toward the store, Mogotsi stopped abruptly.

"What is it?" Willson asked.

"I'm sorry," he said, turning back around toward the truck, "I just remembered that I don't have any money. This is what I was wearing when they arrested me."

Willson smiled. "Don't worry about it. We'll get whatever you want, since we're going to delay you from getting home for a bit."

At the anti-poaching unit office, after Mogotsi had devoured a bag of spicy biltong, two cans of cola, and an apple, they got down to work. The two women sat across from him. Willson had a notebook open in front of her, and a small digital voice recorder sat on the table between them, its red light blinking.

"Let's start with the arrest, Sam," she said, a pencil poised in her right hand. "Tell us what happened."

"They came before dawn," he said. "They got me out of bed. They said nothing other than that I was under arrest for the murder of Chioto Shipanga."

"Did you say anything to them at that time?"

"I told them I didn't kill Chioto! I reminded them that *I* found his body and reported it."

"How did they respond?" asked Muafangejo. It was the first time she'd spoken since they'd arrived at the office.

"They told me I could tell my story to a magistrate."

"And did that happen?"

"No. I've been sitting in that cell for two days."

"Anything else when you were arrested?" Willson asked.

"No, other than I asked my wife to call a lawyer, the one my sister was using. But he never did show up."

"So, you haven't spoken with a lawyer?"

"Not yet."

Willson looked at Muafangejo, who gave a subtle nod.

"Do you want to talk to one now?" asked Willson.

"You two are helping me now, so that can wait."

"I want to be clear, Sam: we got you out of jail so we could talk freely with you, to find out what you know, to uncover the truth. Please don't mistake that for helping you or being on your side."

Mogotsi felt his emotions rising and falling. "Okay, I'm sorry. I'm confused by all of this. I don't understand how I ended up in this situation. And I don't have a lawyer yet."

"I get that, Sam," Willson said. "We'll do what we can to explain things to you as we go along. But you really should talk to a lawyer about how you will defend yourself as soon as possible. We can't do that for you. But I have spoken with a friend of mine, Dinnah Usiku. She's a top defence lawyer from Keetmanshoop, and she's willing to defend you based on what I've told her so far."

"Thank you very much, Jenny," said Mogotsi, tears in his eyes again. "I will talk to my wife to see if she has spoken to anyone yet. If not, then I would like to talk to your friend."

Willson moved forward in her chair. "Did the officers say anything while they were driving you here to Kamanjab?" she asked.

"They told me they'd found my rifle, that it matched the bullet that killed Chioto and the rhino. They gave me the impression that it proved my guilt."

"Did you say *anything* else while you were being arrested?" asked Muafangejo.

Mogotsi paused for a moment, thinking back to the confusion and shock of that morning. "I asked my wife to contact you, Jenny. It was the last thing I said before they drove me away."

"And why did you do that?" asked Willson, cocking her head to one side. "Why me?"

"Because you seemed interested in finding out what happened, and might be willing to help me. I was scared and did not know what to do."

"Like I said, Sam, for me it's all about finding out what the hell is going on. If that ends up helping you, great. But if it doesn't, then it's nothing personal."

"I understand," said Mogotsi.

The stress and uncertainty of the last three days weighed on him increasingly, like big rocks on his chest. "Are we finished yet? Can I go home now?"

"When you got to the station, what questions did the police ask you?" Willson said, ignoring his plea.

Mogotsi sighed loudly. "Once I got in the cell, Inspector Nashili always asked the questions. Most of the time he came to see me alone. But sometimes he brought in Sergeant Kugara. Seemed like his job was to scare me."

"How so?"

"He always came in and stood close to me with his big arms across his chest, watching every move I made."

"And?"

"And what?"

"What questions did the inspector ask you?"

"He asked the same ones every time. Why did I kill Chioto. Why did I try to hide the rifle I used to kill him. What did I know about the people poaching rhinos. What did I do with the rhino horn I took in Klip River. Who was I working with, and where did the rhino horn go after I sold it. What did I do with the money."

"How did you answer those questions?"

"I denied everything repeatedly. I told him I knew nothing about any of it."

"And he didn't believe you?"

"It seemed like he'd already made up his mind that I was guilty of all those things, and there was nothing I could say to change that."

"Did he ever show you any evidence?"

Mogotsi shook his head. "No. Like I said, he told me they had found my rifle, although he wouldn't say where they found it. I did ask him. He said they'd matched it with the bullet that killed Chioto, and the rhino, so I guess they must have done a test of some kind. But he never showed me anything." He saw Willson and Muafangejo exchange a quick glance. "What is it?"

"They do have a rifle, Sam," said Muafangejo. "I saw it. What kind was yours?"

"It's an old .303 my father gave me."

Muafangejo nodded. "That's the calibre of rifle they now have as evidence, but I can't say whether it was yours or not."

Willson slammed her fist on the table. Mogotsi jumped. "Come on, Sam," she said, rising to stand with her hands on the back of her chair, "something is not adding up here. They've got your rifle, and it appears to be the weapon used to kill Chioto. *You* found the body. The rifle also appears to be the weapon that was used to shoot the rhino cow. It's more than a little suspicious, isn't it? And yet, you say you know nothing, that you're not involved?"

Mogotsi raised his hands to cover the top of his head, shocked at Willson's outburst. "I'm telling the truth! A few days after Chioto was murdered, the police told me that when they searched my place, the rifle wasn't there. Now, suddenly, they have it? It makes no sense. The longer I was in jail, the more I began to wonder. Where did they find it? And if it really *was* used to kill Chioto, then who pulled the trigger? If they were so sure that I killed him, why didn't they get me in front of a magistrate? It seems to me that someone is trying to make it look like I killed my brother-in-law."

"Did you mention that to Nashili?" said Muafangejo.

"I did, and he laughed. He just wanted me to admit to everything. He said he would go easier on me if I did, but there'd be serious consequences if I didn't."

"What do you think he meant by that?"

"He kept mentioning that my wife and family were at home, alone …"

"You felt threatened?"

"I did. I was frightened. But I wasn't going to admit to something I didn't do. That would be worse for my family."

Willson closed her notebook, turned off the recorder, and stood up. "I think we've done enough for the morning," she said. "Let's get you home, Sam. I appreciate your patience with our questions."

Mogotsi stood, too, but his head started to spin. He grabbed the table to keep from falling.

"Are you okay?"

"Yes," he said as the room slowly came back into focus. "I normally walk every day, so I don't think my body liked sitting in a cell for so long, under stress. I need food, rest, and fresh air. And I need all this to go away." He began to move toward the door, carefully and slowly. "What happens next, Jenny?"

"You should talk to a lawyer, Sam, as soon as you can. Once Nashili hears that his main murder suspect has been released, he won't be happy. I don't know what he'll do next."

"Do you believe me?"

"I'm getting there," said Willson, opening the main door for him. The morning sun flooded in, followed by a wave of warm air. "If you *are* telling the truth, then we've got a lot of work to do to figure out what the hell's going on."

CHAPTER 19

JULY 18

The large entrance signs and imposing rock wall at Galton Gate, the western doorway to Etosha National Park, were still in darkness when Jenny Willson and Veronica Muafangejo rolled up in the early morning. They'd left Kamanjab at 3:00 a.m. and, with no traffic on the paved road, had made good time on the 190-kilometre journey north, their eyes constantly on the watch for animals big and small.

When they reached the closed entrance gate, Muafangejo sounded the horn once, then a second time. Finally, a sleepy-looking police officer appeared on the other side. He shook his head and waved his arms back and forth, indicating that the park was still closed. But when Muafangejo pushed her badge out the truck window, the man rushed to slide the gate out of the way.

They waved at the officer, who was still straightening his hat as they went by, and passed a castle-like tower to the right of the gate. The Namibian flag, with its distinctive blue, red, and green bands topped by a bright yellow sun, hung limply on a pole at its apex. At the base of the tower, another officer was fast asleep, sitting in a chair tilted against the stone wall. Muafangejo pushed the palm of her hand hard against the truck's horn, and the man fell forward with a start.

"Rude start to his day," said Willson, grinning.

"It's hard to find people who'll take this job seriously," the inspector said, slowing the truck as she checked out the buildings. "Those posted here are at the bottom of our hierarchy. They'll learn. And there's a crafty old sergeant here who'll do his best to whip them into shape."

"This is a pretty fancy entrance gate and facility. Someone spent a lot of money on this."

"Looks can be deceiving. An American aid agency helped build this back in 2014. It includes staff houses, offices, an administration building, a conference hall with kitchen and ablution facilities. They widened the intersection back there, paved this entrance, and installed a reverse osmosis plant for water. But from what I hear, there wasn't any money in the deal for operating costs. So, sometimes, they don't have drinking water. That's not the first time this kind of thing has happened here."

Muafangejo continued driving up the main road and explained that, until 2014, it had been open only to park personnel and visitors staying at the private Dolomite Camp. It was open to the public now, though not this early in the day.

The road was bumpy and dusty, and it climbed steadily past a tall mountain. On the way they spotted Hartmann's mountain zebras, red hartebeest, and a pair of large eland — Willson's first Namibian sighting of the largest member of the antelope family. After fourteen kilometres of bouncing around, they rounded a sharp corner and came to a major crossroad.

Willson was surprised by the number of military and police vehicles parked at the junction. "Holy shit, Veronica, this is a big deal."

"They're somewhere out here almost every day," Muafangejo said. "As you know, our government is taking poaching extremely seriously now, and there's no more high-profile place than Etosha. It's been a reserve or park of some form since 1907 and has become the main reason visitors come to the northern part of the country. While we're doing our investigations, there are hundreds of officers out here all year round, acting as a deterrent as much as anything else." She smiled. "They were out yesterday on camels, so I'm glad today is on foot. We can see what they're doing without having to deal with those horrid beasts."

"What have you got against camels? I hear they work well in the deserts and near-deserts out here."

"You mean aside from the fact that they're ugly, ungainly, smelly, and have a bad attitude?"

The women pulled their packs from behind their seats, then walked over to join a group of police officers and Defence Force personnel standing around a makeshift table. Willson studied the circle of officers, counting a total of ten. They bristled with assault rifles, their belts and vests bulged with gear and ammunition, and some had night-vision binoculars hanging around their necks. Everyone had at least one semi-automatic pistol on their belt — some were Rugers, others Russian-made Makarovs. Willson saw one CZ 75 pistol, built in the Czech Republic. The diversity of weaponry in front of her reflected the unique history of Namibia, a history of international influence that was still unfolding. Willson had her own semi-automatic on her belt. This *was* serious.

Willson saw Ben Mushimba and Gaby Bohitile, who had driven up from Kamanjab the night before. They each gave her a quick nod. Neus stood beside Ben, his eyes shining brightly in the light of the group's headlamps. He tugged at his leash, and his tail beat the air like a high-speed metronome. He was ready to go.

An army major stood at the centre of the circle. He was obviously leading the planning for the day's exercise, so Willson and Muafangejo moved closer and listened carefully.

"Good morning. Today, we will break into two patrols of six," the major said, "and head in parallel tracks in a north-northeast direction from our present location." He pointed with two fingers to a map spread on the table and traced a course northward. "Here and here. We'll try to stay about three kilometres apart throughout the day, one group on the west side of this small peak, the other to the east."

He looked around the circle at the officers. "I want three of my officers and three police officers in each group. Ben, I'd like you and Neus in the western group, please. Because it's closest to the park boundary, that's where we'll likely pick up spoor first, if there is any." He assigned each officer to one of the two patrol groups, then reached for the portable radio hooked on his bulletproof vest. "We'll all use the same tactical frequency today." He gave them the frequency number, and all the officers keyed it in to their radios. "For those of you out with us yesterday, please note that it's a different frequency today. Earpieces are mandatory. Keep the noise to a bare minimum. Call only when you see something. I don't need to remind you of the importance of stealth in our approach."

The major pulled a camouflage-patterned baseball cap firmly down onto his head. "A final reminder: unlike last week, when we were working outside the park, we are now *inside* Etosha National Park. There should be no one here on foot in the park other than us, particularly in the closed area we're patrolling today. Therefore, if you see fresh human tracks, that is our clue that someone is where he should not be. Go on high alert, advise us by radio, and follow the tracks as long and far as you need to. I want to know who it is, where they are, and what they're doing. If that means multiple nights out in the bush, so be it. Arresting poachers is our preference, and our police colleagues are here to do that if needed. However, all of you know the rules of engagement: we do not fire our weapons unless we are threatened. If we *are* threatened with weapons or are fired upon, then your orders are to immediately return fire and eliminate the threat. Understood?" He looked at every officer, awaiting a nod. "Let's do this."

The two groups left the junction on their designated parallel routes. Willson brought up the rear of their group, with Muafangejo and Bohitile ahead of her in the single-file line, and Mushimba and Neus in the lead. Willson loved seeing man and dog at work; they were a team, Neus doing what he did best with his nose, Mushimba watching for the subtlest of signals that Neus had picked up a scent. In between Bohitile and Willson were two army sergeants, one male, one female. As they entered the sparse forest, Willson found it somewhat familiar, even comforting. After a kilometre, she realized that it reminded her of an abandoned orchard she'd seen back in the Okanagan region of British Columbia. The mopane and acacia trees were well spaced and almost looked as if they'd been planted in rows, then left to fend for themselves. But she knew they hadn't been planted; this was a natural forest type in this part of the savanna. Unlike areas farther to the east, around the salty Etosha pan, this area received enough rain to be lusher and greener. But under the trees, grass was turning brown under the increasing drought conditions. It had been nearly three months since the last rains. Thorny shrubs waited to tear their clothing.

The patrol walked in silence for hours, listening, watching for animals, searching the ground for human footprints. They stopped at regular intervals, nibbling on food in the shade of larger acacia trees, sipping from water bottles, always quiet. The other patrol, a few kilometres to their right, would be doing the same.

It was midafternoon when their patrol spotted the first set of human tracks. Ben Mushimba and Neus had dropped back to walk behind Willson, so it was Bohitile who was the first to see them. She held up a fist to stop the group, then crouched down. Everyone gathered around. No words were spoken. She studied the ground for a few moments, looked repeatedly to her left and right, then held up two fingers and pointed to the east. Her assessment was clear: two humans, coming from the west and heading east, in the last few hours. Studying the tracks, Willson assumed that the two people were likely not heading somewhere specific, but meandering, looking for something. Hunting? She couldn't help but wonder if these were the rhino poachers they'd been searching for since she'd arrived in Kamanjab. Could she be that lucky?

She watched Bohitile first check her GPS unit, then cup her left hand around her shoulder-mounted microphone. "Alpha to Bravo," she said softly. "Two tracks, eastbound." Her transmission was short and clipped. She then gave the military grid reference for their location. "Alpha tracking. Out."

Willson heard a double-click on the radio, indicating the second patrol's acknowledgement of the transmission. She also knew that the second patrol leader would at that moment be sending a text message to the pilot of a helicopter that was on standby near Otjetjekua, just outside the park boundary. He'd be ready to take off at a moment's notice if they needed to track the suspects from the air.

Bohitile stood and pointed to the east. She began to walk parallel to the footprints, and the patrol followed her, Mushimba and Neus right at her heels, Neus at the end of his leash, nosing along the tracks. One set was marginally larger than the other. In a practised motion, Bohitile and the two sergeants slid their assault rifles from their backs and held them across their chests. Like they had been choreographed, their index fingers moved to the outside of the trigger guards. Willson opened the nylon holster on her pistol and rested her right hand on it. In front of her, she saw Muafangejo do the same.

Thirty minutes later, they heard a single shot, then two more in rapid succession. It was the sound of a large-calibre weapon, loud and sharp and close. Willson was certain the other patrol would have heard it, too. They stopped and knelt, listening for a hint of direction, of distance. Bohitile was scanning the tops of the trees to the east. After a moment, she pointed. A group of large birds — vultures or perhaps hornbills — rose up and circled in the sky. They had either been disturbed by the shots or were attracted by the potential for a meal.

Bohitile motioned with her outstretched arm, indicating that they should proceed slowly. Like her two colleagues, she raised her rifle so that it pointed down and ahead of her. Willson slid her pistol out of its holster but kept it beside her leg, also pointing at the ground.

The team stood and moved forward excruciatingly slowly, one small step at a time, their eyes shifting ahead, left, and right, looking for movement. Fingers were now on triggers. The tension was palpable. For Willson, this was unlike anything she'd ever experienced in Canada's national parks. She had tranquilized and relocated grizzly bears, wrestled drunken campers, rescued hapless hikers from precipitous cliffs, and, perhaps most dangerous of all, faced down federal bureaucrats determined not to do anything useful.

But now, her heart was pounding in her chest, and adrenalin pumped through her system like a drug. Every sense was working overtime, it seemed: her vision was crystal clear, and she could smell the sun beating on the red soil around them. The sound of her footsteps banged in her ears. Most of all, fear was a metallic taste on her tongue. Funny how the possibility of a gun battle had woken up her entire sensory system.

The two sets of footprints remained on their right. Willson saw that the spaces between the prints were now smaller, as if the humans who'd made them had also slowed down.

Bohitile again raised her fist in the air slowly and held it there. In mid-stride, she carefully lowered one knee to the ground. When the patrol had stopped, she moved her fist downward slightly, then pointed with her thumb and index finger at an opening in the scrub forest to the right of a bushy mopane tree. Willson looked over Bohitile's shoulder and spotted two men kneeling on the ground with their backs to the patrol. A large animal lay on the ground in front of them, only about a metre from one of them. From her viewpoint, she couldn't see what it was, but she feared the worst. A rifle lay across the animal's flank.

Bohitile raised her rifle. Her two army colleagues slowly stepped to each side of her and did the same. When they were ready, Bohitile yelled at the men, starting in Oshiwambo, the local language, then repeating herself in English. The men had very dark skin, so Bohitile had assumed they were locals.

"Police! Slowly raise your arms above your heads and get on your knees."

Despite Bohitile's demand, the two men's heads whipped around simultaneously. When they saw the three assault rifles pointed at them, they froze, their eyes wide with fear and surprise. In the excitement, Neus began barking.

"Get those hands high," said Bohitile calmly. "Stay on your knees and turn your heads so you are facing away from me. Then, move backward slowly toward the sound of my voice, keeping your arms in the air."

The officers watched the men shuffle awkwardly backward, their hands straining toward the sky. It was no easy task given their kneeling position, the rocky ground, and their not being allowed to use their arms. Neus continued to bark. Mushimba did nothing to stop him, probably knowing the sound would add to the men's fear.

"Keep coming toward the sound of my voice," Bohitile said. "No sudden movements."

When the two men were about five metres away from the animal carcass and out of reach of the rifle, Bohitile ordered them to lie face down on the ground, and then she nodded to Willson and Muafangejo. "Cuff them," she said calmly.

Willson and Muafangejo holstered their weapons, pulled handcuffs from their belts, and moved toward the men. Willson pulled the larger man's arms behind his back and handcuffed him; Muafangejo did the same with the smaller man. The simultaneous ratcheting clicks of the metal cuffs were followed by the sounds of breath escaping from the watching officers.

"Alpha to Bravo," said Bohitile into her microphone. "Targets acquired."

"Roger that," said the voice of the army major. "We're already on the way. Be there in two."

Willson turned her attention to the dead animal. It was not, as she had feared, a black or white rhino. Instead, it was a massive kudu bull, one of the largest members of the antelope family. Its skin was a tawny grey with whitish stripes running from its spine toward its stomach. Between the animal's eyes was the distinctive white chevron marking. The twin spiralling horns, a metre and a half in length, lay in the red dust. The sight brought back stark memories of the bull elk that had triggered her poaching investigation back in Banff National Park. But this time, the culprits were right in front of her, caught in the act. In custody.

As the patrol members circled the two men, now pulled up into a sitting position, the second patrol arrived.

"What are you doing out here?" Muafangejo asked the two men.

They looked to still be in shock, but the larger one spoke. "We need meat for our families."

"Do you know that you are not allowed to hunt in the park?"

"We didn't know we were in a park," said the smaller man. "We didn't. There are no animals near our village, and we are very hungry. We have no money to buy food."

"You had to go through a fence, and you walked past signs, so you must have known you were in the park."

"We didn't know," the man said, his eyes now teary.

"We consider you to be poachers. You'll spend a long time in jail for this."

Willson studied the men. Neither matched any of the descriptions of the three buyers given to them by the Himba elders, but that meant nothing. They could be first-level sellers, men who killed for a quick buck. She wondered if one or both was responsible for any of the rhino horns they'd discovered.

"What were you going to do with the horns?" asked Willson, curious. She was no expert on kudu, but knew that this bull had grown an imposing set, bigger than any she'd seen in photographs. Someone would want them on their trophy wall.

But the men were thin and hungry-looking, their clothes threadbare. Perhaps they were telling the truth. Willson understood that the distribution of legal game meat to local communities had dropped off recently because of increasing droughts. Maybe this was the other face of poaching. Perhaps these men were not greedy trophy hunters, but simply trying to feed their families in a traditional way that had been practised for many generations.

"We can't eat the horns," said the larger man. "We only want the meat. Our families are starving."

"That makes no difference," said Muafangejo. "You're coming with us."

Willson and Muafangejo pulled the two men to their feet and stood behind them. Normally, they would grip an elbow or hold on to the handcuffs, but with Neus staring at them, pulling at his leash, and armed officers circled around them, the men would be foolish to try to escape.

"Veronica," said the major, "I'll let you take charge of the scene so you can collect whatever evidence you need for court. I'll radio to my men back at the vehicles to bring up two trucks along the closed western road. That's the closest point. Once you're done here, we'll all head west. You can take your prisoners back to your vehicle, then back to Kamanjab ... or wherever you're going to take them for interrogation. We'll continue our patrols through the night."

"You won't just leave the horns here, will you?" said one of the army sergeants.

"No," said Muafangejo. "We'll take them with us as evidence."

It took Willson, Muafangejo, and Mushimba another hour to process the scene. The army officers stayed in a loose circle around them, protecting them from lions, hyenas, and other predators that might try to take ownership of the carcass before they were done with it. Even though they'd caught the two men red-handed and had what amounted to a confession, they took photographs of everything and dug the bullet out of the kudu's shoulder so it could be used in court to link to the seized rifle. As a final step, they chopped the horns from the kudu's head. It was a sad and messy job, but it was necessary. The body would be left for scavengers; they'd be upon it as soon as the humans left the scene. Throughout all this activity, the two handcuffed prisoners sat in the shade of a tree, looking like they wished they were anywhere else.

When they returned to their vehicles three hours later, prisoners in tow and the kudu horns tied to

Bohitile's pack, it was the edge of night. As they loaded the two men into one of the trucks, Mushimba walked over to the others, his cellphone in his hand. The screen lit up his concerned face in the dusky light.

"I got a text from Monica," he said, his eyes wide and darting back and forth between Willson and Muafangejo. "Seems that while we were out here today, someone burned down your apartment in Kamanjab."

"What?" said Willson, thinking immediately of the few personal possessions that had been in the apartment. Luckily, she'd left her laptop at the office. Then, she remembered that the only framed picture of her mother that she'd brought with her from Canada had been in there … it was likely gone.

"The fire started early this morning, maybe right after you left to come up here. The building is a burnt-out shell. The roof is gone, everything inside is crispy, and the walls are black. Monica says the fire truck, such as it is, showed up an hour after the call was made. By then, it was too late."

"How does she know it was arson?" Willson asked.

"I asked her that. She's taken some courses and said it was clear that someone threw something flammable through the window at the back of the building."

Willson looked at Muafangejo. "Seems like we've really pissed someone off," she said, "and they're trying to send us a message."

Willson knew they both had the same list of possible subjects, with Inspector Nashili — who'd recently been embarrassed by their releasing Sam Mogotsi — at the top of that list. If it *was* him, perhaps this was his revenge for being made to look foolish … or was it something deeper? Was he somehow involved?

But if it wasn't him, then who *did* feel threatened by their investigation? What good was a message, even one as dramatic as this, if they didn't know who it was from? Regardless, someone seemed to be telling them to back off. For Willson, that meant they were on the right track. Time to bear down harder.

CHAPTER 20

JULY 28

The sun was on its downward slide toward the horizon, and cicadas filled the air with their tinny calls as Danny Trang and Carolina Musso sat in the shade of the porch outside the Klip River Lodge dining room. Glasses of water sweated on the wooden table between them, leaving circles in the dark wood. Guests splashed in the pool below, ignoring a pair of swallows intermittently using it as a drinking fountain. Trang couldn't keep his eyes off the view to the west, the deep gorge of the Klip River. He'd arrived at the lodge late last night and had found himself staring westward ever since first light. He knew that one of the dramatic images he'd captured on his camera as the sun first came up would be front and centre in his article for *Outside* magazine.

"I've read the annual reports," Trang said to Musso, "and there's plenty of great background there. Thanks for sharing those." He pointed to the stack of *State of Community Conservation in Namibia* reports at his elbow, each of them heavily marked with sticky notes. "What I want to focus on in my article is the link between the conservancies and Save the Rhino Trust Namibia in the context of rhino conservation. It seems like a fascinating story that needs to be told."

"I agree, Danny." Musso's red hair glowed in the afternoon sun.

"Where would you like to start?" Trang asked.

Musso leaned back in her seat and stared out into the distance. Trang could see the passion and determination in her eyes and in the set of her jaw.

"In short," she said, "it's a story about finding innovative and outside-the-box ways to get people to care about rhinos. And by people, I don't just mean Namibians. I mean people across the globe. At the local level, we're finding ways for people to benefit from having the rhinos around — employment, diverse income opportunities, being able to stay here rather than move to the larger cities, support for elders, new water sources, new schools, the ability to practise traditional agriculture ... the list goes on. Beyond that, it's helping them see that everyone in the community is moving further ahead."

"Is it working?"

"We have lots of challenges, but it is. Rhino poaching has dropped dramatically, and we see young people attending local schools, rhino rangers taking pride in their work and what they bring home to their families, and local farmers being compensated when their crops are damaged by elephants or when they lose a goat or a cow to a lion."

"So, this is not just about rhino biology, then."

"Far from it. It's as much psychology, governance, and economics as it is biology. I've had to become more multidisciplinary in my approach than I was when I first got here."

"And what about the international level?"

"There are two sides to that coin. On the one side, we have international aid and conservation organizations providing us with significant funds for social and conservation programs, because this community conservancy model is so unique and so successful. Success attracts money, although we can always use more. We truly appreciate those investments. And there's growing public sentiment across the globe that rhinos and elephants are worth saving."

"What's the downside?" asked Trang, writing furiously.

"Under their management plans, local conservancies decide how to manage wildlife and how to increase their financial and social returns from wildlife. Many have decided that both consumptive hunting — that's hunting to put meat on people's tables — and legal trophy hunting are acceptable *if* done in a sustainable, well-managed way. The Namibian government labels it all as 'conservation hunting.' But there's the rub. Because of international revulsion over the poaching of rhinos and elephants for their horns and ivory, there's growing pressure from other countries and from groups like CITES, the Convention on International Trade in Endangered Species, to stop all trophy hunting — in some cases, *all* hunting. You may have heard that some airlines will no longer transport hunting trophies. That's an example of a well-intentioned action that has unintended consequences. I understand that people don't like hunting on principle, but it's a traditional practice here that contributes to community livelihoods. It's been done for generations. If outsiders are successful in putting pressure on conservancies to stop all hunting, then we lose significant income and one tool in our wildlife management kit. But more importantly, we would lose local support for the whole conservancy concept. That would be very dangerous, and it could then negatively impact the success of our rhino programs. I don't think those well-meaning people understand that."

Trang looked up from his notebook. "International interest is both a blessing and a curse?"

"That might be too strong a characterization," said Musso, smiling slightly, "but I can see how it might be a great headline for you. I'd prefer to say it creates both benefits and challenges for us which need to be addressed."

"You sound like a politician."

"Hey, that's not very nice," Musso said, now smiling broadly. "I'm just trying to give you a sense of the two sides of the coin. We try to keep the coin standing upright, balanced on its edge so it's neither heads nor tails, but an equal measure of both."

Trang laughed, thinking of the caribou head on the Canadian quarter. "That's a great analogy, Carolina. It's those nuances I'm trying to tweak out of this story. It's fascinating." He sipped his water, then flipped back through his notebook. "Tell me more about the role that this lodge plays in rhino conservation."

"How about we go for a drive and I can talk while we look at animals?"

The road from the lodge along the Grootberg Plateau was bumpy, mirroring the boulder-strewn terrain they followed as Musso drove them south. It reminded Trang of the moon, or Mars. It was almost that barren. Even though Musso drove slowly, Trang had to hang on with both hands, which made it tough to take notes. Musso, having driven this rough trail many times before, stayed silent, letting Trang soak up the atmosphere. They saw many Hartmann's mountain zebras, oryx, and springbok, along with the kaleidoscopic colours of the lilac-breasted roller, always perched on the topmost branches of trees or tall shrubs, and the Monteiro's hornbill, with its large reddish beak and hollow-sounding *toak* calls that reminded Trang of the ravens back in B.C. There was so much to see that he finally dropped the notebook on the floor between the seats. It was too bumpy to use binoculars, so, just as he'd done at Walvis Bay, he tried to be in the moment, take in the sights and sounds and smells.

Musso stopped the Toyota truck at a dramatic viewpoint overlooking a different side canyon of Klip River from the one that was visible from the lodge, then she pulled out two camp chairs from the back. They sat and sipped on ice-cold cans of Windhoek Lager that appeared from a cooler.

"What do you think?" asked Musso.

Trang shook his head. "I think it's amazing. Are there rhinos down there?"

"There are. Getting back to what we were talking about before, the local saying is that a dead rhino will feed a family for a week, whereas a live rhino in a valley like this will feed a family for a lifetime."

"That's a heck of a lead sentence for my article," Trang said, transcribing Musso's quote word for word in his notebook.

"If we can continue to show local people through places like our lodge that keeping rhinos and elephants alive is better than shooting them for their horns or ivory, then I believe we can become a conservation success story. Done well, tourism and conservation go together like this," said Musso, crossing the index and middle fingers of her right hand. "The lodge hires people and it gives them hope. It's proof of the direct link between saving rhinos and a better life for locals."

"And I thought the lodge was simply some amazing buildings built on the edge of an incredible landscape."

"It's much more than that. It was built by outside investors, but the lodge has largely been turned over to the local conservancy to run. Everyone who works here now is local; they're earning money, supporting families, learning new skills, and feeling pride. And the more they realize that visitors pay good money to see rhinos and other species, the more they want to do their part to keep it going."

"What a great model," Trang said, nodding. "So how does your organization fit into all of this?"

"Save the Rhino Trust was formed in 1982, and we've actively supported the work of Namibia's Ministry of Environment and Tourism since the 1990s. Our funds have helped cover the costs of annual rhino translocations from risky areas to less risky areas, of ear-notching operations so animals can be monitored, and of the radio transmitter implanting program. The Minnesota Zoo pays me to be here and to act as a resource for local conservancy managers. In addition, we've bought various pieces of rhino monitoring equipment, and of course we're the main player in the rhino tracker program. These rangers, mostly former poachers, spend twenty-one days in the field at a time, following rhinos and keeping animal observation records. They're like rhino babysitters."

"You mentioned a transmitter program — what's that?"

"We'll tranquilize a rhino, drill a small hole in its horn, place a radio transmitter in the hole and cover it back up with cement, then release the animal. This way, we can track their locations and movements, which supports the observations of the rangers, and we hope that the modified horns are of less interest to poachers."

"And you mentioned the Minnesota Zoo. Why are they involved in rhino conservation here?"

"There's a growing tendency for zoos to demonstrate more direct support of 'in-country' conservation efforts, especially for rare and endangered species. It's driven by internal and external pressures, but more importantly, having a bigger vision for wild animals beyond zoo fences is the right thing to do. The Minnesota Zoo joined forces with SRT in 2009 to support the Namibian government and local communities in protecting and restoring the critically endangered desert black rhino."

"I had no idea, but it all makes sense. I'm impressed." Trang paused to stare at the changing light in the canyon. Every moment was different. "With all that going on, what are you most worried about?"

"My list of worries is shorter, but no less significant. Another beer?"

"Please." Trang readily accepted a second cold can. He popped the tab and swallowed deeply.

"I'm worried about climate change ... that it will cause severe droughts that could decimate our wildlife populations," Musso said. "I'm worried that poor management, weak governance, or lack of capacity in some of our conservancies will force the government to pull its support for all of them. I'm worried that one government department is trying to put an extra five percent levy on our eco-lodges, which may make some of them unviable. I'm worried about international pressure to stop all kinds of hunting. But most of all, I'm worried about poaching and the increased sophistication of organized crime. If we don't find a way to stop it through our community conservancies *and* aggressive law enforcement and support from magistrates and judges, eventually we won't have anything unique to offer visitors. And then all of this" — Musso spread her arms wide — "will be in serious trouble."

"Are you aware of the new anti-poaching unit working in the area?" asked Trang.

Musso nodded.

"What do you think of it?"

"I met the team in a meeting in Kamanjab a couple of weeks ago. I'm excited they're here. And the fact that most of them are women is shaking things up in a good way. The women in the community often know what's really going on, who's doing what, and they'll be more likely to talk to female officers."

"Have you met the Canadian park warden who's here on a secondment?" Trang asked, trying to sound nonchalant. "I think her name is Willson?"

"Yeah, I met her briefly at that same meeting. She didn't say much. Let her Namibian colleagues take the lead, which was smart. But she struck me as no-nonsense. Apparently, she and her team have been here, to the lodge, a few times, doing patrols in the area, but I've missed her every time. And the locals are talking about them. I heard that they got one of our guides, Sam Mogotsi, out of jail simply by vouching for him. And he'd been arrested for murder, even though I don't believe he's guilty. Why do you ask about her, anyway?" asked Musso, lifting her eyebrows.

"No real reason," Trang said, looking away. "Just, well, while I was in Walvis Bay, I learned some things that I thought might be of interest to her. About poaching. I met her on a safari trip a while ago, and we talked a bit … exchanged a few emails."

"Her team's office is in Kamanjab, if you want to connect with her. I'm heading there the day after tomorrow, if you want to come along."

Trang smiled. "I think I'll take you up on that."

CHAPTER 21

"They can do it?" asked Veronica Muafangejo.

Jenny Willson pointed to the long email on her laptop from Professor Robin King of UBC's school of biomedical engineering. In it, he said that making an artificial rhino horn was possible.

"Do we order them on Amazon, or what?"

"Not yet," said Willson, laughing. "So, first, I had to get the good professor to trust me. It took a call from one of my old professors to convince him I was legitimate, that I wasn't on the wrong side of the law on this. He seems to see the obvious value in making artificial horns, and he's going to start working on some prototypes as soon as he can. He's even made a few phone calls and says he already has funding in place from a wealthy Vancouver philanthropist, someone who's been over here a few times and made it his life's mission to help rhinos."

Willson ran her finger down the screen of the laptop. "King says that 'keratin is a structural protein made of thin filaments joined together by chemical bonds called crosslinks,' so he feels he can replicate it, then build it into fake horns using the 3-D printers. He talks about calcium and melanin and keratin in a gelatinous state, which all confuses the hell out of me. But he says it's much easier than having to do a Dr. Frankenstein and print a new body part with living cells, like a heart or a kidney."

"But will the horns look real? The buyers we're chasing are pretty sophisticated."

"That's what'll take some testing: getting the size, consistency, texture, and colour right. But if he can do it, they'll essentially be the real deal — the key difference being that they're not cut off a murdered rhino."

"What about your idea of implanting GPS trackers into the horns?"

Willson nodded. "He said that would be the easy part."

"How long is this going to take?"

"I'm an optimist," Willson said, lifting her eyes from the screen, "but the reality is, it will take time to get it right … and to get samples to us. But once King and his team get the system perfected, they can theoretically create as many as we need."

Muafangejo grinned. "Brilliant, Jenny. Can you imagine what this will do to buyers at every level? They won't have a clue whether they're buying or selling real horns or fakes. That confusion could cause the price to drop in a dramatic way, especially if the market is flooded. And if the GPS chips work, we can track the fake horns up the supply chain and grab everyone who handles them. Could this be the end of rhino poaching?"

"Now *you're* being the optimist. Let's take this one step at a time. And there are other proposed solutions out there, you know. Some want to legalize the trade in horn because they say the international ban has only sent the whole thing underground, into the realm of criminals. They suggest rhinos be grown on farms and have their horns removed humanely, so they can grow back. Apparently, the amount of horn used in traditional medicines is so small it could be controlled by a legal market, which could kill off the black market."

"That makes some sense to me."

"But while the two sides debate that, we've got to put all our energy into finding the bastards killing rhinos *now*, in this area, and put their nuts in a wringer."

Jenny rose and crossed to the far side of the office. Now that their apartment was a blackened shell, she and Muafangejo were sleeping on foamies and sleeping bags in the opposite corner of the office from Ben and Neus. It was Sunday, and the rest of the team had taken the day off. "Any luck finding us new accommodations?"

"Nothing yet. I've been pushing my bosses in Windhoek to rent us a cabin at the Oppi-Koppi Camp. But they're balking at the cost."

"Well, they wouldn't want us to be comfortable, would they?"

Muafangejo's laugh was interrupted by a loud knock at the door. There was a pause, then both women reached for their pistols. The arson had made them all too aware that someone who was unhappy with their presence was targeting them. Willson cautiously opened the door, holding her pistol beside her leg, her finger on the trigger.

"Danny! What are you doing here?"

Trang took a step back when he noticed Willson's pistol. His eyes widened even more when he saw Veronica standing behind her in a combat stance, her own pistol drawn.

"Jesus," said Trang. "If I'd known you'd react like this, I'd have called first. Except I didn't, you know, have your number ..."

Willson waved Trang in with her pistol. When he hesitated, she laughed. "Don't worry, I'm not going to shoot you. We thought you might be someone else." She introduced Trang and Muafangejo and offered to make coffee.

"How did you find me?" she asked.

"I'm staying at the Klip River Lodge for a while, working on a story. I mentioned your name to Carolina Musso from the SRT when I interviewed her yesterday. She said you were staying here in town and offered to drive me in, so I thought I'd come say hi."

"Well, as you've probably noticed, things are a bit tense around here right now."

A few minutes later, Willson was passing around mugs of coffee. She inhaled the rich aroma and felt a sense of calm creep down to her toes.

"So, what did you want to see me about?" she asked.

Trang flushed at the question. "I sent you a few emails," he said, "and I wasn't sure if you'd want to see me or not ... me being an evil journalist and all. But besides just wanting to catch up with a fellow Canuck, I recently learned something about the rhino poaching that might be of interest to you."

"Right, you did say something in your email about information. Okay, let's talk." Willson offered him one of the chairs at their main work table. She and Muafangejo joined him, unconsciously taking the positions they used in suspect interviews. They both pulled out notebooks and pencils. "What have you got?"

Trang seemed nervous, but perhaps that was because he'd very recently had two guns pointed at him. In Willson's experience, people didn't react to that well. "When I was in Walvis Bay, I met a kayak guide called Jason," he said, sipping his coffee. "He sees what's going on and has lots of great contacts. We went for a beer after a day of paddling and talked about all sorts of things, including why some people here don't seem to like me. Apart from all the other beefs people have with the Chinese, he told me that Asians are getting an increasingly bad reputation for being involved in poaching and illegal trade here in Namibia … and elsewhere in Africa. Not only as foreign buyers of traditional medicines using illegal animal products, but as buyers and shippers right here in the country."

"And so …"

"Jason thinks that rhino horns and elephant tusks are being covertly shipped from the interior of the country to the coast via the TransNamib railway. Being hidden in railcars carrying materials like copper or charcoal. He's got a buddy who works on the Walvis Bay docks. Apparently, every so often this buddy sees guys, Asian guys, hanging around waiting for trains. They show up to the docks in their fancy cars, supposedly hush-hush, but people notice. Jason's buddy said they never seem to take anything when they leave, so he thinks they're there to confirm the arrival of their cargo, make sure it gets on the ships."

"And where are the ships going?"

"Somewhere in Asia," Trang said, shrugging. "Jason claims if people are seeing what's going on but not reporting it, there must be some 'official' involvement."

"He could be right," said Muafangejo, shaking her head. "Did he mention the local police at all?"

Trang nodded. "Jason's sure it's an open secret on the docks, so someone posted at the port's Namibian Police station must be involved somehow. People stay quiet about it because they're afraid of losing their jobs ... or worse."

Willson sat back, her mind racing. She stared at Trang, but her eyes were unfocused. She and the team had always talked about the supply chain for rhino horn, and recently, she'd begun to imagine it as a literal chain, one link connected to the next link, to the next. One end of that chain started right here in northwestern Namibia, in the Kunene region. They had only a few vague descriptions of some of the links at this end. Three men — two local, one Asian — who were allegedly active horn buyers. Others doing the killing of human and rhino — as yet unidentified. Now, Trang had painted them an imprecise picture of the links at the other end of the chain, and he'd added the cross-country railway as a steel link between the two. Walvis Bay wasn't really the end of the chain. It stretched off across the ocean, on ships carrying rhino horn to those final buyers who created the demand.

"This is good stuff, Danny," Willson said. "Really good. But why are you telling me? What's in it for you?" Like being hit with a hammer, she had another powerful flashback of her previous betrayal. Idaho-based reporter Mike Berland had gained her trust, then abused it by writing about her investigation of a shady ski hill developer. It had not only deeply hurt her, but caused her case to implode, and almost killed the investigation and her career. Ultimately, it had also led indirectly to her mother's death. She couldn't forgive … or forget.

"Jenny," Trang said, his hands folded in front of him, "there's nothing in this for me. I told you that in my email. I'm an adventure travel writer, not an investigative journalist. I'm sharing this with you because I believe in what you're doing. I have no interest in this as a story whatsoever. None. I'm not sure why you don't believe me."

"Because I've heard that shit before," Willson blurted.

In the red haze of anger that filled her vision, she registered the surprise and hurt in Trang's eyes, but she didn't care. She felt a hand on her arm.

"Jenny," Muafangejo said, with an edge to her voice, "can I talk to you outside?"

"There's nothing to talk about."

The grip on her arm became more forceful. "Outside. Now."

Without looking at Trang, Willson followed her colleague outside to the street. They waited while a mule-drawn two-wheeled buggy of the sort ubiquitous in this part of Namibia, known by locals as a "Kalahari Ferrari," clattered past them, the two men inside bouncing on the bench seat.

"What's up with you?" Muafangejo asked. "I thought you were good at reading people."

"What's *your* problem? You know I'm good."

"You were burned in the past, I get that. But I believe this guy."

"Fuckin' journalists are all the same."

"Bullshit, Jenny. He came out of his way to bring us really good information that we didn't have, and he's not asking for anything in return."

"They always want something. It's always quid pro quo with them. They use people and they don't care who gets hurt."

"You need to calm down. Your anger is blinding you professionally *and* personally. Trang may want something, but I don't think it's quid pro quo. If anything, I think his motivation is personal."

"What the hell do you mean?"

"I mean, you dense Canadian knucklehead, that he likes you."

"Are you kidding me?"

"He's clearly interested in you. Although after your little outburst, I'm surprised he hasn't left."

Willson stared at Muafangejo as though she were speaking a foreign language. Confusion had killed off her anger, and now a hint of embarrassment began to creep in.

"You really think so?" she said.

"I'd put money on it."

"Shit. I'm a dumbass."

"That is accurate. But there's only one way to know for sure."

"What's that?"

"Go back inside and apologize for being a jerk. I'll find a reason to disappear for a while so you two can talk. Maybe take him out for a beer …"

Just then, Carolina Musso pulled up in her SRT truck, and Trang came out the office door to meet her. Willson had lost her chance to apologize.

CHAPTER 22

AUGUST 20

The morning sun had yet to crack the distant plane of the horizon when Sam Mogotsi left Klip River Lodge with eight guests in an open-sided safari truck. Luckily, the lodge manager, deVilliers, had covered his short absence, since he believed Mogotsi had been unfairly jailed. But Mogotsi knew that if the charges against him ended up in court, deVilliers wouldn't have the same reaction.

The guests had wrapped their faces in scarves or upturned collars and pulled their hats down low to ward off the morning chill. Here on the high edge of the canyon, at 5,300 feet in elevation, it took time for the heat to make its presence known. But when it did later in the morning, it would be hard to ignore.

Mogotsi briefed the guests in the dining room while they finished their breakfast, explaining how the day would unfold. Because it would be a long day, however, he'd kept his speech short; he would add more detail when they stopped for their first break.

The road from the lodge down to the C40 was bumpy and boulder-strewn, but that made it easier for the lodge to keep track of who arrived or departed. Mogotsi took it slow to ensure the still-sleepy guests wouldn't suffer any concussions or broken bones. He slowed even more when he saw on the hill above them a pair of klip-springers, the small, stocky antelopes that inhabited cliff bands around the lodge. For guests with binoculars, he pointed out the short horns on the male, and in both animals, the noticeable black scent glands in front of the eyes that they used to mark their territories.

Once they reached the smooth gravel of the C40 and turned east, Mogotsi stopped the running commentary; as their speed increased, so did the noise, making it hard to hear. In the rear-view mirror, he saw that most of the guests had nodded off to the motion of the vehicle. Unfortunately, the obnoxious British woman who continually asked complex and obscure questions that she already knew the answers to was still awake. One of his fellow guides had warned him about her and her family after having spent time with them the previous day. Mogotsi owed the man a beer — it was just as common for guides not to warn each other about guests like these. A guide walking obliviously into a challenging situation for which he had no notice was always cause for laughter and ribbing in the next evening's guide meeting. The woman's two daughters, who mirrored their mother's habit of annoying interrogation, were asleep. The husband was smiling in his slumber, perhaps because it was the first time his family had been quiet since Mogotsi had met them the night before. *His life with those three females must be hellish*, Mogotsi thought.

He caught the mother looking at him, opening her mouth to ask a question, and immediately dropped his eyes, then pushed his foot down on the gas pedal. Her question was drowned out by the rush of the wind and the crunch of the tires on gravel. He smiled. It was only a short reprieve, but a reprieve nonetheless. However, he might still pay for it.

Twenty minutes later, Mogotsi turned right onto the D2646, the secondary route that led past his house. The change in motion caused his guests to stir. He tooted the horn as he passed his house, waving at his sons where they stood waiting for the school bus. He heard camera shutters snapping behind him. It was always an internal debate for him: wave at the boys and subject them to being photographed like zoo animals? Or pass by without waving? Most often, his pride overrode his common sense.

A few kilometres later, he saw flashing lights and sensed trouble. This was neither a common time nor place for a roadblock. He rolled to a stop in front of the V formed by two police trucks.

Sergeant Kugara strolled over to his side of the safari truck. "Sam Mogotsi," he said with a smug smile, "what are *you* doing out here at this time of the morning?"

"Good morning, Sergeant. I'm taking a group of lodge guests into the Klip River on a tour."

The obnoxious British woman piped up from her place two rows behind Mogotsi. "Why are you stopping us, officer?"

"Keep your questions to yourself, madam," the sergeant said, glaring at her. "If I want to talk to you, you will know it."

Mogotsi considered using the same line on her later, but knew it would be a career-limiting move.

"But you have no right —"

"Keep your mouth shut, lady, or you'll be coming back with us to the station."

In the mirror, Mogotsi saw the woman sit back with a motion that bounced the entire vehicle. "Well, I never ..."

With so many witnesses in the truck, it was unlikely that anything unpleasant would happen. But Mogotsi decided to be extra polite so that the sergeant would have no reason to do anything but let them continue. "Sergeant, my apologies for my guest. What can I do for you today?"

"I need to see your driver's licence and a copy of your tourism permit."

"Uh, I have my driver's licence here in my pocket." Mogotsi slid his hand slowly around to his back pocket. "But I don't know anything about a tourism permit ..."

"Your lodge is required to have a permit in order to operate a tourism business in this country, and because you are the lodge's representative here, you need to have that permit with you."

"That's news to me. No one has ever told me that before."

The smug smile returned. "I can't comment on what others may or may not have told you. I am telling you now that you need to carry a copy of that permit with you always if you are the company's representative. If you don't have it with you, I'll have to send you back to the lodge."

Mogotsi's anger was growing, but he tried to keep it in check. He handed the man his driver's licence. "Sergeant, could we speak privately?" he said, pointing toward the police vehicles.

After an awkward pause, the sergeant nodded his head, then turned and walked back toward his three other colleagues. Mogotsi followed.

"Come on, Sergeant Kugara," he said, "you know as well as I do that guides aren't required to carry all their employer's permits with them when they're out in the field. If I were really required to do that, I'd have to carry a box of papers around with me wherever I went. I'm a registered tourist guide here in Namibia, and I have the right to work for Klip River Lodge."

"Sam," said the sergeant, shaking his head, "you seem to be confused. Let me clear that up for you. This is not about your permits or your guide certification. This is about you being a suspected murderer and poacher. This is about you walking around free instead of being a guest in our jail. This is about us making sure that you know we're watching every move you make. You seem to have friends in high places, and those friends forced us to release you from custody. But those friends can't help you if you break the law again."

"But I'm not breaking the law now."

"Again, you are confused. You're breaking the law if *I* say you're breaking the law."

"Is this just a cheap way of getting back at me, harassing me?"

The sergeant glared at Mogotsi. "I recommend you don't try my patience this morning. I'm in no mood for it. If you don't have the permit in your possession, then I need you to turn the truck around and go straight back to the lodge."

"But I have guests who've paid for a day with the rhino trackers."

"That is unfortunate, but it's not my problem. Turn around and go, Sam. Your family will be pleased that you chose to co-operate with me." He handed the driver's licence back to Mogotsi without even looking at it.

Mogotsi felt his anger rise. "Why did you mention my family?"

"You need to understand that your actions, lawless or otherwise, affect more people than just yourself."

"Don't you dare mention my family again," said Mogotsi, stepping closer to the sergeant, despite the difference in their size and authority. "Do you understand me?"

The sergeant dropped his arms to his sides, making fists with his massive hands. "Are you threatening me, Sam Mogotsi?"

"I'm suggesting to you that my family play no part in this, Sergeant, and I ask you to keep that in mind."

"And *I* suggest that you turn around, get in your truck, turn *it* around, and go back to the lodge before you are arrested."

Realizing that he was seconds away from another visit to the Kamanjab cells, Mogotsi turned and walked stiffly back to the truck. He took in large breaths to try to calm his temper. "I'll advise the lodge manager of this harassment," he called over his shoulder. "He won't be happy, and I'm sure your supervisor will get a complaint from both him and the conservancy executive."

"A complaint?" the sergeant asked, bursting into laughter that was echoed by his colleagues.

With laughter at his back and his face red with anger and embarrassment, Mogotsi got in the truck, turned it around, and drove away without saying a word to his guests. He would explain and apologize to them when they reached the lodge. Then, after advising his manager of what had transpired, he'd go see Jenny Willson again. He had information to share with her. It was time to come clean.

"They must have known I would be there with a group of guests," said Mogotsi, sitting across from Willson in the Kamanjab office. "It was like they were waiting for me."

"What do you think Kugara wanted?" Willson asked.

"I have no idea. He's trying to send me a message ... or maybe he was trying to get me to react so he could rearrest me. He almost got his wish."

Mogotsi could see that Willson was skeptical. "Maybe they decided to set up the roadblock as part of a regular enforcement check in the area? Could it have been a coincidence?"

Mogotsi shook his head. "Then why did they turn off their flashing lights, get in their vehicles, and follow me back to the C40 as soon as I turned around?"

"Okay, it does seem likely that he was waiting for you. Has this happened to you before, Sam? Have you ever been stopped and asked for ID and a tourism permit?"

"No. The guests were angry, and my manager gave me grief once I got back to the lodge. He must be wondering if this will happen to all the guides, or just to me. If this continues, I'll lose my job."

Mogotsi saw that Willson was staring at him, a curious expression on her face. "What?" he asked.

"I met that sergeant. I don't think he's smart enough to be doing this on his own. Once I tell her, I'm guessing that Inspector Muafangejo will speak with Inspector Nashili here in Kamanjab about why he's doing what he's doing. But …"

"But what?"

"But why did you come here to see me, Sam? What do you think I can do for you?"

In an instant, Mogotsi wondered if he'd made the right decision. If he talked to Willson, he would be crossing a line. Once crossed, he could never return things to the way they were. He couldn't jump back across and assume things would be the same again. But if he said nothing, his family, his job, and his security would all unravel. He knew he had no choice.

"I … I wasn't completely honest with you the last time we met," he said, "when you and Inspector Muafangejo interviewed me."

Willson subtly shifted forward in her seat. "Yes?"

"When you asked if I knew anything about my brother-in-law's murder, I didn't tell you everything."

"Really." It was more of a statement than a question, like she'd been expecting him to come clean at some point. "Did you tell any of this to the local police?"

"No, I told them even less than I told you."

"How about we start at the beginning, Sam?"

"Everything I did tell you was true. I did find Chioto's body. I did not kill him, despite what the local police seem to believe. And I didn't kill that rhino. I don't know how the police got my rifle after they said they couldn't find it. And I don't know who the killer is or how they got my rifle — if it *was* my rifle that was used."

"So, what didn't you tell us?"

Mogotsi stared out the window for a moment. "I didn't tell you what happened to Chioto about a week before he was killed." He hesitated before continuing. "He said it happened in Outjo, in the parking lot outside the new coffee shop. He was getting into his truck when he was approached by two men."

"Did he know them?"

"No. He said he'd never seen them before. Through the truck window, one of them asked if he had anything he wanted to sell. At first, he didn't know what they meant. But then he realized they were asking if he had any rhino horn to sell, or if he knew where they could get some."

Mogotsi saw that Willson was taking notes. "What did these guys look like?" she asked.

"He told me that one guy was maybe Chinese. The other guy, who didn't say anything, looked to Chioto like he was of the San Bushmen, not very tall, with those distinct facial features."

"What did Chioto say?"

"He hates poachers even more than I do, so he told them to get lost."

"Was that the end of it?"

"No. Chioto said the Chinese guy got more aggressive then. He said he knew Chioto worked for the lodge and that he would pay Chioto more than twice his annual salary, in cash, to get even one big rhino horn for him. He said he didn't care where Chioto got it … or how."

"And then?"

"Chioto said he asked how the guy knew where he worked. The guy told him he had 'connections.'"

"That's the word he used, *connections*? What did he mean by that?"

"Chioto had no idea at that point, but told them again to get lost, or he'd report them to the police. When he said that, the man laughed."

"He laughed?"

"Yes, which made Chioto even angrier. So, he drove out of the parking lot and waited a block away. He said he watched them for at least an hour through his binoculars. They came in and out of the coffee shop, approaching others the same way they had approached him. When they finally got in their truck, with the Chinese guy driving, Chioto followed them and got their licence plate number."

"Did they see him?"

"He said they did. I think it was when he was behind them at a stop sign. Chioto saw the passenger turn around and point at him, cocking his hand like a gun."

"Why didn't he tell the police, either in Outjo or here? Why didn't you?"

"For the same reason," Mogotsi said. "Because neither of us trusts the police. Never have. Chioto was really suspicious when the Chinese guy laughed about Chioto going to the police."

"Maybe the guy just didn't believe him."

"And maybe he didn't care. You've got to wonder why."

"Huh. Do you have the licence plate number?"

Mogotsi slid a crumpled piece of paper across the table. He'd kept it in a safe place at his house after Chioto had written it down for him. Willson glanced at it, then placed it on top of her notebook, smoothing the paper with her fingertips. She looked up, and suddenly Mogotsi felt the power of her stare.

"Why do you trust me ... us ... with this now?" Willson asked. She was probably wondering why he would trust her, a white foreigner.

"Because you seem to care about the truth. Because I'm sure that the inspector is trying to pin Chioto's murder on me. And because Chioto was killed only a week after threatening to turn in the Chinese man and his friend."

"You think there's a connection."

"Don't you?"

Willson's mouth was a thin line. Her forehead was furrowed. She didn't answer his question.

CHAPTER 23

AUGUST 26

Willson stood wringing her hands outside the tiny Kamanjab health centre as the red-and-white ambulance raced away, its lights flashing, but its siren silent. The setting sun was a slice of bright orange on the horizon behind her. A wall of black clouds boiled above, hinting at an impending storm.

Monica Hauwanga and Gaby Bohitile followed behind the speeding ambulance in their own vehicle. It would take up to ninety minutes for them to get to the hospital in Outjo, and Willson was still trying to decide whether to follow. Indecision was an abnormal state for her, but she was still in shock from hearing her colleague's desperate radio transmission. She'd responded to many urgent calls in her career, but none so personal or unexpected.

She turned to see Danny Trang striding across the gravel parking lot.

"What the hell happened?" he said. "I was in the garage getting a tire fixed and heard that a police officer had been hurt. I was worried it might be you."

"No, Danny. I'm okay, thanks. It was Veronica. Inspector Muafangejo. They just took her away in the ambulance. They're taking her to hospital in Outjo because the centre here wasn't equipped to deal with it. She might end up in Windhoek, depending on what the emergency doctors in Outjo decide."

"Is she okay? What happened to her?"

Willson turned to walk back toward the office two blocks away. She felt Trang fall in step behind her. "She was visiting the Khaimaseni Women's Craft Centre" — she pointed across the street — "to interview an old woman there who claimed to know something about poachers working in this area." Willson felt as if she were in a trance. She tripped on a low curb, and Trang grabbed her arm to steady her, but she shook him off.

"Jenny," he said again, this time more quietly, "what happened?"

"I only spoke to her for a second because she was in so much pain. She said she went out to her truck after the interview. She opened the door to get in, saw a snake coiled on the front seat, then felt a searing pain in her eyes."

"What? What was it?"

Willson stopped walking to look at Trang. "We think it was a spitting cobra. When she fell back, the snake slithered out of the vehicle and disappeared. So, we don't know for sure."

"A spitting cobra? What the hell —?"

"There are a few species in Africa, but only one is native to this area. I was warned about them when I arrived. Locals call them zebra cobras because of their stripes. They can shoot venom up to two and a half metres with incredible accuracy. And they always aim for the face."

"Is she going to be okay?"

"I don't know. The venom is a neurotoxin. If it's completely washed out of the eyes quickly enough, it only causes temporary blindness and no lasting damage. If not, it can lead to permanent blindness. Veronica was able to get off a quick radio call to me before her vision went. I ran over here and found her writhing on the ground, clawing at her eyes. I poured two bottles of water over her eyes as quickly as I could."

"Shit. What the hell was the snake doing in her truck?"

"That is an excellent question. I'm pretty sure it didn't crawl in there on its own."

"You think someone put it there? On purpose?"

"There's no other obvious explanation."

"Who would do that?"

"Someone has already shown us that they don't want us here — you heard about our apartment. Now this."

"I get the sense this isn't going to make you back off your investigation."

Willson flashed a grim smile. "You're a perceptive guy. In my experience, this sort of thing means we're getting closer, and it's time for me to put my foot on the gas. And this attack on Veronica has really pissed me off. Someone's going to be very sorry they decided to take us on."

"Are you going to go to Outjo?"

Willson stared down the C40 in the direction the ambulance had disappeared. Her hands were shaking. "No. I don't think so. Two of our team are with her, and they'll call me once they know anything. I won't help the situation any by being there."

"What are you going to do?"

"I think … I think I'm going to buy you a beer. Like I wanted to do the last time you were here. I need to calm down, start thinking about next steps." She began walking again.

"Is my life at risk if I hang out with you, Jenny?"

"No guarantees."

Suddenly, rain began to fall. At the first crack of thunder, they raced up the street toward the Oppi-Koppi bar.

Willson sat looking out at the rain falling on the swimming pool beside the patio. They were sitting outside, but were protected from the rain by the thatched roof. She couldn't stop thinking about the sounds Veronica had made when she was rolling on the ground beside her truck. When the server dropped off two large bottles of beer at the table, Willson turned to Trang, who was clearly waiting for her to speak.

"Cheers, Danny. This was certainly a day I'd never want to repeat."

They toasted. "Here's to that," Danny added.

"When we passed by here on the Wild Dog trip," she said, "I never would have guessed that you and I would be sitting here three months later, having a drink together. A hell of a lot has happened since then."

"I never thought we'd meet up again, either. You're really not keen on email, are you?"

Willson looked at him without expression. She never apologized for detesting electronic communication. Early in her career, as smartphones were becoming more common, she'd decided that email, Facebook, and Twitter were not worth wasting time on — unless it was necessary for her job. "Always best to talk in person, I say."

"And here we are ... talking. Just you and me." He paused. "Hey, as we were running up here, I noticed the Impala Meat Market. I know everyone eats game meat here, loves their braais, but does that place really only sell impala meat?"

Willson chuckled. "No, you can get almost any kind of meat there — domestic or wild."

"And just up the hill, is that blackened shell behind the barbed-wire fences your old apartment?"

"Yep. Not much left, eh?"

"Someone really did a number on it. I'm glad you weren't hurt."

"Thanks. Me, too. We're pretty sure it's tied to our investigation. I've just got to figure out how the pieces fit together. They're —" she paused midsentence as Trang put his hand up.

"Stop," he said.

"What?"

"Jenny, I'm a good listener. And I'd gladly listen to you all day. But I don't think I want to hear about your investigation."

"You don't?"

"No. I want you to trust me. And the best way I can think of to start that process is for me to prove that I have no interest in your case as a journalist. None."

"Huh."

"In good faith, I shared what I learned in Walvis Bay with you because I believe in what you're doing. I'd love to see you catch the bad guys, whoever they are. There's no hidden agenda."

Willson remembered Muafangejo's claim that Trang's interest in her was personal. She smiled at him. He was studying her, the calm expression on his face punctuated by eyes that seemed secure ... and kind.

Willson swallowed hard. "So, tell me more about Kimberley."

"Kimberley?" he asked. "Why?"

"A conservation officer job is opening in the East Kootenay, based out of Cranbrook. I'm giving it some serious thought, so I'd love to hear about what it's like in that part of the world."

Trang smiled and shook his head, as though he knew she was changing the subject because she'd felt flustered. He took a sip of his beer and sat back. "Well, I think that Kimberley, and the East Kootenay region generally, is one of the best places in all of B.C. And I've seen most of it. You've got the Purcells on the western side of the Rocky Mountain Trench and the Rockies on the other. I've heard that Cranbrook, which is about twenty minutes away, gets the most hours of sunshine in all of British Columbia. That makes a huge difference in people's dispositions. No matter the season, it always seems sunny. And people seem to smile more there than in other places I've been."

"Sounds good so far ..."

"It is. You've got world-class skiing, fly-fishing, mountain biking, hiking, river rafting ... the list goes on. And the new Rails-to-Trails cycle route to Cranbrook is great. There's an airport that's serviced by three different airlines now, so you can get anywhere in the world with relative ease ... though not as cheaply as I'd like."

"What about house prices?"

"Compared to Calgary or Vancouver or Toronto, they're excellent. A person could cash out of the Vancouver or Toronto market, buy a beautiful house on an acreage, and still have money left in their pocket."

"No downsides?"

"Other than the fact it's a long drive to somewhere like Vancouver, not really. Maybe that people in the Lower Mainland sometimes forget that we're part of B.C. The one-hour time difference doesn't help. My parents are down there, and I don't see them that much — usually only when I'm on my way through for assignments. And they rarely come up to see me; they seem to think the highway only goes in one direction. But to be honest, I don't see myself moving away now that I'm settled there. It's a special place. I love it."

"Good to know."

Willson glanced down at her watch some time later and was surprised to see that they'd been sitting there for over an hour. The time had passed quickly. She checked her phone. No word on Muafangejo's condition yet. They were probably just arriving at the hospital now.

"Do you want to order dinner?" she suggested to Trang. After a quick look at the menu, Willson waved the server over. They ordered the biggest hamburgers available, along with two more large beers. It was raining harder now, and Willson watched large drops fall from the edge of the thatched roof.

"Look," she said, bringing her gaze back to Trang, "I … I need to apologize."

"For what?"

"For acting like an asshole, and for treating you worse than you deserved to be treated."

"You *were* kinda harsh. I'm not sure what I did."

"You did nothing. It's not you, it's me." She laughed. "How's that for a cliché?"

Their beers arrived, and she waited until the server had gone back inside to speak. Willson and Trang were the only ones sitting outside, and Willson liked it that way.

"As you can probably tell," she said, "I'm not a touchy-feely kind of person. So, I don't like talking about this kind of stuff." Trang nodded, and Willson continued, "I've always had trouble trusting people. I guess that comes with the job, because so many people have lied to me over the years." She began ripping a corner of the label off her bottle, using the distraction to decide whether or not to say any more. "Ever since my dad died, I've become more alert to loyalty, or a lack of it. I expect others to be as loyal to me as I am to them. But then they don't always meet my expectations. I don't know … maybe it's a character flaw."

"Not at all."

"That's why I was so pissed off when that American journalist I told you about, Mike, betrayed me. I trusted him and he took advantage of that. In hindsight, trusting him was an incredibly stupid decision. I'll also admit, he took a small chunk of my heart with him when he left town, and he almost destroyed my career."

"He hurt you."

"I've rarely admitted it to anyone, but yes, he did. And then, when my mother took her own life shortly afterward, I was devastated. I went through the early stages of grieving … I'm not big on all that psychological mumbo-jumbo, but I kept coming back to the fact that she left me … without explaining why, before I could say goodbye, she left me all alone. I've been everything from numb to guilty, thinking that I could have done something to stop it, to pissed off with her for being so selfish. Now, I don't know what I am."

"Geez, Jenny, I'm so sorry to hear about your mother. They say that a suicide leaves many victims."

"It does. Beyond that, though, it was all those things together — my mother, Mike, how I was treated by my own agency. It was like my whole idea of loyalty was being put to the biggest test of my life."

"And then I came along …"

"Not quite," said Willson, finally tearing the last of the label off the bottle. She crumpled it into a ball. "I got away from all that crap by taking this assignment. But soon after I got here, the friend I came with, Tracy, chose to go to the northeast to work with elephants. So, even here, I felt like I'd been abandoned."

"Was that the Tracy who was on our safari?"

"The same. And I'm not proud of how I reacted to her decision. The more time that goes by, the more I realize I was being selfish and stupid. I haven't seen her since then, and we've only exchanged a few brief emails."

Trang looked up and smiled. "I know the feeling … But I've been on the road for most of the last month, so maybe I missed an email or two from you along the way."

"You didn't, and I really am sorry about that. I hope you can understand how I was feeling, even if I don't understand it myself."

"So, you were dealing with all of that, *then* I came along — this unknown, *extremely* handsome, yet friendly journalist who appeared to be inserting himself into your investigation."

Willson laughed. "Yes, and then you came along …"

"Sorry, eh."

Willson laughed again. "I've missed having other Canadians around." She looked at Trang but didn't know what to say next. Luckily, at that moment, their server slid plates of tall burgers and skinny fries in front of them. Ravenous, Willson was just reaching for a fry when her phone buzzed. She jammed the fry into her mouth and grabbed her phone. It was a text from Gaby.

> Veronica OK. In less pain. Doctor hopeful her blindness temporary but will take time to confirm. They want her to see Windhoek eye specialist ASAP. No ambulance available so we're taking her now. Keep you posted.

Willson turned the phone around so Trang could see the message.

"That's good, right? By washing out her eyes, you may have saved her sight."

Willson nodded. "If what they're saying is true, that *is* good." She looked back at the pool again. The rain had stopped, and she saw stars in a slice of the now-dark sky visible between the roof and distant cabins. The storm had rolled past. But a storm of a different kind, in which the lives of people and rhinos were at risk, was still gathering around her.

"Veronica would have done the same for me," she added wistfully, before biting into her burger.

"I only met her the one time, but from what you've said, I bet she would. And I bet she's thankful as hell that you arrived when you did."

Between mouthfuls, Willson dabbed at the ketchup, mayonnaise, and burger juices at the corners of her mouth and dripping down her chin. It was a very good burger. "We're getting closer, I know we are. I've just got to figure out how to keep going with Veronica out of the picture for who knows how long."

"We agreed not to talk about this, didn't we?" said Trang with a smile.

"Right."

Trang tipped his beer back, draining it, then wiped his mouth and held up two fingers to their server, ordering another round. "Do you think you make a difference with what you do, Jenny?"

"Wow, that's a deep question. Is that the beer talking?"

Trang sighed and laughed at the same time. "No, I've actually been thinking about that for the last year or so."

"You've been thinking, for a year, about whether *I* make a difference? We haven't known each other that long —"

"No, no," said Trang, "I meant —" He stopped when he saw Willson's smile.

"Do you mean here in Namibia, or more broadly?"

"I guess both," he said. "You work hard to protect parks back in Canada, and now, to protect rhinos here. That's got to be a satisfying way to make a living."

"It can be. Like when I put someone away for damaging a park, or even better, when I stop them before they do it. Then, I feel like I make a difference. But other days, when I see things happening that I have no control over — animals killed on highways, highways that have been constructed through our best wildlife habitats, parks that are loved to death by waves of visitors — or when I see the political and legal systems failing what we're trying to protect, then I do stop and wonder if what I'm doing has value." She accepted her beer from the server with a nod of thanks. "What about you?"

"I guess I'm not much different," he said. They banged the necks of their bottles together. "There's more and more over-tourism happening in places around the world, more negative impacts on the environment and on the social fabric of communities. I often question whether the pieces I write are making it better or worse … whether I'm part of the problem or part of the solution."

Willson caught herself musing that this man was increasingly fascinating, perhaps even a tad sexy. He was asking the right questions — questions that made him seem vulnerable and sincere — yet at the same time, his questions went directly to the heart of who *she* was, what she did, and why. Tough questions looking for answers in a faulty world. And he seemed genuinely interested in what she had to say. "Have you been able to answer your own question?" she asked. "Are you the problem ... or the solution?" Deep down, she recognized that his question was also her question. Was he her problem, or her solution?

"Not consistently," Trang said, shaking his head. "Some days are clearer than others. More and more, I seek out businesses and destinations that are trying to do things right, sharing special places with visitors in ways that put the environment and local cultures on an equal footing with profit. That's what the best adventure travel is all about."

"Are you finding these places?"

"I am. I think we're in one of them right now. In some ways, I believe Namibians are braver than we are in Canada."

"How so?"

"They turned the system on its head, and they're showing the courage to do things we wouldn't dream of doing, like putting economic interests where they belong, finding ways to move past the economy-versus-environment bullshit, building an economy through tourism, based on protecting and sharing natural values."

Who is this man?

"From what I've seen so far, I agree," she said. "And what's ironic, and more than a little hypocritical, is that countries from around the globe are demanding that Namibia protect its rhinos and elephants and lions, and yet, most of them aren't making much progress in protecting their own endangered wildlife."

"That's where the courage comes in," Trang said.

Willson raised her bottle. "Here's to courage."

CHAPTER 24

AUGUST 28

Willson could hear Tracy Brown's voice, but it was distant and tinny and fragmented through the cellphone speaker. "You broke up there, Jenny," Brown said. "*What do you need?*"

"We've lost the leader of our unit for a few weeks, if not longer. She was hurt in an attack … an attack that I believe is related to our work. I'm going to take over the team temporarily, but I need someone to fill my spot. I wondered if you'd be willing to come down and work with us. With me."

Willson didn't hear an immediate response, so thought she might have lost the signal. "Did you —"

Brown's voice suddenly came through loud and clear. "*I'm surprised by the call, Jenny. I kinda thought you'd written me off.*"

Willson paced back and forth across the concrete floor of the unit office. "Look, I'm sorry for being such a jerk. After losing my mother, and all the other stuff, I felt bad that you wanted to head north rather than stay and work with me. But that was selfish of me."

Another pause, this time longer. "I guess we both have things to apologize for. I've been thinking about you lately, and I realize I should've been more sensitive to what you were going through, and how my decision could impact you. My interest in working with elephants wasn't something you and I had discussed properly. And the way I brought it up at dinner that night wasn't cool. I blindsided you, and you had the right to be angry. We did come over here to work together, and I'd like the chance to do that."

Willson stopped pacing. She hadn't expected this, although she'd hoped for it. The heart-to-heart with Danny Trang had done her good. "What's going on there, Tracy? Can you really get away?"

"I've been spending most of my time in and around Bwabwata National Park. The Namibians I'm work-ing with are making some truly impressive progress in protecting elephants, and they really do care. But you remember how this part of Namibia is a narrow pan-handle connected to a much larger ecosystem to the east, including the Okavango Delta? As a result, there are three neighbouring countries involved aside from Namibia: Botswana, Zambia, and Angola. They don't need me for my enforcement background as much as for skills in negotiation and dispute resolution. And that ain't me. It's not that the countries aren't getting along, it's that we seem to spend more time trying to reach a consensus than we do saving elephants. Time is a limited commodity here. I'm certainly learning about the challenges of cross-border conservation, but even from what little you've told me in your emails, I think I could do more good working with you over there."

Willson grimaced. "Yeah, sorry about those emails. I was recently told by someone else that my emails suck."

Brown chuckled. "Let's just say they were … succinct."

"So," Willson said, laughing, "how soon can you get away?"

"Let me talk to the folks here. I'll let you know by tomorrow."

"Deal."

"I really appreciate your call, Jenny. It'll be good to work together again."

At that moment, the signal died, prematurely ending the call. But Willson had heard all she needed to hear. She smiled, realizing that she owed a big thanks to Danny Trang. As the evening at the Oppi-Koppi had worn on, he'd encouraged her, in a roundabout way, to call Tracy to fill the vacant spot. He hadn't come right out and suggested it, but he'd somehow helped her come to that conclusion on her own.

The office door banged open behind her. She jumped and whirled around, her hand automatically going to her weapon.

"Whoa, Jenny," said Ben Mushimba. Neus scrambled across the floor to greet her. "Sorry, I thought you would've heard Neus barking out there. When he sees a jackal, he goes nuts."

"It's fine," said Willson, momentarily shaken. "I was deep in thought and you startled me. I have to keep my head up and my ears open." The attack on Muafangejo had impacted her more than she'd realized. "How did it go out there?"

"Good. Betty and I dug up those two rhino horns like you asked, the ones the Himba women told you about. Here they are. We made it look obvious that someone had taken them by leaving the hole open, though I still don't know why." He placed a black canvas duffle bag on the floor and unzipped it to reveal the two dirty rhino horns.

Betty Tjikuzu came through the door carrying her electronic gear as Willson moved toward the open bag.

"But before I ask you to explain why you had us dig them up," Mushimba said, "how's Veronica doing, boss?" It was his subtle signal that he'd accepted Willson as the new leader of the unit.

"Her vision was a bit hazier today, so they're keeping her in hospital for a few more days."

"Is the prognosis still good?"

"It is, but she could be away from the job for weeks or months yet. We just don't know."

"What about Monica and Gaby?" asked Tjikuzu. "Are they on their way back?"

"They should be back by tomorrow."

Willson picked up one of the horns. It was heavier than she expected, and just under a metre in length. She brushed dirt off the surface. It was surprisingly smooth. The tip was very sharp, while the base showed the marks of whatever tool had been used to remove it. The second horn was much smaller than the first, and Willson assumed it had come from the same animal.

"So, why dig these up and bring them here?" Mushimba asked again.

Willson motioned to the main table. "Let's sit. I'm thinking that it's time to get more proactive."

"What do you mean?" Tjikuzu asked.

"First, I'm excited to tell you I've found someone to replace Veronica on the team, at least until she comes back."

"Who'd you find on such short notice?"

"I came to Namibia with a friend, Tracy Brown. She's a very experienced investigator from the U.S. Fish and Wildlife Service who's been working on elephant poaching in the Caprivi. She's willing to come down and work with us."

Willson saw the two Namibians share a quick glance.

"Look," said Willson, "I know this is not ideal. It would be better to have another Namibian officer join the team. I get that. But I don't feel we have enough time to find someone we can trust, pry them loose from whatever they're doing now, and then get them up to speed quickly enough. Brown is very good, and she's ready. I guarantee you that this is only temporary, just until Veronica comes back."

Mushimba stared at Willson for an uncomfortably long time. "Okay," he said finally. "If you think she's good, then let's get on with it."

Willson looked at Tjikuzu. "Betty?"

"Even though I met her at Waterberg, I'll reserve judgment until I actually work with her."

"Fair enough."

"But don't let my hesitation stand in the way, Jenny," Tjikuzu said. "Let's get these bastards. What are you thinking?"

"I'm thinking it's time we take the fight to the dog. We know there are people at this end of the supply chain doing the actual poaching, but we don't know who they are. We know that three unidentified people in this area, maybe more, are doing the buying. By buying and offering considerable sums of money, they're overtly encouraging the murder of rhinos. We did get a licence plate number from one of our informants, but it led nowhere. And then we have other people, apparently Asian, but also unidentified, allegedly shipping horn by rail to the coast."

"What we don't have is any way to identify any of them, or to link them together," said Mushimba.

"Exactly," said Willson, nodding her head, "and that's where we need to be more proactive. I think the time for a well-planned sting is now. If we do it right, we can identify those responsible *and* link them all together."

"And put them in jail for a long time," Tjikuzu said, smiling.

"That's the goal. I'm tired of dancing on the outside of this. We dug up that first horn and put surveillance on the site, but as far as we know, the guy never came back for it. And from the DNA analysis, we know it wasn't from the Klip River Valley. That was a bust, and in hindsight, a waste of time and resources. I want to put the pieces together before we lose even one more rhino."

"What's the plan?"

"The plan is we use Sam Mogotsi."

"Sam? We just got him out of jail. He may still be facing murder charges," said Tjikuzu.

"Why would he even agree to this, Jenny?" asked Mushimba.

"Two reasons," said Willson. "The first is that he has a history of poaching, and is now working as a ranger in an area with rhinos. He has a background and a job that would make him a believable poacher."

"Okay," said Tjikuzu, "but people know he was arrested and released. Won't that make them suspicious of him?"

"Perhaps, but he tells me that very few people know what happened — only a few members of his family, and his boss. The local police kept it very quiet … probably because they were embarrassed about having to release him."

"So, that part's believable, then. What's your second reason?"

"It's about the local police. Sam continues to claim his innocence. He truly believes that Nashili and his sergeant not only have it out for him and are trying to pin Shipanga's murder on him, but also that they could be directly involved in the murder, and maybe the poaching, too."

"That's a heck of an accusation," Mushimba said. "Why does he think that?"

"He says it's the only thing that explains all the strange events. The fact that he was aggressively questioned after the murder even though he found the body and had no motive to do it. The missing rifle that suddenly was no longer missing. His arrest that didn't lead to an appearance in front of a magistrate. The pressure on him while he was in custody to admit his guilt. And the police harassment of him ever since."

Willson could see that Mushimba wasn't convinced. "Couldn't they just be overzealous investigators?" he asked. "Why do you think the police might be involved in the poaching, too?"

"Good question," Willson said. "Other than noting the inspector's claim at our first meeting that everything here is under control, when it clearly isn't, I can't say for certain. But Sam believes they are. He thinks they're as interested in the rhino horn as they are the murder."

Tjikuzu nodded. "He thinks it's all a cover-up, with him as the scapegoat."

"Scapegoat?" asked Mushimba, his head tilted like Neus's when he was confused.

"The fall guy," Willson said, smiling. "Or, as they used to say in old gangster movies, the patsy."

"Scapegoat? Patsy? ... Are you two speaking English?"

Both women laughed.

"He thinks they're trying to send him to jail for something he didn't do," explained Willson, "to draw the blame away from those who did."

"Ah, why didn't you say that? How will involving him in the sting clarify that?" he asked.

"I've got an idea for how we can kill two or more birds with one stone. If we do this right, we can find out who our poachers are, who the buyers are, who the shippers are, and how they're all connected."

"And the local police's involvement?"

"I think there's a way to force them out into the light, too."

Mushimba and Tjikuzu both sat up noticeably straighter. "Tell us more," Tjikuzu said, her eyes bright with anticipation.

"We've now got three rhino horns, right?"

Tjikuzu nodded.

"The guy who buried that first one may or may not know that it's gone," Willson said. "If he has figured it out, he's going to be angry."

"And these ones?" Mushimba said, pointing to the bag.

"It's very likely that the person who buried them doesn't know that they're gone yet. What if we get the word out that someone 'found' them and now is looking to sell?"

"And that someone is Sam?"

"Exactly. If he starts showing up in places like Outjo or Opuwo, suggesting he might have three horns to sell — horns that he *found* — it's likely that word will reach not only potential buyers, but also the guys who are missing their horns."

"That puts Sam in a fair bit of danger, though, doesn't it?"

"Yes, if he does it alone. But if someone like Tracy Brown is always with him or near him, then it's a different situation. He couldn't have better backup."

"So," Mushimba said, beginning to understand Willson's thinking, "if this works, Sam could have two groups of people looking for him: one that sees him as a threat, the other as an opportunity. And we'd be there to see who they are. Those are two key links in your chain."

"Right, Ben. And of course, if we ensure that our horns have GPS transmitters implanted in them before we start, then we can track them all the way to their final destination in Namibia — perhaps at Walvis Bay. And, through GPS tracking, we'll know all the people who touch them along the way."

"Do you really think Sam will do this?" asked Mushimba.

"I can't say for sure, but he seems awfully eager to make all this go away and get his life back again."

"His biggest problem right now is the local police. You mentioned somehow smoking them out," Tjikuzu said. "What's the plan? Sam will need to see a benefit to agreeing to this level of risk."

"I'm still thinking that through," Willson said pensively. She rose and walked across the office to pour a coffee from the machine in the corner. "I've got ideas on how to make it work. We need to move quickly, though, because the guy who buried those two horns could show up at any time and discover they're gone. I don't want him to think that his only option is to shoot another rhino. I want him to be pissed off enough to seek out the guy who ripped him off and is allegedly boasting about it." She leaned against the counter, coffee cup in hand.

Mushimba slowly tapped his fingers together — once, twice, three times. "This plan certainly has a lot of risk attached to it," he said, "not only for Sam and your friend Tracy, but for our work here, and our reputations."

"It does," said Willson. "But as they say, no risk, no reward."

CHAPTER 25

SEPTEMBER 4

Sam Mogotsi sat in the staff lounge at Klip River Lodge, his feet on the table, an ice-cold soda in his hand. It had been a long day in the field for him following a male rhino in the upper part of the canyon, and one of the few in recent times that the local police hadn't shown up somewhere along his route to hassle him. He'd seen a police truck near the spot where the rough access road turned off the D2646, but the officer inside had only glared at him as he drove by. Perhaps he'd been given a pass because there hadn't been any guests in the vehicle with him, no way to embarrass him … or maybe they were leaving him alone for a while. He doubted that.

The door to the kitchen swung open. "Sam," said a young woman from the hospitality team, "there's someone here asking for you?"

"Who is it?" asked Mogotsi.

"She wouldn't say, but she said you'd want to see her?"

Mogotsi pulled his feet off the table with a bang. "Okay, be right out." He finished his drink in one deep swallow, dropped the can in the recycling bin, and pushed open the door to the reception area. "Jenny," he said, surprised to see the Canadian officer. "What brings you out here?"

"We need to talk, Sam," Willson said quietly. "Let's go for a drive before anyone else sees us together."

"Uh, okay." *This is strange*, he thought. "Let's take my truck. I just gassed it up."

"Is Danny Trang still here?" asked Willson as they headed for the front door.

"No," said Mogotsi, holding the door open for her. "I saw him early this morning. He said he was moving on again, to Hobatere Lodge, west of Etosha, to spend time with the AfriCat researchers there. Something about lions and their tourism concession. Why?"

"Just wondering."

They bounced across the rocky plateau and stopped at a west-facing viewpoint.

Mogotsi, filled with an unexpected sense of foreboding, put the truck in park and turned off the engine. His mouth was dry despite having just downed the cold soda. "What did you want to talk to me about?" He twisted in his seat to face her.

"I've been thinking about our last conversation, when you told me what happened to Chioto before he was killed."

"And?"

"You think that you're being framed for Chioto's murder, and you insist that you had nothing to do with that poached rhino, and that the local police are involved."

"That's right," he said, the dread growing. "I thought you believed me."

"I think you're being honest about what you believe, Sam. But all the same, the evidence just doesn't add up. On balance, it still points to your guilt rather than your innocence."

Mogotsi gripped the steering wheel, his knuckles white. "I … I … what do I need to do to make you believe me?" This was not what he had expected to hear. What had changed since he'd gone to Kamanjab to see her? He'd told her about Chioto's experience in Outjo and given her a licence plate number for the horn buyers. He had left the office feeling that she *did* believe him. But if she hadn't … for a moment, he wondered if Willson was here to arrest him. But wouldn't she already have put the handcuffs on him if she were? He was frightened by the look he saw in her eyes. They were piercing, no-nonsense eyes, like two high-intensity spotlights shining on him, probing for answers.

She shook her head slowly. "Unfortunately, there are many questions yet to be answered. It troubles me that Chioto's murder seems linked to our poaching investigations. It's like you're the eye of the storm, Sam. And yet, you claim to be innocent."

"I *am* innocent. I don't know what else I can tell you."

"The magistrate who gave us the authority to release you from jail continues to ask me if we're still investigating and if we're confident that you will come to court when called."

"What do you tell her?"

"That we're in constant contact with you and your lawyer."

"And she's comfortable with that?"

Willson nodded once. "Did you hear about Inspector Muafangejo?"

"No," Mogotsi said, caught off guard by the sudden change of subject. "Why, what happened to her?"

"Someone planted a spitting cobra in her truck. It got her with its venom. She could be out of commission for weeks, or months."

"Oh my god. That's horrible. Was she blinded?"

"She'll probably be okay eventually, but it's too early to tell for sure. But it's clear to me that someone around here wants us to stop looking under rocks. You don't know anything about that, do you?" Her eyes blazed even brighter.

"No!" Mogotsi said emphatically, holding his hands up to make the point. "I have no idea who would do something like that. I really don't know what to say."

"You're probably right that there may not be anything you could *say* to prove your innocence. What we need is evidence to back up your story, or at least some means to rule out other possibilities."

"What can I do? I'm willing to do anything!" His voice cracked with fear and apprehension. When he'd chosen to lay his cards on the table to Willson, he felt he was crossing a point of no return. But that had been nothing compared to how he was feeling now.

Willson stared out the truck window like she was thinking. Cirrus clouds lit by the setting sun filled the sky above the canyon in undulating waves of red and orange. They looked like they were ablaze. "We need your assistance, Sam," she said finally, turning back to him. "If you're willing to help us, then it might help Veronica and me to feel more … confident that you are innocent. If things work out like I hope they will, then we'll all know the truth."

"Didn't you say Inspector Muafangejo is out of commission for a while?"

"Don't you remember from that meeting at the Kamanjab station, Sam, there are six of us? You may not have met everyone that day, but we're a group of police, army, and MET investigators working as a special unit. I've taken charge while Veronica is away."

"So … tell me what you want me to do."

"We're taking our investigation to another level, and you're going to play a key role."

"How?"

"Before I say any more, you must give me your word that you will not share what I am about to tell you with anyone — not your wife, not your friends, not your fellow rangers. Not even your boss. It can't leave this truck."

"I swear, I won't tell anyone." He unconsciously put up one hand as though swearing an oath in a courtroom — a place he hoped never to see the inside of. "What do you want me to do?"

"You're going to work with a friend and colleague of mine. Her name is Tracy Brown."

"Who is that?"

"She's a U.S. Fish and Wildlife investigator who, like me, is here in Namibia on a secondment."

"What are we going to do?"

"You'll go into Outjo the day after tomorrow, and maybe a few other towns in the Kunene region over the next day or two, and you will quietly spread the word that you have rhino horns for sale. Three big ones."

"What? But I don't have any rhino horns."

"We want people to think you do."

"What people?"

"People who might be interested in buying them from you ... and the people you stole them from."

"This is crazy. I didn't steal any rhino horns!" Mogotsi's brain was racing. He was having serious second thoughts about agreeing to Willson's request.

Willson smiled. "Oh, but you did. You stole one horn from one place, and two from another. They were buried, and you dug them up. You've been busy, Sam. And now you're trying to make some money off them."

"Why would I do that? It's dangerous."

"First, you *will* have access to horns. We've got them in our possession now — these are what you'll be trying to sell. So that part will be true."

"So, I *will* actually have horns to sell ..." Mogotsi paused, trying to connect all the dots. "You're trying to flush out the buyers. Are they the same men Chioto spoke to before he died?"

"We won't know for sure until you talk to them." Willson paused, her gaze hard again. "Those men don't know *you*, do they?"

Mogotsi paused. "No. I cannot think how they would. I have no idea who they are besides the description I gave you from Chioto."

"Good," said Willson. "Just checking. This would not work if they knew you. In fact, it could make things even more dangerous for you."

"Speaking of dangerous," Mogotsi said, his voice shaky, "the men who will think I stole from them — they will be furious with me, thinking I've potentially cost them a lot of money. They'll want their horns back, or they'll make me pay some serious price ... in money or otherwise."

"And that's where Tracy comes in. She'll be with you, or at least nearby, every step of the way."

"Great. How's having an American woman with me going to help?"

"She's a complete unknown around here, she's darker than you are, and she'll be armed. Why does everyone here assume that North Americans are all white? Anyway, depending on the situation, Tracy might accompany you when you interact with some of the people we're talking about, as if she's your partner in crime. That's not my preference, however, because if you run into people in Outjo who know you and your wife, then word might get back to her, and your story would unravel in a hurry. It'll be better for Tracy to stay somewhere close by. You might not see her, but she'll be there. And the rest of us will be watching from a distance, but close enough that we can get there in a hurry if something goes wrong."

"Something going wrong is exactly what I'm worried about," Mogotsi said, now wringing his hands.

"These could be very dangerous people. Look what happened to Chioto."

"Do you know of anyone who might be in the back pocket of Nashili and his men, Sam, someone who might be acting as an informant for them?"

Mogotsi reacted without thinking. "I'm not an informant. Why would they trust me?"

"No, I don't mean you," Willson said, shaking her head. "Is there someone you could talk to, who might in turn repeat what you've said to them?"

Mogotsi was getting more and more confused by the woman's questions. "But I thought you just told me not to tell anyone about what you're planning to do?"

Willson laughed. "I did say that," she said. "What I'm thinking is, if we let slip to the local police that you're selling rhino horns, it'll be very interesting to see how they react."

"Oh. Uh … I've got a cousin who was caught trying to sell dope. He was never charged, yet every so often, I see him talking to Nashili. I know he hates the police, so there must be some special reason he's willing to spend any time with them at all."

"Are you two friendly?"

"We're not friends, but I see him at the occasional family event."

Willson nodded. "What if you found a way to let him know that you might have something to sell — something illegal — if he's interested. Do you think he'd tell Nashili?"

"If the inspector does have something over him, then I have no doubt he'll tell him."

"Okay. Tomorrow, then, I want you to find a way to tell your cousin what you're doing … confide in him, but ask him not to tell the police."

"If you say so."

"I do, and I want you to tell me when you've done it."

"Okay, so you want me to piss off some buyers and sellers *and* the police. At this rate, I'm going to have everyone chasing me."

"I've thought this through, Sam, and I firmly believe that this is the best way for us to find out who these people are so we can put them in jail for a very long time. We'll keep you safe."

Mogotsi pondered the implications of what he was being asked to do. "Is there anything else I could do to get you to believe me? Something less dangerous?"

"No, I'm afraid not. We're committed to this course of action, and I appreciate your agreeing to assist us."

"I don't really have any choice, do I?"

"Not if you want your life back," Willson said, smiling in a way that reminded Mogotsi of a crocodile.

"How do I explain this to my family and my boss?"

"In the short term, you'll need to come up with something to tell your wife that she'll believe and won't question. Start thinking about that now. As for your boss, because all this will be going on during your off-hours, I don't think you need to tell him anything."

"Then I guess we start tomorrow?"

"We do. We'll spend time first thing in the morning going over what we want you to say. I'll show you a picture of Tracy, too. She's heading to Outjo now."

Mogotsi's mind continued to race; competing thoughts battled in his brain. "What I can't figure out is how *my* helping *you* will get Nashili off my back."

Willson's smile was sincere and full of pleasure for the first time that evening.

"Let *me* worry about that," she said. "If this works out like I think it will, we'll have a lot more information about the inspector than we do now."

CHAPTER 26

"Can you see him, Tracy?" asked Willson.

"Roger that," said Tracy Brown over the radio. They were using a scrambled tactical channel. "I've got a window table in the bakery and can see the whole parking lot. The lunch rush in here is winding down, but the lot is still busy. And by the way, the coffee is very good here."

Willson grinned. "We'll get some later. What's Sam doing?"

"Like we asked, he parked his truck where I can see it, and now he's outside talking to one of the car guards. They're standing on the sidewalk near the bank. Unlike the one he spoke to down at the OK Foods earlier this morning, this guy hasn't sent him away. They're having quite the animated chat."

"Ten-four," said Willson. "Keep us posted." She heard the double-click in response, then turned to Gaby Bohitile, who sat in the passenger seat of their unmarked truck.

This was their second day working the streets of Outjo. Through binoculars, Bohitile was staring down Tuni Road toward the parking lot at the corner of Hage Geinbob Street. Monica Hauwanga and Betty Tjikuzu were a block away in the other direction, in the parking lot of the Outjo Post Office. Willson had decided to leave Ben Mushimba and Neus to hold down the fort in Kamanjab; they didn't want to lose their office to another suspicious fire.

"Gaby, can you see Sam?"

"No. He must be over closer to the Standard Bank. But if Tracy can see him, we're good."

"I don't know about you," said Willson, "but I'm damn glad we're finally moving. We probably should've done something like this sooner, but there we are."

"I'm glad, too, Jenny," Bohitile said, dropping the binoculars to her chest. "You were right to suggest that we take back control after the attack on Veronica. Do you think focusing on the car guards is the right way to go?"

"I do." In their meeting with Sam Mogotsi and Tracy Brown the night before, they had all agreed that the most efficient way for Sam to spread the word about selling horns in Outjo was to cautiously chat with the car guards, the young men with fluorescent vests and *tonfas* — wooden batons with a handle on the side that were originally used in martial arts — whose job it was to guard parked cars for a few Namibian dollars per car. These men saw the comings and goings of people on both sides of the law in the commercial areas of towns and cities across Namibia. Locals knew that the sense of security the car guards provided was something of an illusion. But it made visitors feel safe enough to wander and spend money, and it created employment that didn't otherwise exist. It also meant sets of eyes on the street that saw what the police didn't see.

Under the watchful eye of Brown, who had arrived in Outjo two nights ago and kept a low profile since, Mogotsi would make veiled references to having something to sell, something he'd found that might be of value, and carefully ask if there were any buyers around who might be interested. If he found a guard who seemed receptive, who didn't immediately wave him away, he'd show them a picture of one of the horns. And share his cellphone number, if they asked. They'd given him a burner phone that would be used only for this operation. And that included calling his cousin to hint at what he was doing.

"Speaking of Veronica, any news?" asked Willson, her index fingers tapping a rhythm on the steering wheel.

"I spoke to her before we left Kamanjab. She thinks she'll be out of hospital in Windhoek in the next five to seven days, but it will be at least a month before they know whether her vision has fully returned. They're also worried about infection."

"How do you think she's doing?"

Bohitile tilted her head to the side. The straight line of her mouth showed uncertainty. "Better, I think. When we first took her to hospital, she was anxious about going blind. I can't imagine how frightened she must have been. But as her prognosis improves, she seems to be calming down, becoming her optimistic old self again."

Willson shuddered, thinking for a moment how terrifying it would be to lose her vision. "I definitely would've been freaking out."

The radio crackled, and they heard Brown's voice. "Jenny, Tracy."

Willson picked up the hand mic and responded. "Go."

"Sam just gave the hand signal that he has a contact."

"What's he doing?"

"He's on the cellphone. He only touched one button when he picked it up, so someone must have phoned him. The car guard is right beside him."

Willson stared at Bohitile, her eyebrows raised. "Okay," she said to Brown, "once he's done with the call, he should come in to the bakery as we agreed. Let us know."

Five long minutes later, as Bohitile silently watched the back door of the bakery, Willson was starting to get antsy. A phone call about the horn shouldn't last this long, should it?

"Okay," said Bohitile, the binoculars still up to her eyes, "he just went in. Now we wait to hear from Tracy."

Willson pictured the scene inside. Mogotsi would enter the bakery, look around as though it was his first time there, and head for the slatted doors that led to the washrooms. Brown would wait for a moment, then follow him through the same door. They would have a very quick conversation there, then separate. Brown would return to her table and report in, pretending to be talking on her cellphone. Instead, she'd be talking to Willson and Bohitile; the earpiece in her left ear was hidden behind her thick, dark hair, and the mic on the cord below was small and unobtrusive.

The radio call from Brown came just as Willson was debating whether to walk down the street and enter the bakery herself. "Jenny, from Tracy."

"What have you got, Trace?"

"Sam got a call from a very angry man who claims that Sam stole something from him … and he wants it back."

"Wow," said Willson, looking at Bohitile, "word got around fast." Her colleague pumped her fist, and Willson smiled. "That car guard must have called someone after talking to Sam. Or maybe it was the car guard from earlier. Either way, it looks like we've made contact with someone who's missing a horn. How did Sam react?"

Brown's voice crackled through the radio. Willson could hear voices and clinking cups in the background. "I'm glad we prepped him for this scenario. Sam said he told the man he hadn't stolen anything, but he should come see him if he was interested in purchasing what he had to offer."

"And what did the man say?"

"At first, he wanted Sam to come to *him,* but Sam refused because he doesn't know who the guy is. He insisted the man meet him in the parking lot here." Brown chuckled on the phone. "And then he improvised by telling the guy he has two hours to get here, or the item will be sold to someone else."

"Seriously? Nicely done, Sam. What happened then?"

"Sam said the man swore at him in two different languages, then said he wouldn't need two hours to come down and kick his ass."

"Thanks, Tracy," said Willson. "Stand by while Gaby and I talk this through. We won't have enough time to get Sam out of there to plan for what happens next. The caller could show up at any time. He might even be close by, somewhere here in Outjo."

"Ten-four," said Brown, "standing by."

Willson shifted in her seat so she was looking along the truck's bench seat at Bohitile. She glanced at her watch, knowing they had only minutes to figure out their next steps. "We've got to remember our goal here," Willson said. "We *want* this caller, whoever he is, to get his hands on the rhino horn so we can track it. If he's certain now that it's no longer buried where he left it, that likely means that he'd gone to the burial spot with the intention of retrieving it to take somewhere else, possibly to a buyer. He's not going to want to pay for it, at least not willingly, so this could get nasty based on what he said on the phone. But we can't let Sam get hurt. Thoughts?"

Bohitile hesitated before speaking. "The car guard is somehow involved, even if only as a go-between. So, we can't have more people like you or me in the parking lot, because the guard may see us and warn off the caller. We've got to rely on Sam and Tracy."

Willson knew that Bohitile was right. "Okay. Sam knows what we want. We'll assume that when the caller arrives, the guard will somehow point Sam out to him. So, we should get Tracy out to the parking lot now, ready to move closer to Sam when she sees his signal. She can jump in if he needs help, but hang back if he doesn't. We can't do much more than that. We've got to just let this play out. I can't imagine that the caller will do anything too violent in such a public place. I hope Sam remembers that we want him out where you and I can see what's going on."

"We've got to let this man get his hands on the horn if we want to follow his trail," Bohitile said. "It's our only choice. Let's hope he doesn't do anything stupid — or if he tries to, that Tracy can react in time."

Willson grabbed the mic to advise Brown.

Brown's response was immediate. "Roger that," she said. "Agreed and moving now."

"Copy that," said Hauwanga. "Second team standing by. Vehicle running in case we have to move."

Ten minutes later, Brown came back on the radio, her transmission short. "Signal received from Sam. Subject approaching him. Moving closer."

"I see them," said Bohitile, the binoculars back at her face. "The subject is a tall black man. Dressed in brown pants, red T-shirt, and knitted cap, Rastafarian style. A big boy. He must have thirty or forty pounds on Sam. They're talking now. Tracy is about twenty feet away; she's grabbed a shopping cart and is fumbling in her purse, acting like she's lost her wallet or keys."

Willson smiled. She was so pleased to be working with her friend again. Brown was cool and experienced, having worked as an undercover agent for years.

"The subject is waving his arms and looking agitated. Sam seems to be staying cool, shaking his head as though disagreeing. So far, so good," Bohitile said. Then, a few second later: "Sam is motioning toward his truck … they're both walking over that way."

Willson clicked the radio mic. "Stand by. Sam and subject walking toward his truck." More double-clicks in response.

"Sam is opening the canopy door and lowering the tailgate," Bohitile reported. A pause. "He's showing the subject the duffel bag ... he's unzipping it."

Willson watched the scene unfold, her heart speeding up.

In an instant, even from a block away, she saw the subject's arm move swiftly. A punch to the side of Mogotsi's head dropped him to the ground. The man lifted the duffle bag from the bed of Mogotsi's truck and, without looking back at the now-prone Mogotsi, sprinted away, disappearing behind the red-and-white Spar store, out of Willson and Bohitile's view.

"Mogotsi down, but stand by," Willson shouted into the mic. "We need to let the subject leave unmolested. Tracy — get a vehicle licence plate if you can."

Bohitile continued to watch the scene through binoculars. "Okay. I just saw an older-model white Toyota truck leave the parking lot in a hurry. He's turning right off Tuni, heading north on C38."

"Roger that," said Brown. "That's him. Plate number is November-two-two-zero-four-two-Whiskey. Sam's already getting up. I'll look after him."

"Ten-four, Tracy, and good work," said Willson. "Say the same to Sam. Wander over as if you're asking if he needs help, then drive him to the hospital in his truck. Monica and Betty will meet you there. We don't want to raise the car guard's suspicions, or he may phone our suspect. Keep me posted on Sam's condition." Bohitile was bent over the GPS receiver. She gave a thumbs-up, and Willson clicked the mic again. "All units: signal live. We'll follow the subject."

Willson bumped fists with Bohitile. "As long as Sam is okay, that went as well as we could've hoped. Here's hoping the subject isn't suspicious. I just wish our UBC contact had been able to get us a fake horn, so we wouldn't be watching a real one drive away." She turned the truck ignition on, put it in gear, and began rolling down Tuni Street toward the C38. Grinning, she pounded the steering wheel with both hands. "Finally! We've got a traceable rhino horn in play. Let's get these bastards."

CHAPTER 27

Danny Trang sat in the back of the five-row safari truck, his Nikon camera on the tan vinyl seat beside him. He had one hand on the telephoto lens to keep it safe and had wrapped the camera strap around his wrist. His other hand tightly gripped the steel grab bar beside him. Based on his experience thus far with Namibian safaris, the back-row seat in a vehicle like this made for the best wildlife viewing. The back row was the highest, offering optimum visibility. And when Liberty, the guide, turned to tell them what they were seeing, Trang could hear him as clearly as if he was sitting directly behind Liberty.

The only downside was that the back row also gave the most punishing "African massage," the full-body workout passengers received as the truck bounced along the rough bush roads. But Trang could deal with that; normally he had the whole row to himself, with fewer possible obstructions to ruin his images, such as other tourists' hats, cellphones, or meaty shoulders.

They bounced through a low, wet area north of Hobatere Lodge, crossing a rough rock bridge. Trang smelled wild sage in a slight breeze coming from the west. In this area close to the lodge's water hole, moisture and generations of animal dung combined to support thick patches of the herb. The smell was sweet and tangy, opening his nasal passages like freshly ground coffee beans did.

Liberty turned right at the lodge's gravel airstrip, pausing to point out the small, roofless concrete structure that was jokingly called the "arrivals terminal," and the bucket of sand that was the "fire response system." They cruised along the north side of the strip, the guide's head swivelling back and forth as he drove, searching for animals.

They watched two male giraffes feeding on the slope above them, then Liberty turned in to a low forest of mopane trees and began to drive in large, searching circles. They spooked a group of helmeted guinea fowl, their greyish plumage spotted with white, their heads crested. Instead of flying, though, the startled birds scattered in every direction, running like the world was ending. "We call them government chickens," Liberty said. "Their other name is 'bird who has forgotten he can fly.' Not very smart."

Finally, the guide pulled to a quiet stop and pointed to the left. Trang grabbed his camera and swung the long lens in that direction. It took a few seconds of searching, but the autofocus eventually locked on a pride of lions lolling in the shade of a copse of mopane. It was the eyes of the big male that Trang saw first. Golden in the early evening sun, the eyes watched him through branches as though they were seeing through him. The long mane was hidden by the tree trunks, but Trang knew it was there framing the face. The lion's mouth was open. He was panting in the heat of late afternoon. Beside him lay a lioness, and behind her, just beyond her right shoulder, were the ears of two cubs.

"Normally there's a second lioness with them," said Liberty quietly. "She must be out hunting."

"How did you know they were here?" asked Trang in an equally quiet voice. Through the telephoto lens, he could see radio collars on both the male and the female, but he hadn't seen the guide use an antenna to track them.

Liberty pointed to the dirt beside the truck. "I saw them out in this area this morning, and I was following their tracks as I was circling. I knew they'd be here somewhere." Trang looked down to see paw prints in the dust, two large sets and two small.

"How old are cubs?" asked a woman in the front seat. She sat close to the guide in the first row, with her head wrapped in a silky scarf. And she was Asian. Trang had noticed her earlier, when they'd first entered the vehicle. Her eyes had widened upon seeing him. He wondered why. Had they met before, or was it just the surprise of seeing another Asian out here? He could tell that she wasn't Vietnamese. Maybe Chinese, or Korean? He'd said a quick hello, then moved to the back.

"We think they're between six and eight weeks old," replied the guide. "They are a little on the thin side, so we think the pride has not been as successful in hunting as they need to be. The cubs must be hungry."

"You have rhinos here?" asked the same woman, pointing out the opposite side of the truck to where the lions were.

"No, ma'am, we don't. This is not really the best habitat for them, and because the tourism concession we work in is not fenced or actively patrolled, we would quickly lose them to poachers. So, we translocated them elsewhere."

"Where?"

Liberty looked at her sharply. "Uh … where the habitat is much better, and where they are better protected."

Trang noticed the exchange, the guide's suspicious glance, how he evaded answering the woman's question directly. He'd seen and experienced this before.

They spent another ten minutes with the pride, but when the male lion moaned a few times, the guide took that as a signal to move on. Trang knew that the lodge followed very strict protocols for how long to view a pride — more evidence of tourism that was focused on conservation.

Liberty drove them along a rough track that paralleled the airstrip, then turned north through a narrow gap between the hills. They passed oryx, which the guide said surprised him because the hunting lioness would likely be very near here. Above them, African star-chestnut trees, their massive trunks white and marbled and bony, clung to the rocks on a low ridge.

Passing through the gap was like passing into another ecosystem, another world. Trang dropped his camera to his lap and stared. The forest had thinned to reveal a wide savanna dotted with dozens of termite mounds, some as high as fifteen or twenty feet. Between them, large herds of zebras grazed. There were thousands, and amongst them, hundreds of springbok and one lone wildebeest, standing by himself as if wondering whether he'd shown up to the wrong party. In the setting sun, some zebras fought, kicking up clouds of dust that, for Trang, made the scene even more otherworldly. He immediately saw the photographic opportunities and brought up his camera quickly.

"Welcome to Termite City," Liberty said. He stopped the truck. "Let's get out here for a while."

"Are you sure it's okay?" asked an American woman, looking at her husband for reassurance. He shrugged as if to say, *Why are you asking me? I'm from Philadelphia.*

Liberty smiled. "We *should* be okay out here."

One nervous guest at a time slowly stepped down from the vehicle. Trang jumped off the side and immediately began shooting images of the sparring zebras silhouetted against the setting sun. The clouds of dust created an eerie monochromatic haze that Trang knew would make a great potential cover shot. Some of the zebras came closer, as if curious.

When he returned to the truck, Liberty handed him an ice-cold gin and tonic with a slice of lemon. Trang had come to love the African sundowner tradition and had decided some weeks ago that he would continue it back in Kimberley whenever the sun dipped below the Purcell Mountains. After he'd sampled from the plate of cheeses, sliced meats, vegetables, and samosas on the truck's back bumper, he approached the Asian woman. She wasn't having a drink, and she was standing by herself. Now that he was closer, Trang realized that she was older than he'd first thought, perhaps in her late forties, if not early fifties. Her short, dark hair, visible around the edge of the scarf, showed a touch of grey, and she wore glasses with wide, dark frames.

He wondered if the woman spoke more English than she'd demonstrated with her simple questions earlier. "Hi, where are you from? I'm guessing … South Korea?" he tried.

The woman looked at him, nodded once, and climbed back into her seat on the truck. *So much for international relations*, thought Trang. Maybe she'd thought he was trying to flirt with her. In fact, he'd only just been thinking about Jenny Willson and wishing he could share this moment with her. So, whatever. Still, the older woman's cool response was unexpected. And unnecessary.

He turned back to the guide and listened to the same American woman telling him that, on their last safari, she'd seen a zebra in a tree.

"But zebras can't climb trees," Liberty said patiently.

"I saw it with my own eyes. Didn't I, Bill?" she said, turning to her husband. "It was lying up in the branches. It must have gone up there to get away from the lions."

The guide was trying hard not to laugh. Trang could see it in his face, in his long blink and the quivering at the corners of his mouth. "Perhaps a leopard dragged it up there after killing it."

"Oh, I don't think so. There were no leopards anywhere around. I'm quite sure it climbed up there on its own."

"Well, that would certainly be a first," he said, turning away. "Let's go, everyone. If you can put your empty glasses here, we'll head back to the lodge for dinner."

Trang walked around the driver's side of the truck and winked at the guide. "Well done back there," he said quietly.

Liberty smiled and shrugged his shoulders. "All in a day's work."

"Why were those zebras so curious about us tonight?" asked Trang. "Don't they see these trucks almost every day?"

"I guess they haven't seen any white people in a while," Liberty said, winking back at him.

It took the truck about thirty minutes to bounce its way back to the lodge's gate. Like most safari lodges in Africa, Hobatere was circled by an electric fence to keep unwanted and dangerous animals out of the human spaces.

Trang dropped off his camera gear and notebook in his cabin, freshened up, then walked down to the dining room for dinner, using his headlamp to illuminate the rock-lined path.

When he reached the dining room, one of the servers approached him. "Good evening, Mr. Trang. There are two gentlemen waiting for you." She pointed to the veranda.

Trang walked through the open glass doors to the veranda, passing a blazing firepit on the way. "Hello," he said when he reached the candlelit table. "Are you the researchers from the AfriCat Foundation?"

The two men rose to meet Trang. "That's us," said one of them. "You must be Danny. Welcome."

The first man, Frank, introduced himself as the lead researcher in the Hobatere concession; the other was his assistant. Over the next hour and multiple courses, Trang listened to the men talk about their work. Their primary focus was to track lions in the concession area, in western Etosha National Park, and in surrounding communal farmlands. Like the lions he'd seen that afternoon, many in the area were radio-collared. Trang learned that for every lion sighting at Hobatere, not only would the guides share the observation data with AfriCat researchers, the lodge would also make a voluntary payment into a community conservation fund. The fund was then used to undertake more wildlife research, build predator-proof *kraals* (enclosures for livestock), and, just like at Klip River Lodge, compensate farmers who lost livestock to the lions.

"Sorry," said Trang, "but can you please explain to me what a tourism concession is? I've spent time at joint venture lodges in community conservancies such as Klip River, but this is clearly something different."

Frank responded to Trang's question. He was a tall and lanky Brit in his late thirties who was working on his Ph.D. "This place was Namibia's first tourist concession, and it dates back to when the country was still called South West Africa. The concession is thirty-two thousand hectares and is owned by members of the ≠Khoadi-//Hôas Conservancy, where Klip River Lodge is. It's on essentially a ninety-nine-year lease, which allows the owners to make investments in the lodge and chalets. Years ago, it was private. And it was once the best of the country's tourist lodges before it closed and fell into disrepair. Luckily, it was reopened in 2015."

"I heard from our guide today that the concession is not fenced," Trang said. "How do you prevent poaching?"

Frank smiled. "It's mostly a collaborative effort. Besides the lodge guides, people like us are out here every day in different parts of the concession, tracking the lions. We record everything we see. There are also patrols by police, the Ministry, and the army. We never know when we might see them. They show up unannounced, and they're very good about being covert in what they do."

"How does the local community benefit?"

"They get not only a percentage of the profits, but also jobs, career training, improved water holes to keep wildlife away from houses and gardens and grazing areas, and even education funds for schools. It's a very successful model."

Trang madly took down notes as Frank spoke. When he glanced up at one point, he noticed that the Korean woman he'd spoken to earlier was sitting at the adjacent table. There was something about her — besides her chilly response earlier — that bothered him, but he couldn't figure out what. Frank paused, and Trang urged him to continue.

An hour later, when Trang and the two researchers were enjoying an after-dinner beer, he noticed the woman again. She had finished her dinner and was speaking into her tablet, using FaceTime or Skype or something like that. Her face was close to the screen.

"No," the woman whispered, shaking her head animatedly. "No rhinos. I waste time. I leave in morning."

Trang couldn't see who she was talking to; he could only hear a muffled male voice coming from the tablet's speaker. He tried not to be too obvious about listening in.

"No, I leave lodge in morning. I come back to Opuwo." As she closed the tablet case with a bang, she lifted her eyes. Trang turned his head quickly, uncertain if the woman had noticed his attention. She got up from the table and left the dining area.

After Trang had paid for dinner to express his thanks to the two researchers, he stopped at the lodge's reception desk. Over the past couple of nights, he'd become friendly with Samuel, the man sitting behind the wooden counter, by always stopping to chat with him.

"Samuel," he said quietly, leaning over the desk, "could you please tell me who that Korean woman is … the one who sat near us at dinner and who came on the game drive earlier?"

"Mr. Danny," the man said, looking apologetic, "we try to respect our guests' privacy."

"I understand that, it's just that I spoke to her on the game drive today and she wanted me to send her a copy of the magazine article I'm writing. I got her email address, but I've already forgotten her name. I'm very embarrassed and hoping you can help me."

Samuel looked over his shoulder to ensure that no one was watching him, then quickly skimmed his finger down a list in front of him. "Please don't tell anyone I told you this. Her name is Won Hua Suk. She is leaving in the morning with a private driver right after breakfast."

Trang wrote the name in his notebook, asking Samuel to repeat it twice so that he had it spelled right. "And she is from South Korea, right?"

"When she checked in today, she showed me a diplomatic passport from the Democratic People's Republic of Korea. That is South Korea, right?"

Trang frowned, his mind reeling. "Uh, no. She's from *North* Korea." He instantly recalled the conversation he'd had with the kayak guide, Jason; he'd talked about countries on top of the list for buying illicit rhino horn. China. Vietnam. Laos. And North Korea, which allegedly used horn as a source of funds to bypass western trade embargoes.

Trang knew in an instant that this information might be of value to Jenny Willson. But first, he had to be sure. If Won Hua Suk was leaving in the morning on her way to Opuwo, about a two-hour drive north, he could follow her in his truck. Then, once he knew what she was doing, he'd have something interesting and potentially useful to report. It was another way — he hoped — to prove to Willson that he could be trusted. At the same time, however, she might see his discovery and surveillance of the North Korean woman as proof that he *couldn't* be trusted, that he *was* running his own investigation, despite his claims to the contrary. After a moment of hesitation, he made his decision. It was the lesser of two evils.

"I won't check out in the morning, Samuel, but I think I'll take a drive. If all goes well, I should be back for dinner."

The clerk looked concerned. "Is everything okay, Mr. Danny? I'm sorry you won't be with us tomorrow."

Trang smiled. "Everything is just fine, Samuel. I appreciate your help tonight."

CHAPTER 28

Jenny Willson awoke with a start, trying to remember where she was. She'd done a few stakeouts in her career, long nights of surveillance stuck in a vehicle, often with an unapologetically farting male partner, and the word *uncomfortable* was a wholly inadequate description. In comparison, Gaby Bohitile was a dream stakeout partner.

"He's moving again." Bohitile's voice was calm and surprisingly bright, so early in the morning. She was staring at the GPS receiver in her lap.

Willson looked at the digital clock on the dash: 5:45 a.m. "Thanks for taking that second shift, Gaby. I couldn't stay awake any longer." She rolled her shoulders, groaned, swallowed a few times in an unsuccessful attempt to wet her throat, and thought about how good a cup of Kick Ass would taste right now. "Jesus. I feel like I've been trampled by a water buffalo. And I need to pee."

They were parked in a picnic site on the south side of the C40 highway, under a massive acacia tree about four hundred metres from the turnoff to the Otjikandero Himba Village, twenty kilometres east of Kamanjab.

The night before, their suspect had turned off the highway toward the village, forcing Willson and Bohitile to decide whether to pursue or to wait. They were about to turn left to follow the suspect down the dusty red southbound track when the GPS icon for his truck — or, more accurately, for the rhino horn in his truck — stopped moving on the screen, just on the edge of the village. They'd quickly decided to park in the picnic area and wait. That would give them the option of following the suspect if he continued south, beyond the village, on the spiderweb of roads there, or if he came back to the highway. The fact that he'd spent the night in the village meant that he was either a Himba man who lived there, or had a friend in the village who'd put him up for the night.

They'd also received a call from Monica Hauwanga to say that the licence plate of the truck they were following had originally been registered by NaTIS — the Namibian Traffic Information System — to a car belonging to an elderly Windhoek couple who had recently passed away in a traffic accident. Hauwanga had learned that the car had been sold by the couple's son after their death, and the licence plate stolen soon after. So, they still didn't know who they were following. Hauwanga had also informed them that Mogotsi had been checked by a doctor in Outjo, then immediately released. Other than a slight headache and a bruise on one elbow, he was no worse for wear. And, surprisingly, he was keen to continue working with them.

Willson leaned over Bohitile's shoulder to look at the GPS display. "What is this place?" she asked, pointing to the spot on the screen where the icon had stopped moving.

"It's been a Himba village for generations, as far as I know. But it's also an orphanage. AIDS remains a problem here, but adults also die of other health issues, or in accidents. Some children are simply abandoned. There's a small school here with a teacher and an assistant, and local guides host village tours for tourists. Visitors are not only encouraged to donate money to the school and the orphanage, but to bring school supplies and toys with them when they come from Kamanjab or Outjo. It's mostly safari tour groups, but other travellers come, too. I'm not one for mushy stuff, but it's heartwarming to see how well-treated these little ones are. They're lucky, given their horrible circumstances."

Willson recalled her visit to Chioto Shipanga's village near Omarumba and her interview with the Himba elders. Mostly, though, she thought about the little children she'd seen there, smiling, playing, running free amongst the adults. Now having lost both of her own parents, she could commiserate a little with the orphans. She hoped their lives were almost as good as the lives of those children still living with their parents. She couldn't fathom what it would be like to be so small and so alone.

"Jenny," said Bohitile, her finger tracing the icon's route on the screen, "you better pee fast. He's getting close to the highway."

Glad it was still dark, Willson jumped out and sprinted to the edge of the picnic area. Dropping her pants, she squatted and emptied her full bladder in record time. She saw the flash of the suspect's headlights in the distance as the truck bounced down the last section of the access road.

She returned to the truck, doing up her belt. Bohitile was watching the turnoff and the back of the suspect's truck through her binoculars. "There he is ... and ... he's turning west onto the highway."

"The GPS chip has a two-kilometre range, right?"

"Yup, as long as the battery doesn't die on us."

"Okay, I'll wait until he gets a good kilometre ahead of us before I start to follow. He's obviously still got the horn with him. That's a good thing. I was concerned he was going to give it to someone in the village."

Willson and Bohitile followed the suspect into Kamanjab, Willson now fully awake and at the wheel. They watched him from a block away as he filled his truck with gas. She still couldn't get over how the young men who worked as gas station attendants would first vigorously rock every vehicle so they could pump the maximum amount of fuel into each tank. They did it with the suspect's truck, too. Every drop and every dollar was counted here.

"South, north, or west?" asked Willson, wondering which of three highways the suspect would take. Or, would he meet with someone here in Kamanjab?

They had their answer when the suspect drove past them, forcing them to quickly slouch down in their seats as he went by.

"North," Bohitile said, rising back to an upright seated position. "I wonder what he's up to."

"He's got to be heading somewhere like Opuwo, or to one of the towns near the border with Angola." Willson opened a map and traced the highways with her index finger. "If he was heading toward Helao Nafidi, or up toward the Caprivi Strip and Zambia or Botswana, then he would've gone the other way when he left Outjo."

"Agreed. You don't think he's going to rebury the horn, do you?"

"That wouldn't make any sense, because he knows that someone already found it. He thinks that was Sam. So I can't imagine why he would take the same chance again." Bohitile nodded in agreement.

Willson continued to skim the map. "Where in the 'O' are we going, Gaby? Jesus. Outapi. Okahao. Omulonga. It looks like every bloody town and village up here starts with an O."

"Oh, you noticed that, did you?" Bohitile said with a grin.

As they headed north out of Kamanjab, the suspect just over a kilometre ahead of them, they passed by the unit office. Willson thought of the bags of Kick Ass coffee that were waiting for her, calling her name. She'd only just received this second shipment after the remaining bags from the first had gone up in flames with the rest of their apartment. Aside from the picture of her mother, the coffee had been the possession she'd most hated losing.

As she drove, thoughts of her mother and Kicking Horse Coffee evolved into reflections on her Skype interview two days earlier with Conservation Officer Brad Jenkins, his sergeant, and the inspector in charge of the East Kootenay. The conversation had been marred by voice delays and small breaks in connection, but given the great distance, it was a reasonable way to do a face-to-face job interview.

They sped by the rolling, rocky hills at a hundred kilometres an hour as Willson played over the questions the trio had asked her. She had expected typical government interview questions, but it was clear that Jenkins had briefed his colleagues on her background, experience, and capabilities. Rather than quiz her on wildlife, firearms, investigative techniques, or how to deal with aggressive hunters who didn't like "lady COs," they'd pushed her on why she wanted to leave her career as a warden with Parks Canada and join the Conservation Officer Service in B.C. instead.

She'd given the answer that had formed in her mind during the weeks since Jenkins's first email. She'd been expecting this very question, and she'd also needed to truly understand the answer for herself. Her response had evolved only through her asking herself the tough questions that had swirled in her brain since the day she drove away from Golden months ago. Why *was* she ready to leave her dream job at Parks Canada? What was it about moving to B.C. and an enforcement job there that was so interesting to her? Was she running away from loss and betrayal, or from the deep disappointment over her treatment by the higher-ups in the federal government food chain? They'd disrespected her, thrown barriers in her way, and forced her to make impossible choices. Would working for the B.C. government really be any different?

"I'm interested in this job," she'd said without hesitation, "because I'm ready for a change, a new challenge. And, quite frankly, I'm excited about the idea of settling down in a new place in the mountains and getting to know it on a deeper level, personally and professionally, than I have been able to do by bouncing around a bunch of national parks." It was the first time she'd stated this out loud to anyone, and as soon as she'd said the words, she understood that she truly was being honest, with them and with herself. Perhaps for the first time in a long time.

Now, she was waiting for their decision. As someone who loved to be in control, having to wait like this made her uncomfortable. She'd also been thinking about Danny Trang. She'd enjoyed spending the evening with him at the Oppi-Koppi bar. They had talked and shared and drank, then talked and shared and drank some more before parting company with a handshake, Trang returning to his campsite at Oppi-Koppi, Willson stumbling back to her apartment in the dark. The next morning, with a hangover and a scraped knee that she'd gotten from falling after trying to find the Southern Cross in the night sky, she'd remembered the handshake. *A handshake? Jesus.* Was she that cold, that unwilling to show emotion? What must Danny think of her? If Muafangejo had been right about his interest, then she might have seen the last of him.

"He's stopping," said Bohitile, breaking Willson's train of thought. "Let's wait to see what he does."

It was now midmorning, and they were within a kilometre of a major crossroad northwest of Etosha

Park. Willson pulled to the side of the highway. Deep in thought, she'd completely missed the fact that they'd passed the Galton Gate nearly an hour ago.

Bohitile turned to look at Willson and smiled. "Welcome back from your daydreams, Jenny," she said. "So, once again, our guy could go in one of three directions. Have you got a three-headed coin on you?"

Willson's phone buzzed. She looked down to see a text from Tracy Brown: *Sam called by car guard in Outjo. Another buyer interested in horns. Going back with team to set up again. Same place. Will keep you posted.*

"Now that's interesting," said Willson. She showed the phone to her colleague.

Bohitile's eyebrows rose. "Maybe we've finally contacted a real buyer. I'm thinking the guy we're following now has got to be just a low-level seller. Who else would work so hard to recover a horn except someone desperate for cash? This last call to Mogotsi might be the break we've been looking for."

"Maybe you're right. I wish we were there with the rest of the team, because I'd love to see who shows up. But we've committed to following this guy. We have to see it through."

Willson typed a response to Brown, her thumbs flying on the small keyboard: *We'll stick with our guy. We're near Opuwo, still following. Your news huge. Keep us posted & keep Sam safe. I know you'll kick ass.*

Five minutes later, their suspect had not moved from the intersection ahead of them. "What the hell is he doing?" asked Willson impatiently. "Making a phone call? Deciding which way to go? Taking a leak?"

Bohitile sat up straighter. "Okay, here we go. He's moving again, turning left, toward Opuwo. Let's give him a moment, and then we'll go." She grabbed the map and ran her finger toward Opuwo, then north toward Angola. "He must be meeting someone in Opuwo, because there's nothing north of that other than a rough road for almost two hundred kilometres to Epupa Falls on the Kunene River. But there's no border crossing there to Angola. At least, I don't think there is. I guess he could turn south again toward Sesfontein when he gets to Opuwo, but that wouldn't make sense … it's the long way around."

As they rolled up to the same intersection less than a minute later, Willson saw the sign: *Opuwo: 56 kilometres.* "In about thirty minutes, we should find out."

The streets of Opuwo were busy with cars, but not as busy as the sidewalks were with pedestrians. Through the dusty windshield, Willson looked along the main street and saw a continuous procession on both sides. Pairs and groups of Himba women, their traditional dress and semi-nakedness a stark contrast to the pavement, curbs, and concrete sidewalks fronting the houses, stores, and lower-end rest camps. One woman had a massive vinyl bag balanced on her head and a baby bouncing on her back. When she lifted her feet, Willson saw that her sandals were made from a car tire. Farther along, Herero women walked with husbands and sons, their unique, colourful headpieces in the shape of cattle horns swaying as they moved. And everywhere, individual men walked slowly, as if without purpose, but all were on their cellphones. *Who are they talking to*, she wondered, *and about what?*

"The suspect just turned off the highway to the right, Jenny. Take it slow."

Willson gently braked and followed Bohitile's gaze.

"He pulled into the Kaokoland Restaurant on the side street there," said Bohitile, pointing. "He's either stopping for lunch, or he's meeting someone."

"I see a parking lot ahead, also to the right," said Willson. "We can park there, then walk back to the restaurant, past that bank. Our guy doesn't know who we are, but he might have seen the truck. He did pass us this morning, and we've been following him since yesterday. Who knows how observant he might be."

Willson found a parking space in front of a coffee shop. The two officers worked their way past the bank, a grocery store, and a computer repair shop, dodging Himba women sitting on the ground behind spread blankets covered in carvings and bracelets.

They reached the parking area beside the restaurant and saw the suspect's truck parked near a window, perhaps located so he could see it from inside.

Willson paused. She couldn't risk peering inside the suspect's truck for fear of spooking him. They'd have to go into the restaurant to see what the man was doing, whether he had the duffle bag with him, who he might be talking to. She worked her way around the passenger side of a rental truck with a dusty, khaki-coloured tent folded on top, heading for the front door of the restaurant. But as she passed the rental, there, sitting in the driver's seat, was Danny Trang.

CHAPTER 29

Sam Mogotsi chose not to tell the officers about his headaches. Since he'd been sucker-punched by the man in the parking lot, he'd suffered from an intermittent banging pain behind his eyes. It wasn't always there. If he sat quietly in a dark room, like he'd done the night before, it was tolerable. But if he stood up or moved too quickly, or if he went outside without his sunglasses, the pain came back in waves, bringing tears to his eyes. And his vision wasn't quite as clear as it was before the assault. Because he worked in the bush and his job was to search for rhinos and other game, the vision problem was the thing that scared him the most.

But despite all that, he knew he couldn't turn back or pull out now. Despite the risks, he was too far in. He desperately needed the anti-poaching team to believe him, to trust him, so he could get his life back. So he didn't have to worry about his family's safety. He hoped that, by pretending to be a horn seller, his troubles would soon disappear, although he couldn't understand yet how that would happen. As much as he hoped the team would trust him, he hoped that he could trust them.

"Are you ready, Sam?" Tracy Brown looked at him across the hood of her truck. Their two vehicles were parked side by side forty kilometres west of Outjo, one kilometre down a rough D road. The rest of the team had gone ahead to set up surveillance, with Ben Mushimba replacing Betty Tjikuzu for the day.

"I am," Mogotsi said. "I understand what you want me to do, and I'm ready."

"Let's do one final microphone check. Monica and Ben, can you read Sam?" Brown spoke into the mic on the edge of her collar, then listened. "Okay, Sam, we're good. Everything you say, and everything that's said within about twenty feet of you, depending on background noise, will be heard and recorded."

Mogotsi nodded, feeling somewhat comforted that the others would be able to hear what was going on. But he would have felt better if he could somehow hear what *they* were saying, too, although he knew that wouldn't be possible.

"You'll remember not to turn your back on anyone today, right?" Brown asked.

Mogotsi smiled. The action made him wonder if the two sides of his face were working properly, or working together. He touched his cheek with his hand. Did he look like he was having a stroke? "I will. I don't want to end up in hospital again. The next time, I might not be so lucky."

"If it's any consolation, I'll be closer to you this time."

"It's good to know you'll be there," he said, and he meant it.

The man who'd phoned yesterday hadn't given his name, but had simply said word had gotten around that Sam had something of value for sale, and he was interested. When asked what he was willing to pay, the man had said he'd have to look at the merchandise first. He would know how to find Sam when he got to Outjo.

The two rhino horns were packed into two separate opaque plastic bins, the larger one in the back of his truck, the smaller horn in the space behind the bench seat. Each horn was covered in bubble wrap and then nestled in crumpled sheets from the *Namibian* newspaper.

"Let's make this happen. Good luck, Sam."

Thirty minutes later, Mogotsi turned in to the parking lot beside the Outjo coffee shop, the same place where he'd been assaulted and the first horn stolen. He circled the lot once, then found an empty spot and sat for a moment, collecting himself. This was the moment of truth, when things could go as hoped ... or go sideways. He touched his head where he'd been hit. He already knew what going sideways looked and felt like.

He stepped from the truck, then walked back to lean against the tailgate, his arms crossed over his chest and his legs crossed at the ankles, trying to look relaxed despite his pounding heart and pounding head. He swept his gaze around the parking lot and waited.

It was at least twenty minutes before he glimpsed, out of the corner of his eye, the same car guard he'd talked to the last time he was here. Still wearing his fluorescent green vest, the man peered around the large red support column outside the Spar store, looking at Mogotsi and talking on his cellphone, presumably letting his contact know that Mogotsi was here. When the call was done, the man disappeared.

What Mogotsi didn't expect was the two police vehicles that sped into the parking lot, one to his right and one to his left. He stood up straighter, hoping he was mistaken, that they were there for someone else. But when the vehicles stopped, facing each other so that he couldn't back his truck out of the parking space, he knew that things were quickly going sideways again, but in a way he had not anticipated. And when Inspector Nashili, from Kamanjab, stepped out of the vehicle on the right, Sergeant Kugara from the one on the left, Mogotsi knew that his situation had taken a turn for the worse.

"Sam Mogotsi," Nashili said, smiling a wolf-like smile, "funny meeting you here."

Mogotsi stared at the inspector, imagining the radio chatter that was going on between the anti-poaching unit members. He knew that Tracy Brown was watching from somewhere close by, no doubt incredulous at what was happening, but unable to intervene. He glanced around to look for her. Unsuccessful, he turned back to the inspector.

"Were you expecting someone else?" asked Nashili.

"I'm waiting for a friend. What are you doing so far from Kamanjab, Inspector Nashili?"

"I have jurisdiction throughout the Kunene region, so you never know where I'll appear. That's the way I like it."

The inspector leaned against the front grille of his truck, mirroring Mogotsi's stance. "Who are you waiting for?"

"I told you, a friend. We're going to grab a coffee." He nodded his head toward the coffee shop.

"What's your friend's name?"

"I … I don't think that's any of your business."

"Everything around here is my business if I choose to make it so."

Mogotsi stared at the inspector, wondering how this would play out.

"Do you mind if Sergeant Kugara searches your truck, Sam?"

"What if I do?"

"He'll search it anyway. And I will arrest you for obstructing an officer."

Mogotsi's mind raced. Was there any way out of this? He hoped to stall, giving the anti-poaching team enough time to come up with a plan. They couldn't just show up and tell the inspector to back off, especially not with a parking lot full of people watching the confrontation. That would blow the entire operation. "Do you have the right to search my vehicle even if I don't want you to?"

Nashili laughed. "Of course. It comes with the job." He motioned the sergeant toward Mogotsi's truck.

"I want it on the record that I did not give you permission to search my vehicle."

This time, both officers laughed. Kugara pushed Mogotsi away from the back of the truck, then lifted the canopy door and dropped the tailgate. He spotted the first plastic box and slid it out onto the lowered tailgate.

"What's in here, Sam?" asked Kugara.

It was then that Mogotsi realized he'd been set up, that these two police officers already knew what he was carrying in his truck; someone had told them what they would find when they searched it. For a moment, he wondered if the car guard was working with the police, if he had informed them that Mogotsi was back with more horn. That was a possibility. He also wondered briefly if the anti-poaching unit had set him up. But that made no sense. They were looking to catch buyers and sellers of rhino horn, not police officers who held a grudge against him. Then, he remembered Willson's request that he contact his cousin.

"Inspector ... take a look at this." The sergeant had pulled back the newspaper in the plastic bin and removed some of the bubble wrap to expose the large horn inside.

"Is this what I think it is?" said Nashili, pulling back more of the bubble wrap. He turned to Mogotsi. "This is contraband and a serious offence. Sergeant Kugara: arrest this man for illegal possession of rhino horn. Put him in the back of your vehicle, please, then thoroughly search the rest of this truck."

As Kugara pushed him toward one of the police vehicles, Mogotsi desperately searched the parking lot for any sign of Tracy Brown or any of the other team members. Nothing. They must still be watching this scene unfold, listening via his hidden microphone, but unable — or unwilling — to intervene. *Had* they set him up?

Seated in the back seat of Kugara's SUV, Mogotsi watched through the barred windows as the officers searched his truck. They dragged the second bin from the passenger compartment to the tailgate, next to the first bin, and opened it. When they saw what was inside, they both turned toward him, victory on their faces. They transferred the two bins to the inspector's vehicle, then each officer returned to his own. Both vehicles left the parking lot, but when they reached the intersection of highways C38 and C39, the sergeant turned north onto C39. Mogotsi twisted toward the back window to see the inspector head south on the same highway.

"Where is *he* going?"

"That's none of your concern. *You're* going with me to Kamanjab. Back to your home sweet home in our comfortable jail cells."

Ninety minutes later, Kugara pulled Mogotsi from the back seat of his SUV and marched him through the front doors of the Kamanjab station, directly into the prisoner processing area outside the cell block.

"We already have your fingerprints on file, don't we?" said Kugara, smirking. "So, we won't bother with those." He took a step back and pointed to a blank concrete block wall. "Turn and put your hands on the wall and spread your legs. I have to make sure you don't take anything unauthorized into the cell with you."

Mogotsi did as he was told. He felt the sergeant's hands run aggressively across his shoulders, down his arms and back, then around to his chest. When the hands paused, he knew that Kugara had felt the wire leading from the microphone under his collar down to the small transmitter about the size of a cellphone that was hidden in the front of his pants.

The sergeant yanked the wire, hard. The microphone ripped away from Mogotsi's collar, and the transmitter was pulled out of his untucked shirt, falling to the concrete floor with a crash and breaking into pieces.

Kugara grabbed Mogotsi's shoulder and spun him around. "What the hell is this?" he yelled, looking down at the pieces on the floor. "What have you done?"

In the sergeant's face, Mogotsi saw anger, but also shock and confusion. "You don't have to tell your boss about this," Mogotsi said, hopeful.

"No," said Kugara, "I'm not sure that I do."

CHAPTER 30

Danny Trang had seen Won Hua Suk being dropped off by her driver outside the Kaokoland Restaurant in Opuwo, a small suitcase in her hand, so he'd backed his truck into a nearby parking spot to consider what to do. He'd stared at the restaurant's front window, but wasn't able to see inside due to the reflection of the glass. Decision time.

If he went in, there was a good chance she would see him and recognize him, and then, the trip would have been a waste of time. Even if he went in and she didn't see him, he might end up seeing nothing more than the woman eating her lunch. He'd have nothing to offer Jenny. As he sat pondering his next move, he began to rethink his decision to follow the woman. The idea, perhaps hatched a little too quickly, had been to see where she went in order to get a clue or lead that would reveal what she was up to, something useful he could impress

Willson with, with no strings attached. Now, sitting in his car, utterly clueless as to what to do next, he simply felt foolish.

A sharp rapping sounded on the passenger-side window. He whipped his head around and saw Jenny Willson peering in, banging her knuckles on the glass. She looked angry. Trang froze. What the hell was she doing here? She rapped again, this time more forcefully, so he hit the button to roll down the window. "What are you do—"

"Get the hell out of there, Danny, and come with me," she said in a whisper.

Trang reached for the handle, but the door began to open on its own. He looked up to see Gaby Bohitile holding the door open. She said nothing and didn't look at him. Her eyes were locked on the restaurant.

Trang slid out and walked toward the back of the metal canopy, its myriad locked panels protecting his camping gear. Bohitile slid into the driver's seat and closed the door quietly.

Willson was waiting for him behind the truck. She grabbed his elbow and pulled him away from the restaurant, not looking back. "You and I are going for a walk."

"Listen —"

"Not here," she interrupted.

Trang had no idea what was going on, but he was smart enough to do what he was told.

They passed the computer repair store, the grocery store, and a coffee shop before turning in to an alley. She finally stopped in the narrow space between two parked delivery trucks and spun around to face him. "What the hell are you doing here, Danny?" Speechless, Trang was still reeling at her sudden appearance. "I asked you a question." For an instant, he wondered if she was going to grab him.

"It's a long story ... but I was trying to help you, Jenny." He raised his hands as if in supplication or surrender.

"How in the hell is being in this place, at this time, helping me at all?"

Willson grabbed at her ponytail with both hands, aggressively tightening the hair tie, which had loosened during their fast walk over. Her biceps flexed, the veins in her arms popping. *Better her hair than my neck*, he thought.

"I'll start from the beginning."

"Hell of an idea."

"Okay, I've been staying at the Hobatere Lodge, and yesterday, on a game drive, this woman, another guest at the lodge, seemed awfully interested in rhinos. Once she discovered that there aren't any in the Hobatere concession, she left the lodge. I found that kind of strange."

Willson didn't appear to be moved by anything he'd said so far. She shrugged and made a face. "What's so strange about wanting to see a rhino, then leaving when you can't?"

"It was more than that. I overhead her video chatting with someone last night. She said she was wasting her time there and was going to leave in the morning, to come back to Opuwo."

"And?" Willson said impatiently.

"And then I found out from the desk clerk that she's North Korean."

"North Korean?" For the first time, Willson sounded more interested than angry.

"Yes. And here on a diplomatic passport."

"A North Korean diplomat." Willson hesitated, so Trang ploughed forward.

"That kayak guide I met a few weeks ago, Jason, told me about the countries most commonly linked to illicit rhino horn sales. I just thought a North Korean woman interested in rhinos, here on her own, was more than a little suspicious. So, I followed her to the restaurant to see if she was up to something."

"I thought you said you were an adventure tourism journalist, not an investigative reporter. What has a Korean diplomat got to do with adventure travel, Danny? Why would you follow someone like that unless you were chasing a story?" Her face reddened. "I just caught you doing exactly what you assured me you weren't here to do!"

"The only reason I did it was to find out whether she was relevant to your investigation, Jenny. I just didn't want to contact you until I knew for sure. I only wanted to help you."

"Do you know how lame that sounds?"

"Well, it's the truth."

"So you inserted yourself right here, in the middle of our investigation, to *help* me?" she said sarcastically.

Trang suddenly realized that he was missing something. "Wait a minute, why *is* your team here?"

"Like you don't already know."

Trang considered himself a reasonably calm guy, but Willson's suspicious attitude was really starting to annoy him. He took a deep breath. "Look, I told you the truth. Yeah, it was a stupid idea, but I really was trying to help you. If that was wrong, forget it." He turned and began to walk away.

"Danny, wait," Willson said. He felt Willson touch his arm, this time less forcefully. Trang turned back toward her. "You *really* don't know why we're here?"

"I honestly have no idea. Whatever it is, I sincerely hope I didn't screw it up for you."

Willson leaned against one of the parked trucks, rubbing her hands together pensively. She finally lifted her eyes to his, and Trang matched her gaze. "Let's go over again who this woman is, and why you were following her."

He recounted his story and described the woman as best he could. He gave Willson the woman's full name, spelling it out as she wrote it down in her notebook.

"And you said the clerk saw her diplomatic passport from North Korea?"

"That's what he said. I got the impression he doesn't see very many of them, so it stood out."

"And the passport was what made you think something wasn't right?"

Trang nodded. "Why would a North Korean diplomat wander around Namibia alone, asking about rhinos?"

Willson slowly clicked her pen, closed her notebook, and put both back in her hip pocket. "For some reason," she said, staring at him intently, "I believe you."

"Good."

"All I can tell you is that we tracked someone — and something — to this very restaurant. The fact that your mystery woman showed up at the same time probably means the two are connected. It's too much of a coincidence otherwise. For now, that's all I'll say."

"Fair enough. I don't need to know any more," Trang said, shaking his head. "What do you want me to do?"

"For now, I want you to go sit in that coffee shop we passed and wait. Keep your phone handy and give me your truck keys." She stretched out her hand.

"Why do you need my keys?"

"One, because we're using your truck to watch the front of the restaurant and might need to move in a hurry. And two, because I don't want you doing anything silly like trying some more novice surveillance."

"But all my stuff's in there."

"Have you got your wallet?"

"Yeah ..."

"Don't you trust me, Danny?" She smiled — it was the first smile he'd seen that day — and handed him her own keys. She pointed at a truck parked near the coffee shop. "We're parked over there, if we have to take yours. The white Toyota without the canopy."

"Okay."

"But hopefully we won't need to —" Willson was interrupted by her cellphone. She looked at the screen and put the phone to her ear. "Willson here. Talk to me, Trace."

As she listened, she paced between the trucks, kicking small rocks with her boot, then stopped short. "They arrested him? Again? What about the horns?" A pause. "Where's he heading?" Willson turned to look at Trang with a smile on her face. "Intriguing," she said into the phone. "I wondered if something like this might happen." A longer pause. "No. We've got to stay … things just got interesting here. I'll fill you in when I can. Not sure how long we'll be. Keep tracking him and keep me posted. I'll let you know when Gaby and I are on our way back. Great work, Trace. Okay, bye." She returned the phone to her pocket.

"Tracy Brown?" asked Trang with a smile.

"Yeah. Thanks … for that advice, I mean."

"You're welcome. Although I think you already knew what you needed to do." He turned toward the coffee shop. "I better grab that coffee and let you get back to work."

"I'm not sure how long I'll be. I'll come get you when we're done."

"I'll be waiting."

They exchanged smiles, and then he saw a frown cross her face. "Why is it that I always have so much trouble believing you?" Willson asked.

"Only you know the answer to that, Jenny," Trang replied.

CHAPTER 31

Willson opened the door to Trang's truck, slid into the passenger seat, and quietly pulled the door closed.

"So, what's he doing here?" asked Bohitile. "And what did you do with him? Is he still alive?"

Willson smiled. "First things first, Gaby. Anything happen since I left?"

Bohitile shook her head. "Nothing. Our guy is still in there, his truck is still parked where he left it, and no one has left the building with the duffle bag. The GPS signal shows that the horn is still in there, too. Maybe he *is* just having an early lunch and wants to keep it close."

"No," said Willson, "I think it's more than that." She told Bohitile about her conversation with Danny and that she had left him cooling his heels in the nearby coffee shop.

"So, you think our guy is meeting the woman Danny followed?"

"Exactly. We've got a guy desperate to unload a rhino horn he just stole back from someone who stole it from him and a diplomat from North Korea who's been inquiring about rhinos … in the same restaurant. It can't be a coincidence."

"Did Danny give you a description of the woman?" asked Bohitile, opening her notebook.

"Yes. She's in her late forties or early fifties. Black shoulder-length hair with a tinge of grey. Carrying a leather purse and a small suitcase. When Danny saw her this morning, she was wearing black pants and a blue blouse, with a patterned scarf loose around her neck. He says she's probably five feet, four inches tall, although if she's sitting down, that won't help us."

Bohitile closed her notebook. "I think one of us has to go in there to see whether the two of them are together and find out what they're up to. He's been in there a while now."

"Agreed," Willson said. She looked around the messy interior of Trang's truck and grabbed a road map and a guidebook. "I'm going in. I'll pretend I'm a tourist. If they're together, I'll sit as close as I can to them."

"And if they're not together?"

"Then I'll find a seat somewhere between the two and keep my eye on the duffle bag. Stay on your phone. I'll keep you updated by text."

"Roger that," Bohitile said.

Willson got out and walked quickly over to the front door of the restaurant. She glanced at the open-air seating area as she passed, but didn't see either of the two persons of interest, so she continued into the restaurant. She grabbed a menu from a stack at the front, found an empty table near the rear, and ordered a cup of coffee from the server. Then she unfolded the large highway map, using it as a screen behind which she surveyed the room.

She saw their suspect first, the man wearing the colourful knitted cap. He was alone at a table in the far corner. Willson quickly realized that he was sitting with his back to a woman who matched Trang's description of the Korean diplomat. They were sitting less than a foot apart, back to back, with the duffel bag against the wall between them.

When her coffee arrived, Willson sipped slowly, watching the suspects over the rim of the cup. Both had remnants of a meal in front of them, and both were talking on their cellphones. At a glance, no one in the place would give them any thought. They were two single travellers sitting at adjacent tables, nothing more. But Willson was certain they were conversing with each other while probably just holding their phones to their ears, trying to appear as if they were in no way connected. Willson typed a text to Bohitile: *Two suspects here. Not sitting together but very close. I think they're talking to each other but pretending to be on phone. Duffle still here. Stand by.*

Her phone dinged softly with a thumbs-up icon in response. For the next ten minutes, Willson watched the two suspects. One would talk while the other listened. Willson had no doubt they were communicating. Negotiating. At one point, the man vigorously shook his head, disagreeing with something the woman had said. The next time he spoke, he waved his free arm to make a point, even though the woman still had her back to him.

By the time she started on her second cup of coffee, Willson sensed that the conversation was winding down. There appeared to be less arguing and more agreeing. Willson raised her cellphone as if she were reading something on the screen and switched it to camera mode.

The man nodded his head. Once. Twice. Then he reached down and grabbed an envelope that the woman passed to him with her left hand. It was quick and surreptitious. *Click. Click. Click.* Willson captured the moment for posterity and, perhaps, a future court proceeding. The man tucked the envelope down the front of his shirt. Seconds later, the woman reached down and pulled the duffle bag toward her, very subtly and very slowly.

Click. Click. Click.

Willson would have to decide soon. Now that the deal was complete, the two suspects would likely be getting up and leaving separately. The horn was the priority, so she and Gaby would stick with the woman. But they still didn't have an ID for the male suspect. As the man rose to pay his bill, Willson pounded out a quick text to Danny: *Black man coming out of restaurant now in red shirt & bright knitted cap. He'll be in white Toyota truck. Grab our vehicle quick! Follow him, tell me where he goes. I need address if he's from around here. Don't approach — dangerous. Go now! I'll stay in touch.*

The Korean woman was back on her phone. Was she calling someone to confirm the deal was done, or just phoning for a ride? Willson wrote another text, this time to Bohitile, who was still out in the parking lot, sitting in Trang's truck: *Male suspect leaving. Trang will follow him w our vehicle. Woman here. Has package. Start truck. I'll come out when she does. Stand by. We'll follow her.*

Watching the male suspect walk out the door, Willson felt a momentary sense of panic — had she made the right decision, relying on Danny? Would he be able to follow the guy without being seen? Could he get an address for the suspect without being observed or hurt? He was not a trained police officer. Had she just put him in danger?

The two suspects were heading in different directions, and Willson's team had only two vehicles to work with. Willson had two choices: either join Bohitile in following the woman with the horn, or run to her truck and follow the male suspect with Trang. She made her decision: follow the horn.

When the woman began to gather her belongings, including the new duffle bag she'd inherited, Willson tossed twenty Namibian dollars on the table, waited until the woman had paid her bill at the till, then followed her out the door.

A black Mercedes sedan was parked directly in front of the restaurant. Waves of heat shimmered from the hood. Willson walked toward Bohitile, but turned her head slightly to watch as a man climbed out of the driver's seat of the sedan and placed the woman's belongings in the open trunk. Willson made a mental note of the licence plate number, along with the fact that the Korean woman kept the duffle bag with her as she slid into the back seat.

Willson walked quickly over to Trang's truck and jumped into the passenger's seat. By the time she'd put on her seatbelt, Bohitile already had them moving.

"Follow that car," said Willson, grinning. "Is the signal strong?"

"It was a second ago," Bohitile said as she passed Willson the GPS receiver. "Did you see the licence plate?"

"Yep, I got the number."

"No, I mean did you notice the colour? It was red. That means it's a diplomatic vehicle."

"So, that part of the story, at least, is true."

"Also, the car will be easy to follow ... though it may be tougher for us to take action."

"Why?" asked Willson as they turned out of the parking lot. She looked at the receiver and saw the blinking icon ahead of them.

"There's an unwritten rule that we don't stop or bother vehicles with diplomatic plates."

"Oh. We'll sort that out later. Can you tell from the plate number which country it's from?"

Bohitile looked at Willson and nodded.

"And where is this one from?" They were now turning right onto C41. The black sedan was a long block ahead.

"Believe it or not, it's from Russia. North Korea doesn't have an embassy in Namibia, so our suspect must have caught a ride with the next best thing."

"What the hell is going on, Gaby?" asked Willson.

This case was getting stranger by the second.

Three hours later, still following the black sedan and thankful that Trang's gas tank had been almost full when they left Opuwo, Willson and Bohitile reached the edge of Helao Nafidi, the border town that was formed when five smaller Namibian communities amalgamated. It was clear that the North Korean woman and the rhino horn on the seat beside her were heading across the border to Angola.

While Bohitile drove, Willson had received several texts from Danny Trang. He had followed their male suspect to a house in Oukongo, a small village a few kilometres north of Opuwo. Under the guise of a lost tourist, he had approached the house and asked the man for directions. Two little girls there called the man "Daddy," so Trang knew this was actually the man's home. The directional information Trang reported back would be enough for one of them to arrest the man later, once they had the woman in custody.

Trang had asked Willson via text what she wanted him to do next. She'd replied: *Stay around Opuwo for a while until we know what we're doing? We may be coming back there. Don't know yet. Shouldn't be too long.*

"We're going to have to make a call here, Jenny," said Bohitile. "That's the border," she said, lifting one finger off the steering wheel to point. "If we don't stop them soon, they're going to sail right through. And if that happens, then the horn is gone for good. I have no jurisdiction in Angola, and we'll lose the signal once the car is more than two kilometres beyond the border."

"Shit!" said Willson. "I've never been up here before — I had no idea we were this close. It's now or never. At the next intersection, pull out in front of them. Jump out and flash your badge at the driver, and I'll go for the woman in the back seat."

"Understood," Bohitile said. When the black sedan slowed for the intersection, she accelerated past, then turned her wheel hard to the right, putting the truck perpendicular to the sedan's front grille. Bohitile's past training — most of which she couldn't talk about — had clearly kicked in.

The truck was still moving when Willson began to open her door. She felt Bohitile slam the gearshift into park, stopping Trang's rental truck with a lurch. By then, Willson's feet were on the ground, and she was pulling herself out of the seat. She took three quick steps toward the sedan's passenger's side ... then it began to roll forward. "He's moving. He's moving!"

Willson saw Bohitile try unsuccessfully to grab a door handle as the sedan roared by; its side mirror clipped her on the hip. With her other hand, she was trying to clear her pistol, so the sudden impact spun her sideways. As the car moved away, Willson caught a glimpse of the North Korean diplomat in the back seat: her face stared out the passenger-side window without expression, like this kind of thing had happened before. Willson saw the duffle bag beside her, with the woman's right hand placed on top of it protectively. The diplomat would have no idea who Willson's team was or why they'd tried to stop her. But that no longer mattered. She had to know that, whoever they were, they'd failed in their attempt.

With a bang, the black sedan jumped the curb. Then, with a squeal of tires, it was back on the street, heading north. It happened so quickly, so smoothly, that Willson knew the driver must have professional experience in evading pursuit and capture. Bohitile had her pistol trained on the sedan, but just then, a bus full of children crossed the intersection. She raised her pistol to the sky, making a split-second decision not to fire. Willson knew her partner had had no other choice.

Willson and Bohitile could do nothing but watch as border officers waved the black sedan through and into Angola. The car barely slowed down. The horn and its implanted tracking chip were gone.

"Shit!" Willson yelled. "We lost them! The last two days — everything we've done — a complete waste of time."

Bohitile had her hands on her head. "All we got out of this is a guy we can arrest for illegal possession and the assault on Sam."

"And unless that woman comes back into Namibia, we have no way of going after her."

Bohitile turned her head. "Was this just a one-off? One foreign buyer buying a single horn? Or do you think this is the tip of an iceberg?"

Willson shook her head. "I have no idea. But now we've got to concentrate on tracking the other two horns that Inspector Nashili has in his grubby little hands." She pounded a fist on the dashboard. "Son of a bitch, I can't believe she got away."

CHAPTER 32

As the door at the end of the hallway banged open, Sam Mogotsi sat up on the concrete bunk. He hadn't seen or heard from anyone since he'd been arrested, and he hoped that Jenny Willson or one of the other anti-poaching unit members had told his wife where he was and why. Maybe today would be the day he'd be allowed to see her.

But he heard only one set of footsteps coming down the hall. It was most likely one of the officers coming to harass him again, trying to get him to confess to something. Like the last time, the officers had been relentless, using every trick in the book to get him to talk. Kugara had continued to demand to know why he had been wearing a wire and who had been on the other end listening. But Mogotsi was just as determined to stay silent. He didn't dare ask about his family in case the police used that against him. So far there'd been no appearance by the inspector.

Kugara appeared at the door of his cell. "Sam," he said, "your lawyer is here to see you."

"My lawyer? I don't have a lawyer."

"This woman says she's your lawyer and she's here to see you."

"What is her name?"

"Dinnah Usiku. Do you want to see her or not?"

Mogotsi smiled. He remembered the name from his interview with Willson and Veronica Muafangejo after they had forced his release the last time. Willson had told him that Usiku was a top defence lawyer from some-where south of Windhoek — Keetmanshoop, maybe? — and that she had agreed to represent him. Because he'd been released and because he hadn't heard anything more from Kamanjab police since then, there'd been no reason to speak to her. But now was as good a time as any.

"I'll definitely talk to her. Are you bringing her in here?"

"No. She demanded to meet with you in an interview room." Kugara put the key in the door but looked in at Mogotsi without turning it. "I'm going to ask you one last time, Sam, who was listening on the other end of the wire?"

"Why are you so worried about that?" Mogotsi asked. "Is this you asking, or your boss?"

The sergeant's face shifted to something between a smile and a grimace. "I haven't told him what I found yet," he said. "I'm still trying to decide."

"Tell me, Sergeant," said Mogotsi, "were you one of the guys who came to my house that night to frighten my family?"

"I don't know what you're talking about."

Mogotsi was about to speak, to tell Kugara that no matter who'd been listening on the wire, he'd now been openly implicated in the theft of two rhino horns. Before he could say anything, though, a woman's voice came from down the hall. "Where's my client?"

Looking resigned, Kugara opened the door and motioned him down the hall.

Mogotsi smiled as he rose from the bunk. He liked this lawyer's style already. She was taking charge of the situation, forcing the sergeant to do what she wanted. He stretched slowly and deliberately, obliging the sergeant to stand and wait for him. If the lawyer was taking charge, then he'd play his part, too.

Dinnah Usiku was a large woman, wider than she was tall, with thick, dark hair framing a pretty face. She pushed a pair of thick-framed, bejewelled eyeglasses onto her head when Mogotsi entered the room, then gave him a wide smile as she stood and reached across the table to shake his hand. "Pleased to meet you, Sam, I am Dinnah Usiku. Jenny Willson sent me."

"Thanks very much for coming to see me, Miss Usiku, and for agreeing to represent me."

"My pleasure, Sam. Jenny said you needed my assistance, so here I am. Please, call me Dinnah."

Mogotsi started to speak, but was interrupted by the lawyer.

"Sergeant, you can leave us now. I wish to meet with my client in private."

Kugara paused in the doorway, clearly uncertain as to how to respond. "But my inspector said that I was supposed to stay with the prisoner ..."

"I don't care what he said. I drove all the way up here to have a private and confidential meeting with my client, and that's what I intend to do. Do you want me to contact a magistrate and get your charges, however weak they may be, thrown out because of a lack of due process?"

"No, ma'am, but I'm following orders."

Usiku waved her hand at the man, as if trying to rid herself of a bothersome insect. "Leave us now."

Mogotsi couldn't help but smile as the sergeant backed out of the room and closed the door behind him. The lawyer motioned for him to take a seat.

"Miss … Dinnah," Mogotsi said, "I must tell you that I don't have any money to pay you. I appreciate your coming, but I'm sure I cannot afford you."

"That should not be your worry, Sam. I understand from Ms. Willson that you were helping her and her unit and were arrested as a result."

"I was trying to prove to her that I was telling the truth about not killing my brother-in-law or being involved in poaching. So, I agreed to be part of what they called their sting operation. But it backfired on me. I was not only assaulted, but I also ended up here in jail again."

"Well, I'm here to try to turn things around for you."

Mogotsi sat forward in the chair. "Where do we start?"

The lawyer opened a file folder. "First," she said, "tell me what led to your arrest, and what the police said when they arrested you."

The memory of the arrest in the Outjo parking lot was still fresh in Mogotsi's mind. "This was my second time in Outjo. The first time, I tried to sell a horn, but a man showed up who claimed it was his. He punched me and took the it. After I got out of the hospital, the unit sent me back there. This time, I was to sell two rhino horns."

"And what happened?"

"I contacted another buyer through a car guard. I spoke to him on the phone and he said he would come to see me. But instead, the police showed up."

"And what happened when they showed up?"

"It was like they knew I had the horns. They searched my truck and found them right away. Sergeant Kugara," Mogotsi said, pointing with his thumb toward the closed door, "was the guy who arrested me. He cuffed me and put me in his vehicle. But Inspector Nashili was there, too, and he took the horns with him in his truck."

"That matches exactly with what Ms. Willson told me on the phone, Sam. So, that's good." She clicked her pen a few times. "How is it that the police showed up, do you think?"

"Well, Ms. Willson told me to tell my cousin about what we were doing."

"Why your cousin?"

"I told her I thought he might be a police informant. He was in trouble with them once, but was never charged."

"So, she told you to tell someone who might then tell the police?" Miss Usiku smiled and made a note in the file.

"What happens now?" he asked.

Usiku looked up from her notes. "When they arrested you, what did they say was the reason?"

"Inspector Nashili told the sergeant to arrest me for illegal possession of rhino horn."

"And when you got here?"

"Sergeant Kugara found the wire on me. It broke into pieces when it hit the floor after he pulled it off me. He kept asking who put it on me, who was listening, but I said nothing."

"Good. And then what?"

"After that, the sergeant looked like he'd seen a ghost. He went quiet, then he finally told me he was holding me on suspicion of murdering Chioto."

"No mention of the rhino horn?"

"None. It was like he forgot all about it once he knew I'd been wearing a wire." Mogotsi looked at the door, then dropped his voice. "In fact, the sergeant asked me again about the wire just before he brought me in here. He hasn't told his boss about it yet. And when I asked if he had been one of the men who had come to my house to scare my family one night, he wouldn't answer."

Usiku smiled widely. "This is good, Sam. I bet the sergeant is trying to figure out where to place his bets, where his allegiances should lie. But if he said you were arrested on the murder charge, it works in your favour. There's already a previous magistrate's ruling in place on that same charge for you to be released into the custody of Muafangejo and Willson."

"But I'm back in jail again."

"Not for long, not once the magistrate hears that the inspector rearrested you, contrary to her ruling."

"How will she hear that?"

"I'll tell her as soon as we've finished here."

"So, I might get out of here?"

"Unless something goes wrong, you should be out no later than tomorrow morning. They won't be able to hold you on the murder charge, and they sure as hell don't seem to want to hold you on the possession charge. If they do, there's a long list of questions I'm going to ask. Like how police from Kamanjab knew you had those horns in Outjo, and when you'd be there, and where those horns are now."

"My wife will be happy to hear that, I think. She's tired of me being in jail. Has she been told where I am?"

"Yes, we contacted her to let her know the situation and that you would be home soon." Usiku pulled her glasses from her head and twirled them around the fingers of her left hand as she stared at him. "While I've got you here, let's talk about this murder charge, Sam. I've read your file in detail, and it seems that while the police haven't handled it as professionally as I would have liked, every piece of evidence they have points to you as having murdered your brother-in-law."

"But I didn't!"

The glasses kept twirling. "If I'm going to represent you, Sam, then I need the truth from you. You know and I know that the evidence makes you look guilty, very guilty. If this were going before a magistrate or a jury right now, I'd give you only fifty-fifty odds, at best, that you wouldn't be facing a long prison sentence."

Mogotsi slumped forward on the table, his head in his hands. "I don't know what I can say. No one seems to believe me. That's why I agreed to help Ms. Willson and her team ... so they'd believe me."

Usiku put her glasses back on and picked up her pen. "Let's start at the beginning, shall we?"

For the next two hours, Mogotsi answered every question the lawyer asked. It was an exhausting experience, and he had to keep his wits about him. Usiku's questions came like bullets from a machine gun, covering a wide range of topics. Mogotsi found it confusing and upsetting to go over everything again. He felt off-balance. The more he told the story, the less sense it made. And if that was how *he* perceived things, then he could only imagine what the lawyer might be thinking.

"Explain to me again how it is that the ballistics evidence confirms that it was *your* gun used to murder Shipanga, and the rhino ... and that your fingerprints were on the gun."

"I don't know," Mogotsi said, now almost in tears. "I told the police that I hadn't used my gun in a few years, not since I stopped ... uh ... shooting the animals."

"Stopped *poaching*, you mean?"

"Yes, stopped poaching."

"And when was the last time you'd seen your gun before Chioto's death?"

"I told the police that it was probably a few weeks. I couldn't remember for sure. I kept it locked in my shed ... I just don't know when I last saw it."

"So, it could have been at your house ... or not."

"That's true. The police said it wasn't there when they searched that first day. I can't say whether it was or wasn't. But then, later, they said they had found it. I don't know what to believe, and they've never told me where or when they found it."

"All of a sudden, they had the gun."

"Right."

"That doesn't make a lot of sense, does it?"

"No."

"What do you think happened?"

"The only thing I can think of is that they *did* find it when they first searched my place, but wouldn't say so — not to me or anyone else. Then they held on to it for some reason."

"You think something funny is going on with the police?"

"I keep thinking they're trying to frame me, make it look like I killed Chioto."

"Why would they do that?"

"Maybe because they know who *did* do it, and they're protecting them?"

"What about the murdered rhino?"

"What about it?"

"Did you have anything to do with that, Sam? Did Chioto maybe get in your way when you decided to get back into the poaching game? Did he try to stop you?"

"No!" Mogotsi yelled. This interview was not going the way he had expected it to. Wasn't this lawyer supposed to be on his side? "I'm done with killing rhinos now. My job is to protect them, and I take that very seriously. Chioto and I both felt the same way about our new jobs. It's changed my life, and my family's life …"

"Speaking of Chioto, you said in your statement that you couldn't have killed him because you were with your wife in Outjo."

Mogotsi was challenged by the pace of the lawyer's questions, and the many changes of direction. He couldn't imagine what it would be like to be in a courtroom with her. "That's right."

"But I reviewed the evidence, Sam, and it looks like there's a twenty-four- to thirty-six-hour window when Chioto could have been killed. You have a confirmed alibi for only part of that time."

"I thought Chioto was killed when Natasha and I were in Outjo?"

Usiku stared hard at Mogotsi. "I'm not sure where you heard that, Sam, but that was never confirmed. Because wild animals had their way with the body after he died, the investigators can't absolutely pin the time of death down to anything less than a thirty-six-hour window."

"Oh." Mogotsi felt a bead of sweat running down his back. "What does that mean for me?"

"It means that my defence of you is not going to be easy, Sam. I still think there are things you're not telling me. This does *not* add up."

Fear and uncertainty ran through Mogotsi's body like adrenalin. He'd assumed that working with Jenny Willson and her team would somehow make this all go away. He realized now how foolish he'd been. This was far from over.

CHAPTER 33

"Trace," said Willson, "give me some good news. I'm stuck in O-hell up here."

Willson and Bohitile were parked in the shade of a massive acacia tree outside the Protea Hotel in Ondangwa, sixty kilometres south of the Namibia–Angola border.

Brown's voice was crisp over the cellphone speaker, although they could hear highway noises in the background. "Sorry about losing the horn, Jenny. Shit happens, but I know you both tried. I do have some interesting news for you, though. Where are you?"

"We're in Ondangwa, trying to decide which direction to go. I wanted to hear what was happening down there before we chose."

"Head south on the B1 toward Tsumeb. And hurry. If I were you, I'd ignore the speed limits."

Willson, now in the driver's seat, put the truck into gear and accelerated out of the parking lot. "Why Tsumeb?" She punched the gas pedal to pass a loaded truck that looked like it could be a pain in the ass on the highway. Better to get past it now.

"Like you asked, we followed the inspector and the horns he took from Sam. If it had been a legit seizure, he would have gone back to his station and logged the horns in as evidence. Instead, he drove to Otjiwarongo, less than an hour away from Outjo. He sat in a parking lot there for more than three hours, using his cellphone periodically. We were watching him from the next block."

"Was he setting up a meeting with someone?"

"We don't know," Brown said. "He didn't head back to Kamanjab with the horns. After one final phone call, he drove off, so it must have been something important. We're now following him north on the B1, which leads toward Otavi, Tsumeb, and Grootfontein ... or he could be headed to one of the borders to Angola, Zambia, or Botswana."

"Who's we?"

"I'm riding with Ben and Neus. Betty and Monica are behind us in a second vehicle. They'll follow him when we stop for gas, and then we'll catch up again. We'll do that all the way to the border if we have to."

"Good. Do you really think he's headed toward us?"

"He could be heading anywhere in the north or northeast. But at some point, you and he are bound to cross paths. I'm following a very strong signal from the horns."

"Okay, Tracy, we're on our way. I'm not going to let another goddamned set of horns leave Namibia."

"Roger that."

"Hey, Tracy?"

"Yeah?"

"Have you heard how Veronica's doing?"

"Good. I'm told she's out of hospital and back home with her parents near Windhoek. She has to wear dark sunglasses for a few more weeks until the doctors are sure there's no permanent damage to her eyes. But the prognosis is excellent."

"Fantastic. I look forward to seeing her again … and to her being able to see me."

As they drove, Willson stared out the window, her mind partly on the passing landscape and partly on the twists and turns of the investigation. For weeks they'd been chasing shadows, pursuing unknown people who were executing rhinos, mutilating their bodies, selling their horns for cash. As if they were the few remaining dinosaurs of an earlier era, rhinos were in danger of disappearing forever. And yet, these men (and, they now knew, at least one woman) did not care. They were driven by greed, no matter what the consequences were. If this police inspector was involved, was pure greed his motivation? Or something else? No matter — Willson had come from Canada to make a difference, and she wasn't going to let this case unravel; she wouldn't leave this amazing country with nothing to show for it but a bunch of failed intentions. Even with an enticing job offer in hand from the Conservation Officer Service in B.C. She'd received the offer by email, but had yet to respond; she'd vowed to remain in Namibia until this investigation was done.

With that decision settled in her mind, the landscape came into sharper focus for her. In this part of Namibia, the highway traversed a flat land dotted with remote homesteads. Some were the traditional rondavels, circular huts with conical thatched roofs, that she'd seen elsewhere. Many had kraals of upright mopane stems, dry, strong, and predator-proof. Others were built of concrete blocks and used aluminum and plastic for roofs and windows. Domestic goats were common, as were thin, lop-eared cattle, their ribs showing through their taut skin. Everywhere, abandoned plastic shopping bags blew in the wind, sticking to fences and gathering in sad multi-hued piles.

While the sandy soils did support some scattered patches of mopane, fig, and marula trees, Willson was struck by a sense that this whole area was deforested, overgrazed, degraded. Besides being hot, dusty, and arid, it seemed to her that it had been used and abused by humans for decades. Not unlike the rhinos.

Over an hour into their drive, Willson looked ahead to the northern edge of the Etosha Pan, the vast salt pan that was the dominant feature of Etosha National Park. Even though it was now dry, it presented a white, shimmering expanse in the distance, a giant mirage that must have surprised and disappointed early travellers.

Bohitile's voice broke the silence. "They say you can easily see the pan from space. Did anyone tell you its original names?"

Willson nodded. "We caught a glimpse of it on our first tour with Wild Dog Safaris. They told us then, but I had no idea it was this big."

"During the short time of year when there's water in it, it's like a massive mirror on the sky. It's impressive as hell. Every time I see it, I'm still in awe."

They soon passed the turnoff to Etosha's Von Lindequist Gate and Namutoni Camp. Willson had been asleep the last time she came through here, so it was all new country to her. The closer they drove to Tsumeb, the denser the congregation of small homesteads. Many were no more than piles of lumber and sheets of corrugated metal. Goats, chickens, dogs, and soccer-playing children were everywhere, as were exhausted-looking mothers talking on cellphones. As she had with the pedestrians on the streets of Opuwo, Jenny wondered who these women were talking to, what kind of life they led.

"Gaby," said Willson, "could you give Tracy a call to see where they are?"

Bohitile punched Brown's number into her phone, then put it on the seat between them. The phone's screen lit up the cab. The sky outside had shifted to twilight.

"He just turned right at Otavi," Brown said when she answered, "which means he's heading northwest toward Grootfontein."

"Do you think he's heading to the border?" Willson asked.

"Still no way to know. It's about ninety kilometres to Groot for him, and just over fifty for you from Tsumeb. If you hustle, you can easily beat him there."

"What's he driving?"

"He's in a marked police vehicle, a white Toyota Tundra crew cab with a black metal push-grille on the front and a light bar on top."

"You're sure he still has the horns?"

"I am. We've had him in our sight — or on GPS — since we left Outjo. Both signals are strong."

"Okay," Willson said. "He's met all of us, so we'll have to stay well back. We can't risk him seeing us. What's he doing up here? He's so far out of his district that there's no doubt he's no longer on police business."

"Agreed. I'll keep you posted. There are lots of side roads between Otavi and Groot, so we'll stay a bit closer to him."

With Willson driving, it took only twenty minutes to reach Grootfontein. They drove toward the downtown area, passing agricultural fields on the way in, filled their gas tank quickly, then parked at a car dealership so they could keep an eye on the main highway into town. They were close enough to the rest of the team that they could again communicate on the tactical radio channel.

"Brown from Willson."

"Go ahead."

"Where are you?"

"Just reached the edge of town. Subject is three cars ahead of us."

"Roger that. We're sitting in Maroela Motors on the corner of Okavango Road and Sam Nujoma Street."

"We'll reach you in two minutes."

"Ten-four."

Bohitile spotted the police vehicle first. "There he is! He's turning off the highway onto Sam Nujoma, heading south."

Willson pulled out of the parking spot, waved curtly at a night security guard who was approaching them from the office, then drove south on Sam Nujoma. Waiting at a stop sign, she saw the team's two unmarked vehicles, a private vehicle in between, take the same turn as the inspector had, only a few hundred metres behind him. For a moment, Willson wondered if the inspector knew he was being followed and was purposefully leading them on a wild goose chase across northeastern Namibia. But he wouldn't do that while carrying the two horns, would he? It was more likely that he was so arrogant, so sure of himself, that he had no idea that his movements were under a microscope.

While Bohitile searched her phone for a street map of Grootfontein, Willson crossed the highway and followed the other vehicles.

"There's a police station down here somewhere," said Bohitile. "I was here once before for an … operation. I can't see him going there."

The radio crackled with Brown's voice. "Subject is turning in to the industrial area. Stay back, because the road curves here, and he might see you."

Willson slowed the vehicle. It was now dark. She could see the headlights of the inspector's truck to the right, through the fence of an auto body shop.

Brown's voice again: "Suspect now turning left. Looks like he's at the offices of a construction firm. There's what looks like a repair yard on the east side filled with dump trucks and other highway equipment."

"Roger that," Willson said. "We're going to hang back in a small office complex around the corner. We can see the front of the building through a narrow alley. Do you have eyes on the suspect?"

"Ten-four. The lot is well-lit. Our guy's heading into the main office — without the package. Repeat: suspect inside building without package. Standing by."

"Can you keep eyes on the truck?"

"Ten-four. One of us will set up to the east, and one to the west."

Willson turned to Bohitile, whose fingers were flying on her cellphone keyboard. "Can you get any intel on what that place is, Gaby?"

"Working on that now. Stand by."

Willson drummed her fingers on the steering wheel. After the debacle at the Angolan border, they couldn't afford to lose two more horns, or the opportunity to catch a perpetrator in the act. Or, in this case, to put the inspector's nuts in a wringer. She was now certain he was directly involved in rhino poaching, somehow — perhaps not in the actual shooting of the animals, but he sure as hell was a link in the supply chain.

"I've got it," said Bohitile. "The company is China Tengum Construction Group. Like many, it's a Chinese state-owned company. This is their head office, but they have many branches. There was one in Helao Nafidi, where we just were. They've recently bid on and won several high-profile highway construction projects throughout Namibia. They also have a number of concrete plants in the country."

"A Chinese construction company? This just got interesting again."

"The news website I'm looking at suggests that the company gets its contracts by significantly underbidding

Namibian firms. Allegedly, they do it by bringing in Chinese prisoners."

"Chinese prisoners?"

"Yes, they apparently offer prisoners in China a reduced sentence if they volunteer to come here to work on road projects for no wages. I know of one highway contract they won between Swakopmund and Henties Bay on the coast. They're turning a salt road into a paved road, or, as we say here, 'bringing it up to bitumen standards.' When they're working, all the trucks have Chinese symbols on them, and there's not a black or brown face anywhere on the crews."

"Huh. If working in the hot Namibian sun for nothing is better than being in a Chinese prison, what does that say about their penal system?"

"Yeah …"

"Why does the Namibian government allow it?"

"Because the Chinese companies do the work cheap and fast, and because they promise to hire young local men who don't have jobs. They do some of that, for sure. But of course, they also pay them slave wages and break every labour law we have."

"That's got to make it tough for Namibian companies to compete. Is there money changing hands, as well?"

"I can't say. There's some talk of that, but our current president is cracking down hard on corruption. If bribes are being paid, I assume it's farther down the food chain."

"China Tengum. Tengum doesn't sound Chinese."

"I don't know about that," Bohitile said, gazing back down at the phone screen, "but it says here that the company's CEO is a man by the name of Tengum Li. Here's a picture." She shifted the phone so Willson could see the photo. Tengum Li was unremarkable, a dark-haired, stern-looking man in his late fifties, thin in the face, wearing a dark suit and no expression.

Willson shook her head. "What the hell is Nashili doing *here*? He's in uniform and driving a marked police vehicle. This can't be anything official, can it?"

"Unlikely. This guy makes me sick. I'm sure looking forward to taking him down."

CHAPTER 34

It was an hour of sitting and waiting before the radio again crackled to life. "All teams. Suspect and two men are coming out of the building," Brown said, the excitement in her voice evident.

"Roger that," said Willson, "we see them."

Bohitile had already pulled out a pair of specialized binoculars. Willson wondered what other goodies her colleague had in her ever-present pack.

"What do you see, Gaby?"

"One of them is definitely the inspector, but I don't recognize the other two. They appear to be black males, both in their twenties or thirties. Very large."

"What are they doing?" Willson thought back to her meeting with the Himba women and their story of an Asian man and two locals showing up in towns in the Kunene region, offering to buy rhino horns. Could these be the same two local guys?

Bohitile offered a running commentary. "They're approaching Nashili's truck ... he's opening the passenger door ... he is passing the bins to one of the men ... he's shut the door ... he's moving around to the driver's side ... he's getting in ... and he's moving."

"Can you see the man with the bins? Where are the bins?" Willson was almost shouting.

"I lost them," Bohitile said. "They moved to where I can't see them."

Willson grabbed the radio mic. "Tracy. Can you see the man with the packages?"

"Roger that. The two men are approaching a black truck. They're putting the packages behind the seats in the crew cab."

"Are they getting in the vehicle?"

"Negative. They're heading back inside the building. But be advised, the subject will pass your location in less than fifteen seconds."

Willson dropped the mic. "Duck!"

Both officers dropped down sideways to the seat, almost banging heads, then waited until they heard a vehicle pass by on the adjacent street. When they popped back up again, they saw the tail lights of the inspector's truck moving away from them.

"Isn't surveillance glamorous?" Bohitile said. She again raised the binoculars to better follow the inspector's trail. "Looks like he's going back the way he came. Yup, he's turning left onto the B8 back toward Otavi."

Willson was immediately back on the radio. "Tracy, what are the GPS signals telling you? Are the packages still in the black truck?"

"Both packages are definitely in the truck now," Brown said. "They're not in the building, and they did not depart the scene in our subject's truck."

"Ten-four. Tracy, can you and Ben come to where we are ASAP? Monica and Betty, please stay there and keep eyes on that truck."

Willson heard two sets of double-clicks on the radio.

"I don't know about you, Gaby," she said, "but it looks like Nashili just gave two seized rhino horns to people who have no business possessing them."

As the other team vehicle backed into a space beside them, Bohitile turned to Willson. "Funny you should say that. This may be all about business. I wonder who the inspector met with, and whether he drove past us with a large chunk of cash in his pocket."

Tracy Brown, in the passenger seat, rolled down her window. Willson did the same on her side.

"Did we see what I think we just saw?" asked Brown. "Did a Namibian police officer hand over a pair of seized rhino horns — horns that are potential evidence in a crime — to an unknown subject?"

"It appears so," Willson said. "We were just discussing whether he might have handed them over or sold them. And if he sold them, whether he now has a pocket full of cash."

Brown nodded. "What are you thinking, Jenny?"

"At first, I thought we should continue to sit on the horns. Because the two men put them in the truck there, it seems likely they'll take them somewhere sooner or later. We've got to follow them and identify anyone who touches them along the way."

"But for now?"

"We follow the inspector back to Kamanjab, stop him, arrest him, interrogate him, and find out once and for all what the hell he's doing."

"If some of us are going to follow Nashili, we'd better get our asses in gear," said Bohitile.

"I agree," said Willson. "So, here's what we'll do. Gaby and I are going to catch up with Nashili now. We'll stop him as soon as we can. Tracy, you and Ben and Monica and Betty stay here, then follow that truck wherever it goes. Search the web for a picture of Tengum Li, in case he shows up. Good luck, and keep us posted." She turned the rental truck's ignition.

Brown held out her hand and high-fived Willson across the gap between the vehicles. "Give 'em hell, Jenny."

Willson put the truck in gear, then punched the gas pedal. They hurtled around corners and back out onto the B8 highway, now heading west toward Otavi, ignoring the speed limit in order to catch up to the inspector. After months in Namibia, Willson was comfortable with driving on the left side of the road, but she found using the manual transmission in Trang's truck to be tricky. It was never good to mistakenly go from fourth gear to first when travelling at passing speed. Engines didn't like that sort of thing, and they let you know.

They finally caught up to Nashili's truck on the outskirts of the small town of Kombat, halfway between Grootfontein and Otavi. At the same time, Bohitile's cell rang.

"Go for Gaby ... Roger that," she said. "Stay with them."

"What?" asked Willson.

"The same two guys, along with an Asian man, just came out of the office building. The three of them are leaving in the truck, and Tracy advises that the packages are with them."

"Here we go," Willson said. "And they're following?"

Bohitile nodded. "They'll keep us posted. They ran the licence plate, and it's registered to the China Tengum Construction Group. They're pretty sure that the Asian man is Tengum Li." She paused for a moment. "So, what are we doing here, Jenny? Are we going to keep following this guy?" She pointed to the police vehicle, now separated from them by only a single vehicle.

"The more I think about it, the more I think we have to take him down, and soon. We can't wait until he gets out to the B1 because there'll be fewer safe places to stop him. We can't let him get to other towns in case he's got money from Li with him and decides to somehow get rid of it. And to be honest, I really want to know what he's got to say for himself. I've been waiting to confront him for a long time. Other than money, I can't imagine why a police inspector would put his career at risk by getting involved in this."

Bohitile was again looking down at the screen on her phone. "Okay, in less than a kilometre there'll be a road going to the left to what looks like an industrial site, maybe a mill. If you can get beside him and force him in there, it'll be a good spot for us to challenge him. *If* we can get him to stop."

"Let's do it." Willson swung out a bit into the oncoming lane so she could see beyond the inspector's truck and the vehicle in between them. "I can see the lights of a truck coming the other way, and then we're good to go." She sat up straighter in the seat and placed both hands on the wheel. Bohitile rolled down her window.

As soon as the truck passed by them, Willson pounded the gas pedal and dropped the transmission into fourth gear. She passed the first vehicle and came up fast on the inspector's truck. When they were parallel with the truck, Nashili looked over at them. Bohitile motioned with her hand for him to pull over. It was a practised motion, her hand like an arrow. For a moment, he looked surprised and confused. She made the same motion again, her hand well outside the window, strong even in the powerful breeze.

"We've got a vehicle coming at us," Willson yelled. "We've got to get over or back off."

Bohitile's motions toward the inspector became more exaggerated. "Get over, you dumbass!" she yelled into the wind.

It was then Nashili saw the approaching vehicle and realized what was about to happen. He must have seen the mill road on his left, because he turned in at the last minute, his tires spraying gravel and dust. At the same time, Willson hit the brakes and tucked in behind him, both hands still on the wheel, her knuckles white. They heard brakes and a horn behind them as the following driver reacted.

The two vehicles bounced down the gravel road, dust flying, both drivers working hard to maintain control as their speeds dropped. They finally came a stop, the inspector's truck resting against a metal gate, his front grille guard bending it slightly, his headlights shining at a cluster of buildings beyond the gate.

Nashili, Bohitile, and Willson all jumped out of their vehicles simultaneously. The inspector spoke first as he came around the back of his truck.

"What the hell are you trying to …" He hesitated. It was clear that he had not, until that moment, realized who it was that had forced him off the highway. "You two! What's the meaning of this? You almost got us all killed!"

"Hello, Inspector Nashili," said Willson. "Strange place to run into each other, isn't it?" Traffic flew by them on the highway, tail lights fading into the dark.

"It's no time to be cute, Ms. Willson. I'll charge you with reckless driving and anything else relevant I can think of."

"I don't think you'll be laying any charges any time soon, *Inspector*." Willson spoke the officer's title like she was spitting on the ground.

"What are you talking about?" he said indignantly.

"What were you doing in Grootfontein?"

"Where I may or may not have been is none of your business."

Willson smiled. "Speaking of business, how was your meeting with Tengum Li?" She relished the look of shock on Nashili's face. But it was gone almost as quickly as it had appeared. She had no proof that he'd met with the Chinese contractor; she'd just wanted to gauge his response.

"What are you talking about?" he said, his composure regained.

"I'm talking about your meeting with Tengum Li in his office in the industrial park in Grootfontein. The meeting where you sold him the two rhino horns you seized from Sam Mogotsi in Outjo. After which you helped his two assistants load the horns into your buyer's truck."

"I don't know what you're talking about."

"I think you know exactly what I'm talking about. What you don't know, however, is that the two horns you took from Mogotsi had GPS transmitters in them. That allowed us, my team and me, to follow you the entire way. We know exactly what you did."

"You can't be serious. You're making this all up. It's preposterous." He looked around as though desperate for someone to agree with him.

"Is it? Then how do we know that after you took the two horns from Sam — and we recorded that entire incident, by the way — you then drove to Otjiwarongo, then all the way to Grootfontein, just to sell the horns to Tengum Li? How would we know all that?"

The inspector sneered at her. "Even if all of that were true — and it's not — what are you going to do about it?"

"I have no choice but to arrest you for illegal possession and trade of controlled wildlife products under Namibia's Controlled Wildlife Products and Trade Act."

"You can't arrest me! You're just a warden from Canada. You have no authority here." The inspector looked at Bohitile. "And you're just a dyke who plays dress-up as a soldier." He turned back to Willson. "This is a joke. I demand that you move your truck, so I can get on my way and do real police business."

"You're in no position to make any demands," Willson said. "The government of this country gave me a badge that looks very much like yours. It gives me the same powers in Namibia as yours does. One of those is the power of arrest, and I'm using that right now. *You* are under arrest." She pulled a set of handcuffs from her belt and began to move toward the inspector.

Suddenly, Nashili pulled his gun. Willson stopped dead as he swung it toward her, holding it in a two-handed grip, the barrel pointed directly at her chest.

"I order you to get out of my way!" he said.

Willson stood her ground, but held her hands up and to the side, showing she was not a physical threat. "I can't do that. You know I can't. I came to Namibia to do my part to stop poaching. You've put me in the position of having to arrest you. You're clearly part of what's going wrong in this country."

Nashili raised the gun slightly, and Willson could see his finger on the trigger.

"Drop your weapon!" The demand came from Bohitile, who stood to Willson's left in the darkness.

Willson knew that the army captain would have her weapon trained on the inspector, and that if she chose to shoot, she would not miss. It should have given Willson some comfort, but the situation was spiralling quickly out of control. With two weapons in play, anything could happen. She watched the inspector's eyes as they shifted back and forth between them.

"It looks like we have a Namibian standoff here," said Nashili, his eyes momentarily back on Bohitile. "Drop your weapon and your girlfriend here won't get hurt."

"Look, Inspector," Willson said, trying to keep her voice calm. "You don't want to get hurt, and neither do I. Put down your weapon. Let's do this peacefully."

His eyes shifted back to Willson, and they were filled with hate. "I worked too long and too hard to let two women drag me down. I won't do it. I'm going to tell you once more, and only once more: stand down and move your vehicle."

Willson saw his finger tighten on the trigger. Bracing for the worst, she jumped when two shots rang out, one after the other. Startled, she wasn't certain for a moment who had shot whom. But then she saw the inspector drop to the ground, two red holes blossoming on the left side of his chest. She froze and looked over at Bohitile, who was still in a combat stance with her gun pointed at the now-prone man.

"Clear his gun," said Bohitile.

Adrenalin still pumping through her system, Willson moved quickly to kick Nashili's gun well away from his arm, and then bent down to check him for a carotid pulse. As she did so, she turned back to Bohitile. "Jesus, Gaby, you just shot a Namibian police inspector. Do you realize how much paperwork you'll have to fill out?"

"I don't care," said Bohitile, "the son of a bitch called me a dyke. I hate that word."

Willson kept her fingers on the man's neck. "He's still alive, but just barely."

She lowered her head close to the man's mouth. "Where's the money that Tengum Li gave you for the rhino horns?"

The inspector coughed. Blood bubbled from the side of his mouth, staining his teeth and cheek. "Fuck you."

"Why? Why did you do this?"

The same response.

"Who shot the rhinos?"

"I ... don't know."

Willson knew she was losing him. "Chioto Shipanga. Who killed Shipanga?"

"Sam did i—"

Willson watched Nashili die; the light left his eyes, his last breath rattled out of his body. She sat back on her haunches. She'd just heard a deathbed statement accusing Sam Mogotsi of his brother-in-law's murder, reinforcing what the inspector had always claimed. Allegedly, in such confessions, people were at their most honest; they had nothing more to live for, no reason to lie. But could she believe this dying man? Or was it his final attempt to distract them from what had really been going on? She had to find out, and Sam Mogotsi was the only person who had the answers she needed.

CHAPTER 35

SEPTEMBER 8, 3:00 A.M.

The ambulance carrying Nashili's body drove away, lights flashing, siren off. Willson and Bohitile sat on the lowered tailgate of Danny Trang's rental truck, talking to another police inspector, who was asking them probing questions.

"He aimed his pistol at you, correct?"

"That's correct," said Willson, exhausted after two days with little sleep. "I was sure he was going to shoot me. He was furious."

"And your colleague here shot him before he could shoot you."

"That is correct, sir," Bohitile said. "I surrendered my weapon to your warrant officer when he took my statement."

"So, the bullets that killed the inspector came from your gun, and you shot that gun. Correct?"

"Correct again, sir. But I must restate that it was self-defence. Jenny had already clearly indicated to him that he was under arrest, and he wouldn't obey my command to drop his weapon."

"I get that," said the inspector. "I want to be sure I have the facts straight. And why did you decide to stop him here?"

"As we told your colleague," Willson said, "our team followed him to an office in Grootfontein, where he appeared to sell two rhino horns to a Chinese contractor by the name of Tengum Li."

"And why do you think he sold horns to this Tengum Li?"

"Because he had them in two bins when he went to the office, because we saw him give those bins to two of the contractor's associates, and because we found a large sum of money on the inspector's person after he died."

"And when you were following him, how did you know he had the horns with him?"

"We hid GPS transmitters in the horns, which is how we were able to follow and watch him all the way from the point where he took them from our informant."

"Why did your informant have rhino horns on him?"

"Because he was part of a sting operation we'd set up to catch horn buyers."

"And the inspector showed up instead?"

"He did, which made us wonder how he knew what we were doing."

The inspector stared at Willson for a moment. "And if he'd been there on official police business, then he shouldn't have taken the horns directly to this" — he looked at his notes — "Tengum Li."

"Exactly," Willson said. "We've been trying to identify all the links in the supply chain for poached rhinos out of the Kunene region, from killer to buyers. Your colleague seems to be one of those links."

"I see. And how much money was he carrying when he died?"

"He had one hundred thousand Namibian dollars in an envelope tucked in his uniform shirt. If he'd carried it on the left side of his shirt, he might still be alive."

"What did you say?"

"I said, if he'd —"

"No, I mean the amount he was carrying."

"One hundred thousand. It's in our truck for safe-keeping. We decided to stop him here so we could safely confront him, arrest him, and seize the money as evidence."

The inspector's face registered shock. "That's more than four times our annual salary as inspectors."

Willson stared at him. "I know. That was a hell of an incentive for him, wasn't it?"

The inspector shook his head. "We are trying so hard to stop poaching. To find out that one of our people was involved makes me furious."

Bohitile's cellphone rang. "Go for Gaby … She's right here." Bohitile handed Willson the phone. "It's Tracy."

Willson wandered away to take the call. "Hi, Tracy."

"Are you guys okay there? Gaby phoned me earlier to tell me what happened."

"We're good. Things are winding down here. More importantly, what's happening there?"

"We're in Tsumeb, near a railway siding on the edge of town. It's a treed, out-of-the-way spot behind an industrial area. We followed the black truck here."

"Is one of the men there Tengum Li?"

"We think so. But we can't say for sure. We only got a quick glimpse under the lights in the parking lot. It sure looked like him."

"And?" Willson waved a hand at Bohitile, who was by the truck. "Map!" she yelled.

"Okay, after we got here, they wrapped the bins together in multiple plastic bags, sealed them with packing tape, then loaded them on the train between what looks like bags of charcoal. The charcoal is in big white bags, and the horns are tucked in amongst them. Ben got some good pictures with a big telephoto lens of them doing it. And our GPS receiver confirms that the horns are in the train car."

"Holy shit," Willson said. "Danny told me that he'd heard about men shipping horn, and maybe elephant tusks, on trains from up north down to Walvis Bay. Apparently, they then get put on slow boats to China. Literally."

"I guess we've uncovered this end of the supply chain, then," Brown said. "The package is in the third railcar from the back. I've recorded its registration numbers. What do you want us to do?"

"What are they doing now — Li and his boys?"

"The train isn't moving yet, so the three of them are hanging around smoking, watching the railcar. They've made several phone calls since arriving. We think they're waiting for the train to leave."

"So, you're watching them watch the train? Must be like watching paint dry."

"Yup," Brown said. "They said there'd be days like this. And me sitting here with no popcorn. Ben believes they chose a load of charcoal thinking that horns wouldn't be sniffed out by dogs."

"I'd never have thought of that. Smart."

"Not so smart, because Ben says Neus could still find them. So, what say you, boss?"

"I say stay there until they leave. Do Monica and Betty still have tracking gear and drones in their truck?"

"They do."

"Then I'm thinking that when the train finally leaves, I want you and Ben to arrest the three men. Seize their phones and bring the men to Otjiwarongo. I'll have my prosecutor friend, Fred Mokgoro, meet you there. He'll know a place we can put them that isn't compromised by any of our dead inspector's friends. We need them in custody and incommunicado at least until the train reaches Walvis Bay. If it's going that far."

"Sounds good, Jenny. And Betty and Monica?"

"If it's possible, I want them to track the train using the GPS signals and the drone. We're nearly at Otavi, so we'll meet them there, and then we can follow the horns across the country." She ran her finger across the map of Namibia. "In some places, I see that the TransNamib tracks parallel the highway, so we should be able to get good GPS signals and keep the train in sight. In others, however, the tracks are some distance away, so we'll have to rely on the drone to maintain eyes on the train. We can't lose sight of it, not for a moment. And if anyone touches the package along the way, we need to identify them. If they take the package, we follow them and not the train."

"We're on it. I'll pass all that on to Betty and Monica. Once we have the men in custody in Otjiwarongo, should we try to find you?"

"Absolutely. We'll need help tracking the train on the way down, and we don't know what we'll find if and when we get to Walvis Bay."

CHAPTER 36

After eighteen hours, with the three team vehicles alternately tracking the TransNamib train and its precious cargo, they finally arrived at the Walvis Bay docks. Willson and Brown were back together again. They'd taken turns driving and catnapping — two hours here, three hours there — as they drove across the country at the same speed as the train. When it stopped, which was more often than they had anticipated, they stopped. When it moved, they moved. They were certain that no one had approached or taken the packages during the journey; the GPS signals remained strong. Nervous energy kept them awake, despite their deep exhaustion.

Willson, most of all, felt the tension. Her entire time in Namibia seemed to be coming down to this one night on a remote section of these docks on the western edge of the African continent. If they could successfully arrest the men here — men who, if their intel was right, would come to check the horns — and if they could then seize the horns before they were moved onto a ship, they would tie up most of the loose ends in the case. They would, hopefully, be dismantling an entire pipeline for illicit rhino horn and successfully prosecuting the players.

But even if that all happened without incident, there were still two unresolved issues that she'd have to deal with when she returned to Kamanjab: figuring out whether Sam Mogotsi was being honest about his role in Shipanga's murder and the rhino poaching in Klip River … and deciding what to do about Danny Trang.

Two hours earlier, Trang had texted her to say that he'd gone back to Hobatere Lodge to finish the research for his article. He still had her truck and he seemed disillusioned, perhaps even angry. Even though Trang had helpfully discovered the residence of the man who'd assaulted Mogotsi, Willson had absentmindedly left him to cool his heels in Opuwo. She stared at his last text, which had arrived only moments before.

Jenny — back at Hobatere. Here for one more day, then heading to airport and Canada. If I don't hear from you, will drop your truck off at Kamanjab. Pls return my truck to Windhoek airport depot earliest. I assume you'll pay for rental and any damages, and for shipping my gear home. Despite everything, enjoyed meeting and working with you. Maybe see you back home. If not, take care of yourself.

PS — I was always honest with you.

With her gut in a knot, Willson saw that Trang had been surprisingly gracious, though uncharacteristically curt. Deep down, however, she fully understood that even that modicum of grace toward her was more than she deserved for the way she'd treated him. She had used him when it suited her and had mistrusted and mistreated him almost every time they'd met, even though he'd given her every reason to trust him, to treat him with respect.

Willson rolled down the driver's side window. Borne by light breezes, the rank aromas of stale seafood and spilled diesel fuel competed for dominance. For a few seconds, she smelled the sea. Then it was gone, the dueling smells of petrochemicals and fish returning. Willson tossed her phone in the back seat. "Jesus," she said, "why am I so screwed up?"

Brown whistled, shook her head, then smiled. "Where do I begin?"

"Seriously. Danny has been nothing but helpful, nothing but open and honest. And yet, I've treated him like a piece of shit. Why can't I figure out who to trust and who not to? He must think I'm an asshole."

"If I'd gone through what you have, Jenny, I'm not sure if I would know the difference, either."

"That's not a good excuse for being an asshole."

"Will you see him again?"

"I have no idea. He's only in Namibia for one more day, then he's heading home. If I don't get back to Hobatere, or at least Kamanjab, before he goes, I won't get a chance to talk to him, to apologize."

"Did you tell him that you've been offered the conservation officer job?"

"No. And I don't know if that'll be good news for him … or if it'll make him move away."

Brown smiled. "Does it really matter? Before you take that job, Jenny, remember that there'll be lots of new opportunities for you after this. You did a hell of a job back home, and you've now got overseas experience. Many agencies will be interested in you. You could even come work for us in the U.S. Fish and Wildlife Service. Maybe do some undercover work."

Willson turned to look at Brown. She'd already decided to accept the B.C. job offer, although she hadn't yet done so. However, her friend's comments hit her as if she'd come out of a dark tunnel; the sudden illumination was bright, yet overwhelming, the big sky above dramatically expanded her perspective.

"Are you serious?"

"Totally serious. You've got the skills, the drive, and the brains to tackle all sorts of new challenges. I mean, if you really want the B.C. job, take it. But don't feel as though it's your only option. It's not. And we *do* make a good team. Whatever you decide," said Brown with a knowing look, "here's hoping we wrap this up soon so you'll get that chance to chat with Danny before he leaves."

"I don't know what the hell I'll say to him."

"How about a simple 'I'm sorry,' like you did with me?"

"Is that enough?"

"It was the best thing you could've said to me when you did, and — though I barely know Danny — I'm willing to bet he'll think the same."

"Maybe you're right."

Through an eight-foot-high chain-link fence, Willson and Brown were watching a small siding at the south end of the port, far from the massive fuel tanks, ship repair yards, and myriad seafood processors that dominated the rest of the facility. The other two teams, with Bohitile, Mushimba, and Neus in one vehicle and Tjikuzu and Hauwanga in the other, were on the opposite side of the fence. Willson had spaced them so they each had a different view of the three railcars, which a small crew of workers had quietly separated from the rest. They now sat on the isolated siding. All three vehicles were parked close to gates in the fence in case they had to respond quickly. And they'd made sure to cut the locks on those gates, so they would open in a hurry.

Three hours earlier, Willson and her team had entered the docks pretending to be looking for illegal immigrants coming off fishing boats — at least, that was what they'd told the bored port officer at the south gate of NamPort. They'd hoped that the officer, who appeared to have just woken up when they rolled up to his guard office, wouldn't tip off the men who might come for the horns, or the authorities that were allegedly turning a blind eye to the smuggling.

"What I can't figure out," Willson said, "is why these guys chose to ship the horns here by train. Why not simply drive them down?"

"I wondered the same thing," Brown said. "The only thing I can think of is that there was something they were worried about. Maybe it was police checkpoints on the highways? Maybe it was trying to get the horns into the port undetected?"

"I mean, on one hand, it's quite ingenious when you think about it. What police officer is ever going to stop a freight train and go through the cargo from one end to the other? But on the other hand, it's risky because the horns are out of their hands for nearly two days. When they put a horn or a tusk on a train, they lose all control of it … even if they've paid off some of the railway guys."

"I hope they'll tell us when we finally catch them," Brown said. Her eyes were bright in the dark of the truck's cab.

An hour later, just when Willson began to think that her fears had been realized, that the bad guys had somehow been tipped off, the radio crackled.

"I've got movement to the north," said Bohitile, her voice quiet. "Two vehicles. Maybe a car and a truck. All I can see are headlights."

"Roger that," Willson said. "I see them. Everyone stand by."

Double-clicks on the radio in response.

Willson and Brown, because they were closest to the rail cars, slumped down in their seats so their heads weren't silhouetted by the oncoming lights. When the two vehicles stopped about twenty-five metres away, they saw that one of the two was a police SUV, the symbol clearly visible on the driver-side door. The other was a dark-coloured Lexus sedan. For a moment, Willson thought of Tengum Li. But he and his two cronies were in a jail cell in Otjiwarongo. So, the occupants of the car could be yet another link in the horn supply chain. And the man in the police vehicle was at best their protector, at worst, a co-conspirator. Or they could have nothing to do with it at all.

"That's not another police officer, is it?" whispered Willson. "Do we have to shoot this one, too?"

Brown shrugged. "I don't know, but we have to assume it is." She shook her head in disgust. The man in the police SUV stepped out first. He was of medium build and wore dark civilian clothes, a hint that he wasn't here on official business. He circled around the vehicles as if checking to ensure the surroundings were clear. He paused when he saw the rental truck. Willson thought he might approach them, so she shrank down even more, banging her knees against the glove compartment. Her eyes were just able to peer over the dash. After a tense moment, he continued his searching. At that point, Willson realized that using a dusty truck for surveillance — with a fold-up tent on top of the canopy — could have gone badly. A truck geared for camping was significantly out of place in industrial docks. They were lucky.

Finally, Willson saw the lone man nod once toward the sedan. The front doors opened simultaneously, and a man emerged from each side. Together, the three men turned on flashlights and pointed them at the ground, then walked quickly toward the railcars, pausing to check their registration numbers.

"Steady," said Willson on the radio. "We wait until they touch the package. If they unwrap it to check it, even better."

The two men from the sedan climbed up on the railcar and began wrestling with the heavy bags of charcoal. The other, the man who might or might not be a police officer, stood at one end, his head swivelling, still looking for threats.

When Willson saw the men pull something out of a dark gap between the white of the charcoal bags and pass it down to their colleague, she whispered "Go!" into the microphone.

Brown turned on the headlights as Willson exited the truck. The other two teams did the same. The three men were suddenly illuminated in a triangle of brilliant light. As she came around the front of the truck, Willson yelled, "Police! Don't move! Hands above your heads." She heard similar calls from other team members.

As expected, the two men atop the railcar jumped down and began sprinting away from them. Willson didn't care, because she and Brown had already agreed to take down whomever was closest, and that was the man who might or might not be a police officer.

The man saw them coming and hesitated. This gave Willson time to crash through the unlocked gate, Brown right behind her. When the man finally started to run, the two women were only metres behind him. With adrenalin pumping, filled with a fear that she'd lose him, Willson sped up. She reached the running man just as he tried to go around a corner in the fence. Instead, their combined momentum carried them into the chain-link, hard. Willson had her arms around him like he was a tackling dummy in a football practice. But the fence pushed back, rebounding with an equal force. Their two bodies reversed direction, then bounced to the ground, with the man now on top. The impact knocked Willson's breath away and her head cracked against the pavement. But somehow, through the stars and chirping birdies in her head and despite her empty lungs, she hung on to him.

"I've got him," said Brown, dragging the man off Willson by his collar. "You can let go, Jenny."

Willson lay on the ground for a moment, winded, trying to get both her bearings and her breath back. In the distance, she heard a dog barking and a man screaming. She slowly turned on her side and saw Brown straddling the other suspect, who lay face down on the asphalt, squirming and whining. Brown was tightening a plastic zip tie around his wrists.

"You can't do this to me," the man said, struggling to turn over. "I'm a police officer."

Brown put a knee in the centre of the man's back, forcing him back down.

"Tonight," said Brown, holding his head down with her left hand, "you're nothing but a slimy horn smuggler who's under arrest." She turned to Willson. "Are you okay?"

Willson struggled to get up. "I think so. Is that a dog barking?"

Brown turned toward the sound. "I think Ben let Neus take a small rump roast out of one of the other perps. I'm guessing he won't be sitting down for a while."

When Willson could finally stand, she helped Brown lead the officer back toward the railcar. His head was down, his nose bleeding profusely, and he was muttering to himself.

On the opposite side of the car, they met up with Gaby Bohitile, who had one of the other men in custody. He was Asian and appeared to have suffered a similar fate as the officer; his face looked as though he'd been dragged behind a vehicle for a block or two.

Bohitile tried to hide a slight smile. "He wasn't keen on my arresting him, so he chose to resist. It was a bad decision."

Mushimba arrived next. With one hand, he pushed a limping, handcuffed man in his late fifties. Also Asian, he was crying and grimacing at the same time. Neus was back on leash beside Mushimba, but was still straining to take another piece out of the man's hide; Mushimba needed all his strength to hold Neus back.

Tjikuzu and Hauwanga stood beside the railcar, the bags of rhino horns at their feet.

"Good job, everyone," said Willson. She leaned against the railcar as a spell of dizziness hit her.

"Are you okay, Jenny?" asked Bohitile.

"I'm fine ..." she managed to say before she slid to the ground and the railyard began to spin.

"Her head hit the ground like a coconut back there," Brown said, quickly moving to Willson's side. "We need to get her to a doctor."

"I'm better now that I'm sitting down," Willson said. "This ain't my first knock on the head." Rather than move her head, she shifted her eyes slowly and carefully toward Mushimba. "Ben, what did the guys who you arrested in Tsumeb look like?"

"One was Tengum Li. We confirmed it when we found his ID. Thin guy, not much over five foot five."

"And the other two?"

"Both were large, dark-skinned men. Well over six feet tall and at least two hundred pounds. Nothing out of the ordinary about them except that one had a gold front tooth."

Willson smiled. "A gold front tooth, eh?" These descriptions matched those of the three buyers who'd approached the Himba women.

With Brown's help, Willson rose to her feet but continued leaning against the railcar. "It looks like we've now put together almost all the pieces to this puzzle. You guys are an amazing team. Now, what we've got to figure out is what role Sam Mogotsi played in all this. And we still don't know who took the two rhinos from the Uukwaluudhi conservancy." She patted the parcel on the railcar beside her. "The two animals who gave their lives for these."

"Actually," said Betty Tjikuzu, "we do."

"We do what?" Willson asked.

"We do know who killed these two rhinos. Carolina Musso phoned me moments before these guys arrived tonight and told me that members of the conservancy, who were angry that they kept losing rhinos, turned in the guy who was responsible."

"Turned him in?"

"Well," Tjikuzu said, grinning, "that's not quite accurate. They brought him to the police station in Kamanjab, trussed up like a warthog ready for the braai. And I understand that they'd asked reporters from Windhoek to be there when they brought him in. It was their attempt to force the hand of the sergeant who's in command there now, at least until the deceased inspector is replaced. Seems like it's worked so far. The man's arrest on two charges of poaching rhinos will be in every newspaper and on every TV news program in the country by tomorrow."

"How did the community know it was him?" asked Brown.

"It seems they caught him in the act of trying to take another one."

"And he admitted to poaching the other two?"

"From what Carolina told me," Tjikuzu said, waving her right index finger at their three injured prisoners, "he ended up looking worse than any of these guys. Apparently, the locals handed out a bit of frontier justice when they caught him, so he did end up confessing to the other two. I assume that, after that experience, being handed off to the police was a welcome change for him."

"Did anyone ask him about who he was selling the horns to?"

"This is third-hand via Carolina, but apparently, he claimed he didn't know the buyers' names. But he described three guys that sound a lot like Tengum Li and his two associates."

"Interesting," Willson said. "So, it looks like we had two different groups operating in the Kunene. Tengum Li and his group, and our North Korean diplomat and some of her colleagues."

"We got the one group," said Hauwanga, "and I've heard that the North Korean woman, the diplomat, is not allowed back in Namibia. That order came right from our president once he heard what she had done. He also sent a formal note of protest to the North Koreans via his counterpart in Angola."

"I guess that's the best we could hope for," Willson said as she walked slowly toward the truck. "I'm going to sit down for a while. Can I ask you guys to process the scene here?" They all nodded.

"We've got one final mystery to solve," Willson told them, thinking of Sam Mogotsi. But in her slightly addled brain, she was also thinking about solving the other mystery: Danny Trang.

CHAPTER 37

"He's gone?" Willson asked, sitting on the edge of her bed in the Swakopmund hospital. Over the past twenty-four hours, she'd undergone a CT scan and a battery of neurological and cognitive tests. The doctors and nurses who examined her all seemed sure that she had experienced another concussion. The first one had happened toward the end of her poaching investigation in Canada. The fact that she was struggling to get her pants on seemed to confirm their diagnosis.

"Yes," Brown said, straightening an uncooperative pant leg for Willson. "Danny left on a flight from Windhoek this morning, bound for Calgary via Frankfurt." She studied her watch. "He's already a good four hours into the flight."

"Are you sure?"

"Yes, he sent a text while you were inside the CT scanner."

Willson slammed her fist down on the bed controls. The head and foot sections began to rise, threatening to trap her like meat in a taco. Brown reacted quickly, stopping the bed's upward movement with the touch of a button.

"I'm sorry," Brown said. "I didn't mean to read it, but it popped up on your phone while I was waiting for you."

"Shit, shit, shit," Willson said. "No, I don't care about you seeing his text, Tracy. I'm pissed because I wanted to talk to him before he left. We should have gone straight to Windhoek rather than coming here. We might have caught him at the airport." A sudden pain, like a knife in her temple, caused her to pause. "Ouch. Okay, maybe coming here wasn't a bad idea."

"Are you certain you're okay, Jenny?"

"Yeah, yeah. Get me out of here." She slowly stood.

Brown knelt to put on Willson's boots and tie the laces. She straightened up and offered Willson her arm. "I'm driving you back to Kamanjab. Try to forget about Danny for now. Instead, focus on getting healthy again."

The drive back from Swakopmund to Kamanjab was longer than normal because Brown chose to stay on paved roads the entire way to avoid jostling Willson too much. The gravel roads in Namibia were good, but they were long and dusty and sometimes a mass of washboard ruts; it was like driving across an accordion. Willson sat with her eyes shaded behind dark sunglasses, a baseball cap pulled down low. The six-hour drive, with brief stops for gas and food, gave her time to think about what was next. When she dropped off to sleep, Brown would wake her at intervals to ensure she was okay.

Although Willson was elated at having led her team to dismantle a major poaching ring, she still couldn't shake a deep and unexpected sense of loss, of uncertainty. She'd lost her mother, and now she was faced with the thought of going back home, with her mother not there to greet her, to hug her, to ask about her trip. Even though western Canada was home, and even though she was only a visitor here on the west side of the African continent, she felt like she was about to enter unknown territory. Like she'd be a foreigner in her own country.

The debacle with Danny hadn't helped. She wondered what he must have thought as he boarded the plane, and suspected he would be questioning if he would ever see his luggage and camera gear again, not having heard from her, not seeing any responses to his texts or emails. Or perhaps he hadn't thought of her at all.

It was late afternoon when Brown turned off the highway onto the main street of Kamanjab, then took a quick left up the dusty hill to the Oppi-Koppi compound. At their backs, the sun hovered above the horizon as they passed the burnt-out shell of the apartment Willson had shared with Veronica Muafangejo. Willson raised her left hand to block the rear-view mirror on her side; the setting sun was like a laser beam reflecting into her tired eyes. More than anything, she needed sleep. And time to reflect.

"Why are we here?" asked Willson.

Brown smirked. "Veronica told me that, now that

we're almost finished the case, the government gave us the go-ahead to stay here."

"That's very … thoughtful of them."

CHAPTER 38

In the three weeks since she'd returned to Kamanjab, Willson and her team had compiled and organized the files, documents, statements, and photographs that prosecutors would need to take their suspects to court. All of them, eight in total — the Opuwo man who sold the horn to the North Korean diplomat, the man who'd shot two rhinos in the Uukwaluudhi conservancy, Tengum Li and his two associates, and the police officer and the two men they'd arrested with the horns at the Walvis Bay docks — were facing multiple counts of poaching, illegal possession, and illegal transport of protected wildlife parts.

Willson had personally interviewed every one of them, spending hours going over details, movements, and intentions. Some, like Tengum Li, had said nothing, knowing they stood a better chance if they remained silent. His associates had also kept their mouths shut, though Willson figured that was less about being smart than fearing their boss. Others, like the man from Opuwo, told her everything she wanted to know. He was doing anything he possibly could to stay out of jail. His statements alone had led to three North Korean diplomats, including the woman they had followed to the Angolan border, and one Russian diplomat being prohibited from ever re-entering Namibia. And Sergeant Kugara, when faced with the possibility of jail time, had sung like a lilac-breasted roller in the top branch of a tree. He'd told Willson how the now-deceased inspector had ordered him and two of his colleagues to frighten Mogotsi's family, and to hide his rifle. But Kugara had claimed to know nothing about his boss's involvement in selling rhino horns. Without evidence to the contrary, Willson knew they couldn't charge him with poaching. He was fired from his post, however.

In the background, what with one dead officer, another caught red-handed, and a third fired rather than charged, the Namibian police force faced an organizational crisis. High-level politicians were asking tough questions about oversight, accountability, and corruption. Senior officers were scrambling for answers, so their heads wouldn't be the ones to roll. Monica Hauwanga and Ben Mushimba were called back to Windhoek, allegedly to be debriefed, but Willson assumed it was to keep them away from the media. On her way, Hauwanga had volunteered to drive Trang's truck to the rental return depot at the airport there. Someone was going to get a heck of an invoice, because she'd had to pack and ship all his personal belongings, as well.

Veronica Muafangejo, who was claiming near-terminal boredom, had returned to Kamanjab and work two weeks earlier to help Willson with paperwork. Her vision was not back to 100 percent, but it was steadily improving. Willson rightly assumed that Muafangejo had been invited by Tracy Brown to help prevent Willson from doing too much, at least until she had a green light from her doctor. A conspiracy of friends.

Good luck with keeping me quiet, thought Willson, as she drove their truck off the pavement and onto the C40 on the edge of Kamanjab. Muafangejo was in the seat beside her, Brown in the back. Despite the heat of the morning, they had already rolled up the windows to avoid the clouds of dust being kicked bt their tires, and from vehicles passing in the other direction.

"Did you tell Sam we were coming?" asked Muafangejo.

"No," said Willson. "I thought it best to show up unannounced."

"Agreed," said Muafangejo. She was wearing the darkest sunglasses she could find. "In my experience, the most productive interviews are those in which the interviewee is unprepared."

"In light of that, is the rumour true?" Willson asked.

"What rumour?"

"That you've been offered command of a new, permanent, all-female anti-poaching unit, with an impressive budget and all the latest weapons and technological bells and whistles?"

"Where did you hear that?"

"You didn't answer my question."

"Yes, I've been asked to lead a new unit, just like you described. We'll be based in Outjo."

Willson grinned. Amidst the political hand-wringing now happening in Windhoek, someone had obviously realized the power of an all-woman team, and whoever it was had made what Willson considered a courageous and forward-thinking decision. Apart from making men nervous, which wasn't a bad thing, a female unit could undoubtedly achieve success by collaborating with women in the communities — the wives and mothers, sisters and daughters, aunties and grandmothers who always thought about the future — how to build a sustainable economy that didn't leap back and forth between boom and bust, between feast and famine.

"That's excellent, Veronica! Congratulations. Are you going to accept it?"

"After what we achieved in the few months you've been here, absolutely! I'm going to invite Gaby, Monica, and Betty to join me. While Ben and Neus have been great to work with, they've been asked to move up to the Caprivi. So, I've found and contacted the first woman K-9 handler in Namibia. She's agreed to join the team."

"I have no doubt you're going to kick some ass," said Willson. "A smart poacher would look elsewhere."

"I hope you're right. Part of my plan is to work closely with Carolina Musso from SRT so that her work in the conservancies continues to succeed, as well as with local prosecutors and magistrates. Ideally, I'd eventually like to work our team out of a job. But I know we have lots of challenges ahead of us yet."

Willson passed the Hoada campsite, triggering the memory of her late-night conversation with Danny Trang. She felt Muafangejo's eyes on her.

"What would you say if I asked you to stay here, Jenny?" the inspector asked. "To be part of my team? I know you've got at least one other offer …"

Willson glanced back at Brown, receiving an *I told you so* look in return. Her friend had predicted that Willson would have a range of job options from which to choose, and another had just appeared.

"I really appreciate the thought, Veronica," Willson said, turning her attention back to the gravel road ahead. "But at this point, my future is a bit of a mystery, even to me." She paused. "Does that offer have a best-before date on it?"

Muafangejo shook her head. "Consider it always open."

It took the three women just over an hour to reach Sam Mogotsi's house.

"Do you think Sam trusts you, Jenny?" asked Brown.

"I think so. Veronica and I got him out of jail once, and I used my contacts in the prosecutor's department to get him out again after he helped us with the sting in Outjo. I think he feels we're the only ones who believe his story."

"Perfect," said Brown. "This should be interesting."

They pulled through an open gate in the barbed wire fence and parked in the yard in front of the house. The three bangs of closing truck doors clearly reached the house, because a moment later the front door opened.

"Hello, Jenny!" Martha Shipanga stepped out on the front porch. "What are you doing here?" She looked from Willson to the other two officers. She wore a drab, shapeless dress and her dark, unwashed hair hung limp around her shoulders.

Willson walked toward Chioto Shipanga's widow. It had been months since she'd seen the woman. Her face was haggard, and she'd lost weight. Lots of weight. "Martha, how are you?" She grabbed Shipanga's right hand in both of hers.

"Eh," Shipanga said, moving her other hand as if to wave off the question. "Trying to keep things together for my daughter. Natasha and Sam have been very good to me, but every day is tough."

"Are they here today?"

"Natasha is in town shopping. But Sam is here. Why?"

"Where is he?"

"He's in the yard out back. I think he's working on some equipment. He bought a couple of things cheap and now he's trying to fix them."

"We need to talk to him," said Willson. "We'll let you go back to what you were doing."

"Okay," Shipanga said, clearly reading from Willson's face that they weren't on a social call. "The kids are playing inside, so I'll keep them in."

"That would be good."

They found Sam Mogotsi on the shady side of his shed, which sat on the edge of a dry creek draw a hundred metres south of the main house. The spot couldn't be seen from the house and had a dramatic view of the surrounding savanna. He was seated on a board balanced across an old tire rim and was using a rag to wipe dirt and grime from pieces of what looked to be an ancient air conditioner. Beside him, parts of two bicycles were scattered on the ground. When he saw the three women approaching, he wiped his hands, dropped the rag, and stood up.

"Jenny, Veronica, Tracy," he said, glancing at each woman in turn. "I didn't expect to see you today."

"We thought it best to come see you in person," Willson said.

"Have you got news about Chioto?"

"That's what we want to talk about. Is there somewhere we could sit?"

"Oh, sorry. Let me get something for you." He rose and strode to the shed.

After a nod from Willson, Brown followed, just in case. They knew better than to let an interviewee wander off on his own, particularly after he'd been surprised by their appearance. Together, Brown and Mogotsi dragged two wooden boxes and a second tire rim out into the shade.

When all four were seated in a circle, Willson spoke. "Do you want your lawyer here today, Sam?"

"It's fine. We are just talking, I assume? I can't afford to pay Miss Usiku much, so I'm waiting to see if I'll need her for court."

Willson looked sideways at Muafangejo, then back at Mogotsi. "Sam," she said, "you know we've been working hard on our poaching investigations. What you don't know is that we've recently had some good successes."

"That's great," Mogotsi said. "But what does that have to do with Chioto?"

"We arrested eight men in the last month. They're all in jail awaiting trial. And you may have heard that Inspector Nashili, the one you had so much trouble with, was killed while resisting arrest."

"I heard a rumour about that. It's true, is it? I won't miss that man."

"I spoke to him just before he died. I asked him who killed Chioto. Do you know what he said?"

"No." Mogotsi shifted on the tire rim. It almost slipped out from underneath him.

"He said it was you, Sam."

"He always said that. It is not true."

Willson inclined her head to one side. "Why, when Nashili had only seconds to live, would he lie?"

"I have no idea. He was always out to get me. Maybe that was his last attempt to get me in trouble."

"You really think a man would use his dying breath, his final moment, when he has nothing more to lose or gain, to frame you?"

"I can't explain it, except that he obviously hated me. I don't know why."

As planned, Brown spoke next. "Do you know who we arrested, Sam?"

The rapid change of subject and interviewer clearly rattled him. "You mean for the murder of Chioto?"

"No," Brown said, shaking her head slowly. "I mean for illegal possession and transportation of rare wildlife."

"Who?"

"Tengum Li."

The three officers watched Mogotsi's face for a reaction. They saw nothing overt.

"I don't know who that is."

Willson stared at him. "He's the guy who claims you sold him a rhino horn around the time of Chioto's murder."

"What? I did not sell anyone a rhino horn!"

"He told us you sold him a rhino horn when you met him in Outjo. He said you told him your wife was at a doctor's appointment that day and didn't know anything about it … and that he gave you thiry-five hundred dollars U.S. for it … in cash."

Mogotsi stood, knocking the tire rim onto its side. It wobbled in the dust, turning small circles, then settled down. "That is not —"

"Brother! Is that true?" It was Martha Shipanga, who had unexpectedly appeared from around the corner of the shed.

Willson was the first to notice the rifle in the woman's hand, dangling beside her leg. But her finger was inside the trigger guard.

"Martha," said Willson firmly and quickly, "put the gun down." She moved her hand to the weapon on her own belt, popping her holster open, sliding the 9mm out carefully.

"Sam," said Martha again, ignoring Willson. "What did you do?"

"I didn't do anything," Mogotsi said, his voice trembling. "I'm being framed."

Like a gunslinger in a western, Martha flipped the rifle up and held it with both hands, one on the forestock, one around the stock near the trigger. It was now aimed at Mogotsi. "Tell the truth for once! What have you done, Sam?"

"Martha," Willson said, more forcefully now, "please put the gun down." She saw the rifle shaking and raised her own weapon.

Shipanga screamed again. "What did you do to Chioto!"

Mogotsi began to cry, tears rolling down both cheeks. "I ... I didn't mean to hurt him."

In surprise, Willson's head snapped back to Mogotsi. "What happened, Sam?"

"We fought, and my gun went off."

Hearing a grunt, Willson turned back to see that Brown had jumped toward the distraught woman and was wrestling the rifle away from her; the barrel was now pointing upward. The struggle lasted only for a few seconds before the sobbing widow dropped to the ground. Brown removed the lone bullet from the gun, put it in her pocket, then leaned the rifle against the shed.

Willson looked at Mogotsi, sliding her weapon back in the holster. "Sit down, Sam, and start from the beginning. It's time to finally be honest with us."

Mogotsi sat directly on the ground, ignoring the board and rim. He clutched his arms around his knees.

"From the beginning, Sam," Willson said, more softly this time.

Once Mogotsi began to speak, it was like a floodgate opening. "Chioto and I were on patrol in the Klip River that day, but in different areas. We agreed to meet for lunch. He had seen some tire tracks and footprints first thing in the morning. So, rather than stop to eat, we decided to follow whomever it was. We were supposed to be the only ones in the valley, at least as far as we knew. We heard a shot close by, but it didn't sound like a regular gunshot, so we snuck over to see what it was. A young calf came running by us. We found a man standing over the cow rhino, his rifle on the ground beside him. He was already hacking at the rhino with an axe, trying to get the horn off. The animal was still alive; it was making a horrible noise. When we got closer, we could see the dart in the animal's hide. He had only tranquilized it."

"What did you do then?" Willson asked.

"We stood up and yelled at the man. Chioto took a shot over his head to scare him. The man grabbed his rifle, left his axe on the ground, and ran into the bush. He was gone before we got there. We were going to follow him but thought he might take a shot at us. Instead, we decided to see if we could save the animal."

"Had you ever seen the man before?"

"No. Both of us have been around the area our whole lives and we had never seen him."

"And then what did you do?"

"At first, we both agreed that we would radio in to report it."

"But what happened?"

"I started thinking about our next baby. By then, Natasha and I already knew it was going to have some birth defects, that it would need lots of expensive care. I suggested to Chioto that, because the rhino was already dead, or close to it, we take and hide the biggest horn, then report the kill to the authorities. The smaller horn was badly damaged. I could sell the big horn and use the money for the baby."

"What did Chioto say?" Willson asked.

Martha stood nearby, listening to every word. Her entire world centred on what he would say next.

"He refused."

"Then what happened?"

"We got into an argument. I told him I was going to take the horn, and he tried to stop me from doing it. We fought … we were down on the ground wrestling and punching … and the gun went off."

"What gun?"

"We sometimes took guns with us for protection … from poachers, or lions."

"Whose gun was it?"

"Mine."

"Who was holding the gun?"

"We both were. When it went off, the bullet hit him in the side of the head. I knew he was dead right away."

Martha's sobs shifted to wailing. She crumpled against Brown.

"What did you do then?"

"I knew I was in trouble. I didn't know what to do. I must have sat there for an hour. The calf came back twice for its mother. Finally, I decided to put the cow rhino out of her misery, take the horn, and leave Chioto there."

"You left him there?" Martha screamed. "You *left* my husband's body in the bush?"

"I didn't know what to do! You have to believe me." Mogotsi was pleading, trying to get any one of the four women to understand. But none of them ever would understand what he had done. And certainly, none of them would ever forgive him.

"But you claim you found his body ... two days later, was it?" Willson asked. "The day after you went into Outjo with Natasha?"

Mogotsi nodded. "Once the lodge realized he was missing, we all started a search. I volunteered to go back to the same area a day later because I felt so guilty."

Martha shrieked at him. "You killed my husband, and you felt *guilty*?"

Tears continued to run down Mogotsi's face. "I couldn't change what happened, so I wanted to go back to make sure his body wasn't out there any longer."

"Did that make you feel better, Sam? Did it?" Martha struggled with Brown, clearly trying to come at Mogotsi, but Brown held her firm. "You are my brother, you're supposed to look out for me, look out for Chioto!"

Veronica Muafangejo, who had calmly watched events unfold from her seat on the box, spoke next. "So, you really did shoot the rhino. What did you do with the horn, Sam?"

"I sold it when Natasha and I went to Outjo. I had called a contact from ... the old days. He and two other men met me there and gave me thirty-five hundred dollars in cash for the horn."

"Did you know any of the three men?" Willson asked.

"No. I had never seen them before."

"What did the man you sold the horn to look like?"

"He was a small Chinese man with glasses. I didn't know his name ... I only had a phone number for my old contact."

"And what about the gun, Sam? What did you do with the gun?"

"I brought it home with me and buried it ... over there." He pointed to a jumbled pile of weathered lumber.

"When did the police find it?"

"I don't know. When they said they hadn't found it, I didn't know what to think. When I got home, I checked, but it was gone. I guess I hoped someone else had taken it."

Muafangejo shook her head. "After all that, Sam, after all Jenny and I did for you, it turns out that Nashili was right about you all along, about your guilt. You are under arrest for the murder of Chioto Shipanga, and for illegal possession and sale of rhino horn."

Willson placed her cuffs around Mogotsi's wrists, then clicked them tight. But she was still curious. "Why did you help us with the sting operation, when you knew that buyers might show up who could recognize you, Sam?" Willson asked.

"I know it makes no sense. I *was* frightened that the same men would show up again. But I assumed that if I helped you, you could protect me from them, and that this would all go away."

"Didn't work, did it?"

"No. It was stupid."

"And what about the attacks on us?" asked Muafangejo. "The arson at our apartment, the cobra in my truck. What do you know about those?"

"I don't know anything, except that when Nashili interviewed me, he always talked about 'those nosy bitches getting what was coming to them.' I think those were his exact words. I assumed he was talking about you and your team."

"So, you think Nashili did all that, trying to persuade us not to investigate him and his involvement in poaching?"

"I have no idea. But when he showed up at Outjo that second time, when we thought we were dealing with a legitimate buyer, I knew he was involved."

As they walked Mogotsi toward the truck, Martha spat at him as he went by. "*Koolele moheli mona Woshikumbu.*"

Willson shoved Mogotsi into the back seat of the truck. She walked around to lean against the front grille, then looked back at the house. It was a small, neatly kept home for a family with few possessions, trying to do its best. Martha now sat on the front steps, sobbing. The three children encircled her, trying to comfort her, though not understanding why she was crying. Willson glanced at Muafangejo and Brown, who stood on either side of her.

"What did she say to her brother?"

"Loosely translated," Muafangejo said, "she said, 'Rot in hell, you son of a bitch.'"

Willson paused. "That was the last piece of the puzzle, wasn't it? It's done. It's really done."

Both women nodded sadly.

"Then why do I feel like shit?" asked Willson.

"We've been in Namibia for five months," Brown said, her head cocked, "and for the most part, we've done what we set out to do. You should feel good about that."

"On the surface, I guess that's true." Willson motioned with her head toward the grieving family. "But if this is the result, then part of me wonders if we've done any good at all. Should we be proud? Is this what it looks like to help? Perhaps they were better off without us." She ran her fingers through her hair and let out a long breath. A single tear left a track down her left cheek. "I think it's time for me to go home … wherever that is."

AUTHOR'S NOTE

Namibia is a special place, not only because of its people, its landscapes, and its incredible diversity of wildlife species, but because it is — as a relatively young country — showing courageous leadership in building new models for conservation that allow local communities to control their destinies.

Many of Namibia's conservation challenges and opportunities centre around black and white rhinos, two of the world's five rhino species (the other three being the Javan rhino, the Sumatran rhino, and the greater one-horned rhino). On the one hand, rhinos are still threatened by poachers, including international crime syndicates acting with military precision. However, the population of the desert-adapted black rhino has begun to rebound from a point of near-extinction. While it remains on the International Union for the Conservation of Nature's (IUCN's) critically endangered list, the passionate work of organizations such as

Save the Rhino Trust Namibia (SRT) and the people of community conservancies scattered across the Kunene and Erongo regions of Namibia *is* making a difference. Often, it is individual rhino trackers who stand — sometimes literally — between rhinos and a bleak future.

If you'd like to learn more about rhinos, wild cats, or community conservancies, or if you feel inspired to support conservation in Namibia, I encourage you to contact any of the following organizations:

- Save the Rhino Trust Namibia (savetherhinotrust.org)
- Namibian Association of Community Based Natural Resource Management Support Organizations (nacso.org.na)
- The AfriCat Foundation (africat.org)

ACKNOWLEDGEMENTS

Many people helped to bring Jenny Willson's Namibian experiences to life.

Thanks to friend and photographer Jim Barber for being a great travelling companion along many kilometres of gravel roads in Namibia. The friendly team at Wild Dog Safaris — Liz, Memory, Jason, Manfred — helped us immensely; I highly recommend their services.

A very special thanks and hello to the amazing Hooker family — Josh, Cathy, Benjamin, Erin, and Matthew. They not only graciously provided us with a home-away-from-home in Windhoek, but Matthew patiently taught two Canadians how to play cricket, and Cathy was a continuing source of insight, connections, and translations. Her influence on this book is greater than she will ever know.

I sincerely appreciate the time that Ms. Maxi Pia Louis spent with me in her office in Windhoek and in many email exchanges. Maxi is director of the Namibian Association of CBNRM Support Organizations (NACSO), and chair of the board of trustees of Save the Rhino Trust Namibia. She provided me with a wealth of knowledge about community conservancies. Dr. Jeff Muntifering, an inspiring and thoughtful conservation biologist, seconded to Namibia by the Minnesota Zoo, was extremely helpful in explaining the links between rhino conservation and local communities. Bern Brell (and his dog Azaro) shared with me as much as he could about field-level wildlife law enforcement in the country.

This third novel in the Jenny Willson mystery series would not be possible without my beta readers — Darrell Bethune, Heather Butler, Stan Chung, Keith Liggett, and Virginia Rasch; the team at Dundurn Press — Michelle Melski, Tabassum Siddiqui, Synora Van Drine, Allison Hirst, Jenny McWha, Laura Boyle; copy editor Catharine Chen; independent bookstore owners and local librarians who continue to support my books; and, most of all, the many readers (some of whom, knowingly or unknowingly, contributed character names to the book) and reviewers of my novels.

I am filled with gratitude for the opportunity to share my writing with all of you.

Mystery and Crime Fiction from Dundurn Press

Birder Murder Mysteries
by Steve Burrows
(Birding, British Coastal Town Mysteries)
A Siege of Bitterns
A Pitying of Doves
A Cast of Falcons
A Shimmer of Hummingbirds
A Tiding of Magpies
A Dance of Cranes

Amanda Doucette Mysteries
by Barbara Fradkin
(PTSD, Cross-Canada Tour)
Fire in the Stars
The Trickster's Lullaby
Prisoners of Hope

B.C. Blues Crime Novels
by R.M. Greenaway
(British Columbia, Police Procedural)
Cold Girl
Undertow
Creep
Flights and Falls

Stonechild & Rouleau Mysteries
by Brenda Chapman
(First Nations, Kingston, Police Procedural)
Cold Mourning
Butterfly Kills
Tumbled Graves
Shallow End
Bleeding Darkness
Turning Secrets

Jack Palace Series
by A.G. Pasquella
(Noir, Toronto, Mob)
Yard Dog
Coming soon: *Carve the Heart*

Jenny Willson Mysteries
by Dave Butler
(National Parks, Animal Protection)
Full Curl
No Place for Wolverines
In Rhino We Trust

Falls Mysteries
by J.E. Barnard
(Rural Alberta, Female Sleuth)
When the Flood Falls
Where the Ice Falls

Foreign Affairs Mysteries
by Nick Wilkshire
(Global Crime Fiction, Humour)
Escape to Havana
The Moscow Code
Remember Tokyo

Dan Sharp Mysteries
by Jeffrey Round
(LGBTQ, Toronto)
Lake on the Mountain
Pumpkin Eater
The Jade Butterfly
After the Horses
The God Game
Shadow Puppet

Max O'Brien Mysteries
by Mario Bolduc
(Translation, Political Thriller, Con Man)
The Kashmir Trap
The Roma Plot
The Tanzania Conspiracy

Cullen and Cobb Mysteries
by David A. Poulsen
(Calgary, Private Investigators, Organized Crime)
Serpents Rising
Dead Air
Last Song Sung
None So Deadly

Salvage
by Stephen Maher
(NOVA SCOTIA, FAST-PACED THRILLER)

Crang Mysteries
by Jack Batten
(HUMOUR, TORONTO)
Crang Plays the Ace
Straight No Chaser
Riviera Blues
Blood Count
Take Five
Keeper of the Flame
Booking In

Jack Taggart Mysteries
by Don Easton
(UNDERCOVER OPERATIONS)
Loose Ends
Above Ground
Angel in the Full Moon
Samurai Code
Dead Ends
Birds of a Feather
Corporate Asset
The Benefactor
Art and Murder
A Delicate Matter
Subverting Justice
An Element of Risk
Coming soon: *The Grey Zone*

Meg Harris Mysteries
by R.J. Harlick
(CANADIAN WILDERNESS FICTION,
FIRST NATIONS)
Death's Golden Whisper
Red Ice for a Shroud
The River Runs Orange
Arctic Blue Death
A Green Place for Dying
Silver Totem of Shame
A Cold White Fear
Purple Palette for Murder

Thaddeus Lewis Mysteries
by Janet Kellough
(PRE-CONFEDERATION CANADA)
On the Head of a Pin
Sowing Poison
47 Sorrows
The Burying Ground
Wishful Seeing

Cordi O'Callaghan Mysteries
by Suzanne F. Kingsmill
(ZOOLOGY, MENTAL ILLNESS)
Forever Dead
Innocent Murderer
Dying for Murder
Crazy Dead

Endgame
by Jeffrey Round
(MODERN RE-TELLING OF AGATHA
CHRISTIE, PUNK ROCK)

Inspector Green Mysteries
by Barbara Fradkin
(OTTAWA, POLICE PROCEDURAL)
Do or Die
Once Upon a Time
Mist Walker
Fifth Son
Honour Among Men
Dream Chasers
This Thing of Darkness
Beautiful Lie the Dead
The Whisper of Legends
None So Blind

Lies That Bind
by Penelope Williams
(RURAL ONTARIO, AMATEUR SLEUTH)

Border City Blues
by Michael Januska
(PROHIBITION-ERA WINDSOR)
Maiden Lane
Riverside Drive
Prospect Avenue